JOHN MILTON

Paradise Lost and Other Poems

JOHN MILTON

Edited, with Introduction
by MAURICE KELLEY

Published for the Classics Club ® *by*

WALTER J. BLACK, INC. · ROSLYN, N. Y.

Contents

THE SONNETS, *continued*

introduction

> . . . he who would not be frustrate of his hope to
> write well hereafter in laudable things, ought him-
> self to be a true poem, that is, a composition and
> pattern of the best and honorablest things.

TO RESOLVE IN YOUTH that one's life should be a true poem,
and fully to realize that resolution before one dies at sixty
five is, at any time, indeed a triumph of the will and spirit.
But to accomplish such a resolve in an era of civil struggle and
distress argues infinitely greater merit. Such a will, such a spirit,
and such a merit we find in John Milton. Early convinced that
God had marked him for high and lofty works, he confidently
declared his purposes and then proceeded to accomplish them in
an age which, like our own, was fraught with dereliction and dis-
may. If we had not a single line of Milton's writings, the mere
facts of his life would still be of infinite value and worth to men
of the modern world. For they mutely proclaim how much the
creative spirit of man can accomplish even when buffeted about
in stormy periods of history.

From the beginning, Milton showed himself a child of unusual
promise. Born in London, December 9, 1608, he grew up under
the shadow of St. Paul's Cathedral and but a stone's throw from

the Mermaid Tavern, which Shakespeare and Jonson memorial-
ized. His father, a prosperous notary and broker, early destined
this eldest son to the pursuit of literature and the service of the
Church. No narrow sectarian, the father personally instructed
the boy in music, provided him with private tutors at home, and
sent him to St. Paul's, one of the best public schools in London.
To this special attention the child responded in a gratifying man-
ner. So eager was his appetite for learning that from twelve years
on he seldom left his studies before midnight; and at the age of
ten—so his earliest biographers chronicle—he began to evidence
a precocious ability in the composition of verse. No poetry has
come down to us written before Milton's fifteenth year, nor do
we know the exact date on which he began his formal schooling.
But in 1625, well tutored in languages, both ancient and modern,
he entered Christ's College, Cambridge.

Such a childhood did much to make this sixteen-year-old boy
think of himself as one apart from ordinary mortals, and fostered
in him a confidence and self-esteem soon to be felt at Cambridge.
By the end of his first year, he quarreled so violently with his tutor
that he was temporarily sent home to his father; but this rustica-
tion did little to disturb Milton's calm and self-assurance. On his
return to Christ's, he soon manifested that vein of intellectual
courage which was later to make him the spokesman of so many
liberal causes. In his academic exercises, delivered before his col-
lege or the university, he bluntly attacked the medieval sophistry
of the Cambridge curriculum, and apparently lost no opportunity
to show his contempt for it. The undergraduates, he felt, were
"mocked and deluded with ragged notions and babblements'
when they had every right to expect "worthy and delightful knowl-
edge." They were set to mastering scholastic logic and wrangling
over petty, inconsequential questions (such as, "Whether Day or

Night is the more Delightful") when they should be taught
astronomy, geography, history, and other subjects concerned with
the universe and man. Cleansing the Augean stables was a kinder
task, he concluded, than that set for students of the English uni-
versity. But in spite of his early difficulty and his dislike for the
curriculum, Milton spent seven years at Cambridge, was a hard-
working student, "performed the collegiate and academical exer-
cises to the admiration of all, and was esteemed to be a virtuous
and sober person, yet not to be ignorant of his own parts."

Milton received his M.A. in 1632, and when he departed from
Cambridge at the age of twenty-three, he took with him a sheaf of
poems sufficient to form a respectable volume of verse. His first
productive period seems to have commenced about the time that
he quarreled with his tutor, and continued for about a year. With
one exception all of this writing was in Latin. Unfortunately, few
people today read Milton's Latin poetry, even in translation. It
gives us, however, our clearest picture of Milton as an under-
graduate, and Milton himself found considerable pleasure in writ-
ing it. After 1628—when he gave his greatest attention to English
and Italian—he continued to compose in that dead tongue; and
even as late as 1639—two years after *Lycidas*—when the untimely
death of his closest friend offered every inducement for him to
express his grief in the most natural and sincerest way, he chose
to write a pastoral lament in Latin.

In the verses and in the prose academic exercises of Milton's
Cambridge period, we find the first utterance of certain convictions
that were constantly to recur through his later writings and were
to constitute the fundamental articles of his moral and artistic
creed. Most deeply seated of these was his feeling that moral in-
tegrity was an absolute essential for a life of great work. Others
were his belief that God had entrusted to him the stewardship of

a great talent, his readiness to take stock of himself and render an account of that stewardship, his habit of ranking himself, without vainglory or apology, with the great figures of the past, and his passionate assurance of the invincibility of truth. The conclusion to Milton's *Fifth Academic Exercise* could easily pass as an excerpt from the *Areopagitica,* written some fifteen years later.

> "Truth has within herself strength enough and to spare for her own defence, and has no need of any help; and though she may seem to us at times to be hard pressed and beaten to the ground, yet she maintains herself ever inviolate and uninjured by the claws of error, even as the sun, who often shows himself to human eyes obscured and darkened by clouds, but then drawing in his beams and gathering together all his splendor, shines forth again in blazing glory without spot or stain."

Milton's father had early destined him for the Church; but by the time that he was ready to take orders, King Charles I had so subjugated it to royal politics that Milton felt that no sincere and self-respecting Christian could enter the ministry. "He who would take orders must subscribe slave, and take an oath withall, which unless he took with a conscience that would retch, he must either straight perjure, or split his faith." These feelings, John Milton, Senior, could readily understand. His own father, a Catholic, had not hesitated to disinherit him because he embraced Protestantism; and now, as a father himself, he was apparently not one to force his eldest son into commitments that involved a violation of the conscience. And so with his father's consent, Milton retired to the family county place at Horton, where he remained until 1638.

To this period belong *Arcades, Comus, Lycidas,* and perhaps *L'Allegro* and *Il Penseroso;* but we must not err by thinking that

Milton spent these years in loafing and inviting the pastoral and the picturesque. The Horton days were days of hard, systematic study; for poetry, Milton felt, could tolerate no mediocrity, and the great poet must be "instructed and thoroughly finished in a certain circular education of all the arts and all science." They seem, likewise, to have been days of painful self-analysis. Conscience had closed the Church to him. He burned with a desire for fame; but at the same time he was acutely sensitive to the little that he had thus far accomplished, and how far in the future lay that honor and repute for which he thirsted. And aggravating this unjustified self-torment was the fear that death might cut him off before his prime. But a person with the intellectual fiber and sinew of John Milton was not to be everlastingly tortured by fears like these. He faced them and found their solution in *Lycidas,* and with the spring of the next year he left for a trip of almost a year and a half on the Continent.

Lycidas was the last and greatest poem of Milton's youth; and of that youth and of its accomplishment, Milton, as he crossed the Channel, might well have been pardonably proud. In his twenty-nine years he had accomplished much. The Latin poetry—so one reliable classicist tells us—compares favorably with that produced by Virgil at the same age. No native English versifier—before or after—was to surpass him in Italian. He had demonstrated a sensitive response to nature and the world about him, and he had proved his ability to master and to fuse those diverse elements that have always been the essence of Christian humanism. He had rivaled the classic authors in their perfection of form, and had soared above the Christians in purity and elevation. Milton had completed the groundwork of his life and art.

The high and memorable moments of Milton's Continental travel were his meetings with Hugo Grotius, the Dutch jurist, in

Paris, with the various academies of learned men in Italy, and with Galileo, now grown old and a prisoner of the Inquisition. But the beginnings of civil strife called him back again to London, where he took a house and a few boys to tutor, and resumed his ambitious literary projects, musing on some great poetic achievement worthy of memory and imitation, which later generations would not willingly let die. In a manuscript now preserved at Trinity College, Cambridge, Milton has left us a record of his search for a subject suitable for such an undertaking. There in Milton's own handwriting we find a list of ninety-nine topics from Biblical and British history, some merely noted by title and others worked up into tentative outlines. Of greatest interest to us today, however, are four preliminary drafts of a play on the fall of man—the subject to which he was to give an epic treatment two decades later in *Paradise Lost*.

But Milton, the idealist and the champion of causes, could not be content to plan classical dramas and to instruct reluctant boys. As the Puritan Revolution gathered momentum, he saw that a way was opening for the establishment of real liberty; "that the foundation was laying for the deliverance of man from the yoke of slavery and superstition." And so, in 1641, Milton embarked on a career of revolutionary pamphleteering that was to continue until the Restoration and was to make him, during the 1650's, the most feared and respected controversialist in all Europe.

Let no one, however, lament that the poet Milton devoted these two decades almost exclusively to prose and the harsh animosities of his age. Milton himself never did. Without the prose writings there could have been no great and final period of poetry, no *Paradise Lost*, no *Paradise Regained*, no *Samson Agonistes*. These decades brought him into searing contact with the actualities of life. They gave his idealism the temper of a Toledo sword, and made it impossible for him ever again to consider seriously much of the poetic subject matter of which he had mused on his return from Italy—romantic stories of Brutus and Arthur. In these decades, furthermore, Milton was not sacrificing his genius to trivial and forgotten issues. The issues of Commonwealth England were the issues that still vex the world of today. It was no caprice or anomaly of history that Mr. Chamberlain, in the House, should hear thundered at him the identical words that Oliver Cromwell had used, three centuries before, to dismiss a dilatory and ineffectual Parliament: "You have sat too long here for any good you have been doing. Depart, I say, and let us have done with you. In the name of God—go." For these still vital issues—the right to think, to worship, and to print what one pleases—Milton was the finest spokesman of his day; and his pamphlets—almost a score of them—constitute a meditated campaign in the cause of liberty, ecclesiastical, civil, and domestic. Although Milton insists that he wrote prose badly—with his left hand, as he put it—he was able to leave to posterity passage after passage, like these from his *History of Britain* and *Areopagitica*, which deserve, for their eloquence and their truth, a final and ineffaceable place in that democratic tradition to which every English-speaking nation is the heir:

"Liberty hath a sharp and double edge, fit only to be handled by just and virtuous men."

"A good book is the precious life blood of a master spirit, embalmed and treasured up on purpose to a life beyond life."

But Cromwell died, and the government and the principles for which Milton sacrificed his eyesight gave way to the army of General Monck and the dissolute court of Charles II. Thus in 1660, Milton had every cause to be a broken man. His fame, a few years ago trumpeted throughout Europe, was now gone, and he himself was a political outlaw. His pamphlets were publicly burned, and he was imprisoned for a time. Much of his fortune, furthermore, had evaporated—both what he had inherited and what he had saved from his government salary. His first wife had died, leaving him with three motherless children; and his second, to whom he wrote one of his greatest sonnets, had succumbed in childbirth. He, we must likewise not forget, had been blind for eight years. And England herself was about to begin an ordeal comparable to that which she knows today. The dread plague was soon to rage in the land. The Great Fire was to devour the St. Paul's of Milton's youth and much of the City, and Londoners were to hear the thunder of victorious Dutch guns rolling up the Thames estuary. But evil tongues and evil days could not crush his spirit. Again, as in *Lycidas,* he faced his problem and proceeded to dictate, at the rate of twenty or thirty lines a day, the great poem of which he had earlier dreamed.

His great poem was *Paradise Lost,* and his fundamental problem was that which has troubled every great writer from Aeschylus to Melville, the problem of evil. Why should God—if there is one and he is benevolent—permit the laceration of man's soul and the destruction of his body by wars, pestilence, and decay? Milton's answer to this question was the answer of seventeenth-century, Protestant Christendom, the Hebraic account of Adam and Eve. Man suffers today because there is in him an innate perverseness, inherited from the first two representatives of his kind, his ancestors in Eden. Adam and Eve, created perfect and endowed with complete freedom of action, chose to transgress the will of their Creator and to eat of the forbidden fruit. For punishment, God justly deprived them of their perfection and their freedom, and drove them forth to suffer and to die in a world that their own transgression had made hostile. This fate Adam and Eve passed down to their

— if Vertue feeble were
Heaven it selfe would stoope to her.

Cælum non animū muto dū trans mare
curro .

Joannes Miltonius
Anglus .

Junij 10°. 1639 .

Milton's inscription in the Album Amicorum of Camillo Cerdagni
in Geneva. Preserved in the Harvard University Library.

Εν α∂ενεια τελει ὅμαη

Joannos Milto
nius.

Londini 26 Sept
Carus, Sic apposuit Celebri
miltoni

Milton's inscription in the Album Amicorum of Johannes Zolli-
kofer, a Swiss theologian who visited Milton in 1656, four years
after the poet had become blind. Translated, the passage in Greek
reads, "In my weakness I am made perfect." Preserved in the Stadt-
bibliothek, St. Gall.

descendants, from generation to generation, and for this reason today liberty and freedom seem futile dreams, and evil desires tear man from within, while an inimical nature buffets him from without. But Milton does not end on a note of pessimism. Through the grace of God, man can again attain true liberty and perfection of the soul; but this liberty is to be sought, not from without by terror of the sword, but within by sobriety of conduct and integrity of life. This belief Milton was to set forth with greater detail in his short epic, *Paradise Regained*. Adam and Eve, by falling into temptation in the garden, lost for mankind the heritage that God had graciously bestowed on them; Christ, by spurning temptation in the desert, pointed out to man how the paradise lost in the garden could be regained at least partly in this world.

Samson Agonistes, a classical drama, and the third great poem of this final period, presents an equally exalted theme. Milton, who had felt all too keenly the blows of fate and the caprice of circumstance, might well, like Samson, question the wisdom and the justice with which God is supposed to govern man. But through his characters in this poem, Milton can find no fault with the providence of the Creator, and concludes with a Roman confidence that

> *All is best, though we oft doubt,*
> *What the unsearchable dispose*
> *Of highest wisdom brings about,*
> *And ever best found in the close.*

As we look at him today, Milton is indeed a figure of monumental strength and austerity, but those who knew him in life found him also extremely human. Our first picture of him, made at the age of ten, is that of an auburn-haired Puritan boy, intelligent and grave with the lovable gravity that children so often put on when they sit for a portrait. His dislike for his college curricuium is a trait not wanting in many an undergraduate of today; and stripped of the formality that patinates much of seventeenth-century literature, his writings at Cambridge reveal a witty boy touched by springtime emotions of love and capable of broad jokes that still must be printed in their original Latin. In later days, men found him "sweet and affable," and as Aubrey puts it, a "harmonicall and ingeniose soule" dwelling in "a beautiful and well proportioned body." As his contemporary biographers and his private correspondence amply reveal, his circle of friends, both in England and abroad, was always large; and foreigners who came to call on him found him hospitable and gracious. To those who had fallen afoul of the Commonwealth government, he seems to have been particularly generous; and among those he aided were a grandchild of the great Elizabethan poet Spenser and the Restoration writers Marvell and D'Avenant. Among his acquaintances, and particularly at the table, he was amiable in conversation and revealed a ready and sprightly wit. He was a temperate man, and rarely drank between meals. His chief exercise was walking, and he carried his slender, medium-sized body with the erectness and bearing of a gentleman. His voice was delicate and tuneable; he had some proficiency at the organ; and when attacks of gout struck him in the spring and fall, he would be cheerful and sing.

Being human, however, Milton had his failings. He was tenacious in his law suits, merciless in political controversy, and in his nuncupative will he cut off his daughters, condemning them as "unkind." But the great Taskmaster, whom Milton had served so diligently and long, could not have held these faults too seriously against him, for to him on November 8, 1674, death came so quietly "that the time of his expiring was not perceived by those in the room."

Posterity has not denied Milton the fame for which he strove,

Poets as diverse in theory and practice as Pope and Wordsworth have both admired and imitated him; and his reading public has proved to be far more than that "fit audience though few" for which he had dared to hope. *Paradise Lost* was the first English poem to be sold by subscription, the first to have a variorum edition, and the first to be made the subject of a detailed critical study. Between 1700 and 1800, this epic was published over a hundred times; while during the same period, Spenser went through seven editions, and Shakespeare only fifty. Nor was Milton's popularity restricted solely to *Paradise Lost*. In its original form, *Comus* was published thrice; and as adapted for the stage, it saw over fifty printings. *Samson Agonistes* was translated into Greek, was four times revised for the theater, and the version made for Handel's oratorio appeared nine times before 1800. During the eighteenth century, Shakespeare's most popular play, *Macbeth,* saw only thirteen reprintings.

In the nineteenth century, this respect was to grow into something little short of idolatry; and even the increasing materialism of our own age has done little to diminish Milton's gigantic stature. We still rank him with Dante and Shakespeare, and see him, as did Shelley, "the sire of an immortal strain," whose

> *clear sprite*
> *Yet reigns o'er earth; the third among the Sons of Light.*

This is indeed high praise, but nevertheless it is praise well deserved, for Milton himself sought to make his whole life a poem and spared neither flesh nor the spirit to accomplish this aim.

MAURICE KELLEY

JOHN MILTON

The Early Poems

O F MILTON'S EARLY ENGLISH WRITINGS we have today some sixteen poems, beginning with two translations of the Psalms made when he was fifteen, and covering his university and Horton periods. All show unusual promise, and three stand out as productions unusual for a poet of Milton's years. *L'Allegro* and *Il Penseroso* reveal a surprising mastery of form, and the *Nativity Ode,* written when Milton was only twenty-one, is perhaps the greatest Christmas poem in the language.

As one would naturally expect, Milton's early works plainly bear the imprint of the century in which they were written. In them we find the wit and the musings on death and religion that early Stuart England seems to have relished so much. The seven-line stanza form shows the influence of that sweetly singing school that took Spenser for its master; and Milton's couplets have the smoothness and decorum that we should expect from a disciple of Ben Jonson. Here and there are the quaint and ingenious conceits that give seventeenth-century verse its peculiar intellectual piquancy. The dead Shakespeare, according to Milton's lines on him, needs no monument of stone reared by mortal hands. His admirers are so awed by his effortless art that they are turned to marble, and thus Shakespeare creates for himself a monument that even kings should envy.

Already in the poems of Milton's youth we find those qualities that were to characterize his later and supreme work. We find the preoccupation with Christian subject matter and the effortless blending of it with classical materials. We find the untrammeled imagination, the willingness to sing not of earth only, but also of creation, heaven, and eternity. We sense a high type of intellect that readily expresses itself in terms of classical and Biblical allusion.

Likewise evident are the beginnings of Milton's characteristic style. Note, for instance, the following lines from *On the Death of a Fair Infant,* written at the age of seventeen:

> *Down he descended from his snow-soft chair,*
> *But all unwares with his cold-kind embrace*
> *Unhoused thy virgin soul from her fair biding place.*

> *Yet art thou not inglorious in thy fate;*
> *For so Apollo, with unweeting hand*
> *Whilom did slay his dearly-loved mate,*
> *Young Hyacinth born on Eurotas' strand,*
> *Young Hyacinth the pride of Spartan land.*

Here are the compound epithets, the use of words in their archaic form, the fondness for exotic proper names, the employment of apposition, and the carefully manipulated repetition of words and cadence. And elsewhere one may find words used in their Latin etymological meanings, and even occasionally a long periodic sentence or an inversion of words or phrases from their natural order.

In the early poems, Milton has given a clear earnest of what his full maturity will bring.

On the Morning of Christ's Nativity

(Composed 1629)

I

This is the month, and this the happy morn
Wherein the son of heaven's eternal king,
Of wedded maid, and virgin mother born,
Our great redemption from above did bring;
For so the holy sages once did sing,
   That he our deadly forfeit should release,
And with his father work us a perpetual peace.

II

That glorious form, that light insufferable,
And that far-beaming blaze of majesty,
Wherewith he wont at heaven's high council-table,
To sit the midst of trinal unity,
He laid aside; and here with us to be,
   Forsook the courts of everlasting day,
And chose with us a darksome house of mortal clay.

III

Say heavenly muse, shall not thy sacred vein
Afford a present to the infant God?
Hast thou no verse, no hymn, or solemn strain,
To welcome him to this his new abode,
Now while the heaven by the sun's team untrod,
   Hath took no print of the approaching light,
And all the spangled host keep watch in squadrons bright?

IV

See how from far upon the eastern road
The star-led wizards haste with odors sweet:
O run, prevent them with thy humble ode,
And lay it lowly at his blessed feet:

Have thou the honor first, thy Lord to greet,
　And join thy voice unto the angel choir,
From out his secret altar touched with hallowed fire.

The Hymn

I

It was the winter wild,
　While the heaven-born child,
All meanly wrapt in the rude manger lies;
　Nature in awe to him
　Had doffed her gaudy trim,
With her great master so to sympathize:
It was no season then for her
To wanton with the sun her lusty paramour.

II

Only with speeches fair
　She woos the gentle air
To hide her guilty front with innocent snow,
　And on her naked shame,
　Pollute with sinful blame,
The saintly veil of maiden white to throw,
Confounded, that her maker's eyes
Should look so near upon her foul deformities.

III

But he her fears to cease,
　Sent down the meek-eyed peace,
She crowned with olive green, came softly sliding
　Down through the turning sphere
　His ready harbinger,
With turtle wing the amorous clouds dividing,
And waving wide her myrtle wand,
She strikes a universal peace through sea and land.

IV

No war, or battle's sound
Was heard the world around:
The idle spear and shield were high uphung;
The hooked chariot stood
Unstained with hostile blood,
The trumpet spake not to the armed throng,
And kings sat still with awful eye,
As if they surely knew their sovereign Lord was by.

V

But peaceful was the night
Wherein the prince of light
His reign of peace upon the earth began:
The winds with wonder whist,
Smoothly the waters kissed,
Whispering new joys to the mild ocean,
Who now hath quite forgot to rave,
While birds of calm sit brooding on the charmed wave

VI

The stars with deep amaze
Stand fixed in steadfast gaze,
Bending one way their precious influence,
And will not take their flight,
For all the morning light,
Or Lucifer that often warned them thence;
But in their glimmering orbs did glow,
Until their Lord himself bespake, and bid them go.

VII

And though the shady gloom
Had given day her room,
The sun himself withheld his wonted speed,
And hid his head for shame,
As his inferior flame.

The new enlightened world no more should need;
He saw a greater sun appear
Than his bright throne, or burning axletree could bear.

VIII

The shepherds on the lawn,
Or ere the point of dawn,
Sat simply chatting in a rustic row;
Full little thought they then,
That the mighty Pan
Was kindly come to live with them below;
Perhaps their loves, or else their sheep,
Was all that did their silly thoughts so busy keep.

IX

When such music sweet
Their hearts and ears did greet,
As never was by mortal finger struck,
Divinely-warbled voice
Answering the stringed noise,
As all their souls in blissful rapture took:
The air such pleasure loath to lose,
With thousand echoes still prolongs each heavenly close.

X

Nature that heard such sound
Beneath the hollow round
Of Cynthia's seat, the airy region thrilling,
Now was almost won
To think her part was done,
And that her reign had here its last fulfilling;
She knew such harmony alone
Could hold all heaven and earth in happier union.

XI

At last surrounds their sight
A globe of circular light,

That with long beams the shamefaced night arrayed,
   The helmed cherubim
   And sworded seraphim,
Are seen in glittering ranks with wings displayed,
Harping in loud and solemn choir,
With unexpressive notes to heaven's new-born heir.

XII

   Such music (as 'tis said)
   Before was never made,
But when of old the sons of morning sung,
   While the creator great
   His constellations set,
And the well-balanced world on hinges hung,
And cast the dark foundations deep,
And bid the weltering waves their oozy channel keep.

XIII

   Ring out ye crystal spheres,
   Once bless our human ears,
(If ye have power to touch our senses so)
   And let your silver chime
   Move in melodious time;
And let the bass of heaven's deep organ blow,
And with your ninefold harmony
Make up full consort to the angelic symphony.

XIV

   For if such holy song
   Enwrap our fancy long,
Time will run back, and fetch the age of gold,
   And speckled vanity
   Will sicken soon and die,
And leprous sin will melt from earthly mold,
And hell itself will pass away,
And leave her dolorous mansions to the peering day.

XV

Yea truth, and justice then
Will down return to men,
Orbed in a rainbow; and like glories wearing
Mercy will sit between,
Throned in celestial sheen,
With radiant feet the tissued clouds down steering,
And heaven as at some festival,
Will open wide the gates of her high palace hall.

XVI

But wisest fate says no,
This must not yet be so,
The babe yet lies in smiling infancy,
That on the bitter cross
Must redeem our loss;
So both himself and us to glorify:
Yet first to those ychained in sleep,
The wakeful trump of doom must thunder through the deep.

XVII

With such a horrid clang
As on Mount Sinai rang
While the red fire, and smoldering clouds outbrake:
The aged earth aghast
With terror of that blast,
Shall from the surface to the center shake;
When at the world's last session,
The dreadful judge in middle air shall spread his throne.

XVIII

And then at last our bliss
Full and perfect is,
But now begins; for from this happy day
The old dragon under ground
In straiter limits bound,

Not half so far casts his usurped sway,
And wrath to see his kingdom fail,
Swinges the scaly horror of his folded tail.

XIX

The oracles are dumb,
No voice or hideous hum
Runs through the arched roof in words deceiving,
Apollo from his shrine
Can no more divine,
With hollow shriek the steep of Delphos leaving.
No nightly trance, or breathed spell,
Inspires the pale-eyed priest from the prophetic cell.

XX

The lonely mountains o'er,
And the resounding shore,
A voice of weeping heard, and loud lament;
From haunted spring, and dale
Edged with poplar pale,
The parting genius is with sighing sent,
With flower-inwoven tresses torn
The nymphs in twilight shade of tangled thickets mourn.

XXI

In consecrated earth,
And on the holy hearth,
The lars, and lemures moan with midnight plaint,
In urns, and altars round,
A drear and dying sound
Affrights the flamens at their service quaint;
And the chill marble seems to sweat,
While each peculiar power forgoes his wonted seat.

XXII

Peor, and Baalim,
Forsake their temples dim,

With that twice battered god of Palestine,
    And mooned Ashtaroth,
    Heaven's queen and mother both,
Now sits not girt with tapers' holy shine,
The Libyc Hammon shrinks his horn,
In vain the Tyrian maids their wounded Thammuz mourn.

XXIII

And sullen Moloch fled,
    Hath left in shadows dread,
His burning idol all of blackest hue;
    In vain with cymbals' ring,
    They call the grisly king,
In dismal dance about the furnace blue;
The brutish gods of Nile as fast,
Isis and Orus, and the dog Anubis haste.

XXIV

Nor is Osiris seen
    In Memphian grove, or green,
Trampling the unshowered grass with lowings loud:
    Nor can he be at rest
    Within his sacred chest,
Nought but profoundest hell can be his shroud,
In vain with timbreled anthems dark
The sable-stoled sorcerers bear his worshiped ark.

XXV

He feels from Judah's land
    The dreaded infant's hand,
The rays of Bethlehem blind his dusky eyn;
    Nor all the gods beside,
    Longer dare abide.
Not Typhon huge ending in snaky twine:
Our babe to show his Godhead true,
Can in his swaddling bands control the damned crew.

XXVI

So when the sun in bed,
  Curtained with cloudy red,
Pillows his chin upon an orient wave,
  The flocking shadows pale,
  Troop to the infernal jail,
Each fettered ghost slips to his several grave,
And the yellow-skirted fays,
Fly after the night-steeds, leaving their moon-loved maze.

XXVII

But see the virgin blest,
  Hath laid her babe to rest.
Time is our tedious song should here have ending;
  Heaven's youngest teemed star,
  Hath fixed her polished car,
Her sleeping Lord with handmaid lamp attending:
And all about the courtly stable,
Bright-harnessed angels sit in order serviceable.

A Paraphrase on Psalm CXIV

*(The following Psalm was done by the author when fifteen
years old.)*

When the blest seed of Terah's faithful son,
After long toil their liberty had won,
And passed from Pharian fields to Canaan land,
Led by the strength of the almighty's hand,
Jehovah's wonders were in Israel shown,
His praise and glory was in Israel known.
That saw the troubled sea, and shivering fled,
And sought to hide his froth-becurled head
Low in the earth, Jordan's clear streams recoil,
As a faint host that hath received the foil.

The high, huge-bellied mountains skip like rams
Amongst their ewes, the little hills like lambs.
Why fled the ocean? And why skipped the mountains?
Why turned Jordan toward his crystal fountains?
Shake earth, and at the presence be aghast
Of him that ever was, and aye shall last,
That glassy floods from rugged rocks can crush,
And make soft rills from fiery flint-stones gush.

On the Death of a Fair Infant Dying of a Cough

(1628)

I

O fairest flower no sooner blown but blasted,
Soft silken primrose fading timelessly,
Summer's chief honor if thou hadst outlasted,
Bleak Winter's force that made thy blossom dry:
For he being amorous on that lovely dye
   That did thy cheek envermeil, thought to kiss
But killed alas, and then bewailed his fatal bliss.

II

For since grim Aquilo his charioteer
By boisterous rape the Athenian damsel got,
He thought it touched his deity full near,
If likewise he some fair one wedded not,
Thereby to wipe away the infamous blot,
   Of long uncoupled bed, and childless eld,
Which 'mongst the wanton gods a foul reproach was held.

III

So mounting up in icy-pearled car,
Through middle empire of the freezing air
He wandered long, till thee he spied from far.

There ended was his quest, there ceased his care.
Down he descended from his snow-soft chair,
   But all unwares with his cold-kind embrace
Unhoused thy virgin soul from her fair biding place

IV

Yet art thou not inglorious in thy fate;
For so Apollo, with unweeting hand
Whilom did slay his dearly-loved mate,
Young Hyacinth born on Eurotas' strand,
Young Hyacinth the pride of Spartan land,
   But then transformed him to a purple flower;
Alack that so to change thee winter had no power.

V

Yet can I not persuade me thou art dead
Or that thy corpse corrupts in earth's dark womb,
Or that thy beauties lie in wormy bed,
Hid from the world in a low delved tomb;
Could heaven for pity thee so strictly doom?
   Oh no! for something in thy face did shine
Above mortality that showed thou wast divine.

VI

Resolve me then O soul most surely blest
(If so it be that thou these plaints dost hear)
Tell me bright spirit wher'er thou hoverest
Whether above that high first-moving sphere
Or in the Elysian fields (if such there were).
   Oh say me true if thou wert mortal wight
And why from us so quickly thou didst take thy flight

VII

Wert thou some star which from the ruined roof
Of shaked Olympus by mischance didst fall;
Which careful Jove in nature's true behoof

Took up, and in fit place did reinstall?
Or did of late earth's sons besiege the wall
 Of sheeny heaven, and thou some goddess fled
Amongst us here below to hide thy nectared head.

VIII

Or wert thou that just maid who once before
Forsook the hated earth, O tell me sooth
And camest again to visit us once more?
Or wert thou mercy that sweet smiling youth!
Or that crowned matron sage white-robed truth?
 Or any other of that heavenly brood
Let down in cloudy throne to do the world some good

IX

Or wert thou of the golden-winged host,
Who having clad thyself in human weed,
To earth from thy prefixed seat didst post,
And after short abode fly back with speed,
As if to show what creatures heaven doth breed,
 Thereby to set the hearts of men on fire
To scorn the sordid world, and unto heaven aspire.

X

But oh why didst thou not stay here below
To bless us with thy heaven-loved innocence,
To slake his wrath whom sin hath made our foe
To turn swift-rushing black perdition hence,
Or drive away the slaughtering pestilence,
 To stand 'twixt us and our deserved smart?
But thou canst best perform that office where thou art

XI

Then thou the mother of so sweet a child
Her false imagined loss cease to lament,
And wisely learn to curb thy sorrows wild;

Think what a present thou to God has sent,
And render him with patience what he lent;
   This if thou do he will an offspring give,
That till the world's last-end shall make thy name to live.

The Passion

(1630)

I

Erewhile of music, and ethereal mirth,
Wherewith the stage of air and earth did ring,
And joyous news of heavenly infant's birth,
My muse with angels did divide to sing;
But headlong joy is ever on the wing,
   In wintry solstice like the shortened light
Soon swallowed up in dark and long outliving night.

II

For now to sorrow must I tune my song,
And set my harp to notes of saddest woe,
Which on our dearest Lord did seize erelong,
Dangers, and snares, and wrongs, and worse than so,
Which he for us did freely undergo.
   Most perfect hero, tried in heaviest plight
Of labors huge and hard, too hard for human wight.

III

He sovereign priest stooping his regal head
That dropped with odorous oil down his fair eyes,
Poor fleshly tabernacle entered,
His starry front low-roofed beneath the skies;
O what a mask was there, what a disguise!
   Yet more; the stroke of death he must abide,
Then lies him meekly down fast by his brethren's side.

IV

These latter scenes confine my roving verse,
To this horizon is my Phoebus bound,
His godlike acts, and his temptations fierce,
And former sufferings otherwhere are found;
Loud o'er the rest Cremona's trump doth sound;
   Me softer airs befit, and softer strings
Of lute, or viol still, more apt for mournful things.

V

Befriend me night, best patroness of grief,
Over the pole thy thickest mantle throw,
And work my flattered fancy to belief,
That heaven and earth are colored with my woe;
My sorrows are too dark for day to know:
   The leaves should all be black whereon I write,
And letters where my tears have washed a wannish white.

VI

See, see the chariot, and those rushing wheels,
That whirled the prophet up at Chebar flood,
My spirit some transporting cherub feels,
To bear me where the towers of Salem stood,
Once glorious towers, now sunk in guiltless blood;
   There doth my soul in holy vision sit
In pensive trance, and anguish, and ecstatic fit.

VII

Mine eye hath found that sad sepulchral rock
That was the casket of heaven's richest store,
And here though grief my feeble hands uplock,
Yet on the softened quarry would I score
My plaining verse as lively as before;
   For sure so well instructed are my tears,
That they would fitly fall in ordered characters.

VIII

Or should I thence hurried on viewless wing,
Take up a weeping on the mountains wild,
The gentle neighborhood of grove and spring
Would soon unbosom all their echoes mild,
And I (for grief is easily beguiled)
    Might think the infection of my sorrows loud,
Had got a race of mourners on some pregnant cloud.

*This subject the author finding to be above the years he had, when
he wrote it, and nothing satisfied with what was
begun, left it unfinished.*

On Time

(1630-33?)

Fly envious time, till thou run out thy race,
Call on the lazy leaden-stepping hours,
Whose speed is but the heavy plummet's pace;
And glut thyself with what thy womb devours,
Which is no more than what is false and vain,
And merely mortal dross;
So little is our loss,
So little is thy gain.
For whenas each thing bad thou hast entombed,
And last of all thy greedy self consumed,
Then long eternity shall greet our bliss
With an individual kiss;
And joy shall overtake us as a flood,
When everything that is sincerely good
And perfectly divine,
With truth, and peace, and love shall ever shine
About the supreme throne
Of him, to whose happy-making sight alone,
When once our heavenly-guided soul shall climb,

Then all this earthly grossness quit,
Attired with stars, we shall forever sit,
   Triumphing over death, and chance, and thee O time

At a Solemn Music

(1630-33?)

Blest pair of sirens, pledges of heaven's joy,
Sphere-born harmonious sisters, voice, and verse,
Wed your divine sounds, and mixed power employ
Dead things with inbreathed sense able to pierce,
And to our high-raised phantasy present,
That undisturbed song of pure concent,
Aye sung before the sapphire-colored throne
To him that sits thereon
With saintly shout, and solemn jubilee,
Where the bright seraphim in burning row
There loud uplifted angel trumpets blow,
And the cherubic host in thousand choirs
Touch their immortal harps of golden wires,
With those just spirits that wear victorious palms,
Hymns devout and holy psalms
Singing everlastingly;
That we on earth with undiscording voice
May rightly answer that melodious noise;
As once we did, till disproportioned sin
Jarred against nature's chime, and with harsh din
Broke the fair music that all creatures made
To their great Lord, whose love their motion swayed
In perfect diapason, whilst they stood
In first obedience, and their state of good.
O may we soon again renew that song,
And keep in tune with heaven, till God erelong
To his celestial consort us unite,
To live with him, and sing in endless morn of light.

An Epitaph on the Marchioness of Winchester

(1631)

This rich marble doth inter
The honored wife of Winchester,
A viscount's daughter, an earl's heir,
Besides what her virtues fair
Added to her noble birth,
More than she could own from earth.
Summers three times eight save one
She had told, alas too soon,
After so short time of breath,
To house with darkness, and with death.
Yet had the number of her days
Been as complete as was her praise,
Nature and fate had had no strife
In giving limit to her life.
Her high birth, and her graces sweet,
Quickly found a lover meet;
The virgin choir for her request
The god that sits at marriage-feast;
He at their invoking came
But with a scarce-well-lighted flame;
And in his garland as he stood,
Ye might discern a cypress bud.
Once had the early matrons run
To greet her of a lovely son,
And now with second hope she goes,
And calls Lucina to her throes;
But whether by mischance or blame
Atropos for Lucina came;
And with remorseless cruelty,
Spoiled at once both fruit and tree:
The hapless babe before his birth
Had burial, yet not laid in earth,

And the languished mother's womb
Was not long a living tomb.
So have I seen some tender slip
Saved with care from winter's nip,
The pride of her carnation train,
Plucked up by some unheedy swain,
Who only thought to crop the flower
New shot up from vernal shower;
But the fair blossom hangs the head
Sideways as on a dying bed,
And those pearls of dew she wears,
Prove to be presaging tears
Which the sad morn had let fall
On her hastening funeral.
Gentle lady may thy grave
Peace and quiet ever have;
After this thy travail sore
Sweet rest seize thee evermore,
That to give the world increase,
Shortened hast thy own life's lease;
Here besides the sorrowing
That thy noble house doth bring,
Here be tears of perfect moan
Wept for thee in Helicon,
And some flowers, and some bays,
For thy hearse to strew the ways,
Sent thee from the banks of Came,
Devoted to thy virtuous name;
Whilst thou bright saint high sittest in glory,
Next her much like to thee in story,
That fair Syrian shepherdess,
Who after years of barrenness,
The highly favored Joseph bore
To him that served for her before,
And at her next birth much like thee,
Through pangs fled to felicity,
Far within the bosom bright

Of blazing majesty and light,
There with thee, new welcome saint,
Like fortunes may her soul acquaint,
With thee there clad in radiant sheen,
No marchioness, but now a queen.

Song On May Morning

(1630?)

Now the bright morning star, day's harbinger,
Comes dancing from the east, and leads with her
The flowery May, who from her green lap throws
The yellow cowslip, and the pale primrose.
   Hail bounteous May that dost inspire
   Mirth and youth and warm desire,
   Woods and groves are of thy dressing,
   Hill and dale doth boast thy blessing.
Thus we salute thee with our early song,
And welcome thee, and wish thee long.

On Shakespeare

(1630)

What needs my Shakespeare for his honored bones,
The labor of an age in piled stones,
Or that his hallowed relics should be hid
Under a star-ypointing pyramid?
Dear son of memory, great heir of fame,
What needest thou such weak witness of thy name?
Thou in our wonder and astonishment
Hast built thyself a livelong monument.
For whilst to the shame of slow-endeavoring art,

Thy easy numbers flow, and that each heart
Hath from the leaves of thy unvalued book,
Those Delphic lines with deep impression took,
Then thou our fancy of itself bereaving,
Dost make us marble with too much conceiving;
And so sepulchered in such pomp dost lie,
That kings for such a tomb would wish to die.

On the University Carrier

(1631)

*Who sickened in the time of his Vacancy, being
forbid to go to London, by reason of the Plague.*

Here lies old Hobson, death hath broke his girt,
And here alas, hath laid him in the dirt,
Or else the ways being foul, twenty to one,
He's here stuck in a slough, and overthrown.
'Twas such a shifter, that if truth were known,
Death was half glad when he had got him down;
For he had any time this ten years full,
Dodged with him, betwixt Cambridge and The Bull.
And surely, death could never have prevailed,
Had not his weekly course of carriage failed;
But lately finding him so long at home,
And thinking now his journey's end was come,
And that he had taken up his latest inn,
In the kind office of a chamberlain
Showed him his room where he must lodge that night,
Pulled off his boots, and took away the light:
If any ask for him, it shall be said,
'Hobson has supped, and's newly gone to bed.'

L'Allegro

(1630-32?)

Hence loathed melancholy
   Of Cerberus, and blackest midnight born,
In Stygian cave forlorn
   'Mongst horrid shapes, and shrieks, and sights unholy,
Find out some uncouth cell,
   Where brooding darkness spreads his jealous wings,
And the night-raven sings;
   There under ebon shades, and low-browed rocks,
As ragged as thy locks,
   In dark Cimmerian desert ever dwell.
But come thou goddess fair and free,
In heaven yclept Euphrosyne,
And by men, heart·easing mirth,
Whom lovely Venus at a birth
With two sister graces more
To ivy-crowned Bacchus bore;
Or whether (as some sager sing)
The frolic wind that breathes the spring,
Zephyr with Aurora playing,
As he met her once a-Maying,
There on beds of violets blue,
And fresh-blown roses washed in dew,
Filled her with thee a daughter fair,
So buxom, blithe, and debonair.
Haste thee nymph, and bring with thee
Jest and youthful jollity,
Quips and cranks, and wanton wiles,
Nods, and becks, and wreathed smiles,
Such as hang on Hebe's cheek,
And love to live in dimple sleek;
Sport that wrinkled care derides,
And laughter holding both his sides.

Come, and trip it as you go
On the light fantastic toe,
And in thy right hand lead with thee,
The mountain nymph, sweet liberty;
And if I give thee honor due,
Mirth, admit me of thy crew
To live with her, and live with thee,
In unreproved pleasures free;
To hear the lark begin his flight,
And singing startle the dull night,
From his watch-tower in the skies,
Till the dappled dawn doth rise;
Then to come in spite of sorrow,
And at my window bid good-morrow,
Through the sweet-briar, or the vine,
Or the twisted eglantine.
While the cock with lively din,
Scatters the rear of darkness thin,
And to the stack, or the barn-door,
Stoutly struts his dames before,
Oft listening how the hounds and horn
Cheerly rouse the slumbering morn,
From the side of some hoar hill,
Through the high wood echoing shrill.
Sometime walking not unseen
By hedgerow elms, on hillocks green,
Right against the eastern gate,
Where the great sun begins his state,
Robed in flames, and amber light,
The clouds in thousand liveries dight,
While the plowman near at hand,
Whistles o'er the furrowed land,
And the milkmaid singeth blithe,
And the mower whets his scythe,
And every shepherd tells his tale
Under the hawthorn in the dale.
Straight mine eye hath caught new pleasures

Whilst the landscape round it measures,
Russet lawns, and fallows gray,
Where the nibbling flocks do stray,
Mountains on whose barren breast
The laboring clouds do often rest:
Meadows trim with daisies pied,
Shallow brooks, and rivers wide.
Towers, and battlements it sees
Bosomed high in tufted trees,
Where perhaps some beauty lies,
The cynosure of neighboring eyes.
Hard by, a cottage chimney smokes,
From betwixt two aged oaks,
Where Corydon and Thyrsis met,
Are at their savory dinner set
Of herbs, and other country messes,
Which the neat-handed Phillis dresses;
And then in haste her bower she leaves,
With Thestylis to bind the sheaves;
Or if the earlier season lead
To the tanned haycock in the mead,
Sometimes with secure delight
The upland hamlets will invite,
When the merry bells ring round,
And jocund rebecs sound
To many a youth, and many a maid,
Dancing in the checkered shade;
And young and old come forth to play
On a sunshine holiday,
Till the livelong daylight fail,
Then to the spicy nut-brown ale,
With stories told of many a feat,
How Faery Mab the junkets eat,
She was pinched, and pulled she said,
And he by friar's lantern led
Tells how the drudging goblin sweat,
To earn his cream-bowl duly set,

When in one night, ere glimpse of morn,
His shadowy flail hath threshed the corn
That ten day-laborers could not end,
Then lies him down the lubber fiend.
And stretched out all the chimney's length,
Basks at the fire his hairy strength;
And crop-full out of doors he flings,
Ere the first cock his matin rings.
Thus done the tales, to bed they creep,
By whispering winds soon lulled asleep.
Towered cities please us then,
And the busy hum of men,
Where throngs of knights and barons bold,
In weeds of peace high triumphs hold,
With store of ladies, whose bright eyes
Rain influence, and judge the prize,
Of wit, or arms, while both contend
To win her grace, whom all commend,
There let Hymen oft appear
In saffron robe, with taper clear,
And pomp, and feast, and revelry,
With mask, and antique pageantry,
Such sights as youthful poets dream
On summer eves by haunted stream.
Then to the well-trod stage anon,
If Jonson's learned sock be on,
Or sweetest Shakespeare fancy's child,
Warble his native wood-notes wild,
And ever against eating cares,
Lap me in soft Lydian airs,
Married to immortal verse
Such as the meeting soul may pierce
In notes, with many a winding bout
Of linked sweetness long drawn out,
With wanton heed, and giddy cunning,
The melting voice through mazes running;
Untwisting all the chains that tie

The hidden soul of harmony.
That Orpheus' self may heave his head
From golden slumber on a bed
Of heaped Elysian flowers, and hear
Such strains as would have won the ear
Of Pluto, to have quite set free
His half-regained Eurydice.
These delights, if thou canst give,
Mirth, with thee I mean to live.

Il Penseroso

Hence vain deluding joys,
   The brood of folly without father bred,
How little you bested,
   Or fill the fixed mind with all your toys;
Dwell in some idle brain,
   And fancies fond with gaudy shapes possess,
As thick and numberless
   As the gay motes that people the sunbeams,
Or likest hovering dreams
   The fickle pensioners of Morpheus' train.
But hail thou goddess, sage and holy,
Hail divinest melancholy,
Whose saintly visage is too bright
To hit the sense of human sight;
And therefore to our weaker view,
O'erlaid with black staid wisdom's hue.
Black, but such as in esteem,
Prince Memnon's sister might beseem,
Or that starred Ethiop queen that strove
To set her beauty's praise above
The sea-nymphs, and their powers offended,
Yet thou art higher far descended,
Thee bright-haired Vesta long of yore,
To solitary Saturn bore;

His daughter she (in Saturn's reign,
Such mixture was not held a stain)
Oft in glimmering bowers, and glades
He met her, and in secret shades
Of woody Ida's inmost grove,
Whilst yet there was no fear of Jove.
Come pensive nun, devout and pure,
Sober, steadfast, and demure,
All in a robe of darkest grain,
Flowing with majestic train,
And sable stole of cypress lawn,
Over thy decent shoulders drawn.
Come, but keep thy wonted state,
With even step, and musing gait,
And looks commercing with the skies,
Thy rapt soul sitting in thine eyes:
There held in holy passion still,
Forget thyself to marble, till
With a sad leaden downward cast,
Thou fix them on the earth as fast.
And join with thee calm peace, and quiet,
Spare fast, that oft with gods doth diet,
And hears the muses in a ring,
Aye round about Jove's altar sing.
And add to these retired leisure,
That in trim gardens takes his pleasure;
But first, and chiefest, with thee bring,
Him that yon soars on golden wing,
Guiding the fiery-wheeled throne,
The cherub contemplation,
And the mute silence hist along,
'Less Philomel will deign a song,
In her sweetest, saddest plight,
Smoothing the rugged brow of night,
While Cynthia checks her dragon yoke,
Gently o'er the accustomed oak;
Sweet bird that shunnest the noise of folly,

Most musical, most melancholy!
Thee chantress oft the woods among,
I woo to hear thy even-song;
And missing thee, I walk unseen
On the dry smooth-shaven green,
To behold the wandering moon,
Riding near her highest noon,
Like one that had been led astray
Through the heaven's wide pathless way;
And oft, as if her head she bowed,
Stooping through a fleecy cloud.
Oft on a plat of rising ground,
I hear the far-off curfew sound,
Over some wide-watered shore,
Swinging slow with sullen roar;
Or if the air will not permit,
Some still removed place will fit,
Where glowing embers through the room
Teach light to counterfeit a gloom,
Far from all resort of mirth,
Save the cricket on the hearth,
Or the bellman's drowsy charm,
To bless the doors from nightly harm:
Or let my lamp at midnight hour,
Be seen in some high lonely tower,
Where I may oft outwatch the bear,
With thrice great Hermes, or unsphere
The spirit of Plato to unfold
What worlds, or what vast regions hold
The immortal mind that hath forsook
Her mansion in this fleshly nook:
And of those demons that are found
In fire, air, flood, or underground,
Whose power hath a true consent
With planet, or with element.
Sometime let gorgeous tragedy
In sceptered pall come sweeping by,

Presenting Thebes, or Pelops' line,
Or the tale of Troy divine.
Or what (though rare) of later age,
Ennobled hath the buskined stage.
But, O sad virgin, that thy power
Might raise Musaeus from his bower,
Or bid the soul of Orpheus sing
Such notes as warbled to the string,
Drew iron tears down Pluto's cheek,
And made hell grant what love did seek.
Or call up him that left half told
The story of Cambuscan bold,
Of Camball, and of Algarsife,
And who had Canace to wife,
That owned the virtuous ring and glass,
And of the wondrous horse of brass,
On which the Tartar king did ride;
And if aught else, great bards beside,
In sage and solemn tunes have sung,
Of tourneys and of trophies hung;
Of forests, and enchantments drear,
Where more is meant than meets the ear.
Thus night oft see me in thy pale career,
Till civil-suited morn appear,
Not tricked and frounced as she was wont,
With the Attic boy to hunt,
But kerchieft in a comely cloud,
While rocking winds are piping loud,
Or ushered with a shower still,
When the gust hath blown his fill,
Ending on the rustling leaves,
With minute drops from off the eaves.
And when the sun begins to fling
His flaring beams, me goddess bring
To arched walks of twilight groves,
And shadows brown that Sylvan loves
Of pine, or monumental oak,

Where the rude axe with heaved stroke,
Was never heard the nymphs to daunt,
Or fright them from their hallowed haunt.
There in close covert by some brook,
Where no profaner eye may look,
Hide me from day's garish eye,
While the bee with honeyed thigh,
That at her flowery work doth sing,
And the waters murmuring
With such consort as they keep,
Entice the dewy-feathered sleep;
And let some strange mysterious dream,
Wave at his wings in airy stream,
Of lively portraiture displayed,
Softly on my eyelids laid.
And as I wake, sweet music breathe
Above, about, or underneath,
Sent by some spirit to mortals good,
Or the unseen genius of the wood.
But let my due feet never fail,
To walk the studious cloisters pale,
And love the high embowed roof,
With antique pillars massy proof,
And storied windows richly dight,
Casting a dim religious light.
There let the pealing organ blow,
To the full voiced choir below,
In service high, and anthems clear,
As may with sweetness, through mine ear
Dissolve me into ecstasies,
And bring all heaven before mine eyes.
And may at last my weary age
Find out the peaceful hermitage,
The hairy gown and mossy cell,
Where I may sit and rightly spell
Of every star that heaven doth show,

And every herb that sips the dew;
Till old experience do attain
To something like prophetic strain.
These pleasures melancholy give,
And I with thee will choose to live.

Comus

I𝕹 THE ENGLAND of Milton's youth the masque was a form of private, dramatic entertainment popular at court and among the nobility. People then—no less than today—liked to don costumes and act their parts in pageantry and plays. The masque commonly celebrated some important occasion. Its purpose was compliment, and its tone lyric and courtly. Poetic dialogue, song, and dance were the chief components of the form, with comic and grotesque dances, called antimasques, furnishing the spice of liveliness and contrast.

Early in the 1630's, Milton wrote two masques. The first, apparently, was *Arcades,* which formed a part of an entertainment honoring the Countess Dowager of Derby at Harefield, some twelve miles distant from Horton. The second was *Comus,* which celebrated the inauguration of the Countess's stepson, the Earl of Bridgewater, as Lord President of Wales, at Ludlow Castle, September 29, 1634. *Arcades,* though complete in itself, is too brief to offer much material for criticism, and so it is upon *Comus* that Milton must primarily depend for his reputation as a writer of masques.

Here he has adapted his form admirably to the occasion for which it was intended. The plot concerns the adventures of three children journeying to the inauguration of their father. The Earl, his Lady, his two sons and one daughter all have parts in the entertainment. Henry Lawes, music master of the Earl's family and friend of Milton, played Thyrsis, the attendant spirit; and guests of the Earl had an opportunity to appear in the rout of Comus or in the dances at the end. Added to these virtues were a dramatic situation, a dialogue rich in allusion and poetic imagery, and songs of fluent beauty, which all combine to make this masque still—to those who have seen it acted—a "dainty piece of entertainment" three centuries after the event which Milton meant it to celebrate.

Comus, moreover, illustrates one of the chief qualities of Milton's greatness: his ability not merely to master a conventional form, but in addition to put it to uses and purposes peculiarly his own. In his hands, the masque transcends mere compliment and gallantry and becomes an instrument of moral instruction. The theme is the inviolability of the virtuous mind, and the specific virtue illustrated is that of chastity. The Lady personifies purity; Comus, vice in its sensuous and most seductive form, while his rout of monsters show the true brutishness of evil. Thyrsis is the divine protection that guards the pure. The elder brother represents the mature philosopher, who has come to understand the sage and serious doctrine of virginity; while the second brother is the neophyte, who is not yet perfected and secure in his belief that

> *So dear to heaven is saintly chastity,*
> *That when a soul is found securely so,*
> *A thousand liveried angels lackey her,*
> *Driving far off each thing of sin and guilt.*

This idealistic faith in the "sun-clad power of chastity" was not for Milton the profession of a passing moment. It recurs elsewhere in his writing. And five years after he had written *Comus,* when a newly-met acquaintance in Switzerland asked Milton for his auto-

graph, the poet complied and wrote in the proffered album not only
his name but also the two final lines of his masque:

If virtue feeble were,
Heaven itself would stoop to her.

Comus

(1634)

A Masque Presented at Ludlow Castle, 1634, &c.

THE PERSONS

THE ATTENDANT SPIRIT *afterwards in the habit of* THYRSIS.
COMUS *with his Crew.*
THE LADY.
1ST BROTHER.
2D BROTHER
SABRINA *the Nymph.*

The chief persons which presented were

The Lord Brackley.
Mr. Thomas Egerton his Brother.
The Lady Alice Egerton.

The first scene discovers a wild wood.

The ATTENDANT SPIRIT *descends or enters*

Before the starry threshold of Jove's court
My mansion is, where those immortal shapes
Of bright aerial spirits live insphered
In regions mild of calm and serene air,
Above the smoke and stir of this dim spot,
Which men call earth, and with low-thoughted care

Confined, and pestered in this pinfold here,
Strive to keep up a frail, and feverish being
Unmindful of the crown that virtue gives
After this mortal change, to her true servants
Amongst the enthroned gods on sainted seats.
Yet some there be that by due steps aspire
To lay their just hands on that golden key
That opes the palace of eternity:
To such my errand is, and but for such,
I would not soil these pure ambrosial weeds,
With the rank vapors of this sin-worn mold.
　　But to my task. Neptune besides the sway
Of every salt flood, and each ebbing stream,
Took in by lot 'twixt high, and nether Jove,
Imperial rule of all the sea-girt isles
That like to rich, and various gems inlay
The unadorned bosom of the deep,
Which he to grace his tributary gods
By course commits to several government,
And gives them leave to wear their sapphire crowns,
And wield their little tridents, but this isle
The greatest, and the best of all the main
He quarters to his blue-haired deities,
And all this tract that fronts the falling sun
A noble peer of mickle trust, and power
Has in his charge, with tempered awe to guide
An old, and haughty nation proud in arms:
Where his fair offspring nursed in princely lore,
Are coming to attend their father's state,
And new-entrusted scepter, but their way
Lies through the perplexed paths of this drear wood,
The nodding horror of whose shady brows
Threats the forlorn and wandering passenger.
And here their tender age might suffer peril,
But that by quick command from sovereign Jove
I was despatched for their defense, and guard;

And listen why, for I will tell you now
What never yet was heard in tale or song
From old, or modern bard in hall, or bower.
   Bacchus that first from out the purple grape,
Crushed the sweet poison of misused wine
After the Tuscan mariners transformed
Coasting the Tyrrhene shore, as the winds listed,
On Circe's island fell (who knows not Circe
The daughter of the sun? Whose charmed cup
Whoever tasted, lost his upright shape,
And downward fell into a groveling swine)
This nymph that gazed upon his clustering locks,
With ivy berries wreathed, and his blithe youth,
Had by him, ere he parted thence, a son
Much like his father, but his mother more,
Whom therefore she brought up and Comus named,
Who ripe, and frolic of his full grown age,
Roving the Celtic, and Iberian fields,
At last betakes him to this ominous wood,
And in thick shelter of black shades imbowered,
Excels his mother at her mighty art,
Offering to every weary traveler,
His orient liquor in a crystal glass,
To quench the drought of Phoebus, which as they taste
(For most do taste through fond intemperate thirst)
Soon as the potion works, their human countenance,
The express resemblance of the gods, is changed
Into some brutish form of wolf, or bear,
Or ounce, or tiger, hog, or bearded goat,
All other parts remaining as they were,
And they, so perfect in their misery,
Not once perceive their foul disfigurement,
But boast themselves more comely than before
And all their friends, and native home forget
To roll with pleasure in a sensual sty.
Therefore when any favored of high Jove,

Chances to pass through this adventurous glade,
Swift as the sparkle of a glancing star,
I shoot from heaven to give him safe convoy,
As now I do: But first I must put off
These my sky robes spun out of Iris' woof,
And take the weeds and likeness of a swain,
That to the service of this house belongs,
Who with his soft pipe, and smooth-dittied song
Well knows to still the wild winds when they roar,
And hush the waving woods, nor of less faith,
And in this office of his mountain watch,
Likeliest, and nearest to the present aid
Of this occasion. But I hear the tread
Of hateful steps, I must be viewless now.

COMUS *enters with a charming-rod in one hand, his glass in the*
other, with him a rout of monsters, headed like sundry sorts of
wild beasts, but otherwise like men and women, their apparel
glistering, they come in making a riotous and unruly noise, with
torches in their hands.

Comus. The star that bids the shepherd fold,
Now the top of heaven doth hold,
And the gilded car of day,
His glowing axle doth allay
In the steep Atlantic stream,
And the slope sun his upward beam
Shoots against the dusky pole,
Pacing toward the other goal
Of his chamber in the east.
Meanwhile welcome joy, and feast,
Midnight shout, and revelry,
Tipsy dance, and jollity.
Braid your locks with rosy twine
Dropping odors, dropping wine.
Rigor now is gone to bed,
And Advice with scrupulous head,

Strict Age, and sour Severity,
With their grave saws in slumber lie.
We that are of purer fire
Imitate the starry choir,
Who in their nightly watchful spheres,
Lead in swift round the months and years.
The sounds, and seas with all their finny drove
Now to the moon in wavering morris move,
And on the tawny sands and shelves,
Trip the pert fairies and the dapper elves;
By dimpled brook, and fountain brim,
The wood-nymphs decked with daisies trim,
Their merry wakes and pastimes keep:
What hath night to do with sleep?
Night hath better sweets to prove,
Venus now wakes, and wakens love.
Come let us our rites begin,
'Tis only daylight that makes sin
Which these dun shades will ne'er report.
Hail goddess of nocturnal sport
Dark veiled Cotytto, to whom the secret flame
Of midnight torches burns; mysterious dame
That ne'er art called, but when the dragon womb
Of Stygian darkness spits her thickest gloom,
And makes one blot of all the air,
Stay thy cloudy ebon chair,
Wherein thou ridest with Hecat', and befriend
Us thy vowed priests, till utmost end
Of all thy dues be done, and none left out,
Ere the blabbing eastern scout,
The nice morn on the Indian steep
From her cabined loop-hole peep,
And to the tell-tale sun descry
Our concealed solemnity.
Come, knit hands, and beat the ground,
In a light fantastic round.

The Measure

Break off, break off, I feel the different pace,
Of some chaste footing near about this ground.
Run to your shrouds, within these brakes and trees,
Our number may affright: Some virgin sure
(For so I can distinguish by mine art)
Benighted in these woods. Now to my charms,
And to my wily trains, I shall ere long
Be well stocked with as fair a herd as grazed
About my mother Circe. Thus I hurl
My dazzling spells into the spongy air,
Of power to cheat the eye with blear illusion,
And give it false presentments, lest the place
And my quaint habits breed astonishment,
And put the damsel to suspicious flight,
Which must not be, for that's against my course;
I under fair pretense of friendly ends,
And well-placed words of glozing courtesy
Baited with reasons not unplausible
Wind me into the easy-hearted man,
And hug him into snares. When once her eye
Hath met the virtue of this magic dust,
I shall appear some harmless villager
And hearken, if I may her business hear.
But here she comes, I fairly step aside

THE LADY *enters*

Lady. This way the noise was, if mine ear be true,
My best guide now, methought it was the sound
Of riot, and ill managed merriment,
Such as the jocund flute, or gamesome pipe
Stirs up among the loose unlettered hinds,
When for their teeming flocks, and granges full
In wanton dance they praise the bounteous Pan,
And thank the gods amiss. I should be loath
To meet the rudeness, and swilled insolence

Of such late wassailers, yet O where else
Shall I inform my unacquainted feet
In the blind mazes of this tangled wood?
My brothers when they saw me wearied out
With this long way, resolving here to lodge
Under the spreading favor of these pines,
Stepped as they said to the next thicket side
To bring me berries, or such cooling fruit
As the kind hospitable woods provide.
They left me then, when the gray-hooded even
Like a sad votarist in palmer's weed
Rose from the hindmost wheels of Phoebus' wain.
But where they are, and why they came not back,
Is now the labor of my thoughts, 'tis likeliest
They had engaged their wandering steps too far,
And envious darkness, ere they could return,
Had stole them from me, else O thievish night
Why should thou, but for some felonious end,
In thy dark lantern thus close up the stars,
That nature hung in heaven, and filled their lamps
With everlasting oil, to give due light
To the misled and lonely traveler?
This is the place, as well as I may guess,
Whence even now the tumult of loud mirth
Was rife, and perfect in my listening ear,
Yet nought but single darkness do I find.
What might this be? A thousand fantasies
Begin to throng into my memory
Of calling shapes, and beckoning shadows dire,
And airy tongues, that syllable men's names
On sands, and shores, and desert wildernesses.
These thoughts may startle well, but not astound
The virtuous mind, that ever walks attended
By a strong siding champion conscience.
O welcome pure-eyed faith, white-handed hope,
Thou hovering angel girt with golden wings,
And thou unblemished form of chastity.

I see ye visibly, and now believe
That he, the supreme good, to whom all things ill
Are but as slavish officers of vengeance,
Would send a glistening guardian if need were
To keep my life and honor unassailed.
Was I deceived, or did a sable cloud
Turn forth her silver lining on the night?
I did not err, there does a sable cloud
Turn forth her silver lining on the night,
And casts a gleam over this tufted grove.
I cannot hallo to my brothers, but
Such noise as I can make to be heard farthest
I'll venture, for my new enlivened spirits
Prompt me; and they perhaps are not far off.

Song

Sweet Echo, sweetest nymph that livest unseen
     Within thy airy shell
   By slow Meander's margent green,
And in the violet embroidered vale
   Where the love-lorn nightingale
Nightly to thee her sad song mourneth well.
Canst thou not tell me of a gentle pair
    That likest thy Narcissus are?
     O if thou have
   Hid them in some flowery cave,
    Tell me but where
 Sweet queen of parley, daughter of the sphere,
  So mayest thou be translated to the skies,
And give resounding grace to all heaven's harmonies.

Comus. Can any mortal mixture of earth's mold
Breathe such divine enchanting ravishment?
Sure something holy lodges in that breast,
And with these raptures moves the vocal air
To testify his hidden residence;

How sweetly did they float upon the wings
Of silence, through the empty-vaulted night
At every fall smoothing the raven down
Of darkness till it smiled: I have oft heard
My mother Circe with the sirens three,
Amidst the flowery-kirtled naiades
Culling their potent herbs, and baleful drugs,
Who as they sung, would take the prisoned soul,
And lap it in Elysium, Scylla wept,
And chid her barking waves into attention,
And fell Charybdis murmured soft applause:
Yet they in pleasing slumber lulled the sense,
And in sweet madness robbed it of itself,
But such a sacred, and home-felt delight,
Such sober certainty of waking bliss
I never heard till now. I'll speak to her
And she shall be my queen. Hail foreign wonder
Whom certain these rough shades did never breed
Unless the goddess that in rural shrine
Dwellest here with Pan, or Sylvan, by blest song
Forbidding every bleak unkindly fog
To touch the prosperous growth of this tall wood.
    Lady. Nay gentle shepherd ill is lost that praise
That is addressed to unattending ears,
Not any boast of skill, but extreme shift
How to regain my severed company
Compelled me to awake the courteous Echo
To give me answer from her mossy couch.
    Comus. What chance good lady hath bereft you thus?
    Lady. Dim darkness, and this leafy labyrinth.
    Comus. Could that divide you from near-ushering guides?
    Lady. They left me weary on a grassy turf.
    Comus. By falsehood, or discourtesy, or why?
    Lady. To seek in the valley some cool friendly spring.
    Comus. And left your fair side all unguarded lady?
    Lady. They were but twain, and purposed quick return.
    Comus. Perhaps forestalling night prevented them.

Lady. How easy my misfortune is to hit!

Comus. Imports their loss, beside the present need?

Lady. No less than if I should my brothers lose.

Comus. Were they of manly prime, or youthful bloom?

Lady. As smooth as Hebe's their unrazored lips.

Comus. Two such I saw, what time the labored ox
In his loose traces from the furrow came,
And the swinked hedger at his supper sat;
I saw them under a green mantling vine
That crawls along the side of yon small hill,
Plucking ripe clusters from the tender shoots,
Their port was more than human, as they stood;
I took it for a faëry vision
Of some gay creatures of the element
That in the colors of the rainbow live
And play in the plighted clouds. I was awe-struck,
And as I passed, I worshiped; if those you seek
It were a journey like the path to heaven,
To help you find them.

    Lady.   Gentle villager
What readiest way would bring me to that place?

    Comus. Due west it rises from this shrubby point.

    Lady. To find out that, good shepherd, I suppose,
In such a scant allowance of star-light,
Would overtask the best land-pilot's art,
Without the sure guess of well-practiced feet.

    Comus. I know each lane, and every alley green
Dingle, or bushy dell of this wild wood,
And every bosky bourn from side to side
My daily walks and ancient neighborhood,
And if your stray attendance be yet lodged,
Or shroud within these limits, I shall know
Ere morrow wake, or the low roosted lark
From her thatched pallet rouse, if otherwise
I can conduct you lady to a low
But loyal cottage, where you may be safe
Till further quest.

Lady.   Shepherd I take thy word,
And trust thy honest offered courtesy,
Which oft is sooner found in lowly sheds
With smoky rafters, than in tapestry halls
And courts of princes, where it first was named,
And yet is most pretended: In a place
Less warranted than this, or less secure
I cannot be, that I should fear to change it,
Eye me blest Providence, and square my trial
To my proportioned strength.
                         Shepherd lead on.

The TWO BROTHERS

Elder Brother. Unmuffle ye faint stars, and thou fair moon
That wontest to love the traveler's benison,
Stoop thy pale visage through an amber cloud,
And disinherit chaos, that reigns here
In double night of darkness, and of shades;
Or if your influence be quite dammed up
With black usurping mists, some gentle taper
Though a rush candle from the wicker hole
Of some clay habitation visit us
With thy long leveled rule of streaming light,
And thou shalt be our star of Arcady,
Or Tyrian Cynosure.
Second Brother.   Or if our eyes
Be barred that happiness, might we but hear
The folded flocks penned in their wattled cotes,
Or sound of pastoral reed with oaten stops,
Or whistle from the lodge, or village cock
Count the night watches to his feathery dames,
'Twould be some solace yet, some little cheering
In this close dungeon of innumerous boughs.
But O that hapless virgin our lost sister
Where may she wander now, whither betake her
From the chill dew, amongst rude burs and thistles?
Perhaps some cold bank is her bolster now

Or 'gainst the rugged bark of some broad elm
Leans her unpillowed head fraught with sad fears.
What if in wild amazement, and affright,
Or while we speak within the direful grasp
Of savage hunger, or of savage heat?

Elder Brother. Peace brother, be not over-exquisite
To cast the fashion of uncertain evils;
For grant they be so, while they rest unknown,
What need a man forestall his date of grief,
And run to meet what he would most avoid?
Or if they be but false alarms of fear,
How bitter is such self-delusion?
I do not think my sister so to seek,
Or so unprincipled in virtue's book,
And the sweet peace that goodness bosoms ever,
As that the single want of light and noise
(Not being in danger, as I trust she is not)
Could stir the constant mood of her calm thoughts,
And put them into misbecoming plight.
Virtue could see to do what virtue would
By her own radiant light, though sun and moon
Were in the flat sea sunk. And wisdom's self
Oft seeks to sweet retired solitude,
Where with her best nurse contemplation
She plumes her feathers, and lets grow her wings
That in the various bustle of resort
Were all too ruffled, and sometimes impaired.
He that has light within his own clear breast
May sit in the center, and enjoy bright day,
But he that hides a dark soul, and foul thoughts
Benighted walks under the midday sun;
Himself is his own dungeon.

Second Brother. 'Tis most true
That musing meditation most affects
The pensive secrecy of desert cell,
Far from the cheerful haunt of men, and herds,
And sits as safe as in a senate house,

For who would rob a hermit of his weeds,
His few books, or his beads, or maple dish,
Or do his gray hairs any violence?
But beauty like the fair Hesperian tree
Laden with blooming gold, had need the guard
Of dragon watch with unenchanted eye,
To save her blossoms, and defend her fruit
From the rash hand of bold Incontinence.
You may as well spread out the unsunned heaps
Of miser's treasure by an outlaw's den,
And tell me it is safe, as bid me hope
Danger will wink on opportunity,
And let a single helpless maiden pass
Uninjured in this wild surrounding waste.
Of night, or loneliness it recks me not,
I fear the dread events that dog them both,
Lest some ill greeting touch attempt the person
Of our unowned sister.
   Elder Brother.   I do not, brother,
Infer, as if I thought my sister's state
Secure without all doubt, or controversy:
Yet where an equal poise of hope and fear
Does arbitrate the event, my nature is
That I incline to hope, rather than fear,
And gladly banish squint suspicion.
My sister is not so defenseless left
As you imagine, she has a hidden strength
Which you remember not.
   Second Brother.   What hidden strength,
Unless the strength of heaven, if you mean that?
   Elder Brother. I mean that too, but yet a hidden strength
Which if heaven gave it, may be termed her own:
'Tis chastity, my brother, chastity:
She that has that, is clad in complete steel,
And like a quivered nymph with arrows keen
May trace huge forests, and unharbored heaths,
Infamous hills, and sandy perilous wilds.

Where through the sacred rays of chastity,
No savage fierce, bandit, or mountaineer
Will dare to soil her virgin purity,
Yea there, where very desolation dwells
By grots, and caverns shagged with horrid shades,
She may pass on with unblenched majesty,
Be it not done in pride, or in presumption.
Some say no evil thing that walks by night
In fog, or fire, by lake, or moorish fen,
Blue meager hag, or stubborn unlaid ghost,
That breaks his magic chains at curfew time,
No goblin, or swart faëry of the mine,
Hath hurtful power o'er true virginity.
Do ye believe me yet, or shall I call
Antiquity from the old schools of Greece
To testify the arms of chastity?
Hence had the huntress Dian her dread bow,
Fair silver-shafted queen forever chaste,
Wherewith she tamed the brinded lioness
And spotted mountain pard, but set at nought
The frivolous bolt of Cupid, gods and men
Feared her stern frown, and she was queen of the woods.
What was that snaky-headed Gorgon shield
That wise Minerva wore, unconquered virgin,
Wherewith she freezed her foes to congealed stone?
But rigid looks of chaste austerity,
And noble grace that dashed brute violence
With sudden adoration, and blank awe.
So dear to heaven is saintly chastity,
That when a soul is found sincerely so,
A thousand liveried angels lackey her,
Driving far off each thing of sin and guilt,
And in clear dream, and solemn vision
Tell her of things that no gross ear can hear,
Till oft converse with heavenly habitants
Begin to cast a beam on the outward shape,
The unpolluted temple of the mind,

And turns it by degrees to the soul's essence,
Till all be made immortal: but when lust
By unchaste looks, loose gestures, and foul talk,
But most by lewd and lavish act of sin,
Lets in defilement to the inward parts,
The soul grows clotted by contagion,
Imbodies, and imbrutes, till she quite lose
The divine property of her first being.
Such are those thick and gloomy shadows damp
Oft seen in charnel vaults, and sepulchers
Lingering, and sitting by a new made grave,
As loath to leave the body that it loved,
And linked itself by carnal sensuality
To a degenerate and degraded state.

    Second Brother. How charming is divine philosophy!
Not harsh, and crabbed as dull fools suppose,
But musical as is Apollo's lute,
And a perpetual feast of nectared sweets,
Where no crude surfeit reigns.

    Elder Brother.   List, list, I hear
Some far off hallo break the silent air.

    Second Brother. Methought so too; what should it be?
    Elder Brother.   For certain
Either someone like us night-foundered here,
Or else some neighbor woodman. or at worst,
Some roving robber calling to his fellows.

    Second Brother. Heaven keep my sister, again, again, and near,
Best draw, and stand upon our guard.

    Elder Brother.   I'll hallo.
If he be friendly he comes well, if not,
Defense is a good cause. and heaven be for us.

      The ATTENDANT SPIRIT *habited like a shepherd*
That hallo I should know, what are you? speak;
Come not too near, you fall on iron stakes else.

    Spirit. What voice is that, my young lord? speak again.
    Second Brother. O brother, 'tis my father's shepherd sure.

Elder Brother. Thyrsis? Whose artful strains have oft delayed
The huddling brook to hear his madrigal,
And sweetened every musk rose of the dale,
How camest thou here good swain? hath any ram
Slipped from the fold, or young kid lost his dam,
Or straggling wether the pent flock forsook?
How couldst thou find this dark sequestered nook?

    Spirit. O my loved master's heir, and his next joy,
I came not here on such a trivial toy
As a strayed ewe, or to pursue the stealth
Of pilfering wolf, not all the fleecy wealth
That doth enrich these downs, is worth a thought
To this my errand, and the care it brought.
But O my virgin lady, where is she?
How chance she is not in your company?

    Elder Brother. To tell thee sadly shepherd, without blame,
Or our neglect, we lost her as we came.

    Spirit. Ay me unhappy then my fears are true.

    Elder Brother. What fears good Thyrsis? Prithee briefly show.

    Spirit. I'll tell ye, 'tis not vain or fabulous,
(Though so esteemed by shallow ignorance)
What the sage poets taught by the heavenly muse,
Storied of old in high immortal verse
Of dire chimeras and enchanted isles,
And rifted rocks whose entrance leads to hell,
For such there be, but unbelief is blind.

    Within the navel of this hideous wood,
Immured in cypress shades a sorcerer dwells
Of Bacchus, and of Circe born, great Comus,
Deep skilled in all his mother's witcheries,
And here to every thirsty wanderer,
By sly enticement gives his baneful cup,
With many murmurs mixed, whose pleasing poison
The visage quite transforms of him that drinks,
And the inglorious likeness of a beast
Fixes instead, unmolding reason's mintage
Charactered in the face; this have I learned

Tending my flocks hard by in the hilly crofts,
That brow this bottom glade, whence night by night
He and his monstrous rout are heard to howl
Like stabled wolves, or tigers at their prey,
Doing abhorred rites to Hecate
In their obscured haunts of inmost bowers.
Yet have they many baits, and guileful spells
To inveigle and invite the unwary sense
Of them that pass unweeting by the way.
This evening late by then the chewing flocks
Had taken their supper on the savory herb
Of knot-grass dew-besprent, and were in fold,
I sat me down to watch upon a bank
With ivy canopied, and interwove
With flaunting honeysuckle, and began
Wrapt in a pleasing fit of melancholy
To meditate my rural minstrelsy,
Till fancy had her fill, but ere a close
The wonted roar was up amidst the woods,
And filled the air with barbarous dissonance,
At which I ceased, and listened them a while,
Till an unusual stop of sudden silence
Gave respite to the drowsy frighted steeds
That draw the litter of close-curtained sleep.
At last a soft and solemn breathing sound
Rose like a steam of rich distilled perfumes,
And stole upon the air, that even silence
Was took ere she was ware, and wished she might
Deny her nature, and be never more,
Still to be so displaced. I was all ear,
And took in strains that might create a soul
Under the ribs of death, but O ere long
Too well I did perceive it was the voice
Of my most honored lady, your dear sister.
Amazed I stood, harrowed with grief and fear.
And 'O poor hapless nightingale' thought I,
'How sweet thou singest, how near the deadly snare!'

Then down the lawns í ran with headlong haste
Through paths, and turnings often trod by day,
Till guided by mine ear I found the place
Where that damned wizard hid in sly disguise
(For so by certain signs I knew) had met
Already, ere my best speed could prevent,
The aidless innocent lady his wished prey,
Who gently asked if he had seen such two,
Supposing him some neighbor villager;
Longer I durst not stay, but soon I guessed
Ye were the two she meant, with that I sprung
Into swift flight, till I had found you here,
But further know I not.
    Second Brother.   O night and shades,
How are ye joined with hell in triple knot
Against the unarmed weakness of one virgin
Alone, and helpless! is this the confidence
You gave me brother?
    Elder Brother.   Yes, and keep it still,
Lean on it safely, not a period
Shall be unsaid for me: against the threats
Of malice or of sorcery, or that power
Which erring men call chance, this I hold firm,
Virtue may be assailed, but never hurt,
Surprised by unjust force, but not enthralled,
Yea even that which mischief meant most harm,
Shall in the happy trial prove most glory.
But evil on itself shall back recoil,
And mix no more with goodness, when at last
Gathered like scum, and settled to itself
It shall be in eternal restless change
Self-fed, and self-consumed; if this fail,
The pillared firmament is rottenness,
And earth's base built on stubble. But come let's on.
Against the opposing will and arm of heaven
May never this just sword be lifted up,
But for that damned magician, let him be girt

With all the grisly legions that troop
Under the sooty flag of Acheron,
Harpies and Hydras, or all the monstrous forms
'Twixt Africa and Ind, I'll find him out,
And force him to return his purchase back,
Or drag him by the curls, to a foul death,
Cursed as his life.

    Spirit.   Alas good venturous youth,
I love thy courage yet, and bold emprise,
But here thy sword can do thee little stead,
Far other arms, and other weapons must
Be those that quell the might of hellish charms,
He with his bare wand can unthread thy joints,
And crumble all thy sinews.

    Elder Brother.   Why prithee shepherd
How durst thou then thyself approach so near
As to make this relation?

    Spirit.   Care and utmost shifts
How to secure the lady from surprisal,
Brought to my mind a certain shepherd lad
Of small regard to see to, yet well skilled
In every virtuous plant and healing herb
That spreads her verdant leaf to the morning ray,
He loved me well, and oft would beg me sing,
Which when I did, he on the tender grass
Would sit, and hearken even to ecstasy,
And in requital ope his leathern scrip,
And show me simples of a thousand names
Telling their strange and vigorous faculties;
Amongst the rest a small unsightly root,
But of divine effect, he culled me out;
The leaf was darkish, and had prickles on it,
But in another country, as he said,
Bore a bright golden flower, but not in this soil:
Unknown, and like esteemed, and the dull swain
Treads on it daily with his clouted shoon,
And yet more medicinal is it than that moly

That Hermes once to wise Ulysses gave;
He called it haemony, and gave it me,
And bade me keep it as of sovereign use
'Gainst all enchantments, mildew blast, or damp
Or ghastly furies' apparition;
I pursed it up, but little reckoning made,
Till now that this extremity compelled,
But now I find it true; for by this means
I knew the foul enchanter though disguised,
Entered the very lime-twigs of his spells,
And yet came off: if you have this about you
(As I will give you when we go) you may
Boldly assault the necromancer's hall;
Where if he be, with dauntless hardihood,
And brandished blade rush on him, break his glass,
And shed the luscious liquor on the ground,
But seize his wand, though he and his cursed crew
Fierce sign of battle make, and menace high,
Or like the sons of Vulcan vomit smoke,
Yet will they soon retire, if he but shrink.

    Elder Brother. Thyrsis lead on apace, I'll follow thee,
And some good angel bear a shield before us.

*The scene changes to a stately palace, set out with all manner of
    deliciousness: soft music, tables spread with all dainties.* COMUS
    appears with his rabble, and THE LADY *set in an enchanted chair
    to whom he offers his glass, which she puts by, and goes about
    to rise.*

    Comus. Nay lady sit; if I but wave this wand,
Your nerves are all chained up in alabaster,
And you a statue, or as Daphne was
Root-bound, that fled Apollo,
    Lady.   Fool do not boast,
Thou canst not touch the freedom of my mind
With all thy charms, although this corporal rind
Thou hast immanacled, while heaven sees good.

Comus. Why are you vexed lady? why do you frown?
Here dwell no frowns, nor anger, from these gates
Sorrow flies far: See here be all the pleasures
That fancy can beget on youthful thoughts,
When the fresh blood grows lively, and returns
Brisk as the April buds in primrose season.
And first behold this cordial julep here
That flames, and dances in his crystal bounds
With spirits of balm, and fragrant syrups mixed.
Not that nepenthes which the wife of Thone,
In Egypt gave to Jove-born Helena
Is of such power to stir up joy as this,
To life so friendly, or so cool to thirst.
Why should you be so cruel to yourself,
And to those dainty limbs which Nature lent
For gentle usage, and soft delicacy?
But you invert the covenants of her trust,
And harshly deal like an ill borrower
With that which you received on other terms,
Scorning the unexempt condition
By which all mortal frailty must subsist,
Refreshment after toil, ease after pain,
That have been tired all day without repast,
And timely rest have wanted, but fair virgin
This will restore all soon.
          Lady.   'Twill not false traitor,
'Twill not restore the truth and honesty
That thou hast banished from thy tongue with lies,
Was this the cottage, and the safe abode
Thou toldest me of? What grim aspects are these,
These ugly-headed monsters? Mercy guard me!
Hence with thy brewed enchantments, foul deceiver,
Hast thou betrayed my credulous innocence
With vizored falsehood, and base forgery,
And wouldst thou seek again to trap me here
With liquorish baits fit to ensnare a brute?
Were it a draught for Juno when she banquets,

I would not taste thy treasonous offer; none
But such as are good men can give good things,
And that which is not good, is not delicious
To a well-governed and wise appetite.

    Comus. O foolishness of men! that lend their ears
To those budge doctors of the Stoic fur,
And fetch their precepts from the Cynic tub,
Praising the lean and sallow abstinence.
Wherefore did nature pour her bounties forth,
With such a full and unwithdrawing hand,
Covering the earth with odors, fruits, and flocks,
Thronging the seas with spawn innumerable,
But all to please, and sate the curious taste?
And set to work millions of spinning worms,
That in their green shops weave the smooth-haired silk
To deck her sons, and that no corner might
Be vacant of her plenty, in her own loins
She hutched the all-worshiped ore, and precious gems
To store her children with; if all the world
Should in a pet of temperance feed on pulse,
Drink the clear stream, and nothing wear but frieze,
The all-giver would be unthanked, would be unpraised,
Not half his riches known, and yet despised,
And we should serve him as a grudging master,
As a penurious niggard of his wealth,
And live like nature's bastards, not her sons,
Who would be quite surcharged with her own weight,
And strangled with her waste fertility;
The earth cumbered, and the winged air darked with plumes,
The herds would over-multitude their lords,
The sea o'erfraught would swell, and the unsought diamonds
Would so emblaze the forehead of the deep,
And so bestud with stars, that they below
Would grow inured to light, and come at last
To gaze upon the sun with shameless brows.
List lady be not coy, and be not cozened
With that same vaunted name virginity,

Beauty is nature's coin, must not be hoarded,
But must be current, and the good thereof
Consists in mutual and partaken bliss,
Unsavory in the enjoyment of itself.
If you let slip time, like a neglected rose
It withers on the stalk with languished head.
Beauty is nature's brag, and must be shown
In courts, at feasts, and high solemnities
Where most may wonder at the workmanship;
It is for homely features to keep home,
They had their name thence; coarse complexions
And cheeks of sorry grain will serve to ply
The sampler, and to tease the housewife's wool.
What need a vermeil-tinctured lip for that
Love-darting eyes, or tresses like the morn?
There was another meaning in these gifts,
Think what, and be advised, you are but young yet.

   Lady. I had not thought to have unlocked my lips
In this unhallowed air, but that this juggler
Would think to charm my judgment, as mine eyes
Obtruding false rules pranked in reason's garb.
I hate when vice can bolt her arguments,
And virtue has no tongue to check her pride:
Imposter do not charge most innocent nature,
As if she would her children should be riotous
With her abundance, she good cateress
Means her provision only to the good
That live according to her sober laws,
And holy dictate of spare temperance:
If every just man that now pines with want
Had but a moderate and beseeming share
Of that which lewdly-pampered luxury
Now heaps upon some few with vast excess,
Nature's full blessings would be well dispensed
In unsuperfluous even proportion,
And she no whit encumbered with her store.

And then the giver would be better thanked,
His praise due paid, for swinish gluttony
Ne'er looks to heaven amidst his gorgeous feast,
But with besotted base ingratitude
Crams, and blasphemes his feeder. Shall I go on?
Or have I said enow? To him that dares
Arm his profane tongue with contemptuous words
Against the sun-clad power of chastity,
Fain would I something say, yet to what end?
Thou hast nor ear, nor soul to apprehend
The sublime notion, and high mystery
That must be uttered to unfold the sage
And serious doctrine of virginity,
And thou art worthy that thou shouldst not know
More happiness than this thy present lot.
Enjoy your dear wit, and gay rhetoric
That hath so well been taught her dazzling fence,
Thou are not fit to hear thyself convinced;
Yet should I try, the uncontrolled worth
Of this pure cause would kindle my rapt spirits
To such a flame of sacred vehemence,
That dumb things would be moved to sympathize,
And the brute Earth would lend her nerves, and shake,
Till all thy magic structures reared so high,
Were shattered into heaps o'er thy false head.
   Comus. She fables not, I feel that I do fear
Her words set off by some superior power;
And though not mortal, yet a cold shuddering dew
Dips me all o'er, as when the wrath of Jove
Speaks thunder, and the chains of Erebus
To some of Saturn's crew. I must dissemble,
And try her yet more strongly. Come, no more,
This is mere moral babble, and direct
Against the canon laws of our foundation;
I must not suffer this, yet 'tis but the lees
And settlings of a melancholy blood;

But this will cure all straight, one sip of this
Will bathe the drooping spirits in delight
Beyond the bliss of dreams. Be wise, and taste.—

THE BROTHERS *rush in with swords drawn, wrest his glass out of
his hand, and break it against the ground; his rout make sign of
resistance, but are all driven in; the* ATTENDANT SPIRIT *comes in.*

Spirit. What, have you let the false enchanter scape?
O ye mistook, ye should have snatched his wand
And bound him fast; without his rod reversed,
And backward mutters of dissevering power,
We cannot free the lady that sits here
In stony fetters fixed, and motionless;
Yet stay, be not disturbed, now I bethink me,
Some other means I have which may be used,
Which once of Meliboeus old I learned,
The soothest shepherd that e'er piped on plains.
   There is a gentle nymph not far from hence,
That with moist curb sways the smooth Severn stream,
Sabrina is her name, a virgin pure,
Whilom she was the daughter of Locrine,
That had the scepter from his father Brute.
The guiltless damsel flying the mad pursuit
Of her enraged stepdame Guendolen,
Commended her fair innocence to the flood
That stayed her flight with his cross-flowing course,
The water nymphs that in the bottom played,
Held up their pearled wrists and took her in,
Bearing her straight to aged Nereus' hall,
Who piteous of her woes, reared her lank head,
And gave her to his daughters to imbathe
In nectared lavers strewed with asphodel,
And through the porch and inlet of each sense
Dropped in ambrosial oils till she revived,
And underwent a quick immortal change
Made goddess of the river; still she retains

Her maiden gentleness, and oft at eve
Visits the herds along the twilight meadows,
Helping all urchin blasts, and ill luck signs
That the shrewd meddling elf delights to make,
Which she with precious vialed liquors heals.
For which the shepherds at their festivals
Carol her goodness loud in rustic lays,
And throw sweet garland wreaths into her stream
Of pansies, pinks, and gaudy daffodils.
And, as the old swain said, she can unlock
The clasping charm, and thaw the numbing spell,
If she be right invoked in warbled song,
For maidenhood she loves, and will be swift
To aid a virgin, such as was herself
In hard-besetting need, this will I try
And add the power of some adjuring verse.

Song

Sabrina fair
   Listen where thou art sitting
Under the glassy, cool, translucent wave,
   In twisted braids of lilies knitting
The loose train of thy amber-dropping hair,
    Listen for dear honor's sake,
    Goddess of the silver lake,
       Listen and save.

    Listen and appear to us
    In name of great Oceanus,
    By the earth-shaking Neptune's mace,
    And Tethys' grave majestic pace,
    By hoary Nereus' wrinkled look,
    And the Carpathian wizard's hook,

    By scaly Triton's winding shell,
    And old soothsaying Glaucus' spell,

Song

Sabrina faire
listen where thou art sitting
the glassie coole translucent wave
in twisted braids of lillies knitting
the loose traine of thy amber dropping haire
listen for deare honours sake
Goddesse of the silver lake
Listen and save

Listen and appeare to us
in name of great Oceanus
by th'earth shaking Neptunes mace
and Tethys grave majestick pace
by hoarie Nereus wrincled looke
and the Carpathian wizards hooke
by scaly Tritons winding shell
and old sooth-saying Glaucus spell
by Leucothea's lovely hands
and her son that rules the strands
by Thetis tinsel-slipper'd feet
and the songs of Sirens sweet
by dead Parthenope's deere tomb
and faire Ligea's golden combe
wherwith she sits on diamond rocks
sleeking her soft alluring locks
by all the nymphs that nightly dance
upon thy streames with wilie glance
rise rise & heave thy rosie head
from thy corall-paven bed
and bridle in thy headlong wave
till thou our summons answer'd have
Listen & save

to be said

Song from *Comus*, in Milton's own hand. From the manuscript of
Milton's minor poems, preserved in the Library of Trinity College,
Cambridge.

By Leucothea's lovely hands,
And her son that rules the strands,
By Thetis' tinsel-slippered feet,
And the songs of sirens sweet,
By dead Parthenope's dear tomb,
And fair Ligea's golden comb,
Wherewith she sits on diamond rocks
Sleeking her soft alluring locks,
By all the nymphs that nightly dance
Upon thy streams with wily glance,
Rise, rise, and heave thy rosy head
From thy coral-paven bed,
And bridle in thy headlong wave,
Till thou our summons answered have.

Listen and save.

SABRINA *rises, attended by water-nymphs, and sings.*
By the rushy-fringed bank,
Where grows the willow and the osier dank,
My sliding chariot stays,
Thick set with agate, and the azurn sheen
Of turquoise blue, and emerald green
That in the channel strays,
Whilst from off the waters fleet
Thus I set my printless feet
O'er the cowslip's velvet head,
That bends not as I tread,
Gentle swain at thy request
I am here.

Spirit. Goddess dear
We implore thy powerful hand
To undo the charmed band
Of true virgin here distressed,
Through the force, and through the wile
Of unblessed enchanter vile.

Sabrina. Shepherd 'tis my office best
To help ensnared chastity;
Brightest lady look on me,
Thus I sprinkle on thy breast
Drops that from my fountain pure,
I have kept of precious cure,
Thrice upon thy finger's tip,
Thrice upon thy rubied lip,
Next this marble venomed seat
Smeared with gums of glutinous heat
I touch with chaste palms moist and cold,
Now the spell hath lost his hold;
And I must haste ere morning hour
To wait in Amphitrite's bower.

SABRINA *descends, and* THE LADY *rises out of her seat*

Spirit. Virgin, daughter of Locrine
Sprung of old Anchises' line
May thy brimmed waves for this
Their full tribute never miss
From a thousand petty rills,
That tumble down the snowy hills:
Summer drouth, or singed air
Never scorch thy tresses fair,
Nor wet October's torrent flood
Thy molten crystal fill with mud,
May thy billows roll ashore
The beryl, and the golden ore,
May thy lofty head be crowned
With many a tower and terrace round,
And here and there thy banks upon
With groves of myrrh, and cinnamon.
Come lady while heaven lends us grace,
Let us fly this cursed place,
Lest the sorcerer us entice
With some other new device.
Not a waste, or needless sound

'Till we come to holier ground,
I shall be your faithful guide
Through this gloomy covert wide,
And not many furlongs thence
Is your father's residence,
Where this night are met in state
Many a friend to gratulate
His wished presence, and beside
All the swains that there abide,
With jigs, and rural dance resort,
We shall catch them at their sport,
And our sudden coming there
Will double all their mirth and cheer;
Come let us haste, the stars grow high,
But night sits monarch yet in the mid sky.

*The scene changes, presenting Ludlow Town and the President's
castle, then come in country dancers, after them the* ATTENDANT
SPIRIT, *with the two* BROTHERS *and* THE LADY.

Song

Spirit. Back shepherds, back, enough your play,
Till next sun-shine holiday,
Here be without duck or nod
Other trippings to be trod
Of lighter toes, and such court guise
As Mercury did first devise
With the mincing Dryades
On the lawns, and on the leas.

This second song presents them to their father and mother.
Noble lord, and lady bright,
I have brought ye new delight,
Here behold so goodly grown
Three fair branches of your own,
Heaven hath timely tried their youth,
Their faith, their patience, and their truth.

And sent them here through hard assays
With a crown of deathless praise,
   To triumph in victorious dance
O'er sensual folly, and intemperance.

The dances ended, the SPIRIT *epiloguizes.*

   Spirit. To the ocean now I fly,
And those happy climes that lie
Where day never shuts his eye,
Up in the broad fields of the sky:
There I suck the liquid air
All amidst the gardens fair
Of Hesperus, and his daughters three
That sing about the golden tree:
Along the crisped shades and bowers
Revels the spruce and jocund spring,
The graces, and the rosy-bosomed hours,
Thither all their bounties bring,
That there eternal summer dwells,
And west winds, with musky wing
About the cedarn alleys fling
Nard, and cassia's balmy smells.
Iris there with humid bow,
Waters the odorous banks that blow
Flowers of more mingled hue
Than her purfled scarf can show,
And drenches with Elysian dew
(List mortals if your ears be true)
Beds of hyacinth, and roses
Where young Adonis oft reposes,
Waxing well of his deep wound
In slumber soft, and on the ground
Sadly sits the Assyrian queen;
But far above in spangled sheen
Celestial Cupid her famed son advanced,
Holds his dear Psyche sweet entranced
After her wandering labors long,

Till free consent the gods among
Make her his eternal bride,
And from her fair unspotted side
Two blissful twins are to be born,
Youth and joy; so Jove hath sworn.
    But now my task is smoothly done,
i can fly, or I can run
Quickly to the green earth's end
Where the bowed welkin slow doth bend
And from thence can soar as soon
To the corners of the moon.
    Mortals that would follow me,
Love virtue, she alone is free,
She can teach ye how to climb
Higher than the sphery chime;
Or if virtue feeble were,
Heaven itself would stoop to her.

Lycidas

ON AUGUST 1, 1637, Edward King, schoolmate of Milton and Fellow of Christ's College, made his will and then left Cambridge for his home in Ireland. Ten days later—in his twenty-fifth year—King was dead, drowned off the coast of Wales. His affection for Christ's he had manifested by bequeathing it the whole of his estate; and the college sought to express its sense of loss by a volume of verses honoring his memory. When an invitation to share in this memorial came to Milton, he was at Horton and—if our surmise is correct—not particularly happy. Perturbed by a desire for fame and by a sense of his present inadequacies, he found in King's untimely death and the presence of the plague a grim reminder that he too might be cut off before his genius could reach its full flower and fruition.

In such a state of mind, Milton sat down and wrote the greatest of English elegies. Based on the pastoral elegiac form as it had developed through Greek, Latin, and Renaissance literatures, *Lycidas* demonstrates Milton's complete mastery and assimilation of that traditional form. His monody is packed with echoes of Theocritus, Virgil, and other masters of the genre, and reveals the ease and dexterity with which he could follow, yet manipulate to his peculiar purpose, the set body of precedents that compose this literary type.

The chief of these are the fictions that the dead man was a shepherd, that all nature mourns for him, the procession of appropriate mourners, and the concluding transition from sorrow to joy because the shepherd lives immortal in another and happier realm. This mastery of convention, combined with a consummate control of a seemingly irregular verse form and his gift of vivid, and often succinct, imagery, indicate that Milton—whatever the sense of his own shortcomings may have been—had attained the full maturity of his art. Milton's *Lycidas,* Shelley's *Adonais,* and Arnold's *Thyrsis* are the three great pastoral elegies of English literature, and of these three *Lycidas* is generally acknowledged the greatest.

Usually this elegy is taken to be about Edward King, but the careful reader will soon discover that the poem to a greater extent is about Milton himself. Just as the two central and most powerful portions of the monody are the meditation on fame and the philippic against the Church, so were the ever impending threat of an untimely death and the corruption of the English Church Milton's chief quarrels with life at the age of twenty-nine.

It is here, in *Lycidas,* that Milton settles these quarrels. True fame, he concludes, is to be attained only in heaven; and a justly indignant God will not leave long unpunished the hirelings who corrupt his holy Church. King's early death, then, is merely the starting point of the poem. What really interests us is how that death helped Milton to resolve his deepest doubts about the wise providence of God and thus to attain a peace of mind before he departed for the Continent and Italy.

Lycidas

(1638)

In this monody the author bewails a learned friend, unfortunately drowned in his passage from Chester on the Irish Seas, 1637. And by occasion foretells the ruin of our corrupted clergy then in their height.

Yet once more, O ye laurels, and once more
Ye myrtles brown, with ivy never sere,
I come to pluck your berries harsh and crude,
And with forced fingers rude,
Shatter your leaves before the mellowing year.
Bitter constraint, and sad occasion dear,
Compels me to disturb your season due:
For Lycidas is dead, dead ere his prime,
Young Lycidas, and hath not left his peer:
Who would not sing for Lycidas? he knew
Himself to sing, and build the lofty rhyme.
He must not float upon his watery bier
Unwept, and welter to the parching wind,
Without the meed of some melodious tear.

Begin then, sisters of the sacred well,
That from beneath the seat of Jove doth spring,
Begin, and somewhat loudly sweep the string.
Hence with denial vain, and coy excuse,
So may some gentle muse
With lucky words favor my destined urn,
And as he passes turn,
And bid fair peace be to my sable shroud.
For we were nursed upon the self-same hill,
Fed the same flock, by fountain, shade, and rill,

Together both, ere the high lawns appeared
Under the opening eyelids of the morn,
We drove afield, and both together heard
What time the gray-fly winds her sultry horn

Battening our flocks with the fresh dews of night,
Oft till the star that rose, at evening, bright,
Toward heaven's descent had sloped his westering wheel
Meanwhile the rural ditties were not mute,
Tempered to the oaten flute,
Rough satyrs danced, and fauns with cloven heel,
From the glad sound would not be absent long,
And old Damaetas loved to hear our song.

But O the heavy change, now thou art gone,
Now thou art gone, and never must return!
Thee shepherd, thee the woods, and desert caves,
With wild thyme and the gadding vine o'ergrown,
And all their echoes mourn.
The willows, and the hazel copses green,
Shall now no more be seen,
Fanning their joyous leaves to thy soft lays.
As killing as the canker to the rose,
Or taint-worm to the weanling herds that graze,
Or frost to flowers, that their gay wardrobe wear,
When first the white-thorn blows;
Such, Lycidas, thy loss to shepherd's ear.

Where were ye nymphs when the remorseless deep
Closed o'er the head of your loved Lycidas?
For neither were ye playing on the steep,
Where your old bards, the famous druids lie,
Nor on the shaggy top of Mona high,
Nor yet where Deva spreads her wizard stream:
Ay me, I fondly dream!
'Had ye been there'—for what could that have done?
What could the muse herself that Orpheus bore.
The muse herself for her enchanting son
Whom universal nature did lament,
When by the rout that made the hideous roar,
His gory visage down the stream was sent,
Down the swift Hebrus to the Lesbian shore.

Alas! What boots it with uncessant care
To tend the homely slighted shepherd's trade,

And strictly meditate the thankless muse,
Were it not better done as others use,
To sport with Amaryllis in the shade,
Or with the tangles of Neaera's hair?
Fame is the spur that the clear spirit doth raise
(That last infirmity of noble mind)
To scorn delights, and live laborious days;
But the fair guerdon when we hope to find,
And think to burst out into sudden blaze,
Comes the blind fury with the abhorred shears,
And slits the thin-spun life. 'But not the praise,'
Phoebus replied, and touched my trembling ears;
'Fame is no plant that grows on mortal soil,
Nor in the glistering foil
Set off to the world, nor in broad rumor lies,
But lives and spreads aloft by those pure eyes,
And perfect witness of all-judging Jove;
As he pronounces lastly on each deed,
Of so much fame in heaven expect thy meed.'

O fountain Arethuse, and thou honored flood,
Smooth-sliding Mincius, crowned with vocal reeds,
That strain I heard was of a higher mood:
But now my oat proceeds,
And listens to the herald of the sea
That came in Neptune's plea,
He asked the waves, and asked the felon winds,
What hard mishap hath doomed this gentle swain?
And questioned every gust of rugged wings
That blows from off each beaked promontory,
They knew not of his story,
And sage Hippotades their answer brings,
That not a blast was from his dungeon strayed,
The air was calm, and on the level brine,
Sleek Panope with all her sisters played.
It was that fatal and perfidious bark
Built in the eclipse, and rigged with curses dark,
That sunk so low that sacred head of thine.

Next Camus, reverend sire, went footing slow,
His mantle hairy, and his bonnet sedge,
Inwrought with figures dim, and on the edge
Like to that sanguine flower inscribed with woe.
'Ah; Who hath reft' (quoth he) 'my dearest pledge?'
Last came, and last did go,
The pilot of the Galilean Lake,
Two massy keys he bore of metals twain,
(The golden opes, the iron shuts amain)
He shook his mitered locks, and stern bespake,
'How well could I have spared for thee, young swain,
Enow of such as for their bellies' sake,
Creep and intrude, and climb into the fold?
Of other care they little reckoning make,
Than how to scramble at the shearers' feast,
And shove away the worthy bidden guest.
Blind mouths! that scarce themselves know how to hold
A sheep-hook, or have learned aught else the least
That to the faithful herdman's art belongs!
What recks it them? What need they? They are sped,
And when they list, their lean and flashy songs
Grate on their scrannel pipes of wretched straw,
The hungry sheep look up, and are not fed,
But swollen with wind, and the rank mist they draw,
Rot inwardly, and foul contagion spread:
Besides what the grim wolf with privy paw
Daily devours apace, and nothing said,
But that two-handed engine at the door,
Stands ready to smite once, and smite no more.'
   Return Alpheus, the dread voice is past,
That shrunk thy streams; Return Sicilian muse,
And call the vales, and bid them hither cast
Their bells, and flowerets of a thousand hues.
Ye valleys low where the mild whispers use,
Of shades and wanton winds, and gushing brooks,
On whose fresh lap the swart star sparely looks,
Throw hither all your quaint enameled eyes,

That on the green turf suck the honeyed showers,
And purple all the ground with vernal flowers.
Bring the rathe primrose that forsaken dies,
The tufted crow-toe, and pale jessamine,
The white pink, and the pansy freaked with jet,
The glowing violet.
The musk-rose, and the well-attired woodbine,
With cowslips wan that hang the pensive head,
And every flower that sad embroidery wears:
Bid amaranthus all his beauty shed,
And daffodillies fill their cups with tears,
To strew the laureate hearse where Lycid lies.
For so to interpose a little ease,
Let our frail thoughts dally with false surmise.
Ay me! Whilst thee the shores, and sounding seas
Wash far away, where'er thy bones are hurled,
Whether beyond the stormy Hebrides,
Where thou perhaps under the whelming tide
Visitest the bottom of the monstrous world;
Or whether thou to our moist vows denied,
Sleepest by the fable of Bellerus old,
Where the great vision of the guarded mount
Looks toward Namancos and Bayona's hold;
Look homeward angel now, and melt with ruth.
And, O ye dolphins, waft the hapless youth.
    Weep no more, woeful shepherds weep no more,
For Lycidas your sorrow is not dead,
Sunk though he be beneath the watery floor,
So sinks the day-star in the ocean bed,
And yet anon repairs his drooping head,
And tricks his beams, and with new-spangled ore,
Flames in the forehead of the morning sky:
So Lycidas sunk low, but mounted high,
Through the dear might of him that walked the waves
Where other groves, and other streams along,
With nectar pure his oozy locks he laves,
And hears the unexpressive nuptial song,

In the blest kingdoms meek of joy and love.
There entertain him all the saints above,
In solemn troops, and sweet societies
That sing, and singing in their glory move,
And wipe the tears forever from his eyes.
Now Lycidas the shepherds weep no more,
Henceforth thou art the genius of the shore,
In thy large recompense, and shalt be good
To all that wander in that perilous flood.

    Thus sang the uncouth swain to the oaks and rills,
While the still morn went out with sandals gray,
He touched the tender stops of various quills,
With eager thought warbling his Doric lay:
And now the sun had stretched out all the hills,
And now was dropped into the western bay;
At last he rose, and twitched his mantle blue:
Tomorrow to fresh woods, and pastures new.

The Sonnets

THE SONNET is an Italian verse form which Wyatt and Surrey introduced into England about 1540. During the fifty years that followed, sonneteering became an extremely popular fashion, and numbered among its devotees poets of no less note than Sidney, Spenser, and Shakespeare. By the end of Elizabeth's reign, however, the vogue had all but spent itself. Later writers tended to make love the sole subject matter and to turn the form itself into a mere verse exercise stuffed with trite metaphors and forced conceits. Milton's contemporaries consequently all but ignored the form.

Milton himself, however, composed twenty-three regular sonnets in Italian and English, and a twenty-fourth in which the conventional fourteen lines are followed by two "tails" consisting of a half line and a couplet each. In these Milton showed a complete disregard for English practices of the past. First, he freed the subject matter from the narrow tradition of amorous writing. He made the sonnet serve for verse epistle, for humorous commentary or serious political attack, for complimentary tribute to those that he honored or respected, as well as for the expression of his most deeply-felt emotions. Second, he liberated the sonnet from the fetters of Elizabethan artificiality, and showed that it was a form capable of expressing serious, sustained, and elevated thought.

Milton wrote the major portion of his sonnets during the two decades that he was engaged in the heat of political controversy, and these poems do much to reveal the essential humanity of their author. They show a cheerful, witty man, courteous and gregarious in his instincts, and not averse to an hour of social relaxation. Sonnet XX, for instance, is to a young friend, Edward Lawrence, and suggests that he and the poet waste an occasional winter day at wine, lute, and song, for

> *He who of those delights can judge, and spare*
> *To interpose them oft, is not unwise.*

Sonnets XVIII, XIX, and XXIII, however, reveal Milton at his greatest. In these poems he conveys to us a righteous indignation, a stoical acceptance of his blindness, and a grief for the loss of his second wife in a manner that fully justifies Wordsworth's high tribute that in Milton's hands the sonnet

> *became a trumpet; whence he blew*
> *Soul-animating strains—alas; too few!*

VII. On His Having Arrived at the Age of Twenty-Three

(1631-1632)

How soon hath time the subtle thief of youth,
    Stolen on his wing my three and twentieth year!
    My hasting days fly on with full career,
    But my late spring no bud or blossom showeth.
Perhaps my semblance might deceive the truth,
    That I to manhood am arrived so near,
    And inward ripeness doth much less appear,
    That some more timely-happy spirits endueth.
Yet be it less or more, or soon or slow,
    It shall be still in strictest measure even,
    To that same lot, however mean, or high,
Toward which time leads me, and the will of heaven;
    All is, if I have grace to use it so,
    As ever in my great task master's eye.

VIII. When the Assault was Intended to the City

(1642)

Captain or colonel, or knight in arms,
    Whose chance on these defenseless doors may seize,
    If ever deed of honor did thee please,
    Guard them, and him within protect from harms;
He can requite thee, for he knows the charms
    That call fame on such gentle acts as these,
    And he can spread thy name o'er lands and seas,
    Whatever clime the sun's bright circle warms.
Lift not thy spear against the muses' bower,
    The great Emathian conqueror bid spare
    The house of Pindarus, when temple and tower
Went to the ground: And the repeated air
    Of sad Electra's poet had the power
    To save the Athenian walls from ruin bare.

How soone hath Time the suttle theef of youth
Stoln on his wing my three & twentith yeere
my hasting days fly on wth full carreer
but my late spring no bud or blossome shewth
Perhaps my semblance might deceave ye truth
that I to manhood am arrivd so neere
& inward ripenesse doth much lesse appeare
That some more tymely-happie spirits indu'th
Yet be it lesse or more, or soone or slow
it shall be still in strictest measure eeven
to that same lot however meane or high
toward wch Tyme leads me, & the will of heaven
all is if I have grace to use it so
as ever in my great task-maisters eye

Sonnet VII, written in Milton's own hand soon after his twenty-third birthday, December 9, 1631. It accompanies a letter to a friend From the manuscript of Milton's minor poems, preserved in the Library of Trinity College, Cambridge.

X. To the Lady Margaret Ley
(1643-1645)

Daughter to that good earl, once president
  Of England's council, and her treasury,
  Who lived in both, unstained with gold or fee,
  And left them both, more in himself content,
Till the sad breaking of that parliament
  Broke him, as that dishonest victory
  At Chaeronea, fatal to liberty
Killed with report that old man eloquent,
Though later born, than to have known the days
  Wherein your father flourished, yet by you,
  Madam, methinks I see him living yet;
So well your words his noble virtues praise,
  That all both judge you to relate them true,
  And to possess them, honored Margaret.

XI On the Detraction Which Followed upon My Writing
Certain Treatises
(After 1645)

A book was writ of late called *Tetrachordon;*
  And woven close, both matter, form and style;
  The subject new: it walked the town a while,
  Numbering good intellects; now seldom pored on.
Cries the stall-reader, 'bless us! what a word on
  A title-page is this!' and some in file
  Stand spelling false, while one might walk to Mile-
End Green. Why is it harder sirs than Gordon,
Colkitto, or Macdonnel, or Galasp?
  Those rugged names to our like mouths grow sleek
  That would have made Quintilian stare and gasp.
Thy age, like ours, O soul of Sir John Cheek,
  Hated not learning worse than toad or asp;
  When thou taughtest Cambridge, and King Edward
    Greek.

XII. On the Same

I did but prompt the age to quit their clogs
 By the known rules of ancient liberty,
 When straight a barbarous noise environs **me**
Of owls and cuckoos, asses, apes and dogs.
As when those hinds that were transformed to **frogs**
 Railed at Latona's twin-born progeny
 Which after held the sun and moon in fee.
But this is got by casting pearl to hogs;
That bawl for freedom in their senseless mood,
 And still revolt when truth would set them **free.**
 License they mean when they cry liberty;
For who loves that, must first be wise and good;
 But from that mark how far they rove we see
 For all this waste of wealth, and loss of blood.

XIII. To Mr. H. Lawes on His Airs

(1646)

Harry whose tuneful and well measured song
 First taught our English music how to span
 Words with just note and accent, not to scan
With Midas ears, committing short and long;
Thy worth and skill exempts thee from the throng,
 With praise enough for envy to look wan;
 To after age thou shalt be writ the man,
 That with smooth air couldst humor best our **tongue.**
Thou honorest verse, and verse must send her wing
 To honor thee, the priest of Phoebus' choir
 That tunest their happiest lines in hymn, **or story.**
Dante shall give fame leave to set thee higher
 Than his Casella, whom he wooed to sing
 Met in the milder shades of Purgatory.

XVI. To the Lord General Cromwell, May 1652, on the
· Proposals of certain Ministers at the Committee for
Propagation of the Gospel

(1652)

Cromwell, our chief of men, who through a cloud
    Not of war only, but detractions rude,
    Guided by faith and matchless fortitude
    To peace and truth thy glorious way hast plowed,
And on the neck of crowned fortune proud
    Hast reared God's trophies and his work pursued,
    While Darwen stream with blood of Scots imbrued,
    And Dunbar field resounds thy praises loud,
And Worcester's laureate wreath; yet much remains
    To conquer still; peace hath her victories
    No less renowned than war, new foes arise
Threatening to bind our souls with secular chains:
    Help us to save free conscience from the paw
    Of hireling wolves whose gospel is their maw.

XVII. To Sir Henry Vane the Younger

(1652)

Vane, young in years, but in sage counsel old,
    Than whom a better senator ne'er held
    The helm of Rome, when gowns not arms repelled
    The fierce Epirot and the African bold,
Whether to settle peace, or to unfold
    The drift of hollow states, hard to be spelled,
    Then to advise how war may best, upheld,
    Move by her two main nerves, iron and gold
In all her equipage; besides to know
    Both spiritual power and civil, what each means,
What severs each, thou hast learned, which few have done
The bounds of either sword to thee we owe.
    Therefore on thy firm hand religion leans
    In peace, and reckons thee her eldest son.

XVIII. On the Late Massacre in Piedmont
(1655)

Avenge O Lord thy slaughtered saints, whose bones
    Lie scattered on the Alpine mountains cold,
    Even them who kept thy truth so pure of old
    When all our fathers worshiped stocks and stones,
Forget not: in thy book record their groans
    Who were thy sheep and in their ancient fold
    Slain by the bloody Piemontese that rolled
    Mother with infant down the rocks. Their moans
The vales redoubled to the hills, and they
    To heaven. Their martyred blood and ashes sow
    O'er all the Italian fields where still doth sway
The triple tyrant: that from these may grow
    A hundredfold, who having learned thy way
    Early may fly the Babylonian woe.

XIX. On His Blindness
(1655)

When I consider how my light is spent,
    Ere half my days, in this dark world and wide,
    And that one talent which is death to hide,
    Lodged with me useless, though my soul more bent
To serve therewith my maker, and present
    My true account, lest he returning chide,
    'Doth God exact day-labor, light denied,'
    I fondly ask; But patience to prevent
That murmur, soon replies, 'God doth not need
    Either man's work or his own gifts, who best
    Bear his mild yoke, they serve him best, his state
's kingly. Thousands at his bidding speed
    And post o'er land and ocean without rest:
    They also serve who only stand and wait.'

XX. To Mr. Lawrence
(1655-1656)

Lawrence of virtuous father virtuous son,
    Now that the fields are dank, and ways are mire,
    Where shall we sometimes meet, and by the fire
    Help waste a sullen day; what may be won
From the hard season gaining: time will run
    On smoother, till Favonius re-inspire
    The frozen earth; and clothe in fresh attire
    The lily and rose, that neither sowed nor spun.
What neat repast shall feast us, light and choice,
    Of Attic taste, with wine, whence we may rise
    To hear the lute well touched, or artful voice
Warble immortal notes and Tuscan air?
    He who of those delights can judge, and spare
    To interpose them oft, is not unwise.

XXI. To Cyriack Skinner
(1655)

Cyriack, whose grandsire on the royal bench
    Of British Themis, with no mean applause
    Pronounced and in his volumes taught our laws,
    Which others at their bar so often wrench;
Today deep thoughts resolve with me to drench
    In mirth, that after no repenting draws;
    Let Euclid rest and Archimedes pause,
    And what the Swede intend, and what the French.
To measure life, learn thou betimes, and know
    Toward solid good what leads the nearest way;
    For other things mild heaven a time ordains,
And disapproves that care, though wise in show,
    That with superfluous burden loads the day,
    And when God sends a cheerful hour, refrains.

XXII. To the Same

Cyriack, this three years' day these eyes, though clear
    To outward view, of blemish or of spot,
    Bereft of light their seeing have forgot;
    Nor to their idle orbs doth sight appear
Of sun or moon or star throughout the year,
    Or man or woman. Yet I argue not
    Against heaven's hand or will, nor bate a jot
    Of heart or hope; but still bear up and steer
Right onward. What supports me, dost thou ask?
    The conscience, friend, to have lost them overplied
    In liberty's defense, my noble task,
Of which all Europe talks from side to side.
    This thought might lead me through the world's
        vain mask
    Content though blind, had I no better guide.

XXIII. On His Deceased Wife

(1658)

Methought I saw my late espoused saint
    Brought to me like Alcestis from the grave,
    Whom Jove's great son to her glad husband gave,
    Rescued from death by force though pale and faint.
Mine as whom washed from spot of child-bed taint,
    Purification in the old law did save,
    And such, as yet once more I trust to have
    Full sight of her in heaven without restraint,
Came vested all in white, pure as her mind:
    Her face was veiled, yet to my fancied sight,
    Love, sweetness, goodness, in her person shined
So clear, as in no face with more delight.
    But O as to embrace me she inclined
    I waked, she fled, and day brought back my night.

On the New Forcers of Conscience Under the Long Parliament

(1645-46)

Because you have thrown off your prelate lord,
　　And with stiff vows renounced his liturgy
　　To seize the widowed whore plurality
　　From them whose sin ye envied, not abhorred,
Dare ye for this adjure the civil sword
　　To force our consciences that Christ set free,
　　And ride us with a classic hierarchy
　　Taught ye by mere A. S. and Rutherford?
Men whose life, learning, faith and pure intent
　　Would have been held in high esteem with Paul
　　Must now be named and printed heretics
By shallow Edwards and Scotch what-d'-ye-call:
　　But we do hope to find out all your tricks,
　　Your plots and packing worse than those of Trent,
　　　　　That so the Parliament
May with their wholesome and preventive shears
Clip your phylacteries, though baulk your ears,
　　　　　And succor our just fears
When they shall read this clearly in your charge
New presbyter is but old priest writ large.

Paradise Lost

THE ADJECTIVE "Miltonic" has now long stood as synonymous with the word "sublime," and the poet, like any other artist, achieves this aesthetic quality of sublimity through his ability to handle vast bodies of material with perfect control and ease. A mere perusal of the arguments of *Paradise Lost* shows the scope of this epic, about which Milton had long dreamed. The subject is the omnipresent problem of the origin of evil. The setting is earth, heaven, and the infinite space beyond. The time is eternity. And into this poem, Milton has poured the results of a lifetime of study and action. He reveals that he knew the Bible almost by heart and had an almost comparable command of Hebrew, patristic, and Renaissance commentary on the Scriptures. Echoes and allusion throughout his verse witness a mastery not only of the classics but also of later European literature. And the characters of *Paradise Lost* show that Milton had not neglected the study of mankind, or wasted the hours during which he listened to the impassioned debate of Commonwealth politicians.

Milton, furthermore, handles this mass of material with consummate control and ease. In its broadest aspect, the narrative technique is that of the long epic of Homer and Virgil, in which the poet begins with an important scene well along in the sequence of events and then, after several books have elapsed, cuts back to happenings which preceded the opening event of the poem, and which really constitute the beginning of the narrative. Within this plan, Milton freely employs the device of parallelism. In picturing hell—with the throne of Satan, the debate of the devils, and the gate and the bridge—Milton repeatedly contrasts it with heaven. Satan, Sin, and Death constitute a trio comparable to the Father Son, and Spirit, and the fall of Satan parallels—often in minute details—the fall of Adam and Eve.

Equally well planned is the debate in hell. Moloch, who stands for blind, instinctive action, speaks first, to be followed by Belial, who represents the other extreme, inertia and inaction. Mammon, the materialist, offers a popular compromise; and it is only then, after the assembly has lost some of its initial vigor, that Satan, through his lieutenant Beelzebub, leads the fallen angels to the decision that he himself desires. This is indeed a true picture of the dialectic by which democratic assemblies work; but behind this picture lies a careful and calculated plan of the poet. A similar control we also find even in the long, Homeric similes, which we are too apt to dismiss as merely digressive purple passages retarding the progress of the narrative. Milton, however, has constructed these figures with great care, for almost without exception every element in the simile subtly parallels and describes the matter that it is called upon to reinforce. *Paradise Lost* is far from a conglomerate and formless poem, for its author was a master craftsman, comparable to those who designed and built the Parthenon or the cathedrals of medieval Europe.

No poet, before or after Milton, has attempted in English so titanic a task or brought it off so well. Fused in the twelve books of *Paradise Lost* are all the great traditions to which Milton was the heir, Hebraic, classic, medieval, and renaissance. The poem stands as a superlative achievement of a great and lofty mind, not without a definitely aristocratic bent, and marks Milton as the finest exemplar of neo-classicism and Christian humanism that England has thus far been able to produce

Paradise Lost

(1658-1665)

A Poem in Twelve Books

BOOK I

The Argument: This first book proposes first in brief the whole
subject, Man's disobedience, and the loss thereupon of Paradise
wherein he was placed: Then touches the prime cause of his fall, the
serpent, or rather Satan in the serpent; who revolting from God,
and drawing to his side many legions of angels, was by the command
of God driven out of heaven with all his crew into the great deep.
Which action passed over, the poem hastes into the midst of things,
presenting Satan with his angels now fallen into hell, described
here, not in the center (for heaven and earth may be supposed as
yet not made, certainly not yet accursed) but in a place of utter
darkness, fitliest called chaos: Here Satan with his angels lying on
the burning lake, thunderstruck and astonished, after a certain space
recovers, as from confusion, calls up him who next in order and
dignity lay by him; they confer of their miserable fall. Satan
awakens all his legions, who lay till then in the same manner
confounded; They rise, their numbers, array of battle, their chief
leaders named, according to the idols known afterwards in Canaan
and the countries adjoining. To these Satan directs his speech, com-
forts them with hope yet of regaining heaven, but tells them lastly
of a new world and new kind of creature to be created, according to
an ancient prophecy or report in heaven; for that angels were long
before this visible creation, was the opinion of many ancient fathers.

To find out the truth of this prophecy, and what to determine
thereon he refers to a full council. What his associates thence
attempt. Pandemonium the palace of Satan rises, suddenly built out
of the deep: The infernal peers there sit in council.

Of man's first disobedience, and the fruit
Of that forbidden tree, whose mortal taste
Brought death into the world, and all our woe,
With loss of Eden, till one greater man
Restore us, and regain the blissful seat,
Sing heavenly muse, that on the secret top
Of Oreb, or of Sinai, didst inspire
That shepherd, who first taught the chosen seed,
In the beginning how the heavens and earth
Rose out of chaos: Or if Sion hill
Delight thee more, and Siloa's brook that flowed
Fast by the oracle of God; I thence
Invoke thy aid to my adventurous song,
That with no middle flight intends to soar
Above the Aonian mount, while it pursues
Things unattempted yet in prose or rhyme.
And chiefly thou O spirit, that dost prefer
Before all temples the upright heart and pure,
Instruct me, for thou knowest; thou from the first
Wast present, and with mighty wings outspread
Dove-like satest brooding on the vast abyss
And madest it pregnant: What in me is dark
Illumine, what is low raise and support;
That to the height of this great argument
I may assert eternal providence,
And justify the ways of God to men.
       Say first, for heaven hides nothing from thy view,
Nor the deep tract of hell, say first what cause
Moved our grand parents in that happy state,
Favored of heaven so highly, to fall off
From their creator, and transgress his will
For one restraint, lords of the world besides?

Who first seduced them to that foul revolt?
The infernal serpent; he it was, whose guile
Stirred up with envy and revenge, deceived
The mother of mankind, what time his pride
Had cast him out from heaven, with all his host
Of rebel angels, by whose aid aspiring
To set himself in glory above his peers,
He trusted to have equaled the most high,
If he opposed; and with ambitious aim
Against the throne and monarchy of God
Raised impious war in heaven and battle proud
With vain attempt. Him the almighty power
Hurled headlong flaming from the ethereal sky
With hideous ruin and combustion down
To bottomless perdition, there to dwell
In adamantine chains and penal fire,
Who durst defy the omnipotent to arms.
Nine times the space that measures day and night
To mortal men, he with his horrid crew
Lay vanquished, rolling in the fiery gulf
Confounded though immortal: But his doom
Reserved him to more wrath; for now the thought
Both of lost happiness and lasting pain
Torments him; round he throws his baleful eyes
That witnessed huge affliction and dismay
Mixed with obdurate pride and steadfast hate:
At once as far as angels' ken he views
The dismal situation waste and wild,
A dungeon horrible, on all sides round
As one great furnace flamed, yet from those flames
No light, but rather darkness visible
Served only to discover sights of woe,
Regions of sorrow, doleful shades, where peace
And rest can never dwell, hope never comes
That comes to all; but torture without end
Still urges, and a fiery deluge, fed
With ever-burning sulphur unconsumed:

Such place eternal justice had prepared
For those rebellious, here their prison ordained
In utter darkness, and their portion set
As far removed from God and light of heaven
As from the center thrice to the utmost pole.
O how unlike the place from whence they fell!
There the companions of his fall, o'erwhelmed
With floods and whirlwinds of tempestuous fire,
He soon discerns, and weltering by his side
One next himself in power, and next in crime,
Long after known in Palestine, and named
Beelzebub. To whom the arch-enemy,
And thence in heaven called Satan, with bold words
Breaking the horrid silence thus began.

'If thou beest he; but O how fallen! how changed
From him, who in the happy realms of light
Clothed with transcendent brightness didst outshine
Myriads though bright: If he whom mutual league
United thoughts and counsels, equal hope
And hazard in the glorious enterprise,
Joined with me once, now misery hath joined
In equal ruin: into what pit thou seest
From what height fallen, so much the stronger proved
He with his thunder: and till then who knew
The force of those dire arms? yet not for those,
Nor what the potent victor in his rage
Can else inflict, do I repent or change,
Though changed in outward luster; that fixed mind
And high disdain, from sense of injured merit,
That with the mightiest raised me to contend,
And to the fierce contention brought along
Innumerable force of spirits armed
That durst dislike his reign, and me preferring,
His utmost power with adverse power opposed
In dubious battle on the plains of heaven,
And shook his throne. What though the field be lost?
All is not lost; the unconquerable will,

And study of revenge, immortal hate,
And courage never to submit or yield:
And what is else not to be overcome?
That glory never shall his wrath or might
Extort from me. To bow and sue for grace
With suppliant knee, and deify his power,
Who from the terror of this arm so late
Doubted his empire, that were low indeed,
That were an ignominy and shame beneath
This downfall; since by fate the strength of gods
And this empyreal substance cannot fail,
Since through experience of this great event
In arms not worse, in foresight much advanced,
We may with more successful hope resolve
To wage by force or guile eternal war
Irreconcilable, to our grand foe,
Who now triumphs, and in the excess of joy
Sole reigning holds the tyranny of heaven.'

So spake the apostate angel, though in pain,
Vaunting aloud, but racked with deep despair:
And him thus answered soon his bold compeer.

'O prince, O chief of many throned powers,
That led the embattled seraphim to war
Under thy conduct, and in dreadful deeds
Fearless, endangered heaven's perpetual king;
And put to proof his high supremacy,
Whether upheld by strength, or chance, or fate,
Too well I see and rue the dire event,
That with sad overthrow and foul defeat
Hath lost us heaven, and all this mighty host
In horrible destruction laid thus low,
As far as gods and heavenly essences
Can perish: for the mind and spirit remains
Invincible, and vigor soon returns,
Though all our glory extinct, and happy state
Here swallowed up in endless misery.
But what if he our conqueror, (whom I now

Of force believe almighty, since no less
Than such could have o'erpowered such force as ours)
Have left us this our spirit and strength entire
Strongly to suffer and support our pains,
That we may so suffice his vengeful ire,
Or do him mightier service as his thralls
By right of war, whate'er his business be
Here in the heart of hell to work in fire,
Or do his errands in the gloomy deep;
What can it then avail though yet we feel
Strength undiminished, or eternal being
To undergo eternal punishment?'
Whereto with speedy words the arch-fiend replied.

   'Fallen cherub, to be weak is miserable
Doing or suffering: but of this be sure,
To do aught good never will be our task,
But ever to do ill our sole delight,
As being the contrary to his high will
Whom we resist. If then his providence
Out of our evil seek to bring forth good,
Our labor must be to pervert that end,
And out of good still to find means of evil;
Which ofttimes may succeed, so as perhaps
Shall grieve him, if I fail not, and disturb
His inmost counsels from their destined aim.
But see the angry victor hath recalled
His ministers of vengeance and pursuit
Back to the gates of heaven: the sulphurous hail
Shot after us in storm, o'erblown hath laid
The fiery surge, that from the precipice
Of heaven received us falling, and the thunder,
Winged with red lightning and impetuous rage,
Perhaps hath spent his shafts, and ceases now
To bellow through the vast and boundless deep.
Let us not slip the occasion, whether scorn,
Or satiate fury yield it from our foe.
Seest thou yon dreary plain, forlorn and wild,

The seat of desolation, void of light,
Save what the glimmering of these livid flames
Casts pale and dreadful? Thither let us tend
From off the tossing of these fiery waves,
There rest, if any rest can harbor there,
And reassembling our afflicted powers,
Consult how we may henceforth most offend
Our enemy, our own loss how repair,
How overcome this dire calamity,
What reinforcement we may gain from hope,
If not what resolution from despair.'
　Thus Satan talking to his nearest mate
With head uplift above the wave, and eyes
That sparkling blazed, his other parts besides
Prone on the flood, extended long and large
Lay floating many a rood, in bulk as huge
As whom the fables name of monstrous size,
Titanian, or earth-born, that warred on Jove,
Briareos or Typhon, whom the den
By ancient Tarsus held, or that sea-beast
Leviathan, which God of all his works
Created hugest that swim the ocean stream:
Him haply slumbering on the Norway foam
The pilot of some small night-foundered skiff,
Deeming some island, oft, as seamen tell,
With fixed anchor in his scaly rind
Moors by his side under the lee, while night
Invests the sea, and wished morn delays:
So stretched out huge in length the arch-fiend lay
Chained on the burning lake, nor ever thence
Had risen or heaved his head, but that the will
And high permission of all-ruling heaven
Left him at large to his own dark designs,
That with reiterated crimes he might
Heap on himself damnation, while he sought
Evil to others, and enraged might see
How all his malice served but to bring forth

Infinite goodness, grace and mercy shown
On man by him seduced, but on himself
Treble confusion, wrath and vengeance poured.
Forthwith upright he rears from off the pool
His mighty stature; on each hand the flames
Driven backward slope their pointing spires, and rolled
In billows, leave in the midst a horrid vale.
Then with expanded wings he steers his flight
Aloft, incumbent on the dusky air
That felt unusual weight, till on dry land
He lights, if it were land that ever burned
With solid, as the lake with liquid fire;
And such appeared in hue, as when the force
Of subterranean wind transports a hill
Torn from Pelorus, or the shattered side
Of thundering Etna, whose combustible
And fueled entrails thence conceiving fire.
Sublimed with mineral fury, aid the winds,
And leave a singed bottom all involved
With stench and smoke: Such resting found the sole
Of unblest feet. Him followed his next mate,
Both glorying to have scaped the Stygian flood
As gods, and by their own recovered strength,
Not by the sufferance of supernal power.
    Is this the region, this the soil, the clime,'
Said then the lost archangel, 'this the seat
That we must change for heaven, this mournful gloom
For that celestial light? Be it so, since he
Who now is sovereign can dispose and bid
What shall be right: farthest from him is best
Whom reason hath equaled, force hath made supreme
Above his equals. Farewell happy fields
Where joy forever dwells: Hail horrors, hail
Infernal world, and thou profoundest hell
Receive thy new possessor: One who brings
A mind not to be changed by place or time.
The mind is its own place, and in itself

To reign is worth ambition though in Hell,
Better to reign in Hell, then serve in Heav'n.
But wherefore let wee then our faithfull friends
Th' Associates and copartners of our loss
Ly thus astonisht on th' oblivious poole,
And call them not to share with us, thir part
In this unhappie Mansion; or once more
With rallied arms to try what may be yet
270 Regaind in Heav'n or what more lost in Hell?
     So Satan spake, and him Beëlzebub
Thus answerd. Leader of those armies bright,
Which but th' Omnipotent none could have foyld,
If once they heare that voice, thir livoliest pledge
Of hope in feares and dangers, heard so oft
In worst extreames, and on the perilous edge
Of battell when it rag'd, in all assaults
Thir surest signall, they will soon resume
New courage and revive, though now they ly
280 Groveling and prostrate on yon lake of fire,
As wee ere while, astounded and amaz'd,
No wonder, fal'n such a pernicious highth.
     Hee scarce had ceast when the superiour fiend
Was moving toward the shore; his ponderous shield
Ethereal temper, massy, large and round,
Behind him cast; the broad circumference
                          Hung on

Twelfth and thirteenth pages from Book I of *Paradise Lost*, written by an amanuensis and corrected by several hands under Milton's direction. Some authorities believe that it was used by the printer in

Hung on his shoulders like the moon whose orb
Through optick glasse the Tuscan Artist views
At eevning from the top of Fesole,
290 Or in Valdarno, to descry new lands,
Rivers or Mountaines in her spotty globe.
His Speare, to equall which the tallest pine
Hewn on Norwegian hills, to be the mast
Of some great Ammirall, were but a wand
He walkt with, to support uneasy steps
Over the burning Marle, not like those steps
On Heavens azure; and the torrid clime
Smote on him sore besides, vaulted with fire;
Nathlesse hee so endur'd, till on the beach
Of that inflamed sea, hee stood and call'd
300 His legions, Angell forms, ~~that~~ who lay intranc't
Thick as Autumnall leaves that strow the brooks
In Vallombrosa, where th' Etrurian shades
High overarcht imbowr: or scatterd sedge
Afloat when with fierce winds Orion arm'd
Hath vext the red-sea coast, whose waves oerthrew
Busiris and his Memphian chivalry
While with perfidious hatred they pursu'd
The sojourners of Goshen, who beheld
310 From the safe shore thir floating carcasses

setting up type for the first edition. Courtesy of Morgan Library,
New York.

Can make a heaven of hell, a hell of heaven.
What matter where, if I be still the same,
And what I should be, all but less than he
Whom thunder hath made greater? Here at least
We shall be free; the almighty hath not built
Here for his envy, will not drive us hence:
Here we may reign secure, and in my choice
To reign is worth ambition though in hell:
Better to reign in hell, than serve in heaven.
But wherefore let we then our faithful friends,
The associates and copartners of our loss
Lie thus astonished on the oblivious pool,
And call them not to share with us their part
'In this unhappy mansion, or once more
With rallied arms to try what may be yet
Regained in heaven, or what more lost in hell?'
  So Satan spake, and him Beelzebub
Thus answered. 'Leader of those armies bright,
Which but the omnipotent none could have foiled,
If once they hear that voice, their liveliest pledge
Of hope in fears and dangers, heard so oft
In worst extremes, and on the perilous edge
Of battle when it raged, in all assaults
Their surest signal, they will soon resume
New courage and revive, though now they lie
Groveling and prostrate on yon lake of fire,
As we erewhile, astounded and amazed,
No wonder, fallen such a pernicious height.'
  He scarce had ceased when the superior Fiend
Was moving toward the shore; his ponderous shield
Ethereal temper, massy, large and round,
Behind him cast; the broad circumference
Hung on his shoulders like the moon, whose orb
Through optic glass the Tuscan artist views
At evening from the top of Fesole,
Or in Valdarno, to descry new lands,
Rivers or mountains in her spotty globe.

His spear, to equal which the tallest pine
Hewn on Norwegian hills, to be the mast
Of some great ammiral, were but a wand,
He walked with to support uneasy steps
Over the burning marl, not like those steps
On heaven's azure, and the torrid clime
Smote on him sore besides, vaulted with fire;
Nathless he so endured, till on the beach
Of that inflamed sea, he stood and called
His legions, angel forms, who lay entranced
Thick as autumnal leaves that strew the brooks
In Vallombrosa, where the Etrurian shades
High over arched embower; or scattered sedge
Afloat, when with fierce winds Orion armed
Hath vexed the Red Sea coast, whose waves o'erthrew
Busiris and his Memphian chivalry,
While with perfidious hatred they pursued
The sojourners of Goshen, who beheld
From the safe shore their floating carcasses
And broken chariot wheels, so thick bestrown
Abject and lost lay these, covering the flood,
Under amazement of their hideous change.
He called so loud, that all the hollow deep
Of Hell resounded. 'Princes, potentates,
Warriors, the flower of heaven, once yours, now lost,
If such astonishment as this can seize
Eternal spirits; or have ye chosen this place
After the toil of battle to repose
Your wearied virtue, for the ease you find
To slumber here, as in the vales of heaven?
Or in this abject posture have ye sworn
To adore the conqueror? who now beholds
Cherub and seraph rolling in the flood
With scattered arms and ensigns, till anon
His swift pursuers from heaven gates discern
The advantage, and descending tread us down
Thus drooping, or with linked thunderbolts

Transfix us to the bottom of this gulf.
Awake, arise, or be forever fallen.'
    They heard, and were abashed, and up they sprung
Upon the wing, as when men wont to watch
On duty, sleeping found by whom they dread,
Rouse and bestir themselves ere well awake.
Nor did they not perceive the evil plight
In which they were, or the fierce pains not feel;
Yet to their general's voice they soon obeyed
Innumerable. As when the potent rod
Of Amram's son in Egypt's evil day
Waved round the coast, up called a pitchy cloud
Of locusts, warping on the eastern wind,
That o'er the realm of impious Pharaoh hung
Like night, and darkened all the land of Nile:
So numberless were those bad angels seen
Hovering on wing under the cope of hell
'Twixt upper, nether, and surrounding fires;
Till, as a signal given, the uplifted spear
Of their great sultan waving to direct
Their course, in even balance down they light
On the firm brimstone, and fill all the plain;
A multitude, like which the populous north
Poured never from her frozen loins, to pass
Rhene or the Danaw, when her barbarous sons
Came like a deluge on the south, and spread
Beneath Gibraltar to the Libyan sands.
Forthwith from every squadron and each band
The heads and leaders thither haste where stood
Their great commander; godlike shapes and forms
Excelling human, princely dignities,
And powers that erst in heaven sat on thrones;
Though of their names in heavenly records now
Be no memorial blotted out and rased
By their rebellion, from the books of life.
Nor had they yet among the sons of Eve
Got them new names, till wandering o'er the earth,

Through God's high sufferance for the trial of man,
By falsities and lies the greatest part
Of mankind they corrupted to forsake
God their creator, and the invisible
Glory of him that made them, to transform
Oft to the image of a brute, adorned
With gay religions full of pomp and gold,
And devils to adore for deities:
Then were they known to men by various names,
And various idols through the heathen world.
Say, muse, their names then known, who first, who last,
Roused from the slumber, on that fiery couch,
At their great emperor's call, as next in worth
Came singly where he stood on the bare strand,
While the promiscuous crowd stood yet aloof?
The chief were those who from the pit of hell
Roaming to seek their prey on earth, durst fix
Their seats long after next the seat of God,
Their altars by his altar, gods adored
Among the nations round, and durst abide
Jehovah thundering out of Sion, throned
Between the cherubim; yea, often placed
Within his sanctuary itself their shrines,
Abominations; and with cursed things
His holy rites, and solemn feasts profaned,
And with their darkness durst affront his light.
First Moloch, horrid king besmeared with blood
Of human sacrifice, and parents' tears,
Though for the noise of drums and timbrels loud
Their children's cries unheard, that passed through fire
To his grim idol. Him the Ammonite
Worshiped in Rabba and her watery plain,
In Argob and in Basan, to the stream
Of utmost Arnon. Nor content with such
Audacious neighborhood, the wisest heart
Of Solomon he led by fraud to build
His temple right against the temple of God

On that opprobrious hill, and made his grove
The pleasant valley of Hinnom, Tophet thence
And black Gehenna called, the type of hell.
Next Chemos, the obscene dread of Moab's sons,
From Aroar to Nebo, and the wild
Of southmost Abarim; in Hesebon
And Horonaim, Seon's realm, beyond
The flowery dale of Sibma clad with vines,
And Eleale to the asphaltic pool.
Peor his other name, when he enticed
Israel in Sittim on their march from Nile
To do him wanton rites, which cost them woe.
Yet thence his lustful orgies he enlarged
Even to that hill of scandal, by the grove
Of Moloch homicide, lust hard by hate;
Till good Josiah drove them thence to hell.
With these came they, who from the bordering flood
Of old Euphrates to the brook that parts
Egypt from Syrian ground, had general names
Of Baalim and Ashtaroth, those male,
These feminine. For spirits when they please
Can either sex assume, or both; so soft
And uncompounded in their essence pure,
Not tied or manacled with joint or limb,
Nor founded on the brittle strength of bones,
Like cumbrous flesh; but in what shape they choose
Dilated or condensed, bright or obscure,
Can execute their airy purposes,
And works of love or enmity fulfill.
For those the race of Israel oft forsook
Their living strength, and unfrequented left
His righteous altar, bowing lowly down
To bestial gods; for which their heads as low
Bowed down in battle, sunk before the spear
Of despicable foes. With these in troop
Came Astoreth, whom the Phoenicians called
Astarte, queen of heaven, with crescent horns;

To whose bright image nightly by the moon
Sidonian virgins paid their vows and songs,
In Sion also not unsung, where stood
Her temple on the offensive mountain, built
By that uxorious king, whose heart though large,
Beguiled by fair idolatresses, fell
To idols foul. Thammuz came next behind,
Whose annual wound in Lebanon allured
The Syrian damsels to lament his fate
In amorous ditties all a summer's day,
While smooth Adonis from his native rock
Ran purple to the sea, supposed with blood
Of Thammuz yearly wounded: the love-tale
Infected Sion's daughters with like heat,
Whose wanton passions in the sacred porch
Ezekiel saw, when by the vision led
His eye surveyed the dark idolatries
Of alienated Judah. Next came one
Who mourned in earnest, when the captive ark
Maimed his brute image, head and hands lopped off
In his own temple, on the grunsel edge,
Where he fell flat, and shamed his worshipers:
Dagon his name, sea monster, upward man
And downward fish: yet had his temple high
Reared in Azotus, dreaded through the coast
Of Palestine, in Gath and Ascalon
And Accaron and Gaza's frontier bounds.
Him followed Rimmon, whose delightful seat
Was fair Damascus, on the fertile banks
Of Abbana and Pharphar, lucid streams.
He also against the house of God was bold:
A leper once he lost and gained a king,
Ahaz his sottish conqueror, whom he drew
God's altar to disparage and displace
For one of Syrian mode, whereon to burn
His odious offerings, and adore the gods
Whom he had vanquished. After these appeared

A crew who under names of old renown,
Osiris, Isis, Orus and their train
With monstrous shapes and sorceries abused
Fanatic Egypt and her priests, to seek
Their wandering gods disguised in brutish forms
Rather than human. Nor did Israel scape
The infection when their borrowed gold composed
The calf in Oreb: and the rebel king
Doubled that sin in Bethel and in Dan,
Likening his maker to the grazed ox,
Jehovah, who in one night when he passed
From Egypt marching, equaled with one stroke
Both her first born and all her bleating gods.
Belial came last, than whom a spirit more lewd
Fell not from heaven, or more gross to love
Vice for itself: To him no temple stood
Or altar smoked; yet who more oft than he
In temples and at altars, when the priest
Turns atheist, as did Eli's sons, who filled
With lust and violence the house of God.
In courts and palaces he also reigns
And in luxurious cities, where the noise
Of riot ascends above their loftiest towers,
And injury and outrage: And when night
Darkens the streets, then wander forth the sons
Of Belial, flown with insolence and wine.
Witness the streets of Sodom, and that night
In Gibeah, when the hospitable door
Exposed a matron to avoid worse rape.
These were the prime in order and in might;
The rest were long to tell, though far renowned,
The Ionian gods, of Javan's issue held
Gods, yet confessed later than heaven and earth
Their boasted parents; Titan Heaven's first born
With his enormous brood, and birthright seized
By younger Saturn, he from mightier Jove
His own and Rhea's son like measure found;

So Jove usurping reigned: these first in Crete
And Ida known, thence on the snowy top
Of cold Olympus ruled the middle air
Their highest heaven; or on the Delphian cliff,
Or in Dodona, and through all the bounds
Of Doric land; or who with Saturn old
Fled over Adria to the Hesperian fields,
And o'er the Celtic roamed the utmost isles.
All these and more came flocking; but with looks
Downcast and damp, yet such wherein appeared
Obscure some glimpse of joy, to have found their chief
Not in despair, to have found themselves not lost
In loss itself; which on his countenance cast
Like doubtful hue: but he his wonted pride
Soon recollecting, with high words, that bore
Semblance of worth, not substance, gently raised
Their fainting courage, and dispelled their fears.
Then straight commands that at the warlike sound
Of trumpets loud and clarions be upreared
His mighty standard; that proud honor claimed
Azazel as his right, a cherub tall:
Who forthwith from the glittering staff unfurled
The imperial ensign, which full high advanced
Shone like a meteor streaming to the wind
With gems and golden luster rich emblazoned,
Seraphic arms and trophies: all the while
Sonorous metal blowing martial sounds:
At which the universal host upsent
A shout that tore hell's concave, and beyond
Frighted the reign of chaos and old night.
All in a moment through the gloom were seen
Ten thousand banners rise into the air
With orient colors waving: with them rose
A forest huge of spears: and thronging helms
Appeared, and serried shields in thick array
Of depth immeasurable: Anon they move
In perfect phalanx to the Dorian mood

Of flutes and soft recorders; such as raised
To height of noblest temper heroes old
Arming to battle, and instead of rage
Deliberate valor breathed, firm and unmoved
With dread of death to flight or foul retreat,
Nor wanting power to mitigate and swage
With solemn touches, troubled thoughts, and chase
Anguish and doubt and fear and sorrow and pain
From mortal or immortal minds. Thus they
Breathing united force with fixed thought
Moved on in silence to soft pipes that charmed
Their painful steps o'er the burnt soil; and now
Advanced in view they stand, a horrid front
Of dreadful length and dazzling arms, in guise
Of warriors old with ordered spear and shield,
Awaiting what command their mighty chief
Had to impose: He through the armed files
Darts his experienced eye, and soon traverse
The whole battalion views, their order due,
Their visages and stature as of gods,
Their number last he sums. And now his heart
Distends with pride, and hardening in his strength
Glories: For never since created man,
Met such embodied force, as named with these
Could merit more than that small infantry
Warred on by cranes: though all the giant brood
Of Phlegra with the heroic race were joined
That fought at Thebes and Ilium, on each side
Mixed with auxiliar gods; and what resounds
In fable or romance of Uther's son
Begirt with British and Armoric knights;
And all who since, baptized or infidel
Jousted in Aspramont or Montalban,
Damasco, or Morocco, or Trebisond,
Or whom Biserta sent from Afric shore
When Charlemain with all his peerage fell
By Fontarabbia. Thus far these beyond

Compare of mortal prowess, yet observed
Their dread commander: he above the rest
In shape and gesture proudly eminent
Stood like a tower; his form had yet not lost
All her original brightness, nor appeared
Less than archangel ruined, and the excess
Of glory obscured: As when the sun new risen
Looks through the horizontal misty air
Shorn of his beams, or from behind the moon
In dim eclipse disastrous twilight sheds
On half the nations, and with fear of change
Perplexes monarchs. Darkened so, yet shone
Above them all the archangel: but his face
Deep scars of thunder had intrenched, and care
Sat on his faded cheek, but under brows
Of dauntless courage, and considerate pride
Waiting revenge: cruel his eye, but cast
Signs of remorse and passion to behold
The fellows of his crime, the followers rather
(Far other once beheld in bliss) condemned
Forever now to have their lot in pain,
Millions of spirits for his fault amerced
Of heaven, and from eternal splendors flung
For his revolt, yet faithful how they stood,
Their glory withered. As when heaven's fire
Hath scathed the forest oaks, or mountain pines,
With singed top their stately growth though bare
Stands on the blasted heath. He now prepared
To speak; whereat their doubled ranks they bend
From wing to wing, and half enclose him round
With all his peers: attention held them mute.
Thrice he assayed, and thrice in spite of scorn,
Tears such as angels weep, burst forth: at last
Words interwove with sighs found out their way.

'O myriads of immortal spirits, O powers
Matchless, but with the almighty, and that strife
Was not inglorious, though the event was dire,

As this place testifies, and this dire change
Hateful to utter: but what power of mind
Foreseeing or presaging, from the depth
Of knowledge past or present, could have feared,
How such united force of gods, how such
As stood like these, could ever know repulse?
For who can yet believe, though after loss,
That all these puissant legions, whose exile
Hath emptied heaven, shall fail to reascend
Self-raised, and repossess their native seat?
For me, be witness all the host of heaven,
If counsels different, or danger shunned
By me, have lost our hopes. But he who reigns
Monarch in heaven, till then as one secure
Sat on his throne, upheld by old repute,
Consent or custom, and his regal state
Put forth at full, but still his strength concealed,
Which tempted our attempt, and wrought our fall.
Henceforth his might we know, and know our own
So as not either to provoke, or dread
New war, provoked; our better part remains
To work in close design, by fraud or guile
What force effected not: that he no less
At length from us may find, who overcomes
By force, hath overcome but half his foe.
Space may produce new worlds; whereof so rife
There went a fame in heaven that he erelong
Intended to create, and therein plant
A generation, whom his choice regard
Should favor equal to the sons of heaven:
Thither, if but to pry, shall be perhaps
Our first eruption, thither or elsewhere:
For this infernal pit shall never hold
Celestial spirits in bondage, nor the abyss
Long under darkness cover. But these thoughts
Full counsel must mature: Peace is despaired,
For who can think submission? War then, war

Open or understood must be resolved.'
   He spake: and to confirm his words, out flew
Millions of flaming swords, drawn from the thighs
Of mighty cherubim; the sudden blaze
Far round illumined hell: highly they raged
Against the highest, and fierce with grasped arms
Clashed on their sounding shields the din of war.
Hurling defiance toward the vault of heaven.
   There stood a hill not far whose grisly top
Belched fire and rolling smoke; the rest entire
Shone with a glossy scurf, undoubted sign
That in his womb was hid metallic ore,
The work of sulphur. Thither winged with speed
A numerous brigade hastened. As when bands
Of pioneers with spade and pickaxe armed
Forerun the royal camp, to trench a field,
Or cast a rampart. Mammon led them on,
Mammon, the least erected spirit that fell
From heaven, for even in heaven his looks and thoughts
Were always downward bent, admiring more
The riches of heaven's pavement, trodden gold,
Than aught divine or holy else enjoyed
In vision beatific: by him first
Men also, and by his suggestion taught,
Ransacked the center, and with impious hands
Rifled the bowels of their mother earth
For treasures better hid. Soon had his crew
Opened into the hill a spacious wound
And digged out ribs of gold. Let none admire
That riches grow in hell; that soil may best
Deserve the precious bane. And here let those
Who boast in mortal things, and wondering tell
Of Babel, and the works of Memphian kings,
Learn how their greatest monuments of fame,
And strength and art are easily outdone
By spirits reprobate, and in an hour
What in an age they with incessant toil

And hands innumerable scarce perform.
Nigh on the plain in many cells prepared,
That underneath had veins of liquid fire
Sluiced from the lake, a second multitude
With wondrous art found out the massy ore,
Severing each kind, and scummed the bullion dross:
A third as soon had formed within the ground
A various mold, and from the boiling cells
By strange conveyance filled each hollow nook,
As in an organ from one blast of wind
To many a row of pipes the soundboard breathes.
Anon out of the earth a fabric huge
Rose like an exhalation, with the sound
Of dulcet symphonies and voices sweet,
Built like a temple, where pilasters round
Were set, and Doric pillars overlaid
With golden architrave; nor did there want
Cornice or frieze, with bossy sculptures graven,
The roof was fretted gold. Not Babylon,
Nor great Alcairo such magnificence
Equaled in all their glories, to enshrine
Belus or Serapis their gods, or seat
Their kings, when Egypt with Assyria strove
In wealth and luxury. The ascending pile
Stood fixed her stately height, and straight the doors
Opening their brazen folds discover wide
Within, her ample spaces, o'er the smooth
And level pavement: from the arched roof
Pendent by subtle magic many a row
Of starry lamps and blazing cressets fed
With naphtha and asphaltus yielded light
As from a sky. The hasty multitude
Admiring entered, and the work some praise
And some the architect: his hand was known
In heaven by many a towered structure high,
Where sceptered angels held their residence,
And sat as princes, whom the supreme king

Exalted to such power, and gave to rule,
Each in his hierarchy, the orders bright.
Nor was his name unheard or unadored
In ancient Greece; and in Ausonian land
Men called him Mulciber; and how he fell
From heaven, they fabled, thrown by angry Jove
Sheer o'er the crystal battlements; from morn
To noon he fell, from noon to dewy eve,
A summer's day; and with the setting sun
Dropped from the zenith like a falling star,
On Lemnos the Aegean isle: thus they relate,
Erring; for he with this rebellious rout
Fell long before; nor aught availed him now
To have built in heaven high towers; nor did I scape
By all his engines, but was headlong sent
With his industrious crew to build in hell.
Meanwhile the winged heralds by command
Of sovereign power, with awful ceremony
And trumpet's sound throughout the host proclaim
A solemn council forthwith to be held
At Pandemonium, the high capital
Of Satan and his peers: their summons called
From every band and squared regiment
By place or choice the worthiest; they anon
With hundreds and with thousands trooping came
Attended: all access was thronged, the gates
And porches wide, but chief the spacious hall
(Though like a covered field, where champions bold
Wont ride in armed, and at the soldan's chair
Defied the best of paynim chivalry
To mortal combat or career with lance)
Thick swarmed, both on the ground and in the air,
Brushed with the hiss of rustling wings. As bees
In springtime, when the sun with Taurus rides,
Pour forth their populous youth about the hive
In clusters; they among fresh dews and flowers
Fly to and fro, or on the smoothed plank,

The suburb of their straw-built citadel,
New rubbed with balm, expatiate and confer
Their state affairs. So thick the airy crowd
Swarmed and were straitened; till the signal **given,**
Behold a wonder! they but now who seemed
In bigness to surpass earth's giant sons
Now less than smallest dwarfs, in narrow room
Throng numberless, like that pygmaean race
Beyond the Indian mount, or faery elves,
Whose midnight revels, by a forest side
Or fountain some belated peasant sees,
Or dreams he sees, while overhead the moon
Sits arbitress, and nearer to the earth
Wheels her pale course, they on their mirth and dance
Intent, with jocund music charm his ear;
At once with joy and fear his heart rebounds.
Thus incorporeal spirits to smallest forms
Reduced their shapes immense, and were at large,
Though without number still amidst the hall
Of that infernal court. But far within
And in their own dimensions like themselves
The great seraphic lords and cherubim
In close recess and secret conclave sat
A thousand demi-gods on golden seats,
Frequent and full. After short silence then
And summons read, the great consult began.

BOOK II

The Argument: The consultation begun, Satan debates whether another battle be to be hazarded for the recovery of heaven: some advise it, others dissuade: A third proposal is preferred, mentioned before by Satan, to search the truth of that prophecy or tradition in heaven concerning another world, and another kind of creature

equal or not much inferior to themselves, about this time to be cre-
ated: Their doubt who shall be sent on this difficult search: Satan
their chief undertakes alone the voyage, is honored and applauded.
The council thus ended, the rest betake them several ways and to
several employments, as their inclinations lead them, to entertain
the time till Satan return. He passes on his journey to hell gates,
finds them shut, and who sat there to guard them, by whom at length
they are opened, and discover to him the great gulf between hell and
heaven; with what difficulty he passes through, directed by chaos,
the power of that place, to the sight of this new world which he
sought.

> High on a throne of royal state, which far
> Outshone the wealth of Ormus and of Ind,
> Or where the gorgeous east with richest hand
> Showers on her kings barbaric pearl and gold,
> Satan exalted sat, by merit raised
> To that bad eminence; and from despair
> Thus high uplifted beyond hope, aspires
> Beyond thus high, insatiate to pursue
> Vain war with heaven, and by success untaught
> His proud imaginations thus displayed.
> 'Powers and dominions, deities of heaven,
> For since no deep within her gulf can hold
> Immortal vigor, though oppressed and fallen,
> I give not heaven for lost. From this descent
> Celestial virtues rising, will appear
> More glorious and more dread than from no fall,
> And trust themselves to fear no second fate:
> Me though just right, and the fixed laws of heaven
> Did first create your leader, next, free choice,
> With what besides, in council or in fight,
> Hath been achieved of merit, yet this loss
> Thus far at least recovered, hath much more
> Established in a safe unenvied throne
> Yielded with full consent. The happier state
> In heaven, which follows dignity, might draw

Envy from each inferior; but who here
Will envy whom the highest place exposes
Foremost to stand against the thunderer's aim
Your bulwark, and condemns to greatest share
Of endless pain? where there is then no good
For which to strive, no strife can grow up there
From faction; for none sure will claim in hell
Precedence, none, whose portion is so small
Of present pain, that with ambitious mind
Will covet more. With this advantage then
To union, and firm faith, and firm accord,
More than can be in heaven, we now return
To claim our just inheritance of old,
Surer to prosper than prosperity
Could have assured us; and by what best way,
Whether of open war or covert guile,
We now debate; who can advise, may speak.'
  He ceased, and next him Moloch, sceptered king
Stood up, the strongest and the fiercest spirit
That fought in heaven; now fiercer by despair:
His trust was with the eternal to be deemed
Equal in strength, and rather than be less
Cared not to be at all; with that care lost
Went all his fear: of God, or hell, or worse
He recked not, and these words thereafter spake.
  'My sentence is for open war: Of wiles,
More unexpert, I boast not: them let those
Contrive who need, or when they need, not now.
For while they sit contriving, shall the rest,
Millions that stand in arms, and longing wait
The signal to ascend, sit lingering here
Heaven's fugitives, and for their dwelling place
Accept this dark opprobrious den of shame,
The prison of his tyranny who reigns
By our delay? no, let us rather choose
Armed with hell flames and fury all at once
O'er heaven's high towers to force resistless way,

Turning our tortures into horrid arms
Against the torturer; when to meet the noise
Of his almighty engine he shall hear
Infernal thunder, and for lightning see
Black fire and horror shot with equal rage
Among his angels; and his throne itself
Mixed with Tartarean sulphur, and strange fire,
His own invented torments. But perhaps
The way seems difficult and steep to scale
With upright wing against a higher foe.
Let such bethink them, if the sleepy drench
Of that forgetful lake benumb not still,
That in our proper motion we ascend
Up to our native seat: descent and fall
To us is adverse. Who but felt of late
When the fierce foe hung on our broken rear
Insulting, and pursued us through the deep,
With what compulsion and laborious flight
We sunk thus low? The ascent is easy then;
The event is feared; should we again provoke
Our stronger, some worse way his wrath may find
To our destruction: if there be in hell
Fear to be worse destroyed: what can be worse
Than to dwell here, driven out from bliss, condemned
In this abhorred deep to utter woe;
Where pain of unextinguishable fire
Must exercise us without hope of end
The vassals of his anger, when the scourge
Inexorably, and the torturing hour
Calls us to penance? More destroyed than thus
We should be quite abolished and expire.
What fear we then? what doubt we to incense
His utmost ire? which to the height enraged,
Will either quite consume us, and reduce
To nothing this essential, happier far
Than miserable to have eternal being:
Or if our substance be indeed divine,

And cannot cease to be, we are at worst
On this side nothing; and by proof we feel
Our power sufficient to disturb his heaven,
And with perpetual inroads to alarm,
Though inaccessible, his fatal throne:
Which if not victory is yet revenge.'
    He ended frowning, and his look denounced
Desperate revenge, and battle dangerous
To less than gods. On the other side uprose
Belial, in act more graceful and humane;
A fairer person lost not heaven; he seemed
For dignity composed and high exploit:
But all was false and hollow; though his tongue
Dropped manna, and could make the worse appear
The better reason, to perplex and dash
Maturest counsels: for his thoughts were low;
To vice industrious, but to nobler deeds
Timorous and slothful: yet he pleased the ear,
And with persuasive accent thus began.
    'I should be much for open war, O peers,
As not behind in hate; if what was urged
Main reason to persuade immediate war,
Did not dissuade me most, and seem to cast
Ominous conjecture on the whole success:
When he who most excels in fact of arms,
In what he counsels and in what excels
Mistrustful, grounds his courage on despair
And utter dissolution, as the scope
Of all his aim, after some dire revenge.
First, what revenge? the towers of heaven are filled
With armed watch, that render all access
Impregnable; oft on the bordering deep
Encamp their legions, or with obscure wing
Scout far and wide into the realm of night,
Scorning surprise. Or could we break our way
By force, and at our heels all hell should rise
With blackest insurrection, to confound

Heaven's purest light, yet our great enemy
All incorruptible would on his throne
Sit unpolluted, and the ethereal mold
Incapable of stain would soon expel
Her mischief, and purge off the baser fire
Victorious. Thus repulsed, our final hope
Is flat despair: we must exasperate
The almighty victor to spend all his rage,
And that must end us, that must be our cure,
To be no more; sad cure; for who would lose,
Though full of pain, this intellectual being,
Those thoughts that wander through eternity,
To perish rather, swallowed up and lost
in the wide womb of uncreated night,
Devoid of sense and motion? and who knows,
Let this be good, whether our angry foe
Can give it, or will ever? how he can
Is doubtful; that he never will is sure.
Will he, so wise, let loose at once his ire
Belike through impotence, or unaware,
To give his enemies their wish, and end
Them in his anger, whom his anger saves
To punish endless? "wherefore cease we then?"
Say they who counsel war, "we are decreed,
Reserved and destined to eternal woe;
Whatever doing, what can we suffer more,
What can we suffer worse?" is this then worst,
Thus sitting, thus consulting, thus in arms?
What when we fled amain, pursued and struck
With heaven's afflicting thunder, and besought
The deep to shelter us? this hell then seemed
A refuge from those wounds: or when we lay
Chained on the burning lake? that sure was worse.
What if the breath that kindled those grim fires
Awaked should blow them into sevenfold rage
And plunge us in the flames? or from above
Should intermitted vengeance arm again

His red right hand to plague us? what if all
Her stores were opened, and this firmament
Of hell should spout her cataracts of fire,
Impendent horrors, threatening hideous fall
One day upon our heads; while we perhaps
Designing or exhorting glorious war,
Caught in a fiery tempest shall be hurled
Each on his rock transfixed, the sport and prey
Of racking whirlwinds, or for ever sunk
Under yon boiling ocean, wrapt in chains;
There to converse with everlasting groans,
Unrespited, unpitied, unreprieved,
Ages of hopeless end; this would be worse.
War therefore, open or concealed, alike
My voice dissuades; for what can force or guile
With him, or who deceive his mind, whose eye
Views all things at one view? he from heaven's height
All these our motions vain, sees and derides;
Not more almighty to resist our might
Than wise to frustrate all our plots and wiles.
Shall we then live thus vile, the race of heaven
Thus trampled, thus expelled to suffer here
Chains and these torments? better these than worse
By my advice; since fate inevitable
Subdues us, and omnipotent decree,
The victor's will. To suffer, as to do,
Our strength is equal, nor the law unjust
That so ordains: this was at first resolved,
If we were wise, against so great a foe
Contending, and so doubtful what might fall.
I laugh, when those who at the spear are bold
And venturous, if that fail them, shrink and fear
What yet they know must follow, to endure
Exile, or ignominy, or bonds, or pain,
The sentence of their conqueror: This is now
Our doom; which if we can sustain and bear,
Our supreme foe in time may much remit

His anger, and perhaps thus far removed
Not mind us not offending, satisfied
With what is punished; whence these raging fires
Will slacken, if his breath stir not their flames.
Our purer essence then will overcome
Their noxious vapor, or inured not feel,
Or changed at length, and to the place conformed
In temper and in nature, will receive
Familiar the fierce heat, and void of pain;
This horror will grow mild, this darkness light,
Besides what hope the never-ending flight
Of future days may bring, what chance, what change
Worth waiting, since our present lot appears
For happy though but ill, for ill not worst,
If we procure not to ourselves more woe.'

    Thus Belial with words clothed in reason's garb
Counseled ignoble ease, and peaceful sloth,
Not peace: and after him thus Mammon spake.

    'Either to disenthrone the king of heaven
We war, if war be best, or to regain
Our own right lost: him to unthrone we then
May hope, when everlasting fate shall yield
To fickle chance, and chaos judge the strife:
The former vain to hope argues as vain
The latter: for what place can be for us
Within heaven's bound, unless heaven's lord supreme
We overpower? Suppose he should relent
And publish grace to all, on promise made
Of new subjection; with what eyes could we
Stand in his presence humble, and receive
Strict laws imposed, to celebrate his throne
With warbled hymns, and to his Godhead sing
Forced hallelujahs; while he lordly sits
Our envied sovereign, and his altar breathes
Ambrosial odors and ambrosial flowers,
Our servile offerings. This must be our task
In heaven, this our delight; how wearisome

Eternity so spent in worship paid
To whom we hate. Let us not then pursue
By force impossible, by leave obtained
Unacceptable, though in heaven, our state
Of splendid vassalage, but rather seek
Our own good from ourselves, and from our own
Live to ourselves, though in this vast recess,
Free, and to none accountable, preferring
Hard liberty before the easy yoke
Of servile pomp. Our greatness will appear
Then most conspicuous, when great things of small,
Useful of hurtful, prosperous of adverse
We can create, and in what place so e'er
Thrive under evil, and work ease out of pain
Through labor and endurance. This deep world
Of darkness do we dread? How oft amidst
Thick clouds and dark doth heaven's all-ruling sire
Choose to reside, his glory unobscured,
And with the majesty of darkness round
Covers his throne; from whence deep thunders roar
Mustering their rage, and heaven resembles hell?
As he our darkness, cannot we his light
Imitate when we please? This desert soil
Wants not her hidden luster, gems and gold;
Nor want we skill or art, from whence to raise
Magnificence; and what can heaven show more?
Our torments also may in length of time
Become our elements, these piercing fires
As soft as now severe, our temper changed
Into their temper; which must needs remove
The sensible of pain. All things invite
To peaceful counsels, and the settled state
Of order, how in safety best we may
Compose our present evils, with regard
Of what we are and were, dismissing quite
All thoughts of war; ye have what I advise.'

He scarce had finished, when such murmur filled
The assembly, as when hollow rocks retain
The sound of blustering winds, which all night long
Had roused the sea, now with hoarse cadence lull
Seafaring men o'erwatched, whose bark by chance
Or pinnace anchors in a craggy bay
After the tempest: Such applause was heard
As Mammon ended, and his sentence pleased,
Advising peace: for such another field
They dreaded worse than hell; so much the fear
Of thunder and the sword of Michael
Wrought still within them; and no less desire
To found this nether empire, which might rise
By policy, and long process of time,
In emulation opposite to heaven.
Which when Beelzebub perceived, than whom,
Satan except, none higher sat, with grave
Aspect he rose, and in his rising seemed
A pillar of state; deep on his front engraven
Deliberation sat and public care;
And princely counsel in his face yet shone,
Majestic though in ruin: sage he stood
With Atlantean shoulders fit to bear
The weight of mightiest monarchies; his look
Drew audience and attention still as night
Or summer's noontide air, while thus he spake.
　'Thrones and imperial powers, offspring of heaven,
Ethereal virtues; or these titles now
Must we renounce, and changing style be called
Princes of hell? for so the popular vote
Inclines, here to continue, and build up here
A growing empire; doubtless; while we dream,
And know not that the king of heaven hath doomed
This place our dungeon, not our safe retreat
Beyond his potent arm, to live exempt
From heaven's high jurisdiction, in new league
Banded against his throne, but to remain

In strictest bondage, though thus far removed,
Under the inevitable curb, reserved
His captive multitude: For he, be sure
In height or depth, still first and last will reign
Sole king, and of his kingdom lose no part
By our revolt, but over hell extend
His empire, and with iron scepter rule
Us here, as with his golden those in heaven.
What sit we then projecting peace and war?
War hath determined us, and foiled with loss
Irreparable; terms of peace yet none
Vouchsafed or sought; for what peace will be given
To us enslaved, but custody severe,
And stripes, and arbitrary punishment
Inflicted? and what peace can we return,
But to our power hostility and hate,
Untamed reluctance, and revenge though slow,
Yet ever plotting how the conqueror least
May reap his conquest, and may least rejoice
In doing what we most in suffering feel?
Nor will occasion want, nor shall we need
With dangerous expedition to invade
Heaven, whose high walls fear no assault or siege,
Or ambush from the deep. What if we find
Some easier enterprise? There is a place
(If ancient and prophetic fame in heaven
Err not) another world, the happy seat
Of some new race called man, about this time
To be created like to us, though less
In power and excellence, but favored more
Of him who rules above; so was his will
Pronounced among the gods, and by an oath,
That shook heaven's whole circumference, confirmed.
Thither let us bend all our thoughts, to learn
What creatures there inhabit, of what mold,
Or substance, how endued, and what their power,
And where their weakness, how attempted best,

By force or subtlety: Though heaven be shut,
And heaven's high arbitrator sit secure
In his own strength, this place may lie exposed
The utmost border of his kingdom, left
To their defense who hold it: here perhaps
Some advantageous act may be achieved
By sudden onset, either with hell fire
To waste his whole creation, or possess
All as our own, and drive as we were driven,
The puny habitants, or if not drive,
Seduce them to our party, that their God
May prove their foe, and with repenting hand
Abolish his own works. This would surpass
Common revenge, and interrupt his joy
In our confusion, and our joy upraise
In his disturbance; when his darling sons
Hurled headlong to partake with us, shall curse
Their frail original, and faded bliss,
Faded so soon. Advise if this be worth
Attempting, or to sit in darkness here
Hatching vain empires.' Thus Beelzebub
Pleaded his devilish counsel, first devised
By Satan, and in part proposed: for whence,
But from the author of all ill could spring
So deep a malice, to confound the race
Of mankind in one root, and earth with hell
To mingle and involve, done all to spite
The great creator? But their spite still serves
His glory to augment. The bold design
Pleased highly those infernal states, and joy
Sparkled in all their eyes; with full assent
They vote: whereat his speech he thus renews.

  'Well have ye judged, well ended long debate,
Synod of gods, and like to what ye are,
Great things resolved, which from the lowest deep
Will once more lift us up, in spite of fate,
Nearer our ancient seat; perhaps in view

Of those bright confines, whence with neighboring arms
And opportune excursion we may chance
Re-enter heaven; or else in some mild zone
Dwell not unvisited of heaven's fair light
Secure, and at the brightening orient beam
Purge off this gloom; the soft delicious air,
To heal the scar of these corrosive fires
Shall breathe her balm. But first whom shall we send
In search of this new world, whom shall we find
Sufficient? who shall tempt with wandering feet
The dark unbottomed infinite abyss
And through the palpable obscure find out
His uncouth way, or spread his airy flight
Upborne with indefatigable wings
Over the vast abrupt, ere he arrive
The happy isle; what strength, what art can then
Suffice, or what evasion bear him safe
Through the strict sentries and stations thick
Of angels watching round? Here he had need
All circumspection, and we now no less
Choice in our suffrage; for on whom we send,
The weight of all and our last hope relies.'

  This said, he sat; and expectation held
His look suspense, awaiting who appeared
To second, or oppose, or undertake
The perilous attempt: but all sat mute,
Pondering the danger with deep thoughts; and each
In other's countenance read his own dismay
Astonished: none among the choice and prime
Of those heaven-warring champions could be found
So hardy as to proffer or accept
Alone the dreadful voyage; till at last
Satan, whom now transcendent glory raised
Above his fellows, with monarchal pride
Conscious of highest worth, unmoved thus spake.

  'O progeny of heaven, empyreal thrones,
With reason hath deep silence and demur

Seized us, though undismayed: long is the way
And hard, that out of hell leads up to light;
Our prison strong, this huge convex of fire,
Outrageous to devour, immures us round
Ninefold, and gates of burning adamant
Barred over us prohibit all egress.
These passed, if any pass, the void profound
Of unessential night receives him next
Wide gaping, and with utter loss of being
Threatens him, plunged in that abortive gulf,
If thence he scape into whatever world,
Or unknown region, what remains him less
Than unknown dangers and as hard escape.
But I should ill become this throne, O peers,
And this imperial sovereignty, adorned
With splendor, armed with power, if aught proposed
And judged of public moment, in the shape
Of difficulty or danger could deter
Me from attempting. Wherefore do I assume
These royalties, and not refuse to reign,
Refusing to accept as great a share
Of hazard as of honor, due alike
To him who reigns, and so much to him due
Of hazard more, as he above the rest
High honored sits? Go therefore mighty powers,
Terror of heaven, though fallen; intend at home,
While here shall be our home, what best may ease
The present misery, and render hell
More tolerable; if there be cure or charm
To respite or deceive, or slack the pain
Of this ill mansion: intermit no watch
Against a wakeful foe, while I abroad
Through all the coasts of dark destruction seek
Deliverance for us all: this enterprise
None shall partake with me.' Thus saying rose
The monarch, and prevented all reply,
Prudent, lest from his resolution raised

Others among the chief might offer now
(Certain to be refused) what erst they feared;
And so refused might in opinion stand
His rivals, winning cheap the high repute
Which he through hazard huge must earn. But they
Dreaded not more the adventure than his voice
Forbidding; and at once with him they rose;
Their rising all at once was as the sound
Of thunder heard remote. Towards him they bend
With awful reverence prone; and as a god
Extol him equal to the highest in heaven:
Nor failed they to express how much they praised,
That for the general safety he despised
His own: for neither do the spirits damned
Lose all their virtue; lest bad men should boast
Their specious deeds on earth, which glory excites,
Or close ambition varnished o'er with zeal.
Thus they their doubtful consultations dark
Ended rejoicing in their matchless chief:
As when from mountain tops the dusky clouds
Ascending, while the north wind sleeps, o'erspread
Heaven's cheerful face, the louring element
Scowls o'er the darkened landscape snow, or shower;
If chance the radiant sun with farewell sweet
Extend his evening beam, the fields revive,
The birds their notes renew, and bleating herds
Attest their joy, that hill and valley rings.
O shame to men! Devil with devil damned
Firm concord holds, men only disagree
Of creatures rational, though under hope
Of heavenly grace: and God proclaiming peace
Yet live in hatred, enmity, and strife
Among themselves, and levy cruel wars,
Wasting the earth, each other to destroy:
As if (which might induce us to accord)
Man had not hellish foes enow besides
That day and night for his destruction wait.

The Stygian council thus dissolved; and forth
In order came the grand infernal peers,
Midst came their mighty paramount, and seemed
Alone the antagonistic of heaven, nor less
Than hell's dread emperor with pomp supreme,
And god-like imitated state; him round
A globe of fiery seraphim enclosed
With bright emblazonry, and horrent arms.
Then of their session ended they bid cry
With trumpet's regal sound the great result:
Toward the four winds four speedy cherubim
Put to their mouths the sounding alchemy
By herald's voice explained: the hollow abyss
Heard far and wide, and all the host of hell
With deafening shout, returned them loud acclaim.
Thence more at ease their minds and somewhat raised
By false presumptuous hope, the ranged powers
Disband, and wandering, each his several way
Pursues, as inclination or sad choice
Leads him perplexed, where he may likeliest find
Truce to his restless thoughts, and entertain
The irksome hours, till this great chief return.
Part on the plain, or in the air sublime
Upon the wing, or in swift race contend,
As at the Olympian games or Pythian fields;
Part curb their fiery steeds, or shun the goal
With rapid wheels, or fronted brigades form.
As when to warn proud cities war appears
Waged in the troubled sky, and armies rush
To battle in the clouds, before each van
Prick forth the airy knights, and couch their spears
Till thickest legions close; with feats of arms
From either end of heaven the welkin burns.
Others with vast Typhoean rage more fell
Rend up both rocks and hills, and ride the air
In whirlwind; hell scarce holds the wild uproar.
As when Alcides from Oechalia crowned

With conquest, felt the envenomed robe, and tore
Through pain up by the roots Thessalian pines,
And Lichas from the top of Oeta threw
Into the Euboic sea. Others more mild,
Retreated in a silent valley, sing
With notes angelical to many a harp
Their own heroic deeds and hapless fall
By doom of battle; and complain that fate
Free virtue should enthrall to force or chance.
Their song was partial, but the harmony
(What could it less when spirits immortal sing?)
Suspended hell, and took with ravishment
The thronging audience. In discourse more sweet
(For eloquence the soul, song charms the sense,)
Others apart sat on a hill retired,
In thoughts more elevate, and reasoned high
Of providence, foreknowledge, will, and fate,
Fixed fate, free will, foreknowledge absolute,
And found no end, in wandering mazes lost.
Of good and evil much they argued then,
Of happiness and final misery,
Passion and apathy, and glory and shame,
Vain wisdom all, and false philosophy:
Yet with a pleasing sorcery could charm
Pain for a while or anguish, and excite
Fallacious hope, or arm the obdured breast
With stubborn patience as with triple steel.
Another part in squadrons and gross bands
On bold adventure to discover wide
That dismal world, if any clime perhaps
Might yield them easier habitation, bend
Four ways their flying march, along the banks
Of four infernal rivers that disgorge
Into the burning lake their baleful streams;
Abhorred Styx the flood of deadly hate,
Sad Acheron of sorrow, black and deep;
Cocytus, named of lamentation loud

Heard on the rueful stream; fierce Phlegeton
Whose waves of torrent fire inflame with rage.
Far off from these a slow and silent stream,
Lethe the river of oblivion rolls
Her watery labyrinth, whereof who drinks,
Forthwith his former state and being forgets,
Forgets both joy and grief, pleasure and pain.
Beyond this flood a frozen continent
Lies dark and wild, beat with perpetual storms
Of whirlwind and dire hail, which on firm land
Thaws not, but gathers heap, and ruin seems
Of ancient pile; all else deep snow and ice,
A gulf profound as that Serbonian bog
Betwixt Damiata and Mount Casius old,
Where armies whole have sunk: the parching air
Burns frore, and cold performs the effect of fire.
Thither by harpy-footed furies haled,
At certain revolutions all the damned
Are brought: and feel by turns the bitter change
Of fierce extremes, extremes by change more fierce.
From beds of raging fire to starve in ice
Their soft ethereal warmth, and there to pine
Immovable, infixed, and frozen round,
Periods of time, thence hurried back to fire.
They ferry over this Lethean sound
Both to and fro, their sorrow to augment,
And wish and struggle, as they pass, to reach
The tempting stream, with one small drop to lose
In sweet forgetfulness all pain and woe,
All in one moment, and so near the brink;
But fate withstands, and to oppose the attempt
Medusa with Gorgonian terror guards
The ford, and of itself the water flies
All taste of living wight, as once it fled
The lip of Tantalus. Thus roving on
In confused march forlorn, the adventurous bands
With shuddering horror pale, and eyes aghast

Viewed first their lamentable lot, and found
No rest: through many a dark and dreary vale
They passed, and many a region dolorous,
O'er many a frozen, many a fiery alp,
Rocks, caves, lakes, fens, bogs, dens, and shades of death.
A universe of death, which God by curse
Created evil, for evil only good,
Where all life dies, death lives, and nature breeds,
Perverse, all monstrous, all prodigious things,
Abominable, inutterable, and worse
Than fables yet have feigned, or fear conceived,
Gorgons and hydras, and chimeras dire.
    Meanwhile the adversary of God and man,
Satan with thoughts inflamed of highest design,
Puts on swift wings, and towards the gates of hell
Explores his solitary flight; sometimes
He scouts the right hand coast, sometimes the left,
Now shaves with level wing the deep, then soars
Up to the fiery concave towering high.
As when far off at sea a fleet descried
Hangs in the clouds, by equinoctial winds
Close sailing from Bengala, or the isles
Of Ternate and Tidore, whence merchants bring
Their spicy drugs: they on the trading flood
Through the wide Ethiopian to the cape
Ply stemming nightly toward the pole. So seemed
Far off the flying fiend: at last appear
Hell bounds high reaching to the horrid roof,
And thrice threefold the gates; three folds were brass,
Three iron, three of adamantine rock,
Impenetrable, impaled with circling fire,
Yet unconsumed. Before the gates there sat
On either side a formidable shape;
The one seemed woman to the waist, and fair,
But ended foul in many a scaly fold
Voluminous and vast, a serpent armed
With mortal sting: about her middle round

A cry of hell hounds never ceasing barked
With wide Cerberean mouths full loud, and rung
A hideous peal: yet, when they list, would creep,
If aught disturbed their noise, into her womb,
And kennel there, yet there still barked and howled,
Within unseen. Far less abhorred than these
Vexed Scylla bathing in the sea that parts
Calabria from the hoarse Trinacrian shore:
Nor uglier follow the night-hag, when called
In secret, riding through the air she comes
Lured with the smell of infant blood, to dance
With Lapland witches, while the laboring moon
Eclipses at their charms. The other shape,
If shape it might be called that shape had none
Distinguishable in member, joint, or limb,
Or substance might be called that shadow seemed,
For each seemed either; black it stood as night,
Fierce as ten furies, terrible as hell,
And shook a dreadful dart; what seemed his head
The likeness of a kingly crown had on.
Satan was now at hand, and from his seat
The monster moving onward came as fast
With horrid strides, hell trembled as he strode.
The undaunted fiend what this might be admired,
Admired, not feared; God and his Son except,
Created thing naught valued he nor shunned;
And with disdainful look thus first began.

'Whence and what art thou, execrable shape,
That darest, though grim and terrible, advance
Thy miscreated front athwart my way
To yonder gates? through them I mean to pass,
That be assured, without leave asked of thee:
Retire, or taste thy folly, and learn by proof,
Hell-born, not to contend with spirits of heaven.'

To whom the goblin full of wrath replied,
'Art thou that traitor angel, art thou he,
Who first broke peace in heaven and faith, till then

Unbroken, and in proud rebellious arms
Drew after him the third part of heaven's sons
Conjured against the highest, for which both thou
And they outcast from God, are here condemned
To waste eternal days in woe and pain?
And reckonest thou thyself with spirits of heaven,
Hell-doomed, and breathest defiance here and scorn
Where I reign king, and to enrage thee more,
Thy king and lord? Back to thy punishment,
False fugitive, and to thy speed add wings,
Lest with a whip of scorpions I pursue
Thy lingering, or with one stroke of this dart
Strange horror seize thee, and pangs unfelt before.'
   So spake the grisly terror, and in shape,
So speaking and so threatening, grew tenfold
More dreadful and deform: on the other side
Incensed with indignation Satan stood
Unterrified, and like a comet burned,
That fires the length of Ophiuchus huge
In the arctic sky, and from his horrid hair
Shakes pestilence and war. Each at the head
Leveled his deadly aim; their fatal hands
No second stroke intend, and such a frown
Each cast at the other, as when two black clouds
With heaven's artillery fraught, come rattling on
Over the Caspian, then stand front to front
Hovering a space, till winds the signal blow
To join their dark encounter in mid-air:
So frowned the mighty combatants, that hell
Grew darker at their frown, so matched they stood
For never but once more was either like
To meet so great a foe: and now great deeds
Had been achieved, whereof all hell had rung,
Had not the snaky sorceress that sat
Fast by hell gate, and kept the fatal key,
Risen, and with hideous outcry rushed between.
   'O father, what intends thy hand,' she cried,

'Against thy only son? What fury O son,
Possesses thee to bend that mortal dart
Against thy father's head? and knowest for whom;
For him who sits above and laughs the while
At thee ordained his drudge, to execute
Whate'er his wrath, which he calls justice, bids,
His wrath which one day will destroy ye both.'
    She spake, and at her words the hellish pest
Forbore, then these to her Satan returned:
    'So strange thy outcry, and thy words so strange
Thou interposest, that my sudden hand
Prevented spares to tell thee yet by deeds
What it intends; till first I know of thee,
What thing thou art, thus double-formed, and why
In this infernal vale first met thou callest
Me father, and that phantasm callest my son?
I know thee not, nor ever saw till now
Sight more destestable than him and thee.'
    To whom thus the portress of hell gate replied:
'Hast thou forgot me then, and do I seem
Now in thine eye so foul, once deemed so fair
In heaven, when at the assembly, and in sight
Of all the seraphim with thee combined
In bold conspiracy against heaven's king,
All on a sudden miserable pain
Surprised thee, dim thine eyes, and dizzy swum
In darkness, while thy head flames thick and fast
Threw forth, till on the left side opening wide,
Likest to thee in shape and countenance bright,
Then shining heavenly fair, a goddess armed
Out of thy head I sprung; amazement seized
All the host of heaven; back they recoiled afraid
At first, and called me Sin, and for a sign
Portentous held me; but familiar grown,
I pleased, and with attractive graces won
The most averse, thee chiefly, who full oft
Thyself in me thy perfect image viewing

Becamest enamored, and such joy thou tookest
With me in secret, that my womb conceived
A growing burden. Meanwhile war arose,
And fields were fought in heaven; wherein remained
(For what could else) to our almighty foe
Clear victory, to our part loss and rout
Through all the empyrean: down they fell
Driven headlong from the pitch of heaven, down
Into this deep, and in the general fall
I also; at which time this powerful key
Into my hand was given, with charge to keep
These gates forever shut, which none can pass
Without my opening. Pensive here I sat
Alone, but long I sat not, till my womb
Pregnant by thee, and now excessive grown
Prodigious motion felt and rueful throes.
At last this odious offspring whom thou seest
Thine own begotten, breaking violent way
Tore through my entrails, that with fear and pain
Distorted, all my nether shape thus grew
Transformed: but he my inbred enemy
Forth issued, brandishing his fatal dart
Made to destroy: I fled, and cried out "Death;"
Hell trembled at the hideous name, and sighed
From all her caves, and back resounded "Death."
I fled, but he pursued (though more, it seems,
Inflamed with lust than rage) and swifter far,
Me overtook his mother all dismayed,
And in embraces forcible and foul
Engendering with me, of that rape begot
These yelling monsters that with ceaseless cry
Surround me, as thou sawest, hourly conceived
And hourly born, with sorrow infinite
To me, for when they list into the womb
That bred them they return, and howl and gnaw
My bowels, their repast; then bursting forth
Afresh with conscious terrors vex me round,

That rest or intermission none I find.
Before mine eyes in opposition sits
Grim Death my son and foe, who sets them on,
And me his parent would full soon devour
For want of other prey, but that he knows
His end with mine involved; and knows that I
Should prove a bitter morsel, and his bane,
Whenever that shall be; so fate pronounced.
But thou O father, I forewarn thee, shun
His deadly arrow; neither vainly hope
To be invulnerable in those bright arms,
Though tempered heavenly, for that mortal dint,
Save he who reigns above, none can resist.'

   She finished, and the subtle fiend his lore
Soon learned, now milder, and thus answered smooth.
'Dear daughter, since thou claimest me for thy sire,
And my fair son here showest me, the dear pledge
Of dalliance had with thee in heaven, and joys
Then sweet, now sad to mention, through dire change
Befallen us unforeseen, unthought of, know
I come no enemy, but to set free
From out this dark and dismal house of pain,
Both him and thee, and all the heavenly host
Of spirits that in out just pretences armed
Fell with us from on high: from them I go
This uncouth errand sole, and one for all
Myself expose, with lonely steps to tread
The unfounded deep, and through the void immense
To search with wandering quest a place foretold
Should be, and, by concurring signs, ere now
Created vast and round, a place of bliss
In the purlieus of heaven, and therein placed
A race of upstart creatures, to supply
Perhaps our vacant room, though more removed,
Lest heaven surcharged with potent multitude
Might hap to move new broils: Be this or aught
Than this more secret now designed, I haste

To know, and this once known, shall soon return,
And bring ye to the place where thou and death
Shall dwell at ease, and up and down unseen
Wing silently the buxom air, embalmed
With odors; there ye shall be fed and filled
Immeasurably, all things shall be your prey.'
He ceased, for both seemed highly pleased, and death
Grinned horrible a ghastly smile, to hear
His famine should be filled, and blessed his maw
Destined to that good hour: no less rejoiced
His mother bad, and thus bespake her sire.
    'The key of this infernal pit by due,
And by command of heaven's all-powerful king
I keep, by him forbidden to unlock
These adamantine gates; against all force
Death ready stands to interpose his dart,
Fearless to be o'er matched by living might.
But what owe I to his commands above
Who hates me, and hath hither thrust me down
Into this gloom of Tartarus profound,
To sit in hateful office here confined,
Inhabitant of heaven, and heavenly-born,
Here in perpetual agony and pain,
With terrors and with clamors compassed round
Of mine own brood, that on my bowels feed:
Thou art my father, thou my author, thou
My being gavest me; whom should I obey
But thee, whom follow? thou wilt bring me soon
To that new world of light and bliss, among
The gods who live at ease, where I shall reign
At thy right hand voluptuous, as beseems
Thy daughter and thy darling, without end.'
    Thus saying, from her side the fatal key,
Sad instrument of all our woe, she took;
And towards the gate rolling her bestial train,
Forthwith the huge portcullis high updrew,
Which but herself not all the Stygian powers

Could once have moved; then in the keyhole turns
The intricate wards, and every bolt and bar
Of massy iron or solid rock with ease
Unfastens: on a sudden open fly
With impetuous recoil and jarring sound
The infernal doors, and on their hinges grate
Harsh thunder, that the lowest bottom shook
Of Erebus. She opened, but to shut
Excelled her power; the gates wide open stood,
That with extended wings a bannered host
Under spread ensigns marching might pass through
With horse and chariots ranked in loose array;
So wide they stood, and like a furnace mouth
Cast forth redounding smoke and ruddy flame.
Before their eyes in sudden view appear
The secrets of the hoary deep, a dark
Illimitable ocean without bound,
Without dimension, where length, breadth, and height,
And time and place are lost; where eldest night
And chaos, ancestors of nature, hold
Eternal anarchy, amidst the noise
Of endless wars, and by confusion stand.
For hot, cold, moist. and dry, four champions fierce
Strive here for mastery, and to battle bring
Their embryon atoms; they around the flag
Of each his faction, in their several clans,
Light-armed or heavy, sharp, smooth, swift or slow,
Swarm populous, unnumbered as the sands
Of Barca or Cyrene's torrid soil,
Levied to side with warring winds, and poise
Their lighter wings. To whom these most adhere,
He rules a moment; chaos umpire sits,
And by decision more embroils the fray
By which he reigns: next him high arbiter
Chance governs all. Into this wild abyss,
The womb of nature and perhaps her grave,
Of neither sea, nor shore. nor air, nor fire,

But all these in their pregnant causes mixed
Confusedly, and which thus must ever fight,
Unless the almighty maker them ordain
His dark materials to create more worlds,
Into this wild abyss the wary fiend
Stood on the brink of hell and looked a while,
Pondering his voyage; for no narrow frith
He had to cross. Nor was his ear less pealed
With noises loud and ruinous (to compare
Great things with small) than when Bellona storms
With all her battering engines bent to rase
Some capital city, or less than if this frame
Of heaven were falling, and these elements
In mutiny had from her axle torn
The steadfast earth. At last his sail-broad vans
He spreads for flight, and in the surging smoke
Uplifted spurns the ground, thence many a league
As in a cloudy chair ascending rides
Audacious, but that seat soon failing, meets
A vast vacuity: all unawares
Fluttering his pennons vain plumb down he drops
Ten thousand fathom deep, and to this hour
Down had been falling, had not by ill chance
The strong rebuff of some tumultuous cloud
Instinct with fire and niter hurried him
As many miles aloft: that fury stayed,
Quenched in a boggy Syrtis, neither sea,
Nor good dry land: nigh foundered on he fares,
Treading the crude consistence, half on foot,
Half flying; behooves him now both oar and sail.
As when a griffin through the wilderness
With winged course o'er hill or moory dale,
Pursues the Arimaspian, who by stealth
Had from his wakeful custody purloined
The guarded gold: So eagerly the fiend
O'er bog or steep, through strait, rough, dense, or rare,
With head, hands, wings or feet pursues his way,

And swims or sinks, or wades, or creeps, or flies:
At length a universal hubbub wild
Of stunning sounds and voices all confused
Borne through the hollow dark assaults his ear
With loudest vehemence: thither he plies,
Undaunted to meet there whatever power
Or Spirit of the nethermost abyss
Might in that noise reside, of whom to ask
Which way the nearest coast of darkness lies
Bordering on light; when straight behold the throne
Of Chaos, and his dark pavilion spread
Wide on the wasteful deep; with him enthroned
Sat sable-vested Night, eldest of things,
The consort of his reign; and by them stood
Orcus and Ades, and the dreaded name
Of Demogorgon; Rumor next and Chance,
And Tumult and Confusion all embroiled,
And Discord with a thousand various mouths.
        To whom Satan turning boldly, thus. 'Ye powers
And spirits of this nethermost abyss,
Chaos and ancient Night, I come no spy,
With purpose to explore or to disturb
The secrets of your realm, but by constraint
Wandering this darksome desert, as my way
Lies through your spacious empire up to light,
Alone, and without guide, half lost, I seek
What readiest path leads where your gloomy bounds
Confine with heaven; or if some other place
From your dominion won, the ethereal king
Possesses late, thither to arrive
I travel this profound, direct my course;
Directed, no mean recompense it brings
To your behoof, if I that region lost,
All usurpation thence expelled, reduce
To her original darkness and your sway
(Which is my present journey) and once more
Erect the standard there of ancient night;

Yours be the advantage all, mine the revenge.'
 Thus Satan; and him thus the anarch old
With faltering speech and visage incomposed
Answered. 'I know thee, stranger, who thou art,
That mighty leading angel, who of late
Made head against heaven's king, though overthrown.
I saw and heard, for such a numerous host
Fled not in silence through the frighted deep
With ruin upon ruin, rout on rout,
Confusion worse confounded; and heaven gates
Poured out by millions her victorious bands
Pursuing. I upon my frontiers here
Keep residence; if all I can will serve,
That little which is left so to defend,
Encroached on still through our intestine broils
Weakening the scepter of old night: first hell
Your dungeon stretching far and wide beneath;
Now lately heaven and earth, another world
Hung o'er my realm, linked in a golden chain
To that side heaven from whence your legions fell:
If that way be your walk, you have not far;
So much the nearer danger; go and speed;
Havoc and spoil and ruin are my gain.'
 He ceased; and Satan stayed not to reply,
But glad that now his sea should find a shore.
With fresh alacrity and force renewed
Springs upward like a pyramid of fire
Into the wild expanse, and through the shock
Of fighting elements, on all sides round
Environed wins his way; harder beset
And more endangered, than when Argo passed
Through Bosporus betwixt the justling rocks:
Or when Ulysses on the larboard shunned
Charybdis, and by the other whirlpool steered.
So he with difficulty and labor hard
Moved on, with difficulty and labor he;
But he once passed, soon after when man fell,

Strange alteration! Sin and death amain
Following his track, such was the will of heaven,
Paved after him a broad and beaten way
Over the dark abyss, whose boiling gulf
Tamely endured a bridge of wondrous length
From hell continued reaching the utmost orb
Of this frail world; by which the spirits perverse
With easy intercourse pass to and fro
To tempt or punish mortals, except whom
God and good angels guard by special grace.
But now at last the sacred influence
Of light appears, and from the walls of heaven
Shoots far into the bosom of dim night
A glimmering dawn; here nature first begins
Her farthest verge, and chaos to retire
As from her outmost works a broked foe
With tumult less and with less hostile din,
That Satan with less toil, and now with ease
Wafts on the calmer wave by dubious light
And like a weather-beaten vessel holds
Gladly the port, though shrouds and tackle torn;
Or in the emptier waste, resembling air,
Weighs his spread wings, at leisure to behold
Far off the empyreal heaven, extended wide
In circuit, undetermined square or round,
With opal towers and battlements adorned
Of living sapphire, once his native seat;
And fast by hanging in a golden chain
This pendent world, in bigness as a star
Of smallest magnitude close by the moon.
Thither full fraught with mischievous revenge,
Accursed, and in a cursed hour he hies.

BOOK III

The Argument: God sitting on his throne sees Satan flying towards this world, then newly created; shows him to the Son who sat at his right hand; foretells the success of Satan in perverting mankind; clears his own justice and wisdom from all imputation, having created man free and able enough to have withstood his tempter; yet declares his purpose of grace towards him, in regard he fell not of his own malice, as did Satan, but by him seduced. The Son of God renders praises to his father for the manifestation of his gracious purpose towards man; but God again declares, that grace cannot be extended towards man without the satisfaction of divine justice; man hath offended the majesty of God by aspiring to Godhead, and therefore with all his progeny devoted to death must die, unless someone can be found sufficient to answer for his offence, and undergo his punishment. The Son of God freely offers himself a ransom for man: the father accepts him, ordains his incarnation, pronounces his exaltation above all names in heaven and earth; commands all the angels to adore him; they obey, and hymning to their harps in full choir, celebrate the Father and the Son. Meanwhile Satan alights upon the bare convex of this world's outermost orb; where wandering he first finds a place since called the limbo of vanity; what persons and things fly up thither; thence comes to the gate of heaven, described ascending by stairs, and the waters above the firmament that flow about it: His passage thence to the orb of the sun; he finds there Uriel the regent of that orb, but first changes himself into the shape of a meaner angel; and pretending a zealous desire to behold the new creation and man whom God had placed here, inquires of him the place of his habitation, and is directed; alights first on Mount Niphates.

Hail holy light, offspring of heaven first-born,
Or of the eternal coeternal beam
May I express thee unblamed? since God is light,
And never but in unapproached light

Dwelt from eternity, dwelt then in thee,
Bright effluence of bright essence increate.
Or hearest thou rather pure ethereal stream,
Whose fountain who shall tell? before the sun,
Before the heavens thou wert, and at the voice
Of God, as with a mantle didst invest
The rising world of waters dark and deep,
Won from the void and formless infinite.
Thee I revisit now with bolder wing,
Escaped the Stygian pool, though long detained
In that obscure sojourn, while in my flight
Through utter and through middle darkness borne
With other notes than to the Orphean lyre
I sung of chaos and eternal night,
Taught by the heavenly muse to venture down
The dark descent, and up to reascend,
Though hard and rare: thee I revisit safe,
And feel thy sovereign vital lamp; but thou
Revisitest not these eyes, that roll in vain
To find thy piercing ray, and find no dawn;
So thick a drop serene hath quenched their orbs,
Or dim suffusion veiled. Yet not the more
Cease I to wander where the muses haunt
Clear spring, or shady grove, or sunny hill,
Smit with the love of sacred song; but chief
Thee Sion and the flowery brooks beneath
That wash thy hallowed feet, and warbling flow,
Nightly I visit: nor sometimes forget
Those other two equaled with me in fate,
So were I equaled with them in renown,
Blind Thamyris and blind Maeonides,
And Tiresias and Phineus prophets old.
Then feed on thoughts, that voluntary move
Harmonious numbers; as the wakeful bird
Sings darkling, and in shadiest covert hid
Tunes her nocturnal note. Thus with the year
Seasons return, but not to me returns

Day, or the sweet approach of even or morn,
Or sight of vernal bloom, or summer's rose,
Or flocks, or herds, or human face divine;
But cloud instead, and ever-during dark
Surrounds me, from the cheerful ways of men
Cut off, and for the book of knowledge fair
Presented with a universal blank
Of nature's works to me expunged and rased,
And wisdom at one entrance quite shut out.
So much the rather thou celestial light
Shine inward, and the mind through all her powers
Irradiate, there plant eyes, all mist from thence
Purge and disperse, that I may see and tell
Of things invisible to mortal sight.
 Now had the almighty father from above,
From the pure empyrean where he sits
High throned above all height, bent down his eye,
His own works and their works at once to view:
About him all the sanctities of heaven
Stood thick as stars, and from his sight received
Beatitude past utterance; on his right
The radiant image of his glory sat,
His only Son; On earth he first beheld
Our two first parents, yet the only two
Of mankind, in the happy garden placed,
Reaping immortal fruits of joy and love,
Uninterrupted joy, unrivaled love
In blissful solitude; he then surveyed
Hell and the gulf between, and Satan there
Coasting the wall of heaven on this side night
In the dun air sublime, and ready now
To stoop with wearied wings, and willing feet
On the bare outside of this world, that seemed
Firm land imbosomed without firmament,
Uncertain which, in ocean or in air.
Him God beholding from his prospect high,

Wherein past, present, future he beholds,
Thus to his only son foreseeing spake.
   'Only begotten son, seest thou what rage
Transports our adversary, whom no bounds
Prescribed, no bars of hell, nor all the chains
Heaped on him there, nor yet the main abyss
Wide interrupt can hold; so bent he seems
On desperate revenge, that shall redound
Upon his own rebellious head. And now
Through all restraint broke loose he wings his way
Not far off heaven, in the precincts of light,
Directly towards the new created world,
And man there placed, with purpose to assay
If him by force he can destroy, or worse,
By some false guile pervert; and shall pervert;
For man will hearken to his glozing lies,
And easily transgress the sole command,
Sole pledge of his obedience: so will fall
He and his faithless progeny: whose fault?
Whose but his own? ingrate, he had of me
All he could have; I made him just and right,
Sufficient to have stood, though free to fall.
Such I created all the ethereal powers
And spirits, both them who stood and them who failed;
Freely they stood who stood, and fell who fell.
Not free, what proof could they have given sincere
Of true allegiance, constant faith or love,
Where only what they needs must do, appeared,
Not what they would? what praise could they receive?
What pleasure I from such obedience paid,
When will and reason (reason also is choice)
Useless and vain, of freedom both despoiled,
Made passive both, had served necessity,
Not me. They therefore as to right belonged,
So were created, nor can justly accuse
Their maker, or their making, or their fate;
As if predestination overruled

Their will, disposed by absolute decree
Or high foreknowledge; they themselves decree
Their own revolt, not I: if I foreknew,
Foreknowledge had no influence on their fault,
Which had no less proved certain unforeknown,
So without least impulse or shadow of fate,
Or aught by me immutably forseen,
They trespass, authors to themselves in all
Both what they judge and what they choose; for so
I formed them free, and free they must remain,
Till they enthrall themselves: I else must change
Their nature, and revoke the high decree
Unchangeable, eternal, which ordained
Their freedom, they themselves ordained their fall.
The first sort by their own suggestion fell,
Self-tempted, self-depraved: Man falls deceived
By the other first: Man therefore shall find grace,
The other none: in mercy and justice both,
Through heaven and earth, so shall my glory excel,
But mercy first and last shall brightest shine.'
    Thus while God spake, ambrosial fragrance filled
All heaven, and in the blessed spirits elect
Sense of new joy ineffable diffused:
Beyond compare the Son of God was seen
Most glorious, in him all his father shone
Substantially expressed, and in his face
Divine compassion visibly appeared,
Love without end, and without measure grace,
Which uttering thus he to his father spake.
    'O father, gracious was that word which closed
Thy sovereign sentence, that man should find grace
For which both heaven and earth shall high extol
Thy praises, with the innumerable sound
Of hymns and sacred songs, wherewith thy throne
Encompassed shall resound thee ever blest.
For should man finally be lost, should man
Thy creature late so loved, thy youngest son

Fall circumvented thus by fraud, though joined
With his own folly? that be from thee far,
That far be from thee, father, who art judge
Of all things made, and judgest only right.
Or shall the adversary thus obtain
His end, and frustrate thine, shall he fulfill
His malice, and thy goodness bring to naught,
Or proud return though to his heavier doom,
Yet with revenge accomplished and to hell
Draw after him the whole race of mankind,
By him corrupted? or wilt thou thyself
Abolish thy creation, and unmake,
For him, what for thy glory thou hast made?
So should thy goodness and thy greatness both
Be questioned and blasphemed without defense.'
    To whom the great creator thus replied.
'O Son, in whom my soul hath chief delight,
Son of my bosom, Son who art alone
My word, my wisdom, and effectual might,
All hast thou spoken as my thoughts are, all
As my eternal purpose hath decreed:
Man shall not quite be lost, but saved who will,
Yet not of will in him, but grace in me
Freely vouchsafed; once more I will renew
His lapsed powers, though forfeit and enthralled
By sin to foul exorbitant desires;
Upheld by me, yet once more he shall stand
On even ground against his mortal foe,
By me upheld, that he may know how frail
His fallen condition is, and to me owe
All his deliverance, and to none but me.
Some I have chosen of peculiar grace
Elect above the rest; so is my will:
The rest shall hear me call, and oft be warned
Their sinful state, and to appease betimes
The incensed Deity while offered grace
Invites: for I will clear their senses dark,

What may suffice, and soften stony hearts
To pray, repent, and bring obedience due.
To prayer, repentance, and obedience due,
Though but endeavored with sincere intent,
Mine ear shall not be slow, mine eye not shut.
And I will place within them as a guide
My umpire conscience, whom if they will hear,
Light after light well used they shall attain,
And to the end persisting, safe arrive.
This my long sufferance and my day of grace
They who neglect and scorn, shall never taste;
But hard be hardened, blind be blinded more,
That they may stumble on, and deeper fall;
And none but such from mercy I exclude.
But yet all is not done; man disobeying,
Disloyal breaks his fealty, and sins
Against the high supremacy of heaven,
Affecting godhead, and so losing all,
To expiate his treason hath naught left,
But to destruction sacred and devote,
He with his whole posterity must die,
Die he or justice must; unless for him
Some other able, and as willing, pay
The rigid satisfaction, death for death.
Say heavenly powers, where shall we find such love,
Which of ye will be mortal to redeem
Man's mortal crime, and just the unjust to save,
Dwells in all heaven charity so dear?'
　　He asked, but all the heavenly choir stood mute,
And silence was in heaven: on man's behalf
Patron or intercessor none appeared,
Much less that durst upon his own head draw
The deadly forfeiture, and ransom set.
And now without redemption all mankind
Must have been lost, adjudged to death and hell
By doom severe, had not the Son of God,

In whom the fulness dwells of love divine,
His dearest mediation thus renewed.
   'Father, thy word is passed, man shall find grace;
And shall grace not find means, that finds her way,
The speediest of thy winged messengers,
To visit all thy creatures, and to all
Comes unprevented, unimplored, unsought,
Happy for man, so coming; he her aid
Can never seek, once dead in sins and lost;
Atonement for himself or offering meet,
Indebted and undone, hath none to bring:
Behold me then, me for him, life for life
I offer, on me let thine anger fall;
Account me man; I for his sake will leave
Thy bosom, and this glory next to thee
Freely put off, and for him lastly die
Well pleased, on me let death wreak all his rage;
Under his gloomy power I shall not long
Lie vanquished; thou hast given me to possess
Life in myself forever, by thee I live,
Though now to death I yield, and am his due
All that of me can die, yet that debt paid,
Thou wilt not leave me in the loathsome grave
His prey, nor suffer my unspotted soul
Forever with corruption there to dwell;
But I shall rise victorious, and subdue
My vanquisher, spoiled of his vaunted spoil;
Death his death's wound shall then receive, and stoop
Inglorious, of his mortal sting disarmed.
I through the ample air in triumph high
Shall lead hell captive mauger hell, and show
The powers of darkness bound. Thou at the sight
Pleased, out of heaven shalt look down and smile,
While by thee raised I ruin all my foes,
Death last, and with his carcass glut the grave:
Then with the multitude of my redeemed
Shall enter heaven long absent, and return,

Father, to see thy face, wherein no cloud
Of anger shall remain, but peace assured,
And reconcilement; wrath shall be no more
Thenceforth, but in thy presence joy entire.'

His words here ended, but his meek aspect
Silent yet spake, and breathed immortal love
To mortal men, above which only shone
Filial obedience: as a sacrifice
Glad to be offered, he attends the will
Of his great father. Admiration seized
All heaven, what this might mean, and whither tend
Wondering; but soon the almighty thus replied:

'O thou in heaven and earth the only peace
Found out for mankind under wrath, O thou
My sole complacence! well thou knowest how dear,
To me are all my works, nor man the least
Though last created, that for him I spare
Thee from my bosom and right hand, to save,
By losing thee a while, the whole race lost.
Thou therefore whom thou only canst redeem,
Their nature also to thy nature join;
And be thyself man among men on earth,
Made flesh, when time shall be, of virgin seed,
By wondrous birth: Be thou in Adam's room
The head of all mankind, though Adam's son.
As in him perish all men, so in thee
As from a second root shall be restored,
As many as are restored, without thee none.
His crime makes guilty all his sons, thy merit
Imputed shall absolve them who renounce
Their own both righteous and unrighteous deeds
And live in thee transplanted, and from thee
Receive new life. So man, as is most just,
Shall satisfy for man, be judged and die,
And dying rise, and rising with him raise
His brethren, ransomed with his own dear life.
So heavenly love shall outdo hellish hate,

Giving to death, and dying to redeem,
So dearly to redeem what hellish hate
So easily destroyed, and still destroys
In those who, when they may, accept not grace.
Nor shalt thou by descending to assume
Man's nature, lessen or degrade thine own.
Because thou hast, though throned in highest bliss
Equal to God, and equally enjoying
God-like fruition, quitted all to save
A world from utter loss, and hast been found
By merit more than birthright Son of God,
Found worthiest to be so by being good,
Far more than great or high; because in thee
Love hath abounded more than glory abounds,
Therefore thy humiliation shall exalt
With thee thy manhood also to this throne;
Here shalt thou sit incarnate, here shalt reign
Both God and man, son both of God and man,
Anointed universal king; all power
I give thee, reign forever, and assume
Thy merits; under thee as head supreme
Thrones, princedoms, powers, dominions I reduce:
All knees to thee shall bow, of them that bide
In heaven, or earth, or under earth in hell;
When thou attended gloriously from heaven
Shalt in the sky appear, and from thee send
The summoning archangels to proclaim
Thy dread tribunal: forthwith from all winds
The living, and forthwith the cited dead
Of all past ages to the general doom
Shall hasten, such a peal shall rouse their sleep.
Then all thy saints assembled, thou shalt judge
Bad men and angels, they arraigned shall sink
Beneath thy sentence; hell, her numbers full,
Thenceforth shall be forever shut. Meanwhile
The world shall burn, and from her ashes spring
New heaven and earth, wherein the just shall dwell

And after all their tribulations long
See golden days, fruitful of golden deeds,
With joy and love triumphing, and fair truth.
Then thou thy regal scepter shalt lay by,
For regal scepter then no more shall need,
God shall be all in all. But all ye gods,
Adore him, who to compass all this dies,
Adore the Son, and honor him as me.'
   No sooner had the almighty ceased, but all
The multitude of angels with a shout
Loud as from numbers without number, sweet
As from blest voices, uttering joy, heaven rung
With jubilee, and loud hosannas filled
The eternal regions: lowly reverent
Towards either throne they bow, and to the ground
With solemn adoration down they cast
Their crowns inwove with amarant and gold,
Immortal amarant, a flower which once
In Paradise, fast by the tree of life
Began to bloom, but soon for man's offense
To heaven removed where first it grew, there grows,
And flowers aloft shading the fount of life,
And where the river of bliss through midst of heaven
Rolls o'er Elysian flowers her amber stream;
With these that never fade the spirits elect
Bind their resplendent locks inwreathed with beams,
Now in loose garlands thick thrown off, the bright
Pavement that like a sea of jasper shone
Impurpled with celestial roses smiled.
Then crowned again their golden harps they took,
Harps ever tuned, that glittering by their side
Like quivers hung, and with preamble sweet
Of charming symphony they introduce
Their sacred song, and waken raptures high;
No voice exempt, no voice but well could join
Melodious part, such concord is in heaven.
   Thee father first they sung omnipotent,

immutable, immortal, infinite,
Eternal king; thee author of all being,
Fountain of light, thyself invisible
Amidst the glorious brightness where thou sittest
Throned inaccessible, but when thou shadest
The full blaze of thy beams, and through a cloud
Drawn round about thee like a radiant shrine,
Dark with excessive bright thy skirts appear,
Yet dazzle heaven, that brightest seraphim
Approach not, but with both wings veil their eyes.
Thee next they sang of all creation first,
Begotten Son, divine similitude,
In whose conspicuous countenance, without cloud
Made visible, the almighty father shines,
Whom else no creature can behold; on thee
Impressed the effulgence of his glory abides,
Transfused on thee his ample spirit rests.
He heaven of heavens and all the powers therein
By thee created, and by thee threw down
The aspiring dominations: thou that day
Thy father's dreadful thunder didst not spare,
Nor stop thy flaming chariot wheels, that shook
Heaven's everlasting frame, while o'er the necks
Thou drovest of warring angels disarrayed.
Back from pursuit thy powers with loud acclaim
Thee only extolled, son of thy father's might,
To execute fierce vengeance on his foes,
Not so on man; him through their malice fallen,
Father of mercy and grace, thou didst not doom
So strictly, but much more to pity incline:
No sooner did thy dear and only son
Perceive thee purposed not to doom frail man
So strictly, but much more to pity inclined,
He to appease thy wrath, and end the strife
Of mercy and justice in thy face discerned,
Regardless of the bliss wherein he sat
Second to thee, offered himself to die

For man's offense. O unexampled love,
Love nowhere to be found less than divine!
Hail Son of God, Saviour of men, thy name
Shall be the copious matter of my song
Henceforth, and never shall my harp thy praise
Forget, nor from thy father's praise disjoin.

Thus they in heaven, above the starry sphere,
Their happy hours in joy and hymning spent.
Meanwhile upon the firm opacous globe
Of this round world, whose first convex divides
The luminous inferior orbs, enclosed
From chaos and the inroad of darkness old,
Satan alighted walks: a globe far off
It seemed, now seems a boundless continent
Dark, waste, and wild, under the frown of night
Starless exposed, and ever-threatening storms
Of chaos blustering round, inclement sky;
Save on that side which from the wall of heaven
Though distant far some small reflection gains
Of glimmering air less vexed with tempest loud:
Here walked the fiend at large in spacious field.
As when a vulture on Imaus bred,
Whose snowy ridge the roving Tartar bounds,
Dislodging from a region scarce of prey
To gorge the flesh of lambs or yeanling kids
On hills where flocks are fed, flies toward the springs
Of Ganges or Hydaspes, Indian streams;
But in his way lights on the barren plains
Of Sericana, where Chineses drive
With sails and wind their cany wagons light:
So on this windy sea of land, the fiend
Walked up and down alone bent on his prey,
Alone, for other creature in this place
Living or lifeless to be found was none,
None yet, but store hereafter from the earth
Up hither like aerial vapors flew
Of all things transitory and vain, when sin

With vanity had filled the works of men:
Both all things vain, and all who in vain things
Built their fond hopes of glory or lasting fame,
Or happiness in this or the other life;
All who have their reward on earth, the fruits
Of painful superstition and blind zeal,
Naught seeking but the praise of men, here find
Fit retribution, empty as their deeds;
All the unaccomplished works of nature's hand,
Abortive, monstrous, or unkindly mixed,
Dissolved on earth, fleet hither, and in vain,
Till final dissolution, wander here,
Not in the neighboring moon, as some have dreamed;
Those argent fields more likely habitants,
Translated saints, or middle spirits hold
Betwixt the angelical and human kind:
Hither of ill-joined sons and daughters born
First from the ancient world those giants came
With many a vain exploit, though then renowned:
The builders next to Babel on the plain
Of Sennaar, and still with vain design
New Babels, had they wherewithal, would build:
Others came single; he who to be deemed
A god, leaped fondly into Etna flames,
Empedocles, and he who to enjoy
Plato's Elysium, leaped into the sea,
Cleombrotus, and many more too long,
Embryos and idiots, eremites and friars
White, black and gray, with all their trumpery.
Here pilgrims roam, that strayed so far to seek
In Golgotha him dead, who lives in heaven;
And they who to be sure of paradise
Dying put on the weeds of Dominic,
Or in Franciscan think to pass disguised;
They pass the planets seven, and pass the fixed,
And that crystalline sphere whose balance weighs
The trepidation talked, and that first moved;

And now Saint Peter at heaven's wicket seems
To wait them with his keys, and now at foot
Of heaven's ascent they lift their feet, when lo
A violent cross wind from either coast
Blows them transverse ten thousand leagues awry
Into the devious air; then might ye see
Cowls, hoods and habits with their wearers tossed
And fluttered into rags, then relics, beads,
Indulgences, dispenses, pardons, bulls,
The sport of winds: all these upwhirled aloft
Fly o'er the backside of the world far off
Into a limbo large and broad, since called
The paradise of fools, to few unknown
Long after, now unpeopled, and untrod;
All this dark globe the fiend found as he passed,
And long he wandered, till at last a gleam
Of dawning light turned thitherward in haste
His traveled steps; far distant he descries
Ascending by degrees magnificent
Up to the wall of heaven a structure high,
At top whereof, but far more rich appeared
The work as of a kingly palace gate
With frontispiece of diamond and gold
Embellished, thick with sparkling orient gems
The portal shone, inimitable on earth
By model, or by shading pencil drawn.
The stairs were such as whereon Jacob saw
Angels ascending and descending, bands
Of guardians bright, when he from Esau fled
To Padan-Aram in the field of Luz,
Dreaming by night under the open sky,
And waking cried, 'This is the gate of Heaven.'
Each stair mysteriously was meant, nor stood
There always, but drawn up to heaven sometimes
Viewless, and underneath a bright sea flowed
Of jasper, or of liquid pearl, whereon
Who after came from earth, sailing arrived,

Wafted by angels, or flew o'er the lake
Rapt in a chariot drawn by fiery steeds.
The stairs were then let down, whether to dare
The fiend by easy ascent, or aggravate
His sad exclusion from the doors of bliss.
Direct against which opened from beneath,
Just o'er the blissful seat of Paradise,
A passage down to the earth, a passage wide,
Wider by far than that of aftertimes
Over Mount Sion, and, though that were large,
Over the promised land to God so dear,
By which, to visit oft those happy tribes,
On high behests his angels to and fro
Passed frequent, and his eye with choice regard
From Paneas the fount of Jordan's flood
To Beersaba, where the Holy Land
Borders on Egypt and the Arabian shore;
So wide the opening seemed, where bounds were set
To darkness, such as bound the ocean wave.
Satan from hence now on the lower stair
That scaled by steps of gold to heaven gate
Looks down with wonder at the sudden view
Of all this world at once. As when a scout
Through dark and desert ways with peril gone
All night; at last by break of cheerful dawn
Obtains the brow of some high-climbing hill,
Which to his eye discovers unaware
The goodly prospect of some foreign land
First seen, or some renowned metropolis
With glistering spires and pinnacles adorned,
Which now the rising sun gilds with his beams.
Such wonder seized, though after heaven seen,
The spirit malign, but much more envy seized
At sight of all this world beheld so fair.
Round he surveys, and well might, where he stood
So high above the circling canopy
Of night's extended shade; from eastern point

Of Libra to the fleecy star that bears
Andromeda far off Atlantic seas
Beyond the horizon; then from pole to pole
He views in breadth, and without longer pause
Down right into the world's first region throws
His flight precipitant, and winds with ease
Through the pure marble air his oblique way
Amongst innumerable stars, that shone
Stars distant, but nigh hand seemed other worlds,
Or other worlds they seemed, or happy isles,
Like those Hesperian gardens famed of old,
Fortunate fields, and groves and flowery vales,
Thrice happy isles, but who dwelt happy there
He stayed not to inquire: above them all
The golden sun in splendor likest heaven
Allured his eye: Thither his course he bends
Through the calm firmament; but up or down
By center, or eccentric, hard to tell,
Or longitude, where the great luminary
Aloof the vulgar constellations thick,
That from his lordly eye keep distance due,
Dispenses light from far; they as they move
Their starry dance in numbers that compute
Days, months, and years, towards his all-cheering lamp
Turn swift their various motions, or are turned
By his magnetic beam, that gently warms
The universe, and to each inward part
With gentle penetration, though unseen,
Shoots invisible virtue even to the deep:
So wondrously was set his station bright.
There lands the fiend, a spot like which perhaps
Astronomer in the sun's lucent orb
Through his glazed optic tube yet never saw.
The place he found beyond expression bright,
Compared with aught on earth, metal or stone;
Not all parts like, but all alike informed
With radiant light, as glowing iron with fire:

If metal, part seemed gold, part silver clear;
If stone, carbuncle most or chrysolite,
Ruby or topaz, to the twelve that shone
In Aaron's breastplate, and a stone besides
Imagined rather oft than elsewhere seen,
That stone, or like to that which here below
Philosophers in vain so long have sought,
In vain, though by their powerful art they bind
Volatile Hermes, and call up unbound
In various shapes old Proteus from the sea,
Drained through a limbec to his native form.
What wonder then if fields and regions here
Breathe forth elixir pure, and rivers run
Potable gold, when with one virtuous touch
The arch-chemic sun so far from us remote
Produces with terrestrial humor mixed
Here in the dark so many precious things
Of color glorious and effect so rare?
Here matter new to gaze the devil met
Undazzled, far and wide his eye commands,
For sight no obstacle found here, nor shade,
But all sunshine, as when his beams at noon
Culminate from the equator, as they now
Shot upward still direct, whence no way round
Shadow from body opaque can fall, and the air
Nowhere so clear, sharpened his visual ray
To objects distant far, whereby he soon
Saw within ken a glorious angel stand,
The same whom John saw also in the sun:
His back was turned, but not his brightness hid;
Of beaming sunny rays, a golden tiar
Circled his head, nor less his locks behind
Illustrious on his shoulders fledge with wings
Lay waving round; on some great charge employed
He seemed, or fixed in cogitation deep.
Glad was the spirit impure; as now in hope
To find who might direct his wandering flight

To Paradise the happy seat of man,
His journey's end and our beginning woe.
But first he casts to change his proper shape,
Which else might work him danger or delay:
And now a stripling cherub he appears,
Not of the prime, yet such as in his face
Youth smiled celestial, and to every limb
Suitable grace diffused, so well he feigned;
Under a coronet his flowing hair
In curls on either cheek played, wings he wore
Of many a colored plume sprinkled with gold,
His habit fit for speed succinct, and held
Before his decent steps a silver wand.
He drew not nigh unheard, the Angel bright,
Ere he drew nigh, his radiant visage turned,
Admonished by his ear, and straight was known
The archangel Uriel, one of the seven
Who in God's presence, nearest to his throne
Stand ready at command, and are his eyes
That run through all the heavens, or down to the ear
Bear his swift errands over moist and dry,
O'er sea and land; him Satan thus accosts.

  'Uriel, for thou of those seven spirits that stand
In sight of God's high throne, gloriously bright,
The first art wont his great authentic will
Interpreter through highest heaven to bring,
Where all his sons thy embassy attend;
And here art likeliest by supreme decree
Like honour to obtain, and as his eye
To visit oft this new creation round;
Unspeakable desire to see, and know
All these his wondrous works, but chiefly man,
His chief delight and favor, him for whom
All these his works so wondrous he ordained,
Hath brought me from the choirs of cherubim
Alone thus wandering. Brightest seraph tell
In which of all these shining orbs hath man

His fixed seat, or fixed seat hath none,
But all these shining orbs his choice to dwell;
That I may find him, and with secret gaze,
Or open admiration him behold
On whom the great creator hath bestowed
Worlds, and on whom hath all these graces **poured**;
That both in him and all things, as is meet,
The universal maker we may praise;
Who justly hath driven out his rebel foes
To deepest hell, and to repair that loss
Created this new happy race of men
To serve him better: wise are all his ways.'
    So spake the false dissembler unperceived;
For neither man nor angel can discern
Hypocrisy, the only evil that walks
Invisible, except to God alone,
By his permissive will, through heaven and **earth**:
And oft though wisdom wake, suspicion sleeps
At wisdom's gate, and to simplicity
Resigns her charge, while goodness thinks no ill
Where no ill seems: Which now for once **beguiled**
Uriel, though regent of the sun, and held
The sharpest sighted spirit of all in heaven;
Who to the fraudulent impostor foul
In his uprightness answer thus returned.
'Fair angel, thy desire which tends to know
The works of God, thereby to glorify
The great work-master, leads to no excess
That reaches blame, but rather merits praise
The more it seems excess, that led thee hither
From thy empyreal mansion thus alone,
To witness with thine eyes what some perhaps
Contented with report hear only in heaven:
For wonderful indeed are all his works,
Pleasant to know, and worthiest to be all
Had in remembrance always with delight;
But what created mind can comprehend

Their number, or the wisdom infinite
That brought them forth, but hid their causes deep.
I saw when at his word the formless mass,
This world's material mold, came to a heap:
Confusion heard his voice, and wild uproar
Stood ruled, stood vast infinitude confined;
Till at his second bidding darkness fled,
Light shone, and order from disorder sprung:
Swift to their several quarters hasted then
The cumbrous elements, earth, flood, air, fire,
And this ethereal quintessence of heaven
Flew upward, spirited with various forms,
That rolled orbicular, and turned to stars
Numberless, as thou seest, and how they move;
Each had his place appointed, each his course,
The rest in circuit walls this universe.
Look downward on that globe whose hither side
With light from hence, though but reflected, shines;
That place is earth the seat of man, that light
His day, which else as the other hemisphere
Night would invade, but there the neighboring moon
(So call that opposite fair star) her aid
Timely interposes, and her monthly round
Still ending, still renewing, through mid-heaven,
With borrowed light her countenance triform
Hence fills and empties to enlighten the earth,
And in her pale dominion checks the night.
That spot to which I point is Paradise,
Adam's abode, those lofty shades his bower.
Thy way thou canst not miss, me mine requires."

Thus said, he turned, and Satan bowing low,
As to superior spirits is wont in heaven,
Where honor due and reverence none neglects,
Took leave, and toward the coast of earth beneath,
Down from the ecliptic, sped with hoped success,
Throws his steep flight in many an airy wheel,
Nor staid, till on Niphates' top he lights.

BOOK IV

The Argument: Satan now in prospect of Eden, and nigh the place where he must now attempt the bold enterprise which he undertook alone against God and man, falls into many doubts with himself, and many passions, fear, envy, and despair; but at length confirms himself in evil, journeys on to Paradise, whose outward prospect and situation is described, overleaps the bounds, sits in the shape of a cormorant on the tree of life, as highest in the garden to look about him. The garden described; Satan's first sight of Adam and Eve; his wonder at their excellent form and happy state, but with resolution to work their fall; overhears their discourse, thence gathers that the tree of knowledge was forbidden them to eat of, under penalty of death; and thereon intends to found his temptation, by seducing them to transgress: then leaves them a while, to know further of their state by some other means. Meanwhile Uriel descending on a sunbeam warns Gabriel, who had in charge the gate of Paradise, that some evil spirit had escaped the deep, and passed at noon by his sphere in the shape of a good angel down to Paradise, discovered after by his furious gestures in the mount. Gabriel promises to find him out ere morning. Night coming on, Adam and Eve, discourse of going to their rest: their bower described; their evening worship. Gabriel drawing forth his bands of night-watch to walk the round of Paradise, appoints two strong angels to Adam's bower, lest the evil spirit should be there doing some harm to Adam or Eve sleeping; there they find him at the ear of Eve, tempting her in a dream, and bring him, though unwilling, to Gabriel; by whom questioned, he scornfully answers, prepares resistance, but hindered by a sign from heaven, flies out of Paradise.

> O for that warning voice, which he who saw
> The Apocalypse, heard cry in heaven aloud,
> Then when the dragon, put to second rout,
> Came furious down to be revenged on men,

'Woe to the inhabitants on earth!' that now,
While time was, our first parents had been warned
The coming of their secret foe, and scaped
Haply so scaped his mortal snare; for now
Satan, now first inflamed with rage came down,
The tempter ere the accuser of mankind,
To wreck on innocent frail man his loss
Of that first battle, and his flight to hell:
Yet not rejoicing in his speed, though bold,
Far off and fearless, nor with cause to boast,
Begins his dire attempt, which nigh the birth
Now rolling, boils in his tumultuous breast,
And like a devilish engine back recoils
Upon himself; horror and doubt distract
His troubled thoughts, and from the bottom stir
The hell within him, for within him hell
He brings, and round about him, nor from hell
One step no more than from himself can fly
By change of place: Now conscience wakes despair
That slumbered, wakes the bitter memory
Of what he was, what is, and what must be
Worse; of worse deeds worse sufferings must ensue.
Sometimes towards Eden which now in his view
Lay pleasant, his grieved look he fixes sad,
Sometimes towards heaven and the full-blazing sun,
Which now sat high in his meridian tower:
Then much revolving, thus in sighs began.
   'O thou that with surpassing glory crowned,
Lookest from thy sole dominion like the god
Of this new world; at whose sight all the stars
Hide their diminished heads; to thee I call,
But with no friendly voice, and add thy name
O sun, to tell thee how I hate thy beams
That bring to my remembrance from what state
I fell, how glorious once above thy sphere;
Till pride and worse ambition threw me down
Warring in heaven against heaven's matchless king:

Ah wherefore! he deserved no such return
From me, whom he created what I was
In that bright eminence, and with his good
Upbraided none; nor was his service hard.
What could be less than to afford him praise,
The easiest recompense, and pay him thanks,
How due! yet all his good proved ill in me,
And wrought but malice; lifted up so high
I 'sdained subjection, and thought one step higher
Would set me highest, and in a moment quit
The debt immense of endless gratitude,
So burdensome still paying, still to owe;
Forgetful what from him I still received,
And understood not that a grateful mind
By owing owes not, but still pays, at once
Indebted and discharged; what burden then?
O had his powerful destiny ordained
Me some inferior angel, I had stood
Then happy; no unbounded hope had raised
Ambition. Yet why not? some other power
As great might have aspired, and me though mean
Drawn to his part; but other powers as great
Fell not, but stand unshaken, from within
Or from without, to all temptations armed.
Hadst thou the same free will and power to stand?
Thou hadst: whom hast thou then or what to accuse,
But heaven's free love dealt equally to all?
Be then his love accursed, since love or hate,
To me alike, it deals eternal woe.
Nay cursed be thou; since against his thy will
Chose freely what it now so justly rues.
Me miserable; which way shall I fly
Infinite wrath, and infinite despair?
Which way I fly is hell; myself am hell;
And in the lowest deep a lower deep
Still threatening to devour me opens wide,
To which the hell I suffer seems a heaven.

O then at last relent: is there no place
Left for repentance, none for pardon left?
None left but by submission; and that word
Disdain forbids me, and my dread of shame
Among the spirits beneath, whom I seduced
With other promises and other vaunts
Than to submit, boasting I could subdue
The omnipotent. Ay me, they little know
How dearly I abide that boast so vain,
Under what torments inwardly I groan:
While they adore me on the throne of hell,
With diadem and scepter high advanced
The lower still I fall, only supreme
In misery; such joy ambition finds.
But say I could repent and could obtain
By act of grace my former state; how soon
Would height recall high thoughts, how soon unsay
What feigned submission swore: ease would recant
Vows made in pain, as violent and void.
For never can true reconcilement grow
Where wounds of deadly hate have pierced so deep:
Which would but lead me to a worse relapse,
And heavier fall: so should I purchase dear
Short intermission bought with double smart.
This knows my punisher; therefore as far
From granting he, as I from begging peace:
All hope excluded thus, behold instead
Of us outcast, exiled, his new delight,
Mankind created, and for him this world.
So farewell hope, and with hope farewell fear,
Farewell remorse: all good to me is lost;
Evil be thou my good; by thee at least
Divided empire with heaven's king I hold
By thee, and more than half perhaps will reign;
As man erelong, and this new world shall know.'

Thus while he spake, each passion dimmed his face
Thrice changed with pale, ire, envy and despair,

Which marred his borrowed visage, and betrayed
Him counterfeit, if any eye beheld.
For heavenly minds from such distempers foul
Are ever clear. Whereof he soon aware,
Each perturbation smoothed with outward calm,
Artificer of fraud; and was the first
That practiced falsehood under saintly show,
Deep malice to conceal, couched with revenge:
Yet not enough had practiced to deceive
Uriel once warned; whose eye pursued him down
The way he went, and on the Assyrian mount
Saw him disfigured, more than could befall
Spirit of happy sort: his gestures fierce
He marked and mad demeanor, then alone,
As he supposed, all unobserved, unseen.
So on he fares, and to the border comes
Of Eden, where delicious Paradise,
Now nearer, crowns with her enclosure green,
As with a rural mound the champaign head
Of a steep wilderness, whose hairy sides
With thicket overgrown, grotesque and wild,
Access denied; and overhead up grew
Insuperable height of loftiest shade,
Cedar, and pine, and fir, and branching palm,
A sylvan scene, and as the ranks ascend
Shade above shade, a woody theater
Of stateliest view. Yet higher than their tops
The verdurous wall of Paradise up sprung:
Which to our general sire gave prospect large
Into his nether empire neighboring round.
And higher than that wall a circling row
Of goodliest trees laden with fairest fruit,
Blossoms and fruits at once of golden hue
Appeared, with gay enameled colors mixed:
On which the sun more glad impressed his beams
Than in fair evening cloud, or humid bow,
When God hath showered the earth; so lovely seemed

That landscape: And of pure now purer air
Meets his approach, and to the heart inspires
Vernal delight and joy, able to drive
All sadness but despair: now gentle gales
Fanning their odoriferous wings dispense
Native perfumes, and whisper whence they stole
Those balmy spoils. As when to them who sail
Beyond the Cape of Hope, and now are past
Mozambic, off at sea north-east winds blow
Sabean odors from the spicy shore
Of Araby the blest, with such delay
Well pleased they slack their course, and many a league
Cheered with the grateful smell old ocean smiles.
So entertained those odorous sweets the fiend
Who came their bane, though with them better pleased
Than Asmodeus with the fishy fume,
That drove him, though enamored, from the spouse
Of Tobit's son, and with a vengeance sent
From Media post to Egypt, there fast bound.

Now to the ascent of that steep savage hill
Satan had journeyed on, pensive and slow;
But further way found none, so thick entwined,
As one continued brake, the undergrowth
Of shrubs and tangling bushes had perplexed
All path of man or beast that passed that way:
One gate there only was, and that looked east
On the other side: which when the arch felon saw
Due entrance he disdained, and in contempt,
At one slight bound high overleaped all bound
Of hill or highest wall, and sheer within
Lights on his feet. As when a prowling wolf,
Whom hunger drives to seek new haunt for prey,
Watching where shepherds pen their flocks at eve
In hurdled cotes amid the field secure,
Leaps o'er the fence with ease into the fold:
Or as a thief bent to unhoard the cash
Of some rich burgher, whose substantial doors

Cross-barred and bolted fast, fears no assault,
In at the window climbs, or o'er the tiles:
So clomb this first grand thief into God's fold:
So since into his church lewd hirelings climb.
Thence up he flew, and on the tree of life
The middle tree and highest there that grew,
Sat like a cormorant; yet not true life
Thereby regained, but sat devising death
To them who lived; nor on the virtue thought
Of that life-giving plant, but only used
For prospect, what well used had been the pledge
Of immortality. So little knows
Any, but God alone, to value right
The good before him, but perverts best things
To worst abuse, or to their meanest use.
Beneath him with new wonder now he views
To all delight of human sense exposed
In narrow room nature's whole wealth, yea more,
A heaven on earth: for blissful Paradise
Of God the garden was, by him in the east
Of Eden planted; Eden stretched her line
From Auran eastward to the royal towers
Of great Seleucia, built by Grecian kings,
Or where the sons of Eden long before
Dwelt in Telassar: in this pleasant soil
His far more pleasant garden God ordained;
Out of the fertile ground he caused to grow
All trees of noblest kind for sight, smell, taste;
And all amid them stood the tree of life,
High eminent, blooming ambrosial fruit
Of vegetable gold; and next to life
Our death the tree of knowledge grew fast by,
Knowledge of good bought dear by knowing ill.
Southward through Eden went a river large,
Nor changed his course, but through the shaggy hil
Passed underneath ingulfed, for God had thrown
That mountain as his garden mold high raised

Upon the rapid current, which through veins
Of porous earth with kindly thirst updrawn,
Rose a fresh fountain, and with many a rill
Watered the garden; thence united fell
Down the steep glade, and met the nether flood,
Which from his darksome passage now appears,
And now divided into four main streams,
Runs diverse, wandering many a famous realm
And country whereof here needs no account,
But rather to tell how, if art could tell,
How from that sapphire fount the crisped brooks,
Rolling on orient pearl and sands of gold,
With mazy error under pendent shades
Ran nectar, visiting each plant, and fed
Flowers worthy of Paradise which not nice art
In beds and curious knots, but nature boon
Poured forth profuse on hill and dale and plain,
Both where the morning sun first warmly smote
The open field, and where the unpierced shade
Imbrowned the noontide bowers: Thus was this place,
A happy rural seat of various view:
Groves whose rich trees wept odorous gums and balm,
Others whose fruit burnished with golden rind
Hung amiable, Hesperian fables true,
If true, here only, and of delicious taste:
Betwixt them lawns, or level downs, and flocks
Grazing the tender herb, were interposed,
Or palmy hillock, or the flowery lap
Of some irriguous valley spread her store,
Flowers of all hue, and without thorn the rose:
Another side, umbrageous grots and caves
Of cool recess, o'er which the mantling vine
Lays forth her purple grape, and gently creeps
Luxuriant; meanwhile murmuring waters fall
Down the slope hills, dispersed, or in a lake,
That to the fringed bank with myrtle crowned.
Her crystal mirror holds, unite their streams.

The birds their choir apply; airs, vernal airs,
Breathing the smell of field and grove, attune
The trembling leaves, while universal Pan
Knit with the graces and the hours in dance
Led on the eternal spring. Not that fair field
Of Enna, where Proserpin gathering flowers
Herself a fairer flower by gloomy Dis
Was gathered, which cost Ceres all that pain
To seek her through the world; nor that sweet grove
Of Daphne by Orontes, and the inspired
Castalian spring might with this Paradise
Of Eden strive; nor that Nyseian isle
Girt with the river Triton, where old Cham,
Whom Gentiles Ammon call and Libyan Jove,
Hid Amalthea and her florid son
Young Bacchus from his stepdame Rhea's eye;
Nor where Abassin kings their issue guard,
Mount Amara, though this by some supposed
True Paradise under the Ethiop line
By Nilus head, enclosed with shining rock,
A whole day's journey high, but wide remote
From this Assyrian garden, where the fiend
Saw undelighted all delight, all kind
Of living creatures new to sight and strange:
Two of far nobler shape erect and tall,
God-like erect, with native honor clad
In naked majesty seemed lords of all,
And worthy seemed, for in their looks divine
The image of their glorious maker shone,
Truth, wisdom, sanctitude severe and pure,
Severe but in true filial freedom placed;
Whence true authority in men; though both
Not equal, as their sex not equal seemed;
For contemplation he and valor formed,
For softness she and sweet attractive grace,
He for God only, she for God in him:
His fair large front and eye sublime declared

Absolute rule; and hyacinthine locks
Round from his parted forelock manly hung
Clustering, but not beneath his shoulders broad.
She as a veil down to the slender waist
Her unadorned golden tresses wore
Disheveled, but in wanton ringlets waved
As the vine curls her tendrils, which implied
Subjection, but required with gentle sway,
And by her yielded, by him best received,
Yielded with coy submission, modest pride,
And sweet reluctant amorous delay.
Nor those mysterious parts were then concealed,
Then was not guilty shame, dishonest shame
Of nature's works, honor dishonorable,
Sin-bred, how have ye troubled all mankind
With shows instead, mere shows of seeming pure,
And banished from man's life his happiest life,
Simplicity and spotless innocence.
So passed they naked on, nor shunned the sight
Of God or angel, for they thought no ill:
So hand in hand they passed, the loveliest pair
That ever since in love's embraces met,
Adam the goodliest man of men since born
His sons, the fairest of her daughters Eve.
Under a tuft of shade that on a green
Stood whispering soft, by a fresh fountain side
They sat them down, and after no more toil
Of their sweet gardening labor than sufficed
To recommend cool zephyr, and make ease
More easy, wholesome thirst and appetite
More grateful, to their supper fruits they fell,
Nectarine fruits which the compliant boughs
Yielded them, sidelong as they sat recline
On the soft downy bank damasked with flowers:
The savory pulp they chew, and in the rind
Still as they thirsted scoop the brimming stream:
Nor gentle purpose, nor endearing smiles

Wanted, nor youthful dalliance as beseems
Fair couple, linked in happy nuptial league,
Alone as they. About them frisking played
All beasts of the earth, since wild, and of all chase
In wood or wilderness, forest or den;
Sporting the lion ramped, and in his paw
Dandled the kid; bears, tigers, ounces, pards
Gamboled before them, the unwieldy elephant
To make them mirth used all his might, and wreathed
His lithe proboscis; close the serpent sly
Insinuating, wove with Gordian twine
His braided train, and of his fatal guile
Gave proof unheeded; others on the grass
Couched, and now filled with pasture gazing sat,
Or bedward ruminating; for the sun
Declined was hastening now with prone career
To the ocean isles, and in the ascending scale
Of heaven the stars that usher evening rose:
When Satan still in gaze, as first he stood,
Scarce thus at length failed speech recovered sad.

'O hell! what do mine eyes with grief behold,
Into our room of bliss thus high advanced
Creatures of other mold, earth-born perhaps,
Not spirits, yet to heavenly spirits bright
Little inferior; whom my thoughts pursue
With wonder, and could love, so lively shines
In them divine rememblance, and such grace
The hand that formed them on their shape hath poured.
Ah gentle pair, ye little think how nigh
Your change approaches, when all these delights
Will vanish and deliver ye to woe,
More woe, the more your taste is now of joy;
Happy, but for so happy ill secured
Long to continue, and this high seat your heaven
Ill fenced for heaven to keep out such a foe
As now is entered; yet no purposed foe
To you whom I could pity thus forlorn

Though I unpitied: League with you I seek,
And mutual amity so strait, so close,
That I with you must dwell, or you with me
Henceforth; my dwelling haply may not please
Like this fair Paradise, your sense, yet such
Accept your maker's work; he gave it me,
Which I as freely give; hell shall unfold,
To entertain you two, her widest gates,
And send forth all her kings; there will be room,
Not like these narrow limits, to receive
Your numerous offspring; if no better place,
Thank him who puts me loath to this revenge
On you who wrong me not for him who wronged.
And should I at your harmless innocence
Melt, as I do, yet public reason just,
Honor and empire with revenge enlarged,
By conquering this new world, compels me now
To do what else though damned I should abhor."

 So spake the fiend, and with necessity,
The tyrant's plea, excused his devilish deeds.
Then from his lofty stand on that high tree
Down he alights among the sportful herd
Of those four-footed kinds, himself now one,
Now other, as their shape served best his end
Nearer to view his prey, and unespied
To mark what of their state he might learn
By word or action marked: about them round
A lion now he stalks with fiery glare,
Then as a tiger, who by chance hath spied
In some purlieu two gentle fawns at play,
Straight couches close, then rising changes oft
His couchant watch, as one who chose his ground
Whence rushing he might surest seize them both
Gripped in each paw: When Adam first of men
To first of women Eve thus moving speech,
Turned him all ear to hear new utterance flow.

'Sole partner and sole part of all these joys,
Dearer thyself than all; needs must the power
That made us, and for us this ample world
Be infinitely good, and of his good
As liberal and free as infinite,
That raised us from the dust and placed us here
In all this happiness, who at his hand
Have nothing merited, nor can perform
Aught whereof he hath need, he who requires
From us no other service than to keep
This one, this easy charge, of all the trees
In Paradise that bear delicious fruit
So various, not to taste that only tree
Of knowledge, planted by the tree of life,
So near grows death to life, whate'er death is,
Some dreadful thing no doubt; for well thou knowest
God hath pronounced it death to taste that tree,
The only sign of our obedience left
Among so many signs of power and rule
Conferred upon us, and dominion given
Over all other creatures that possess
Earth, air, and sea. Then let us not think hard
One easy prohibition, who enjoy
Free leave so large to all things else, and choice
Unlimited of manifold delights:
But let us ever praise him, and extol
His bounty, following our delightful task
To prune these growing plants, and tend these flowers,
Which were it toilsome, yet with thee were sweet.'

    To whom thus Eve replied. 'O thou for whom
And from whom I was formed flesh of thy flesh,
And without whom am to no end, my guide
And head, what thou hast said is just and right.
For we to him indeed all praises owe,
And daily thanks, I chiefly who enjoy
So far the happier lot, enjoying thee
Pre-eminent by so much odds, while thou

Like consort to thyself canst nowhere find.
That day I oft remember, when from sleep
I first awaked, and found myself reposed
Under a shade of flowers, much wondering where
And what I was, whence thither brought, and how.
Not distant far from thence a murmuring sound
Of waters issued from a cave and spread
Into a liquid plain, then stood unmoved
Pure as the expanse of heaven; I thither went
With unexperienced thought, and laid me down
On the green bank, to look into the clear
Smooth lake, that to me seemed another sky.
As I bent down to look, just opposite,
A shape within the watery gleam appeared
Bending to look on me, I started back,
It started back, but pleased I soon returned,
Pleased it returned as soon with answering looks
Of sympathy and love; there I had fixed
Mine eyes till now, and pined with vain desire,
Had not a voice thus warned me, "What thou seest,
What there thou seest fair creature is thyself,
With thee it came and goes: but follow me,
And I will bring thee where no shadow stays
Thy coming, and thy soft embraces, he
Whose image thou art, him thou shalt enjoy
Inseparably thine, to him shalt bear
Multitudes like thyself, and thence be called
Mother of human race:" what could I do,
But follow straight, invisibly thus led?
Till I espied thee, fair indeed and tall,
Under a platane, yet methought less fair,
Less winning soft, less amiably mild,
Than that smooth watery image; back I turned,
Thou following criedst aloud, "Return fair Eve,
Whom fliest thou? whom thou fliest, of him thou art,
His flesh, his bone; to give thee being I lent
Out of my side to thee, nearest my heart

Substantial life, to have thee by my side
Henceforth an individual solace dear;
Part of my soul I seek thee, and thee claim
My other half:" with that thy gentle hand
Seized mine, I yielded, and from that time see
How beauty is excelled by manly grace
And wisdom, which alone is truly fair.'

So spake our general mother, and with eyes
Of conjugal attraction unreproved,
And meek surrender, half embracing leaned
On our first father, half her swelling breast
Naked met his under the flowing gold
Of her loose tresses hid: he in delight
Both of her beauty and submissive charms
Smiled with superior love, as Jupiter
On Juno smiles, when he impregns the clouds
That shed May flowers; and pressed her matron lip
With kisses pure: aside the devil turned
For envy, yet with jealous leer malign
Eyed them askance, and to himself thus plained.

'Sight hateful, sight tormenting! thus these two
Imparadised in one another's arms
The happier Eden, shall enjoy their fill
Of bliss on bliss, while I to hell am thrust,
Where neither joy nor love, but fierce desire,
Among our other torments not the least,
Still unfulfilled with pain of longing pines;
Yet let me not forget what I have gained
From their own mouths; all is not theirs it seems:
One fatal tree there stands of knowledge called,
Forbidden them to taste: Knowledge forbidden?
Suspicious, reasonless. Why should their Lord
Envy them that? can it be sin to know,
Can it be death? and do they only stand
By ignorance, is that their happy state,
The proof of their obedience and their faith?
O fair foundation laid whereon to build

Their ruin! Hence I will excite their minds
With more desire to know, and to reject
Envious commands, invented with design
To keep them low whom knowledge might exalt
Equal with gods; aspiring to be such,
They taste and die: what likelier can ensue?
But first with narrow search I must walk round
This garden, and no corner leave unspied,
A chance but chance may lead where I may meet
Some wandering spirit of heaven, by fountainside,
Or in thick shade retired, from him to draw
What further would be learned. Live while ye may,
Yet happy pair; enjoy, till I return,
Short pleasures, for long woes are to succeed.'
   So saying, his proud step he scornful turned,
But with sly circumspection, and began
Through wood, through waste, o'er hill, o'er dale, his roam.
Meanwhile in utmost longitude, where heaven
With earth and ocean meets, the setting sun
Slowly descended, and with right aspect
Against the eastern gate of Paradise
Leveled his evening rays: it was a rock
Of alabaster, piled up to the clouds,
Conspicuous far, winding with one ascent
Accessible from earth, one entrance high;
The rest was craggy cliff, that overhung
Still as it rose, impossible to climb.
Betwixt these rocky pillars Gabriel sat
Chief of the angelic guards, awaiting night;
About him exercised heroic games
The unarmed youth of heaven, but nigh at hand
Celestial armory, shields, helms, and spears,
Hung high with diamond flaming, and with gold.
Thither came Uriel, gliding through the even
On a sunbeam, swift as a shooting star
In autumn thwarts the night, when vapors fired
Impress the air, and shows the mariner

From what point of his compass to beware
Impetuous winds: he thus began in haste.
  'Gabriel, to thee thy course by lot hath given
Charge and strict watch that to this happy place
No evil thing approach or enter in;
This day at height of noon came to my sphere
A spirit, zealous, as he seemed, to know
More of the almighty's works, and chiefly man
God's latest image: I described his way
Bent all on speed, and marked his airy gait;
But in the mount that lies from Eden north,
Where he first lighted, soon discerned his looks
Alien from heaven, with passions foul obscured:
Mine eye pursued him still, but under shade
Lost sight of him; one of the banished crew
I fear, hath ventured from the deep, to raise
New troubles; him thy care must be to find.'
  To whom the winged warrior thus returned:
'Uriel, no wonder if thy perfect sight.
Amid the sun's bright circle where thou sittest,
See far and wide: in at this gate none pass
The vigilance here placed, but such as come
Well known from heaven; and since meridian hour
No creature thence: if spirit of other sort,
So minded, have o'erleaped these earthy bounds
On purpose, hard thou knowest it to exclude
Spiritual substance with corporeal bar.
But if within the circuit of these walks
In whatsoever shape he lurk, of whom
Thou tellest, by morrow dawning I shall know.'
  So promised he, and Uriel to his charge
Returned on that bright beam, whose point now raised
Bore him slope downward to the sun now fallen
Beneath the Azores; whither the prime orb,
Incredible how swift, had thither rolled
Diurnal, or this less volubile earth
By shorter flight to the east, had left him there

Arraying with reflected purple and gold
The clouds that on his western throne attend:
Now came still evening on, and twilight gray
Had in her sober livery all things clad;
Silence accompanied, for beast and bird,
They to their grassy couch, these to their nests
Were slunk, all but the wakeful nightingale;
She all night long her amorous descant sung;
Silence was pleased: now glowed the firmament
With living sapphires: Hesperus that led
The starry host, rode brightest, till the moon
Rising in clouded majesty, at length
Apparent queen unveiled her peerless light,
And o'er the dark her silver mantle threw.

When Adam thus to Eve: 'Fair consort, the hour
Of night, and all things now retired to rest
Mind us of like repose, since God hath set
Labor and rest, as day and night to men
Successive, and the timely dew of sleep
Now falling with soft slumberous weight inclines
Our eyelids; other creatures all day long
Rove idle unemployed, and less need rest;
Man hath his daily work of body or mind
Appointed, which declares his dignity,
And the regard of heaven on all his ways;
While other animals unactive range,
And of their doings God takes no account.
Tomorrow ere fresh morning streak the east
With first approach of light, we must be risen,
And at our pleasant labor, to reform
Yon flowery arbors, yonder alleys green,
Our walk at noon, with branches overgrown,
That mock our scant manuring, and require
More hands than ours to lop their wanton growth:
Those blossoms also, and those dropping gums
That lie bestrewn unsightly and unsmooth,

Ask riddance, if we mean to tread with ease;
Meanwhile, as nature wills, night bids us rest.'
 To whom thus Eve with perfect beauty adorned.
'My author and disposer, what thou biddest
Unargued I obey; so God ordains,
God is thy law, thou mine: to know no more
Is woman's happiest knowledge and her praise.
With thee conversing I forget all time,
All seasons and their change, all please alike.
Sweet is the breath of morn, her rising sweet,
With charm of earliest birds; pleasant the sun
When first on this delightful land he spreads
His orient beams, on herb, tree, fruit, and flower,
Glistering with dew; fragrant the fertile earth
After soft showers; and sweet the coming on
Of grateful evening mild, then silent night
With this her solemn bird and this fair moon,
And these the gems of heaven, her starry train:
But neither breath of morn when she ascends
With charm of earliest birds, nor rising sun
On this delightful land, nor herb, fruit, flower,
Glistering with dew, nor fragrance after showers,
Nor grateful evening mild, nor silent night
With this her solemn bird, nor walk by moon,
Or glittering starlight without thee is sweet.
But wherefore all night long shine these, for whom
This glorious sight, when sleep hath shut all eyes?'
 To whom our general ancestor replied.
'Daughter of God and man, accomplished Eve,
Those have their course to finish, round the earth,
By morrow evening, and from land to land
In order, though to nations yet unborn,
Ministering light prepared, they set and rise;
Lest total darkness should by night regain
Her old possession, and extinguish life
In nature and all things, which these soft fires
Not only enlighten, but with kindly heat

Of various influence foment and warm,
'Temper or nourish, or in part shed down
Their stellar virtue on all kinds that grow
On earth, made hereby apter to receive
Perfection from the sun's more potent ray.
These then, though unbeheld in deep of night,
Shine not in vain, nor think, though men were none,
That heaven would want spectators, God want praise:
Millions of spiritual creatures walk the earth
Unseen, both when we wake, and when we sleep:
All these with ceaseless praise his works behold
Both day and night: how often from the steep
Of echoing hill or thicket have we heard
Celestial voices to the midnight air,
Sole, or responsive each to other's note
Singing their great creator: oft in bands
While they keep watch, or nightly rounding walk
With heavenly touch of instrumental sounds
In full harmonic number joined, their songs
Divide the night, and lift our thoughts to heaven.'
    Thus talking hand in hand alone they passed
On to their blissful bower; it was a place
Chosen by the sovereign planter, when he framed
All things to man's delightful use; the roof
Of thickest covert was inwoven shade
Laurel and myrtle, and what higher grew
Of firm and fragrant leaf; on either side
Acanthus, and each odorous bushy shrub
Fenced up the verdant wall; each beauteous flower,
Iris all hues, roses, and jessamine
Reared high their flourished heads between, and wrought
Mosaic; underfoot the violet,
Crocus, and hyacinth with rich inlay
Broidered the ground, more colored than with stone
Of costliest emblem: other creature here
Beast, bird, insect, or worm durst enter none;
Such was their awe of man. In shadier bower

More sacred and sequestered, though but feigned,
Pan or Sylvanus never slept, nor nymph,
Nor Faunus haunted. Here in close recess
With flowers, garlands, and sweet-smelling herbs
Espoused Eve decked first her nuptial bed,
And heavenly choirs the hymenaean sung,
What day the genial angel to our sire
Brought her in naked beauty more adorned,
More lovely than Pandora, whom the gods
Endowed with all their gifts, and O too like
In sad event, when to the unwiser son
Of Japhet brought by Hermes, she ensnared
Mankind with her fair looks, to be avenged
On him who had stole Jove's authentic fire.

Thus at their shady lodge arrived, both stood,
Both turned, and under open sky adored
The God that made both sky, air, earth, and heaven
Which they beheld, the moon's resplendent globe
And starry pole: 'Thou also madest the night,
Maker omnipotent, and thou the day,
Which we in our appointed work employed
Have finished happy in our mutual help
And mutual love, the crown of all our bliss
Ordained by thee, and this delicious place
For us too large, where thy abundance wants
Partakers, and uncropped falls to the ground.
But thou hast promised from us two a race
To fill the earth, who shall with us extol
Thy goodness infinite, both when we wake,
And when we seek, as now, thy gift of sleep.'

This said unanimous, and other rites
Observing none, but adoration pure
Which God likes best, into their inmost bower
Handed they went; and eased the putting off
These troublesome disguises which we wear,
Straight side by side were laid, nor turned I ween
Adam from his fair spouse, nor Eve the rites

Mysterious of connubial love refused:
Whatever hypocrites austerely talk
Of purity and place and innocence,
Defaming as impure what God declares
Pure, and commands to some, leaves free to all.
Our maker bids increase, who bids abstain
But our destroyer, foe to God and man?
Hail wedded love, mysterious law, true source
Of human offspring, sole propriety,
In Paradise of all things common else.
By thee adulterous lust was driven from men
Among the bestial herds to range, by thee
Founded in reason, loyal, just, and pure,
Relations dear, and all the charities
Of father, son, and brother first were known.
Far be it, that I should write thee sin or blame,
Or think thee unbefitting holiest place,
Perpetual fountain of domestic sweets,
Whose bed is undefiled and chaste pronounced,
Present, or past, as saints and patriarchs used.
Here love his golden shafts employs, here lights
His constant lamp, and waves his purple wings,
Reigns here and revels; not in the bought smile
Of harlots, loveless, joyless, unendeared,
Casual fruition, nor in court amours,
Mixed dance, or wanton mask, or midnight ball,
Or serenade, which the starved lover sings
To his proud fair, best quitted with disdain.
These lulled by nightingales embracing slept,
And on their naked limbs the flowery roof
Showered roses, which the morn repaired. Sleep on,
Blest pair; and O yet happiest if ye seek
No happier state, and know to know no more.

Now had night measured with her shadowy cone
Halfway uphill this vast sublunar vault,
And from their ivory port the cherubim
Forth issuing at the accustomed hour stood armed

To their night watches in warlike parade,
When Gabriel to his next in power thus spake.
    'Uzziel, half these draw off, and coast the south
With strictest watch; these other wheel the north,
Our circuit meets full west.' As flame they part
Half wheeling to the shield, half to the spear.
From these, two strong and subtle spirits he called
That near him stood, and gave them thus in charge.
    'Ithuriel and Zephon, with winged speed
Search through this garden, leave unsearched no nook,
But chiefly where those two fair creatures lodge,
Now laid perhaps asleep secure of harm.
This evening from the sun's decline arrived
Who tells of some infernal spirit seen
Hitherward bent (who could have thought?) escaped
The bars of hell, on errand bad no doubt:
Such where ye find, seize fast, and hither bring.'
    So saying, on he led his radiant files,
Dazzling the moon; these to the bower direct
In search of whom they sought: him there they found
Squat like a toad, close at the ear of Eve;
Assaying by his devilish art to reach
The organs of her fancy, and with them forge
Illusions as he list, phantasms and dreams,
Or if, inspiring venom, he might taint
The animal spirits that from pure blood arise
Like gentle breaths from rivers pure, thence raise
At least distempered, discontented thoughts,
Vain hopes, vain aims, inordinate desires
Blown up with high conceits engendering pride.
Him thus intent Ithuriel with his spear
Touched lightly; for no falsehood can endure
Touch of celestial temper, but returns
Of force to its own likeness: up he starts
Discovered and surprised. As when a spark
Lights on a heap of nitrous powder, laid
Fit for the tun some magazine to store

Against a rumored war, the smutty grain
With sudden blaze diffused, inflames the air:
So started up in his own shape the fiend.
Back stepped those two fair angels half amazed
So sudden to behold the grisly king;
Yet thus, unmoved with fear, accost him soon.

'Which of those rebel spirits adjudged to hell
Comest thou, escaped thy prison, and transformed,
Why sattest thou like an enemy in wait
Here watching at the head of these that sleep?'

'Know ye not then' said Satan, filled with scorn,
'Know ye not me? ye knew me once no mate
For you, there sitting where ye durst not soar;
Not to know me argues yourselves unknown,
The lowest of your throng; or if ye know,
Why ask ye, and superfluous begin
Your message, like to end as much in vain?'
To whom thus Zephon, answering scorn with scorn.
'Think not, revolted spirit, thy shape the same,
Or undiminished brightness, to be known
As when thou stoodest in heaven upright and pure;
That glory then, when thou no more wast good,
Departed from thee, and thou resemblest now
Thy sin and place of doom obscure and foul.
But come, for thou, be sure, shalt give account
To him who sent us, whose charge is to keep
This place inviolable, and these from harm.'

So spake the cherub, and his grave rebuke
Severe in youthful beauty, added grace
Invincible: abashed the devil stood,
And felt how awful goodness is, and saw
Virtue in her shape how lovely, saw, and pined
His loss; but chiefly to find here observed
His luster visibly impaired: yet seemed
Undaunted. 'If I must contend,' said he,
'Best with the best, the sender not the sent,
Or all at once; more glory will be won,

Or less be lost.' 'Thy fear,' said Zephon bold,
'Will save us trial what the least can do
Single against thee wicked, and thence weak.'
    The fiend replied not, overcome with rage;
But like a proud steed reined, went haughty on,
Champing his iron curb: to strive or fly
He held it vain; awe from above had quelled
His heart, not else dismayed. Now drew they nigh
The western point, where those half-rounding guards
Just met, and closing stood in squadron joined
Awaiting next command. To whom their chief
Gabriel from the front thus called aloud.
    'O friends, I hear the tread of nimble feet
Hasting this way, and now by glimpse discern
Ithuriel and Zephon through the shade,
And with them comes a third of regal port,
But faded splendor wan; who by his gait
And fierce demeanor seems the prince of hell,
Not likely to part hence without contest;
Stand firm, for in his look defiance lours.'
    He scarce had ended, when those two approached
And brief related whom they brought, where found,
How busied, in what form and posture couched.
    To whom with stern regard thus Gabriel spake.
'Why hast thou, Satan, broke the bounds prescribed
To thy transgressions, and disturbed the charge
Of others, who approve not to transgress
By thy example, but have power and right
To question thy bold entrance on this place;
Employed it seems to violate sleep, and those
Whose dwelling God hath planted here in bliss?'
    To whom thus Satan, with contemptuous brow.
'Gabriel, thou hadst in heaven the esteem of wise,
And such I held thee; but this question asked
Puts me in doubt. Lives there who loves his pain?
Who would not, finding way, break loose from hell,
Though thither doomed? Thou wouldst thyself, no doubt,

And boldly venture to whatever place
Farthest from pain, where thou mightest hope to change
Torment with ease, and soonest recompense
Dole with delight, which in this place I sought;
To thee no reason; who knowest only good,
But evil hast not tried: and wilt object
His will who bound us? let him surer bar
His iron gates, if he intends our stay
In that dark durance: thus much what was asked.
The rest is true, they found me where they say;
But that implies not violence or harm.'
    Thus he in scorn. The warlike angel moved,
Disdainfully half smiling thus replied.
'O loss of one in heaven to judge of wise,
Since Satan fell, whom folly overthrew,
And now returns him from his prison scaped,
Gravely in doubt whether to hold them wise
Or not, who ask what boldness brought him hither
Unlicensed from his bounds in hell prescribed;
So wise he judges it to fly from pain
However, and to scape his punishment.
So judge thou still, presumptuous, till the wrath,
Which thou incurrest by flying, meet thy flight
Sevenfold, and scourge that wisdom back to hell,
Which taught thee yet no better, that no pain
Can equal anger infinite provoked.
But wherefore thou alone? wherefore with thee
Came not all hell broke loose? is pain to them
Less pain, less to be fled, or thou than they
Less hardy to endure? courageous chief,
The first in flight from pain, hadst thou alleged
To thy deserted host this cause of flight,
Thou surely hadst not come sole fugitive.'
    To which the fiend thus answered frowning stern.
'Not that I less endure, or shrink from pain,
Insulting angel, well thou knowest I stood
Thy fiercest, when in battle to thy aid

The blasting volleyed thunder made all speed
And seconded thy else not dreaded spear.
But still thy words at random, as before,
Argue thy inexperience what behooves
From hard assays and ill successes past
A faithful leader, not to hazard all
Through ways of danger by himself untried.
I therefore, I alone first undertook
To wing the desolate abyss, and spy
This new created world, whereof in hell
Fame is not silent, here in hope to find
Better abode, and my afflicted powers
To settle here on earth, or in mid-air;
Though for possession put to try once more
What thou and thy gay legions dare against;
Whose easier business were to serve their lord
High up in heaven, with songs to hymn his throne,
And practiced distances to cringe, not fight.'
     To whom the warrior angel, soon replied.
'To say and straight unsay, pretending first
Wise to fly pain, professing next the spy,
Argues no leader but a liar traced,
Satan, and couldst thou "faithful" add? O name,
O sacred name of faithfulness profaned!
Faithful to whom? to thy rebellious crew?
Army of fiends, fit body to fit head;
Was this your discipline and faith engaged,
Your military obedience, to dissolve
Allegiance to the acknowledged power supreme?
And thou sly hypocrite, who now wouldst seem
Patron of liberty, who more than thou
Once fawned, and cringed, and servilely adored
Heaven's awful monarch? wherefore but in hope
To dispossess him, and thyself to reign?
But mark what I aread thee now, avaunt;
Fly thither whence thou fleddst: if from this hour
Within these hallowed limits thou appear,

Back to the infernal pit I drag thee chained,
And seal thee so, as henceforth not to scorn
The facile gates of hell too slightly barred.'
   So threatened he, but Satan to no threats
Gave heed, but waxing more in rage replied.
   'Then when I am thy captive talk of chains,
Proud limitary cherub, but ere then
Far heavier load thyself expect to feel
From my prevailing arm, though heaven's king
Ride on thy wings, and thou with thy compeers,
Used to the yoke, drawest his triumphant wheels
In progress through the road of heaven star-paved.'
   While thus he spake, the angelic squadron bright
Turned fiery red, sharpening in mooned horns
Their phalanx, and began to hem him round
With ported spears, as thick as when a field
Of Ceres ripe for harvest waving bends
Her bearded grove of ears, which way the wind
Sways them; the careful plowman doubting stands
Lest on the threshing floor his hopeful sheaves
Prove chaff. On the other side Satan alarmed
Collecting all his might dilated stood,
Like Teneriff or Atlas unremoved:
His stature reached the sky, and on his crest
Sat horror plumed; nor wanted in his grasp
What seemed both spear and shield: now dreadful deeds
Might have ensued, nor only Paradise
In this commotion, but the starry cope
Of heaven perhaps, or all the elements
At least had gone to wrack, disturbed and torn
With violence of this conflict, had not soon
The eternal to prevent such horrid fray
Hung forth in heaven his golden scales, yet seen
Betwixt Astraea and the Scorpion sign,
Wherein all things created first he weighed,
The pendulous round earth with balanced air
In counterpoise, now ponders all events,

Battles and realms: in these he put two weights
The sequel each of parting and of fight;
The latter quick upflew, and kicked the beam;
Which Gabriel spying, thus bespake the fiend.
    'Satan, I know thy strength, and thou knowest mine,
Neither our own but given; what folly then
To boast what arms can do, since thine no more
Than heaven permits, nor mine, though doubled now
To trample thee as mire: for proof look up,
And read thy lot in yon celestial sign
Where thou art weighed, and shown how light, how weak,
If thou resist.' The fiend looked up and knew
His mounted scale aloft: nor more; but fled
Murmuring, and with him fled the shades of night.

BOOK V

The Argument: Morning approached, Eve relates to Adam her
troublesome dream; he likes it not, yet comforts her: They come
forth to their day labors: Their morning hymn at the door of their
bower. God to render man inexcusable sends Raphael to admonish
him of his obedience, of his free estate, of his enemy near at
hand; who he is, and why his enemy, and whatever else may avail
Adam to know. Raphael comes down to Paradise, his appearance
described, his coming discerned by Adam afar off sitting at the
door of his bower; he goes out to meet him, brings him to his lodge,
entertains him with the choicest fruits of Paradise got together by
Eve; their discourse at table: Raphael performs his message, minds
Adam of his state and of his enemy; relates at Adam's request who
that enemy is, and how he came to be so, beginning from his first
revolt in heaven, and the occasion thereof; how he drew his legions
after him to the parts of the north, and there incited them to rebel
with him, persuading all but only Abdiel a seraph, who in argument
dissuades and opposes him, then forsakes him.

Now morn her rosy steps in the eastern clime
Advancing, sowed the earth with orient pearl,
When Adam waked, so customed, for his sleep
Was airy light from pure digestion bred,
And temperate vapors bland, which the only sound
Of leaves and fuming rills, Aurora's fan,
Lightly dispersed, and the shrill matin song
Of birds on every bough; so much the more
His wonder was to find unwakened Eve
With tresses discomposed, and glowing cheek,
As through unquiet rest: he on his side
Leaning half raised, with looks of cordial love
Hung over her enamored, and beheld
Beauty, which whether waking or asleep,
Shot forth peculiar graces; then with voice
Mild, as when Zephyrus on Flora breathes,
Her hand soft touching, whispered thus. 'Awake
My fairest, my espoused, my latest found,
Heaven's last best gift, my ever new delight,
Awake, the morning shines, and the fresh field
Calls us, we lose the prime, to mark how spring
Our tended plants, how blows the citron grove,
What drops the myrrh, and what the balmy reed,
How nature paints her colors, how the bee
Sits on the bloom extracting liquid sweet.'
    Such whispering waked her, but with startled eye
On Adam, whom embracing, thus she spake.
    'O sole in whom my thoughts find all repose,
My glory, my perfection, glad I see
Thy face, and morn returned, for I this night,
Such night till this I never passed, have dreamed,
If dreamed, not as I oft am wont, of thee,
Works of day past, or morrow's next design,
But of offense and trouble, which my mind
Knew never till this irksome night; methought
Close at mine ear one called me forth to walk
With gentle voice, I thought it thine; it said,

"Why sleepest thou Eve? now is the pleasant time,
The cool, the silent, save where silence yields
To the night-warbling bird, that now awake
Tunes sweetest his love-labored song; now reigns
Full-orbed the moon, and with more pleasing light
Shadowy sets off the face of things; in vain,
If none regard; heaven wakes with all his eyes,
Whom to behold but thee, nature's desire,
In whose sight all things joy, with ravishment
Attracted by thy beauty still to gaze."
I rose at thy call, but found thee not;
To find thee I directed then my walk;
And on, methought, alone I passed through ways
That brought me on a sudden to the tree
Of interdicted knowledge: fair it seemed,
Much fairer to my fancy than by day:
And as I wondering looked, beside it stood
One shaped and winged like one of those from heaven
By us oft seen; his dewy locks distilled
Ambrosia; on that tree he also gazed;
And "O fair plant," said he, "with fruit surcharged,
Deigns none to ease thy load and taste thy sweet,
Nor God, nor man; is knowledge so despised?
Or envy, or what reserve forbids to taste?
Forbid who will, none shall from me withhold
Longer thy offered good, why else set here?"
This said he paused not, but with venturous arm
He plucked, he tasted; me damp horror chilled
At such bold words vouched with a deed so bold:
But he thus overjoyed, "O fruit divine,
Sweet of thyself, but much more sweet thus cropped,
Forbidden here, it seems, as only fit
For gods, yet able to make gods of men:
And why not gods of men, since good, the more
Communicated, more abundant grows,
The author not impaired, but honored more?
Here, happy creature, fair angelic Eve,

Partake thou also; happy though thou art,
Happier thou mayest be, worthier canst not be:
Taste this, and be henceforth among the gods
Thyself a goddess, not to Earth confined,
But sometimes in the air, as we, sometimes
Ascend to heaven, by merit thine, and see
What life the gods live there, and such live thou."
So saying, he drew nigh, and to me held,
Even to my mouth of that same fruit held part
Which he had plucked; the pleasant savory smell
So quickened appetite, that I, methought,
Could not but taste. Forthwith up to the clouds
With him I flew, and underneath beheld
The earth outstretched immense, a prospect wide
And various: wondering at my flight and change
To this high exaltation; suddenly
My guide was gone, and I, methought, sunk down,
And fell asleep; but O how glad I waked
To find this but a dream!' Thus Eve her night
Related, and thus Adam answered sad.

   'Best image of myself and dearer half,
The trouble of thy thoughts this night in sleep
Affects me equally; nor can I like
This uncouth dream, of evil sprung I fear;
Yet evil whence? in thee can harbor none,
Created pure. But know that in the soul
Are many lesser faculties that serve
Reason as chief; among these fancy next
Her office holds; of all external things,
Which the five watchful senses represent,
She forms imaginations, airy shapes,
Which reason joining or disjoining, frames
All what we affirm or what deny, and call
Our knowledge or opinion; then retires
Into her private cell when nature rests.
Oft in her absence mimic fancy wakes
To imitate her; but misjoining shapes,

Wild work produces oft, and most in dreams,
Ill matching words and deeds long past or late.
Some such resemblances methinks I find
Of our last evening's talk, in this thy dream,
But with addition strange: yet be not sad.
Evil into the mind of God or man
May come and go, so unapproved, and leave
No spot or blame behind: Which gives me hope
That what in sleep thou didst abhor to dream,
Waking thou never wilt consent to do.
Be not disheartened then, nor cloud those looks
That wont to be more cheerful and serene
Than when fair morning first smiles on the world,
And let us to our fresh employments rise
Among the groves, the fountains, and the flowers
That open now their choicest bosomed smells
Reserved from night, and kept for thee in store.'
    So cheered he his fair spouse, and she was cheered,
But silently a gentle tear let fall
From either eye, and wiped them with her hair;
Two other precious drops that ready stood,
Each in their crystal sluice, he ere they fell
Kissed as the gracious signs of sweet remorse
And pious awe, that feared to have offended.
    So all was cleared, and to the field they haste.
But first from under shady arborous roof,
Soon as they forth were come to open sight
Of day-spring, and the sun, who scarce uprisen
With wheels yet hovering o'er the ocean brim,
Shot parallel to the earth his dewy ray,
Discovering in wide landscape all the east
Of Paradise and Eden's happy plains,
Lowly they bowed adoring, and began
Their orisons, each morning duly paid
In various style, for neither various style
Nor holy rapture wanted they to praise
Their maker, in fit strains pronounced or sung

Unmeditated, such prompt eloquence
Flowed from their lips, in prose or numerous verse,
More tunable than needed lute or harp
To add more sweetness, and they thus began.
　'These are thy glorious works, parent of good,
Almighty, thine this universal frame,
Thus wondrous fair; thyself how wondrous then!
Unspeakable, who sittest above these heavens
To us invisible or dimly seen
In these thy lowest works, yet these declare
Thy goodness beyond thought, and power divine:
Speak ye who best can tell, ye sons of light,
Angels, for ye behold him, and with songs
And choral symphonies, day without night,
Circle his throne rejoicing, ye in heaven,
On earth join all ye creatures to extol
Him first, him last, him midst, and without end.
Fairest of stars, last in the train of night,
If better thou belong not to the dawn,
Sure pledge of day, that crownest the smiling morn
With thy bright circlet, praise him in thy sphere
While day arises, that sweet hour of prime.
Thou sun, of this great world both eye and soul,
Acknowledge him thy greater, sound his praise
In thy eternal course, both when thou climbest,
And when high noon hast gained, and when thou fallest.
Moon, that now meetest the orient sun, now fliest
With the fixed stars, fixed in their orb that flies,
And ye five other wandering fires that move
In mystic dance not without song, resound
His praise, who out of darkness called up light.
Air, and ye elements the eldest birth
Of nature's womb, that in quaternion run
Perpetual circle, multiform; and mix
And nourish all things, let your ceaseless change
Vary to our great maker still new praise
Ye mists and exhalations that now rise

From hill or steaming lake, dusky or gray,
Till the sun paint your fleecy skirts with gold,
In honor to the world's great author rise,
Whether to deck with clouds the uncolored sky,
Or wet the thirsty earth with falling showers,
Rising or falling still advance his praise.
His praise ye winds, that from four quarters blow,
Breathe soft or loud; and wave your tops, ye pines,
With every plant, in sign of worship wave.
Fountains and ye, that warble, as ye flow,
Melodious murmurs, warbling tune his praise.
Join voices all ye living souls, ye birds,
That singing up to heaven gate ascend,
Bear on your wings and in your notes his praise;
Ye that in waters glide, and ye that walk
The earth, and stately tread, or lowly creep;
Witness if I be silent, morn or even,
To hill, or valley, fountain, or fresh shade
Made vocal by my song, and taught his praise.
Hail universal Lord, be bounteous still
To give us only good; and if the night
Have gathered aught of evil or concealed,
Disperse it, as now light dispels the dark.'
   So prayed they innocent, and to their thoughts
Firm peace recovered soon and wonted calm.
On to their morning's rural work they haste
Among sweet dews and flowers; where any row
Of fruit-trees over-woody reached too far
Their pampered boughs, and needed hands to check
Fruitless embraces: or they led the vine
To wed her elm; she spoused about him twines
Her marriageable arms, and with her brings
Her dower the adopted clusters, to adorn
His barren leaves. Them thus employed beheld
With pity heaven's high king, and to him called
Raphael, the sociable spirit, that deigned

To travel with Tobias, and secured
His marriage with the seven times-wedded maid.
    'Raphael,' said he, 'thou hearest what stir on earth
Satan from hell scaped through the darksome gulf
Hath raised in Paradise, and how disturbed
This night the human pair, how he designs
In them at once to ruin all mankind.
Go therefore, half this day as friend with friend
Converse with Adam, in what bower or shade
Thou findest him from the heat of noon retired,
To respite his day-labor with repast,
Or with repose; and such discourse bring on,
As may advise him of his happy state,
Happiness in his power left free to will,
Left to his own free will, his will though free,
Yet mutable; whence warn him to beware
He swerve not too secure: tell him withal
His danger, and from whom, what enemy
Late fallen himself from heaven, is plotting now
The fall of others from like state of bliss;
By violence, no, for that shall be withstood,
But by deceit and lies; this let him know,
Lest willfully transgressing he pretend
Surprisal, unadmonished, unforewarned.'
    So spake the eternal father, and fulfilled
All justice: nor delayed the winged saint
After his charge received; but from among
Thousand celestial ardors, where he stood
Veiled with his gorgeous wings, upspringing light
Flew through the midst of heaven; the angelic choirs
On each hand parting, to his speed gave way
Through all the empyreal road; till at the gate
Of heaven arrived, the gate self-opened wide
On golden hinges turning, as by work
Divine the sovereign architect had framed.
From hence, no cloud, or, to obstruct his sight,
Star interposed, however small he sees,

Not unconform to other shining globes,
Earth and the garden of God, with cedars crowned
Above all hills. As when by night the glass
Of Galileo, less assured, observes
Imagined lands and regions in the moon:
Or pilot from amidst the Cyclades
Delos or Samos first appearing kens
A cloudy spot. Down thither prone in flight
He speeds, and through the vast ethereal sky
Sails between worlds and worlds, with steady wing
Now on the polar winds, then with quick fan
Winnows the buxom air; till within soar
Of towering eagles, to all the fowls he seems
A phoenix, gazed by all, as that sole bird
When to enshrine his relics in the sun's
Bright temple, to Egyptian Thebes he flies.
At once on the eastern cliff of Paradise
He lights, and to his proper shape returns
A seraph winged; six wings he wore, to shade
His lineaments divine; the pair that clad
Each shoulder broad, came mantling o'er his breast
With regal ornament; the middle pair
Girt like a starry zone his waist, and round
Skirted his loins and thighs with downy gold
And colors dipped in heaven; the third his feet
Shadowed from either heel with feathered mail
Sky-tinctured grain. Like Maia's son he stood,
And shook his plumes, that heavenly fragrance filled
The circuit wide. Straight knew him all the bands
Of Angels under watch; and to his state,
And to his message high in honor rise;
For on some message high they guessed him bound.
Their glittering tents he passed, and now is come
Into the blissful field, through groves of myrrh,
And flowering odors, cassia, nard, and balm;
A wilderness of sweets; for nature here
Wantoned as in her prime, and played at will

Her virgin fancies, pouring forth more sweet,
Wild above rule or art; enormous bliss.
Him through the spicy forest onward come
Adam discerned, as in the door he sat
Of his cool bower, while now the mounted sun
Shot down direct his fervid rays to warm
Earth's inmost womb, more warmth than Adam needs;
And Eve within, due at her hour prepared
For dinner savory fruits, of taste to please
True appetite, and not disrelish thirst
Of nectarous draughts between, from milky stream,
Berry or grape: to whom thus Adam called.

   'Haste hither Eve, and worth thy sight behold
Eastward among those trees, what glorious Shape
Comes this way moving; seems another morn
Risen on mid-noon; some great behest from heaven
To us perhaps he brings, and will vouchsafe
This day to be our guest. But go with speed,
And what thy stores contain, bring forth and pour
Abundance, fit to honor and receive
Our heavenly stranger; well we may afford
Our givers their own gifts, and large bestow
From large bestowed, where nature multiplies
Her fertile growth, and by disburdening grows
More fruitful, which instructs us not to spare.'

   To whom thus Eve. 'Adam, earth's hallowed mold,
Of God inspired, small store will serve, where store,
All seasons, ripe for use hangs on the stalk;
Save what by frugal storing firmness gains
To nourish, and superfluous moist consumes:
But I will haste and from each bough and brake,
Each plant and juiciest gourd will pluck such choice
To entertain our angel guest, as he
Beholding shall confess that here on earth
God hath dispensed his bounties as in heaven.'

   So saying, with dispatchful looks in haste
She turns, on hospitable thoughts intent

What choice to choose for delicacy best,
What order, so contrived as not to mix
Tastes, not well joined, inelegant, but bring
Taste after taste upheld with kindliest change,
Bestirs her then, and from each tender stalk
Whatever earth all-bearing mother yields
In India east or west, or middle shore
In Pontus or the Punic coast, or where
Alcinous reigned, fruit of all kinds, in coat,
Rough, or smooth rinded, or bearded husk, or shell
She gathers, tribute large, and on the board
Heaps with unsparing hand; for drink the grape
She crushes, inoffensive must, and meaths
From many a berry, and from sweet kernels pressed
She tempers dulcet creams, nor these to hold
Wants her fit vessels pure, then strews the ground
With rose and odors from the shrub unfumed.
Meanwhile our primitive great sire, to meet
His godlike guest, walks forth, without more train
Accompanied than with his own complete
Perfections, in himself was all his state,
More solemn than the tedious pomp that waits
On princes, when their rich retinue long
Of horses led, and grooms besmeared with gold
Dazzles the crowd, and sets them all agape.
Nearer his presence Adam though not awed,
Yet with submiss approach and reverence meek,
As to a superior nature, bowing low,
    Thus said. 'Native of heaven, for other place
None can than heaven such glorious shape contain,
Since by descending from the thrones above,
Those happy places thou hast deigned a while
To want, and honor these, vouchsafe with us
Two only, who yet by sovereign gift possess
This spacious ground, in yonder shady bower
To rest, and what the garden choicest bears

To sit and taste, till this meridian heat
Be over, and the sun more cool decline.'
  Whom thus the angelic virtue answered mild.
'Adam, I therefore came, nor art thou such
Created, or such place hast here to dwell,
As may not oft invite, though spirits of heaven
To visit thee; lead on then where thy bower
O'ershades; for these mid-hours, till evening rise
I have at will.' So to the sylvan lodge
They came, that like Pomona's arbor smiled
With flowerets decked and fragrant smells; but Eve
Undecked, save with herself more lovely fair
Than wood-nymph, or the fairest goddess feigned
Of three that in Mount Ida naked strove,
Stood to entertain her guest from heaven; no veil
She needed, virtue-proof, no thought infirm
Altered her cheek. On whom the angel 'Hail'
Bestowed, the holy salutation used
Long after to blest Mary, second Eve.
  'Hail mother of mankind, whose fruitful womb
Shall fill the world more numerous with thy sons
Than with these various fruits the trees of God
Have heaped this table.' Raised of grassy turf
Their table was, and mossy seats had round,
And on her ample square from side to side
All autumn piled, though spring and autumn here
Danced hand in hand. A while discourse they hold;
No fear lest dinner cool; when thus began
Our author. 'Heavenly stranger, please to taste
These bounties which our nourisher, from whom
All perfect good unmeasured out, descends,
To us for food and for delight hath caused
The earth to yield; unsavory food perhaps
To spiritual natures; only this I know,
That one celestial father gives to all.'
  To whom the angel. 'Therefore what he gives
(Whose praise be ever sung) to man in part

Spiritual, may of purest spirits be found
No ingrateful food: and food alike those pure
Intelligential substances require
As doth your rational; and both contain
Within them every lower faculty
Of sense, whereby they hear, see, smell, touch, taste,
Tasting concoct, digest, assimilate,
And corporeal to incorporeal turn.
For know, whatever was created, needs
To be sustained and fed; of elements
The grosser feeds the purer, earth the sea,
Earth and the sea feed air, the air those fires
Ethereal, and as lowest first the moon;
Whence in her visage round those spots, unpurged
Vapors not yet into her substance turned.
Nor doth the moon no nourishment exhale
From her moist continent to higher orbs.
The sun that light imparts to all, receives
From all his alimental recompense
In humid exhalations, and at even
Sups with the ocean: though in heaven the trees
Of life ambrosial fruitage bear, and vines
Yield nectar, though from off the boughs each morn
We brush mellifluous dews, and find the ground
Covered with pearly grain: yet God hath here
Varied his bounty so with new delights,
As may compare with heaven; and to taste
Think not I shall be nice.' So down they sat,
And to their viands fell, nor seemingly
The angel, nor in mist, the common gloss
Of theologians, but with keen dispatch
Of real hunger, and concoctive heat
To transubstantiate: what redounds, transpires
Through spirits with ease; nor wonder; if by fire
Of sooty coal the empiric alchemist
Can turn, or holds it possible to turn
Metals of drossiest ore to perfect gold

As from the mine. Meanwhile at table Eve
Ministered naked, and their flowing cups
With pleasant liquors crowned: O innocence
Deserving Paradise! if ever, then,
Then had the sons of God excuse to have been
Enamored at that sight; but in those hearts
Love unlibidinous reigned, nor jealousy
Was understood, the injured lover's hell.

    Thus when with meats and drinks they had sufficed,
Not burdened nature, sudden mind arose
In Adam, not to let the occasion pass
Given him by this great conference to know
Of things above his world, and of their being
Who dwell in heaven, whose excellence he saw
Transcend his own so far, whose radiant forms
Divine effulgence, whose high power so far
Exceeded human, and his wary speech
Thus to the empyreal minister he framed.

    'Inhabitant with God, now know I well
Thy favor, in this honor done to man,
Under whose lowly roof thou hast vouchsafed
To enter, and these earthly fruits to taste,
Food not of angels, yet accepted so,
As that more willingly thou couldst not seem
At heaven's high feasts to have fed: yet what compare?

    To whom the winged hierarch replied.
'O Adam, one almighty is, from whom
All things proceed, and up to him return,
If not depraved from good, created all
Such to perfection, one first matter all,
Endued with various forms, various degrees
Of substance, and in things that live, of life;
But more refined, more spiritous, and pure,
As nearer to him placed or nearer tending
Each in their several active spheres assigned,
Till body up to spirit work, in bounds
Proportioned to each kind. So from the root

Springs lighter the green stalk, from thence the leaves
More airy, last the bright consummate flower
Spirits odorous breathes: flowers and their fruit
Man's nourishment, by gradual scale sublimed
To vital spirits aspire, to animal,
To intellectual, give both life and sense,
Fancy and understanding, whence the soul
Reason receives, and reason in her being,
Discursive, or intuitive; discourse
Is oftest yours, the latter most is ours,
Differing but in degree, of kind the same.
Wonder not then, what God for you saw good
If I refuse not, but convert, as you,
To proper substance; time may come when men
With angels may participate, and find
No inconvenient diet, nor too light fare:
And from these corporal nutriments perhaps
Your bodies may at last turn all to spirit,
Improved by tract of time, and winged ascend
Ethereal, as we, or may at choice
Here or in heavenly paradises dwell;
If ye be found obedient, and retain
Unalterably firm his love entire
Whose progeny you are. Meanwhile enjoy
Your fill what happiness this happy state
Can comprehend, incapable of more.'
    To whom the patriarch of mankind replied,
'O favorable spirit, propitious guest,
Well hast thou taught the way that might direct
Our knowledge, and the scale of nature set
From center to circumference, whereon
In contemplation of created things
By steps we may ascend to God. But say,
What meant that caution joined, "if ye be found
Obedient?" can we want obedience then
To him, or possibly his love desert
Who formed us from the dust, and placed us here

Full to the utmost measure of what bliss
Human desires can seek or apprehend?'

To whom the angel. 'Son of heaven and earth,
Attend: That thou art happy, owe to God;
That thou continuest such, owe to thyself,
That is, to thy obedience; therein stand.
This was that caution given thee; be advised.
God made thee perfect, not immutable;
And good he made thee, but to persevere
He left it in thy power, ordained thy will
By nature free, not over-ruled by fate
Inextricable, or strict necessity;
Our voluntary service he requires,
Not our necessitated, such with him
Finds no acceptance, nor can find, for how
Can hearts, not free, be tried whether they serve
Willing or no, who will but what they must
By destiny, and can no other choose?
Myself and all the angelic host that stand
In sight of God enthroned, our happy state
Hold, as you yours, while our obedience holds;
On other surety none; freely we serve,
Because we freely love, as in our will
To love or not; in this we stand or fall:
And some are fallen, to disobedience fallen,
And so from heaven to deepest hell; O fall
From what high state of bliss into what woe!'

To whom our great progenitor. 'Thy words
Attentive, and with more delighted ear,
Divine instructor, I have heard, than when
Cherubic songs by night from neighboring hills
Aerial music send: nor knew I not
To be both will and deed created free;
Yet that we never shall forget to love
Our maker, and obey him whose command
Single, is yet so just, my constant thoughts
Assured me, and still assure: though what thou tellest

Hath passed in heaven, some doubt within me move,
But more desire to hear, if thou consent,
The full relation, which must needs be strange,
Worthy of sacred silence to be heard;
And we have yet large day, for scarce the sun
Hath finished half his journey, and scarce begins
His other half in the great zone of heaven.'
    Thus Adam made request, and Raphael
After short assenting, thus began.
    'High matter thou enjoinest me, O prime of men,
Sad task and hard, for how shall I relate
To human sense the invisible exploits
Of warring spirits; how without remorse
The ruin of so many glorious once
And perfect while they stood; how last unfold
The secrets of another world, perhaps
Not lawful to reveal? yet for thy good
This is dispensed, and what surmounts the reach
Of human sense, I shall delineate so,
By likening spiritual to corporal forms,
As may express them best, though what if earth
Be but the shadow of heaven, and things therein
Each to other like, more than on earth is thought?
    'As yet this world was not, and chaos wild
Reigned where these heavens now roll, where earth now rests
Upon her center poised, when on a day
(For time, though in eternity, applied
To motion, measures all things durable
By present, past, and future) on such day
As heaven's great year brings forth, the empyreal host
Of angels by imperial summons called,
Innumerable before the almighty throne
Forthwith from all the ends of heaven appeared
Under their hierarchs in orders bright
Ten thousand thousand ensigns high advanced,
Standards, and gonfalons twixt van and rear
Stream in the air, and for distinction serve

Of hierarchies, of orders, and degrees;
Or in their glittering tissues bear emblazoned
Holy memorials, acts of zeal and love
Recorded eminent. Thus when in orbs
Of circuit inexpressible they stood,
Orb within orb, the father infinite,
By whom in bliss embosomed sat the Son,
Amidst as from a flaming mount, whose top
Brightness had made invisible, thus spake.
    ' "Hear all ye angels, progeny of light,
Thrones, dominations, princedoms, virtues, powers,
Hear my decree, which unrevoked shall stand.
This day I have begot whom I declare
My only Son, and on this holy hill
Him have anointed, whom ye now behold
At my right hand; your head I him appoint;
And by myself have sworn to him shall bow
All knees in heaven, and shall confess him Lord:
Under his great vicegerent reign abide
United as one individual soul
Forever happy: him who disobeys
Me disobeys, breaks union, and that day
Cast out from God and blessed vision, falls
Into utter darkness, deep engulfed, his place
Ordained without redemption, without end."
    'So spake the omnipotent, and with his words
All seemed well pleased, all seemed, but were not all.
That day, as other solemn days, they spent
In song and dance about the sacred hill,
Mystical dance, which yonder starry sphere
Of planets and of fixed in all her wheels
Resembles nearest, mazes intricate,
Eccentric, intervolved, yet regular
Then most, when most irregular they seem,
And in their motions harmony divine
So smooths her charming tones, that God's own ear
Listens delighted. Evening now approached

(For we have also our evening and our morn,
We ours for change delectable, not need)
Forthwith from dance to sweet repast they turn
Desirous; all in circles as they stood,
Tables are set, and on a sudden piled
With angels' food, and rubied nectar flows
In pearl, in diamond, and massy gold,
Fruit of delicious vines, the growth of heaven.
On flowers reposed, and with fresh flowerets crowned,
They eat, they drink, and in communion sweet
Quaff immortality and joy, secure
Of surfeit where full measure only bounds
Excess, before the all bounteous king, who showered
With copious hand, rejoicing in their joy.
Now when ambrosial night with clouds exhaled
From that high mount of God, whence light and shade
Spring both, the face of brightest heaven had changed
To grateful twilight (for night comes not there
In darker veil) and roseate dews disposed
All but the unsleeping eyes of God to rest,
Wide over all the plain, and wider far
Than all this globous earth in plain outspread,
(Such are the courts of God) the angelic throng
Dispersed in bands and files their camp extend
By living streams among the trees of life,
Pavilions numberless, and sudden reared,
Celestial tabernacles, where they slept
Fanned with cool winds, save those who in their course
Melodious hymns about the sovereign throne
Alternate all night long: but not so waked
Satan, so call him now, his former name
Is heard no more in heaven; he of the first,
If not the first archangel, great in power,
In favor and pre-eminence, yet fraught
With envy against the Son of God, that day
Honored by his great father, and proclaimed
Messiah king anointed, could not bear

Through pride that sight, and thought himself impaired,
Deep malice thence conceiving and disdain,
Soon as midnight brought on the dusky hour
Friendliest to sleep and silence, he resolved
With all his legions to dislodge, and leave
Unworshiped, unobeyed the throne supreme
Contemptuous, and his next subordinate
Awakening, thus to him in secret spake.
   ' "Sleepest thou companion dear, what sleep can close
Thy eyelids? and rememberest what decree
Of yesterday, so late hath passed the lips
Of heaven's almighty. Thou to me thy thoughts
Wast wont, I mine to thee was wont to impart;
Both waking we were one; how then can now
Thy sleep dissent? new laws thou seest imposed;
New laws from him who reigns, new minds may raise
In us who serve, new counsels, to debate
What doubtful may ensue, more in this place
To utter is not safe. Assemble thou
Of all those myriads which we lead the chief;
Tell them that by command, ere yet dim night
Her shadowy cloud withdraws, I am to haste,
And all who under me their banners wave,
Homeward with flying march where we possess
The quarters of the north, there to prepare
Fit entertainment to receive our king
The great Messiah, and his new commands,
Who speedily through all the hierarchies
Intends to pass triumphant, and give laws."
   'So spake the false archangel, and infused
Bad influence into the unwary breast
Of his associate; he together calls,
Or several one by one, the regent powers,
Under him regent, tells, as he was taught,
That the most high commanding, now ere night
Now ere dim night had disencumbered heaven,
The great hierarchal standard was to move;

Tells the suggested cause, and casts between
Ambiguous words and jealousies, to sound
Or taint integrity; but all obeyed
The wonted signal, and superior voice
Of their great potentate; for great indeed
His name, and high was his degree in heaven;
His countenance, as the morning star that guides
The starry flock, allured them, and with lies
Drew after him the third part of heaven's host:
Meanwhile the eternal eye, whose sight discerns
Abstrusest thoughts, from forth his holy mount
And from within the golden lamps that burn
Nightly before him, saw without their light
Rebellion rising, saw in whom, how spread
Among the sons of morn, what multitudes
Were banded to oppose his high decree;
And smiling to his only Son thus said.

   " 'Son, thou in whom my glory I behold
In full resplendence, heir of all my might,
Nearly it now concerns us to be sure
Of our omnipotence, and with what arms
We mean to hold what anciently we claim
Of deity or empire, such a foe
Is rising, who intends to erect his throne
Equal to ours, throughout the spacious north;
Nor so content, hath in his thought to try
In battle, what our power is, or our right.
Let us advise, and to this hazard draw
With speed what force is left, and all employ
In our defense, lest unawares we lose
This our high place, our sanctuary, our hill."

   'To whom the Son with calm aspect and clear
Lightning divine, ineffable, serene,
Made answer. "Mighty father, thou thy foes
Justly hast in derision, and secure
Laughest at their vain designs and tumults vain,
Matter to me of glory, whom their hate

Illustrates, when they see all regal power
Given me to quell their pride, and in event
Know whether I be dextrous to subdue
Thy rebels, or be found the worst in heaven."
  'So spake the Son, but Satan with his powers
Far was advanced on winged speed, an host
Innumerable as the stars of night,
Or stars of morning, dewdrops, which the sun
Impearls on every leaf and every flower.
Regions they passed, the mighty regencies
Of seraphim and potentates and thrones
In their triple degrees, regions to which
All thy dominion, Adam, is no more
Than what this garden is to all the earth,
And all the sea, from one entire globose
Stretched into longitude; which having passed
At length into the limits of the north
They came, and Satan to his royal seat
High on a hill, far blazing, as a mount
Raised on a mount, with pyramids and towers
From diamond quarries hewn, and rocks of gold,
The palace of great Lucifer, (so call
That structure in the dialect of men
Interpreted) which not long after, he
Affecting all equality with God,
In imitation of that mount whereon
Messiah was declared in sight of heaven,
The mountain of the congregation called;
For thither he assembled all his train,
Pretending so commanded to consult
About the great reception of their king,
Thither to come, and with calumnious art
Of counterfeited truth thus held their ears.
  ' "Thrones, dominations, princedoms, virtues, powers,
If these magnific titles yet remain
Not merely titular, since by decree
Another now hath to himself engrossed

All power, and us eclipsed under the name
Of king anointed, for whom all this haste
Of midnight march, and hurried meeting here,
This only to consult how we may best
With what may be devised of honors new
Receive him coming to receive from us
Knee-tribute yet unpaid, prostration vile,
Too much to one, but double how endured,
To one and to his image now proclaimed?
But what if better counsels might erect
Our minds and teach us to cast off this yoke?
Will ye submit your necks, and choose to bend
The supple knee? ye will not, if I trust
To know ye right, or if ye know yourselves
Natives and sons of heaven possessed before
By none, and if not equal all, yet free,
Equally free; for orders and degrees
Jar not with liberty, but well consist.
Who can in reason then or right assume
Monarchy over such as live by right
His equals, if in power and splendor less,
In freedom equal? or can introduce
Law and edict on us, who without law
Err not, much less for this to be our lord,
And look for adoration to the abuse
Of those imperial titles which assert
Our being ordained to govern, not to serve?"
    'Thus far his bold discourse without control
Had audience, when among the seraphim
Abdiel, than whom none with more zeal adored
The Deity, and divine commands obeyed,
Stood up, and in a flame of zeal severe
The current of his fury thus opposed.
    ' "O argument blasphemous, false and proud!
Words which no ear ever to hear in heaven
Expected, least of all from thee, ingrate
In place thyself so high above thy peers.

Canst thou with impious obloquy condemn
The just decree of God, pronounced and sworn,
That to his only Son by right endued
With regal scepter, every soul in heaven
Shall bend the knee, and in that honor due
Confess him rightful king? unjust thou sayest
Flatly unjust, to bind with laws the free,
And equal over equals to let reign,
One over all with unsucceeded power.
Shalt thou give law to God, shalt thou dispute
With him the points of liberty, who made
Thee what thou art, and formed the powers of heaver
Such as he pleased, and circumscribed their being?
Yet by experience taught we know how good,
And of our good, and of our dignity
How provident he is, how far from thought
To make us less, bent rather to exalt
Our happy state under one head more near
United. But to grant it thee unjust,
That equal over equals monarch reign:
Thyself though great and glorious dost thou count,
Or all angelic nature joined in one,
Equal to him begotten Son, by whom
As by his word the mighty father made
All things, even thee, and all the spirits of heaven
By him created in their bright degrees,
Crowned them with glory, and to their glory named
Thrones, dominations, princedoms, virtues, powers,
Essential powers, nor by his reign obscured,
But more illustrious made, since he the head
One of our number thus reduced becomes,
His laws our laws, all honor to him done
Returns our own. Cease then this impious rage,
And tempt not these; but hasten to appease
The incensed father, and the incensed Son,
While pardon may be found in time besought."

'So spake the fervent angel, but his zeal
None seconded, as out of season judged,
Or singular and rash, whereat rejoiced
The apostate, and more haughty thus replied.
"That we were formed then sayest thou? and the work
Of secondary hands, by task transferred
From father to his Son? strange point and new!
Doctrine which we would know whence learned: who saw
When this creation was? rememberest thou
Thy making, while the maker gave thee being?
We know no time when we were not as now;
Know none before us, self-begot, self-raised
By our own quickening power, when fatal course
Had circled his full orb, the birth mature
Of this our native heaven, ethereal Sons.
Our puissance is our own, our own right hand
Shall teach us highest deeds, by proof to try
Who is our equal: then thou shalt behold
Whether by supplication we intend
Address, and to begirt the almighty throne
Beseeching or besieging. This report,
These tidings carry to the anointed king;
And fly, ere evil intercept thy flight."
    ' He said, and as the sound of waters deep
Hoarse murmur echoed to his words applause
Through the infinite host, nor less for that
The flaming seraph fearless, though alone
Encompassed round with foes, thus answered bold.
    ' "O alienate from God, O spirit accursed,
Forsaken of all good; I see thy fall
Determined, and thy hapless crew involved
In this perfidious fraud, contagion spread
Both of thy crime and punishment: henceforth
No more be troubled how to quit the yoke
Of God's Messiah; those indulgent laws
Will not be now vouchsafed, other decrees
Against thee are gone forth without recall;

That golden scepter which thou didst **reject**
Is now an iron rod to bruise and break
Thy disobedience. Well thou didst advise,
Yet not for thy advice or threats I fly
These wicked tents devoted, lest the wrath
Impendent, raging into sudden flame
Distinguish not: for soon expect to feel
His thunder on thy head, devouring fire.
Then who created thee lamenting learn,
When who can uncreate thee thou shalt know."

'So spake the seraph Abdiel faithful found,
Among the faithless, faithful only he;
Among innumerable false, unmoved,
Unshaken, unseduced, unterrified
His loyalty he kept, his love, his zeal;
Nor number, nor example with him wrought
To swerve from truth, or change his constant mind
Though single. From amidst them forth he passed,
Long way through hostile scorn, which he sustained
Superior, nor of violence feared aught;
And with retorted scorn his back he turned
On those proud towers to swift destruction doomed.'

BOOK VI

The Argument: Raphael continues to relate how Michael and
Gabriel were sent forth to battle against Satan and his angels. The
first fight described: Satan and his powers retire under night: He
calls a council, invents devilish engines, which in the second day's
fight put Michael and his angels to some disorder; but they at length
pulling up mountains overwhelmed both the force and machines of
Satan: Yet the tumult not so ending, God on the third day sends
Messiah his son, for whom he had reserved the glory of that victory:
He in the power of the father coming to the place, and causing all

nis legions to stand still on either side, with his chariot and thunder
driving into the midst of his enemies, pursues them unable to resist
towards the wall of heaven; which opening, they leap down with
horror and confusion into the place of punishment prepared for
them in the deep: Messiah returns with triumph to his father.

'All night the dreadless angel unpursued
Through heaven's wide champaign held his way, till morn.
Waked by the circling hours, with rosy hand
Unbarred the gates of light. There is a cave
Within the mount of God, fast by his throne,
Where light and darkness in perpetual round
Lodge and dislodge by turns, which makes through heaven
Grateful vicissitude, like day and night;
Light issues forth, and at the other door
Obsequious darkness enters, till her hour
To veil the heaven, though darkness there might well
Seem twilight here; and now went forth the morn
Such as in highest heaven, arrayed in gold
Empyreal, from before her vanished night,
Shot through with orient beams: when all the plain
Covered with thick embattled squadrons bright,
Chariots and flaming arms, and fiery steeds
Reflecting blaze on blaze, first met his view:
War he perceived, war in procinct, and found
Already known what he for news had thought
To have reported: gladly then he mixed
Among those friendly powers who him received
With joy and acclamations loud, that one
That of so many myriads fallen, yet one
Returned not lost: On to the sacred hill
They led him high applauded, and present
Before the seat supreme; from whence a voice
From midst a golden cloud thus mild was heard.
  ' "Servant of God, well done, well hast thou fought
The better fight, who single hast maintained
Against revolted multitudes the cause

Of truth, in word mightier than they in arms;
And for the testimony of truth hast borne
Universal reproach, far worse to bear
Than violence: for this was all thy care
To stand approved in sight of God, though worlds
Judged thee perverse: the easier conquest now
Remains thee, aided by this host of friends,
Back on thy foes more glorious to return
Than scorned thou didst depart, and to subdue
By force, who reason for their law refuse,
Right reason for their law, and for their king
Messiah, who by right of merit reigns.
Go Michael of celestial armies prince,
And thou in military prowess next
Gabriel, lead forth to battle these my sons
Invincible, lead forth my armed saints
By thousands and by millions ranged for fight;
Equal in number to that godless crew
Rebellious, them with fire and hostile arms
Fearless assault, and to the brow of heaven
Pursuing drive them out from God and bliss,
Into their place of punishment, the gulf
Of Tartarus, which ready opens wide
His fiery chaos to receive their fall."
　'So spake the sovereign voice, and clouds began
To darken all the hill, and smoke to roll
In dusky wreaths, reluctant flames, the sign
Of wrath awaked: nor with less dread the loud
Ethereal trumpet from on high gan blow:
At which command the powers militant,
That stood for heaven, in mighty quadrate joined
Of union irresistible, moved on
In silence their bright legions, to the sound
Of instrumental harmony that breathed
Heroic ardor to adventurous deeds
Under their godlike leaders, in the cause
Of God and his Messiah. On they move

Indissolubly firm; nor obvious hill,
Nor straitening vale, nor wood, nor stream divides
Their perfect ranks; for high above the ground
Their march was, and the passive air upbore
Their nimble tread; as when the total kind
Of birds in orderly array on wing
Came summoned over Eden to receive
Their names of thee; so over many a tract
Of heaven they marched, and many a province wide
Tenfold the length of this terrene: at last
Far in the horizon to the north appeared
From skirt to skirt a fiery region, stretched
In battailous aspect, and nearer view
Bristled with upright beams innumerable
Of rigid spears, and helmets thronged, and shields
Various, with boastful argument portrayed,
The banded powers of Satan hasting on
With furious expedition; for they weened
That selfsame day by fight, or by surprise
To win the mount of God, and on his throne
To set the envier of his state, the proud
Aspirer, but their thoughts proved fond and vain
In the midway: though strange to us it seemed
At first, that angel should with angel war,
And in fierce hosting meet, who wont to meet
So oft in festivals of joy and love
Unanimous, as sons of one great sire
Hymning the eternal father: but the shout
Of battle now began, and rushing sound
Of onset ended soon each milder thought.
High in the midst exalted as a god
The apostate in his sun-bright chariot sat
Idol of majesty divine, enclosed
With flaming cherubim, and golden shields;
Then lighted from his gorgeous throne, for now
'Twixt host and host but narrow space was left,
A dreadful interval, and front to front

Presented stood in terrible array
Of hideous length: before the cloudy van.
On the rough edge of battle ere it joined,
Satan with vast and haughty strides advanced,
Came towering, armed in adamant and gold;
Abdiel that sight endured not, where he stood
Among the mightiest, bent on highest deeds,
And thus his own undaunted heart explores.

    ' "O heaven! that such resemblance of the highest
Should yet remain, where faith and realty
Remain not; wherefore should not strength and might
There fail where virtue fails, or weakest prove
Where boldest; though to sight unconquerable?
His puissance, trusting in the almighty's aid,
I mean to try, whose reason I have tried
Unsound and false; nor is it aught but just,
That he who in debate of truth hath won,
Should win in arms, in both disputes alike
Victor; though brutish that contest and foul,
When reason hath to deal with force, yet so
Most reason is that reason overcome."

    'So pondering, and from his armed peers
Forth stepping opposite, half way he met
His daring foe, at this prevention more
Incensed, and thus securely him defied.

    ' "Proud, art thou met? thy hope was to have reached
The height of thy aspiring unopposed,
The throne of God unguarded, and his side
Abandoned at the terror of thy power
Or potent tongue; fool, not to think how vain
Against the omnipotent to rise in arms;
Who out of smallest things could without end
Have raised incessant armies to defeat
Thy folly; or with solitary hand
Reaching beyond all limit, at one blow
Unaided could have finished thee, and whelmed
Thy legions under darkness; but thou seest

All are not of thy train; there be who faith
Prefer, and piety to God, though then
To thee not visible, when I alone
Seemed in thy world erroneous to dissent
From all: my sect thou seest, now learn too late
How few sometimes may know, when thousands err"

   'Whom the grand foe with scornful eye askance
Thus answered. "Ill for thee, but in wished hour
Of my revenge, first sought for thou returnest
From flight, seditious angel, to receive
Thy merited reward, the first assay
Of this right hand provoked, since first that tongue
Inspired with contradiction durst oppose
A third part of the gods, in synod met
Their deities to assert, who while they feel
Vigor divine within them, can allow
Omnipotence to none. But well thou comest
Before thy fellows, ambitious to win
From me some plume, that thy success may show
Destruction to the rest: this pause between
(Unanswered lest thou boast) to let thee know;
At first I thought that liberty and heaven
To heavenly souls had been all one; but now
I see that most through sloth had rather serve,
Ministering spirits, trained up in feast and song;
Such hast thou armed, the minstrelsy of heaven,
Servility with freedom to contend,
As both their deeds compared this day shall prove."

   'To whom in brief thus Abdiel stern replied.
"Apostate, still thou errest, nor end wilt find
Of erring, from the path of truth remote:
Unjustly thou depravest it with the name
Of servitude to serve whom God ordains,
Or nature; God and nature bid the same,
When he who rules is worthiest, and excels
Them whom he governs. This is servitude,
To serve the unwise, or him who hath rebelled

Against his worthier. as thine now serve thee,
Thyself not free, but to thyself enthralled;
Yet lewdly darest our ministering upbraid.
Reign thou in hell thy kingdom, let me serve
In heaven God ever blest, and his divine
Behests obey, worthiest to be obeyed,
Yet chains in hell, not realms expect: meanwhile
From me returned, as erst thou saidst, from flight,
This greeting on thy impious crest receive."
  'So saying, a noble stroke he lifted high,
Which hung not, but so swift with tempest fell
On the proud crest of Satan, that no sight,
Nor motion of swift thought, less could his shield
Such ruin intercept: ten paces huge
He back recoiled; the tenth on bended knee
His massy spear upstayed; as if on earth
Winds under ground or waters forcing way
Sidelong, had pushed a mountain from his seat
Half-sunk with all his pines. Amazement seized
The rebel thrones, but greater rage to see
Thus foiled their mightiest, ours joy filled, and shout
Presage of victory and fierce desire
Of battle: whereat Michael bid sound
The archangel trumpet; through the vast of heaven
It sounded, and the faithful armies rung
Hosanna to the highest: nor stood at gaze
The adverse legions, nor less hideous joined
The horrid shock: now storming fury rose,
And clamor such as heard in heaven till now
Was never, arms on armor clashing brayed
Horrible discord, and the madding wheels
Of brazen chariots raged; dire was the noise
Of conflict; overhead the dismal hiss
Of fiery darts in flaming volleys flew,
And flying vaulted either host with fire.
So under fiery cope together rushed
Both battles main, with ruinous assault

And inextinguishable rage; all heaven
Resounded, and had earth been then, all earth
Had to her center shook. What wonder? when
Millions of fierce encountering angels fought
On either side, the least of whom could wield
These elements, and arm him with the force
Of all their regions: how much more of power
Army against army numberless to raise
Dreadful combustion warring, and disturb,
Though not destroy, their happy native seat;
Had not the eternal king omnipotent
From his stronghold of heaven high overruled
And limited their might; though numbered such
As each divided legion might have seemed
A numerous host, in strength each armed hand
A legion; led in fight, yet leader seemed
Each warrior single as in chief, expert
When to advance, or stand, or turn the sway
Of battle, open when, and when to close
The ridges of grim war; no thought of flight,
None of retreat, no unbecoming deed
That argued fear; each on himself relied,
As only in his arm the moment lay
Of victory; deeds of eternal fame
Were done, but infinite: for wide was spread
That war and various; sometimes on firm ground
A standing fight, then soaring on main wing
Tormented all the air; all air seemed then
Conflicting fire: long time in even scale
The battle hung; till Satan, who that day
Prodigious power had shown, and met in arms
No equal, ranging through the dire attack
Of fighting seraphim confused, at length
Saw where the sword of Michael smote, and felled
Squadrons at once, with huge two-handed sway
Brandished aloft the horrid edge came down
Wide-wasting; such destruction to withstand

He hasted, and opposed the rocky orb
Of tenfold adamant, his ample shield
A vast circumference: At his approach
The great archangel from his warlike toil
Surceased, and glad as hoping here to end
Intestine war in heaven, the arch-foe subdued
Or captive dragged in chains, with hostile frown
And visage all inflamed first thus began.
     ' "Author of evil, unknown till thy revolt,
Unnamed in heaven, now plenteous, as thou seest
These acts of hateful strife, hateful to all,
Though heaviest by just measure on thyself
And thy adherents: how hast thou disturbed
Heaven's blessed peace, and into nature brought
Misery, uncreated till the crime
Of thy rebellion? how hast thou instilled
Thy malice into thousands, once upright
And faithful, now proved false. But think not here
To trouble holy rest; heaven casts thee out
From all her confines. Heaven the seat of bliss
Brooks not the works of violence and war.
Hence then, and evil go with thee along
Thy offspring, to the place of evil, hell,
Thou and thy wicked crew; there mingle broils,
Ere this avenging sword begin thy doom,
Or some more sudden vengeance winged from God
Precipitate thee with augmented pain."
     'So spake the prince of angels; to whom thus
The adversary. "Nor think thou with wind
Of airy threats to awe whom yet with deeds
Thou canst not. Hast thou turned the least of these
To flight, or if to fall, but that they rise
Unvanquished, easier to transact with me
That thou shouldst hope, imperious, and with threat
To chase me hence? err not that so shall end
The strife which thou callest evil, but we style
The strife of glory: which we mean to win.

Or turn this heaven itself into the hell
Thou fablest, here however to dwell free,
If not to reign: meanwhile thy utmost force,
And join him named almighty to thy aid,
I fly not, but have sought thee far and nigh."
    'They ended parle, and both addressed for fight
Unspeakable; for who, though with the tongue
Of angels, can relate, or to what things
Liken on earth conspicuous, that may lift
Human imagination to such height
Of godlike power: for likest gods they seemed,
Stood they or moved, in stature, motion, arms
Fit to decide the empire of great heaven.
Now waved their fiery swords, and in the air
Made horrid circles; two broad suns their shields
Blazed opposite, while expectation stood
In horror; from each hand with speed retired
Where erst was thickest fight, the angelic throng,
And left large field, unsafe within the wind
Of such commotion, such as to set forth
Great things by small; if nature's concord broke,
Among the constellations war were sprung,
Two planets rushing from aspect malign
Of fiercest opposition in mid sky,
Should combat, and their jarring spheres confound.
Together both with next to almighty arm,
Uplifted imminent one stroke they aimed
That might determine, and not need repeat,
As not of power, at once; nor odds appeared
In might or swift prevention; but the sword
Of Michael from the armory of God
Was given him tempered so, that neither keen
Nor solid might resist that edge: it met
The sword of Satan with steep force to smite
Descending, and in half cut sheer, nor stayed,
But with swift wheel reverse, deep entering shared
All his right side; then Satan first knew pain,

And writhed him to and fro convolved; so sore
The griding sword with discontinuous wound
Passed through him, but the ethereal substance closed
Not long divisible, and from the gash
A stream of nectarous humor issuing flowed
Sanguine, such as celestial spirits may bleed,
And all his armor stained erewhile so bright.
Forthwith on all sides to his aid was run
By angels many and strong, who interposed
Defense, while others bore him on their shields
Back to his chariot; where it stood retired
From off the files of war; there they him laid
Gnashing for anguish and despite and shame
To find himself not matchless, and his pride
Humbled by such rebuke, so far beneath
His confidence to equal God in power.
Yet soon he healed; for spirits that live throughout
Vital in every part, not as frail man
In entrails, heart or head, liver or reins;
Cannot but by annihilating die;
Nor in their liquid texture mortal wound
Receive, no more than can the fluid air:
All heart they live, all head, all eye, all ear,
All intellect, all sense, and as they please,
They limb themselves, and color, shape or size
Assume, as likes them best, condense or rare.
    'Meanwhile in other parts like deeds deserved
Memorial, where the might of Gabriel fought,
And with fierce ensigns pierced the deep array
Of Moloch furious king, who him defied,
And at his chariot wheels to drag him bound
Threatened, nor from the holy one of heaven
Refrained his tongue blasphemous; but anon
Down cloven to the waist, with shattered arms
And uncouth pain fled bellowing. On each wing
Uriel and Raphael his vaunting foe,
Though huge, and in a rock of diamond armed,

Vanquished Adramelech, and Asmadai,
Two potent thrones, that to be less than gods
Disdained, but meaner thoughts learned in their flight,
Mangled with ghastly wounds through plate and mail,
Nor stood unmindful Abdiel to annoy
The atheist crew, but with redoubled blow
Ariel and Arioch, and the violence
Of Ramiel scorched and blasted overthrew.
I might relate of thousands, and their names
Eternize here on earth; but those elect
Angels contented with their fame in heaven
Seek not the praise of men: the other sort
In might though wondrous and in acts of war,
Nor of renown less eager, yet by doom
Canceled from heaven and sacred memory,
Nameless in dark oblivion let them dwell.
For strength from truth divided and from just,
Illaudable, nought merits but dispraise
And ignominy, yet to glory aspires
Vainglorious, and through infamy seeks fame:
Therefore eternal silence be their doom.
    'And now their mightiest quelled, the battle swerved,
With many an inroad gored; deformed rout
Entered, and foul disorder; all the ground
With shivered armor strewn, and on a heap
Chariot and charioteer lay overturned
And fiery foaming steeds; what stood, recoiled
O'er-wearied, through the faint Satanic host
Defensive scarce, or with pale fear surprised,
Then first with fear surprised and sense of pain
Fled ignominious, to such evil brought
By sin of disobedience, till that hour
Not liable to fear or flight or pain.
Far otherwise the inviolable saints
In cubic phalanx firm advanced entire,
Invulnerable, impenetrably armed:
Such high advantages their innocence

Gave them above their foes, not to have sinned,
Not to have disobeyed; in fight they stood
Unwearied, unobnoxious to be pained
By wound, though from their place by violence moved.
     'Now night her course began, and over heaven
Inducing darkness, grateful truce imposed,
And silence on the odious din of war:
Under her cloudy covert both retired,
Victor and vanquished: on the foughten field
Michael and his angels prevalent
Encamping, placed in guard their watches round,
Cherubic waving fires: on the other part
Satan with his rebellious disappeared,
Far in the dark dislodged, and void of rest,
His potentates to council called by night;
And in the midst thus undismayed began.
     ' "O now in danger tried, now known in arms
Not to be overpowered, companions dear,
Found worthy not of liberty alone,
Too mean pretense, but what we more affect,
Honor, dominion, glory, and renown,
Who have sustained one day in doubtful fight
(And if one day, why not eternal days?)
What heaven's Lord had powerfullest to send
Against us from about his throne, and judged
Sufficient to subdue us to his will,
But proves not so: then fallible, it seems,
Of future we may deem him, though till now
Omniscient thought. True is, less firmly armed,
Some disadvantage we endured and pain,
Till now not known, but known as soon contemned,
Since now we find this our empyreal form
Incapable of mortal injury
Imperishable, and though pierced with wound,
Soon closing, and by native vigor healed.
Of evil then so small as easy think
The remedy; perhaps more valid arms,

Weapons more violent, when next we meet,
May serve to better us, and worse our foes,
Or equal what between us made the odds,
In nature none; if other hidden cause
Left them superior, while we can preserve
Unhurt our minds, and understanding sound,
Due search and consultation will disclose."
    'He sat; and in the assembly next upstood
Nisroch, of principalities the prime;
As one he stood escaped from cruel fight,
Sore toiled, his riven arms to havoc hewn,
And cloudy in aspect thus answering spake.
"Deliverer from new lords, leader to free
Enjoyment of our right as gods; yet hard
For gods, and too unequal work we find
Against unequal arms to fight in pain,
Against unpained, impassive; from which evil
Ruin must needs ensue; for what avails
Valor or strength, though matchless, quelled with pain
Which all subdues, and makes remiss the hands
Of mightiest. Sense of pleasure we may well
Spare out of life perhaps, and not repine,
But live content, which is the calmest life:
But pain is perfect misery, the worst
Of evils, and excessive, overturns
All patience. He who therefore can invent
With what more forcible we may offend
Our yet unwounded enemies, or arm
Ourselves with like defense, to me deserves
No less than for deliverance what we owe."
    'Whereto with look composed Satan replied.
"Not uninvented that, which thou aright
Believest so main to our success, I bring;
Which of us who beholds the bright surface
Of this ethereous mold whereon we stand,
This continent of spacious heaven, adorned
With plant, fruit, flower ambrosial, gems and gold,

Whose eye so superficially surveys
These things, as not to mind from whence they grow
Deep under ground, materials dark and crude,
Of spiritous and fiery spume, till touched
With heaven's ray, and tempered they shoot forth
So beauteous, opening to the ambient light.
These in their dark nativity the deep
Shall yield us pregnant with infernal flame,
Which into hollow engines long and round
Thick-rammed, at the other bore with touch of fire
Dilated and infuriate shall send forth
From far with thundering noise among our foes
Such implements of mischief as shall dash
To pieces, and o'erwhelm whatever stands
Adverse, that they shall fear we have disarmed
The thunderer of his only dreaded bolt.
Nor long shall be our labor, yet ere dawn,
Effect shall end our wish. Meanwhile revive;
Abandon fear; to strength and counsel joined
Think nothing hard, much less to be despaired."
He ended, and his words their drooping cheer
Enlightened, and their languished hope revived.
The invention all admired, and each, how he
To be the inventor missed, so easy it seemed
Once found, which yet unfound most would have thought
Impossible: yet haply of thy race
In future days, if malice should abound,
Some one intent on mischief, or inspired
With devilish machination might devise
Like instrument to plague the sons of men
For sin, on war and mutual slaughter bent.
Forthwith from council to the work they flew,
None arguing stood, innumerable hands
Were ready, in a moment up they turned
Wide the celestial soil, and saw beneath
The originals of nature in their crude
Conception; sulphurous and nitrous foam

They found, they mingled, and with subtle art,
Concocted and adusted they reduced
To blackest grain, and into store conveyed:
Part hidden veins digged up (nor hath this earth
Entrails unlike) of mineral and stone,
Whereof to found their engines and their balls
Of missive ruin; part incentive reed
Provide, pernicious with one touch to fire.
So all ere day spring, under conscious night
Secret they finished, and in order set,
With silent circumspection unespied.
Now when fair morn orient in heaven appeared
Up rose the victor angels, and to arms
The matin trumpet sung: in arms they stood
Of golden panoply, refulgent host,
Soon banded; others from the dawning hills
Looked round, and scouts each coast light armed scour
Each quarter, to descry the distant foe,
Where lodged, or whither fled, or if for fight,
In motion or in halt: him soon they met
Under spread ensigns moving nigh, in slow
But firm battalion; back with speediest sail
Zophiel, of cherubim the swiftest wing,
Came flying, and in mid air aloud thus cried.
  ' "Arm, warriors, arm for fight, the foe at hand,
Whom fled we thought, will save us long pursuit
This day, fear not his flight; so thick a cloud
He comes, and settled in his face I see
Sad resolution and secure: let each
His adamantine coat gird well, and each
Fit well his helm, grip fast his orbed shield,
Borne even or high, for this day will pour down
If I conjecture aught, no drizzling shower,
But rattling storm of arrows barbed with fire."
So warned he them aware themselves, and soon
In order, quit of all impediment;
Instant without disturb they took alarm.

And onward move embattled; when behold
Not distant far with heavy pace the foe
Approaching gross and huge; in hollow cube
Training his devilish enginry, impaled
On every side with shadowing squadrons deep,
To hide the fraud. At interview both stood
A while, but suddenly at head appeared
Satan: And thus was heard commanding loud.
  ' "Vanguard, to right and left the front unfold;
That all may see who hate us, how we seek
Peace and composure, and with open breast
Stand ready to receive them, if they like
Our overture, and turn not back perverse;
But that I doubt, however witness heaven,
Heaven witness thou anon, while we discharge
Freely our part; ye who appointed stand
Do as you have in charge, and briefly touch
What we propound, and loud that all may hear."
  'So scoffing in ambiguous words he scarce
Had ended; when to right and left the front
Divided, and to either flank retired.
Which to our eyes discovered new and strange,
A triple mounted row of pillars laid
On wheels (for like to pillars most they seemed
Or hollowed bodies make of oak or fir
With branches lopped, in wood or mountain felled)
Brass, iron, stony mold, had not their mouths
With hideous orifice gaped on us wide,
Portending hollow truce; at each behind
A seraph stood, and in his hand a reed
Stood waving tipped with fire; while we suspense,
Collected stood within our thoughts amused,
Not long, for sudden all at once their reeds
Put forth, and to a narrow vent applied
With nicest touch. Immediate in a flame,
But soon obscured with smoke, all heaven appeared,
From those deep throated engines belched, whose roar

Emboweled with outrageous noise the air,
And all her entrails tore, disgorging foul
Their devilish glut, chained thunderbolts and hail
Of iron globes, which on the victor host
Leveled, with such impetuous fury smote,
That whom they hit, none on the feet might stand,
Though standing else as rocks, but down they fell
By thousands, angel on archangel rolled;
The sooner for their arms, unarmed they might
Have easily as spirits evaded swift
By quick contraction or remove; but now
Foul dissipation followed and forced rout;
Nor served it to relax their serried files.
What should they do? if on they rushed, repulse
Repeated, and indecent overthrow
Doubled, would render them yet more despised,
And to their foes a laughter; for in view
Stood ranked of seraphim another row
In posture to displode their second tier
Of thunder: back defeated to return
They worse abhorred. Satan beheld their plight,
And to his mates thus in derision called.
    ' "O friends, why come not on these victors proud?
Erewhile they fierce were coming, and when we,
To entertain them fair with open front
And breast, (what could we more?) propounded terms
Of composition, straight they changed their minds,
Flew off, and into strange vagaries fell,
As they would dance, yet for a dance they seemed
Somewhat extravagant and wild, perhaps
For joy of offered peace: but I suppose
If our proposals once again were heard
We should compel them to a quick result."
    'To whom thus Belial in like gamesome mood,
"Leader, the terms we sent were terms of weight,
Of hard contents, and full of force urged home,
Such as we might perceive amused them all.

And stumbled many, who receives them right,
Had need from head to foot well understand;
Not understood, this gift they have besides,
They show us when our foes walk not upright."
    So they among themselves in pleasant vein
Stood scoffing, heightened in their thoughts beyond
All doubt of victory, eternal might
To match with their inventions they presumed
So easy, and of his thunder made a scorn,
And all his host derided, while they stood
A while in trouble; but they stood not long,
Rage prompted them at length, and found them arms
Against such hellish mischief fit to oppose.
Forthwith (behold the excellence, the power
Which God hath in his mighty angels placed)
Their arms away they threw, and to the hills
(For earth hath this variety from heaven
Of pleasure situate in hill and dale)
Light as the lightning glimpse they ran, they flew,
From their foundations loosening to and fro
They plucked the seated hills with all their load,
Rocks, waters, woods, and by the shaggy tops
Uplifting bore them in their hands: Amaze,
Be sure, and terror seized the rebel host,
When coming towards them so dread they saw
The bottom of the mountains upward turned,
Till on those cursed engines' triple row
They saw them whelmed, and all their confidence
Under the weight of mountains buried deep,
Themselves invaded next, and on their heads
Main promontories flung, which in the air
Came shadowing, and oppressed whole legions armed,
Their armor helped their harm, crushed in and bruised
Into their substance pent, which wrought them pain
Implacable, and many a dolorous groan,
Long struggling underneath, ere they could wind
Out of such prison, though spirits of purest light.

Purest at first, now gross by sinning grown.
The rest in imitation to like arms
Betook them, and the neighboring hills uptore;
So hills amid the air encountered hills
Hurled to and fro with jaculation dire,
That underground they fought in dismal shade;
Infernal noise; war seemed a civil game
To this uproar; horrid confusion heaped
Upon confusion rose: and now all heaven
Had gone to wrack, with ruin overspread,
Had not the almighty father where he sits
Shrined in his sanctuary of heaven secure,
Consulting on the sum of things, foreseen
This tumult, and permitted all, advised:
That his great purpose he might so fulfill,
To honor his anointed Son avenged
Upon his enemies. and to declare
All power on him transferred: whence to his Son
The assessor of his throne he thus began.
      ' "Effulgence of my glory, Son beloved,
Son in whose face invisible is beheld
Visibly, what by deity I am,
And in whose hand what by decree I do,
Second omnipotence, two days are past,
Two days, as we compute the days of heaven,
Since Michael and his powers went forth to tame
These disobedient; sore hath been their fight,
As likeliest was, when two such foes met armed;
For to themselves I left them, and thou knowest,
Equal in their creation they were formed,
Save what sin hath impaired, which yet hath wrought
Insensibly, for I suspend their doom;
Whence in perpetual fight they needs must last
Endless, and no solution will be found:
War wearied hath performed what war can do,
And to disordered rage let loose the reins,
With mountains as with weapons armed, which makes

Wild work in heaven, and dangerous to the main.
Two days are therefore passed, the third is thine;
For thee I have ordained it, and thus far
Have suffered, that the glory may be thine
Of ending this great war, since none but thou
Can end it. Into thee such virtue and grace
Immense I have transfused, that all may know
In heaven and hell thy power above compare,
And this perverse commotion governed thus,
To manifest thee worthiest to be heir
Of all things, to be heir and to be king
By sacred unction, thy deserved right.
Go then thou mightiest in thy father's might,
Ascend my chariot, guide the rapid wheels
That shake heaven's basis, bring forth all my war,
My bow and thunder, my almighty arms
Gird on, and sword upon thy puissant thigh;
Pursue these sons of darkness, drive them out
From all heaven's bounds into the utter deep:
There let them learn, as likes them, to despise
God and Messiah his anointed king."

'He said, and on his Son with rays direct
Shone full, he all his father full expressed
Ineffably into his face received,
And thus the filial Godhead answering spake.

" 'O father, O supreme of heavenly thrones,
First, highest, holiest, best, thou always seekest
To glorify thy son, I always thee,
As is most just; this I my glory account,
My exaltation, and my whole delight,
That thou in me well pleased, declarest thy will
Fulfilled, which to fulfill is all my bliss.
Scepter and power, thy giving, I assume,
And gladlier shall resign, when in the end
Thou shalt be all in all, and I in thee
Forever, and in me all whom thou lovest:
But whom thou hatest, I hate, and can put on

Thy terrors, as I put thy mildness on,
Image of thee in all things: and shall soon,
Armed with thy might, rid heaven of these rebelled,
To their prepared ill mansion driven down
To chains of darkness, and the undying worm,
That from thy just obedience could revolt,
Whom to obey is happiness entire.
Then shall thy saints unmixed, and from the impure
Far separate, circling thy holy mount
Unfeigned hallelujahs to thee sing,
Hymns of high praise, and I among them chief."
So said, he o'er his scepter bowing, rose
From the right hand of glory where he sat,
And the third sacred morn began to shine
Dawning through heaven: forth rushed with whirlwind soun'
The chariot of paternal deity,
Flashing thick flames, wheel within wheel undrawn,
Itself instinct with spirit, but convoyed
By four cherubic shapes, four faces each
Had wondrous, as with stars their bodies all
And wings were set with eyes, with eyes the wheels
Of beryl, and careering fires between;
Over their heads a crystal firmament,
Whereon a sapphire throne, inlaid with pure
Amber, and colors of the showery arch.
He in celestial panoply all armed
Of radiant urim, work divinely wrought,
Ascended, at his right hand victory
Sat eagle-winged, beside him hung his bow
And quiver with three-bolted thunder stored,
And from about him fierce effusion rolled
Of smoke and bickering flame, and sparkles dire;
Attended with ten thousand thousand saints,
He onward came, far off his coming shone,
And twenty thousand (I their number heard)
Chariots of God, half on each hand were seen:
He on the wings of cherub rode sublime

On the crystalline sky, in sapphire throned.
Illustrious far and wide, but by his own
First seen, them unexpected joy surprised,
When the great ensign of Messiah blazed
Aloft by angels borne, his sign in heaven:
Under whose conduct Michael soon reduced
His army, circumfused on either wing,
Under their head embodied all in one.
Before him power divine his way prepared;
At his command the uprooted hills retired
Each to his place, they heard his voice and went
Obsequious, heaven his wonted face renewed,
And with fresh flowers hill and valley smiled.
This saw his hapless foes but stood obdured,
And to rebellious fight rallied their powers
Insensate, hope conceiving from despair.
In heavenly spirits could such perverseness dwell?
But to convince the proud what signs avail,
Or wonders move the obdurate to relent?
They hardened more by what might most reclaim,
Grieving to see his glory, at the sight
Took envy, and aspiring to his height,
Stood re-embattled fierce, by force or fraud
Weening to prosper, and at length prevail
Against God and Messiah, or to fall
In universal ruin last, and now
To final battle drew, disdaining flight,
Or faint retreat; when the great Son of God
To all his host on either hand thus spake.
    " 'Stand still in bright array ye saints, here stand
Ye angels armed, this day from battle rest;
Faithful hath been your warfare, and of God
Accepted, fearless in his righteous cause,
And as ye have received, so have ye done
Invincibly; but of this cursed crew
The punishment to other hand belongs,
Vengeance is his, or whose he sole appoints;

Number to this day's work is not ordained
Nor multitude, stand only and behold
God's indignation on these godless poured
By me, not you but me they have despised,
Yet envied; against me is all their rage,
Because the father, to whom in heaven's supreme
Kingdom and power and glory appertains,
Hath honored me according to his will.
Therefore to me their doom he hath assigned;
That they may have their wish, to try with me
In battle which the stronger proves, they all,
Or I alone against them, since by strength
They measure all, of other excellence
Not emulous, nor care who them excels;
Nor other strife with them do I vouchsafe."
    'So spake the Son, and into terror changed
His countenance too severe to be beheld
And full of wrath bent on his enemies.
At once the four spread out their starry wings
With dreadful shade contiguous, and the orbs
Of his fierce chariot rolled, as with the sound
Of torrent floods, or of a numerous host.
He on his impious foes right onward drove,
Gloomy as night; under his burning wheels
The steadfast empyrean shook throughout,
All but the throne itself of God. Full soon
Among them he arrived; in his right hand
Grasping ten thousand thunders, which he sent
Before him, such as in their souls infixed
Plagues; they astonished all resistance lost,
All courage; down their idle weapons dropped;
O'er shields and helms, and helmed heads he rode
Of thrones and mighty seraphim prostrate,
That wished the mountains now might be again
Thrown on them as a shelter from his ire.
Nor less on either side tempestuous fell
His arrows, from the fourfold visaged four,

Distinct with eyes, and from the living wheels
Distinct alike with multitude of eyes,
One spirit in them ruled, and every eye
Glared lightning, and shot forth pernicious fire
Among the accursed, that withered all their strength,
And of their wonted vigor left them drained,
Exhausted, spiritless, afflicted, fallen.
Yet half his strength he put not forth, but checked
His thunder in mid-volley, for he meant
Not to destroy, but root them out of heaven:
The overthrown he raised, and as a herd
Of goats or timorous flock together thronged
Drove them before him thunderstruck, pursued
With terrors and with furies to the bounds
And crystal wall of heaven, which opening wide,
Rolled inward, and a spacious gap disclosed
Into the wasteful deep; the monstrous sight
Struck them with horror backward, but far worse
Urged them behind; headlong themselves they threw
Down from the verge of heaven, eternal wrath
Burnt after them to the bottomless pit.
    'Hell heard the unsufferable noise, hell saw
Heaven ruining from heaven and would have fled
Affrighted; but strict fate had cast too deep
Her dark foundations, and too fast had bound.
Nine days they fell; confounded chaos roared,
And felt tenfold confusion in their fall
Through his wild anarchy, so huge a rout
Encumbered him with ruin: Hell at last
Yawning received them whole, and on them closed,
Hell their fit habitation fraught with fire
Unquenchable, the house of woe and pain.
Disburdened heaven rejoiced, and soon repaired
Her mural breach, returning whence it rolled.
Sole victor from the expulsion of his foes
Messiah his triumphal chariot turned:
To meet him all his saints, who silent stood

Eye witnesses of his almighty acts,
With jubilee advanced; and as they went,
Shaded with branching palm, each order bright,
Sung triumph, and him sung victorious king,
Son, heir, and lord, to him dominion given,
Worthiest to reign: he celebrated rode
Triumphant through mid heaven, into the courts
And temple of his mighty father throned
On high: who into glory him received,
Where now he sits at the right hand of bliss.
  'Thus measuring things in heaven by things on earth
At thy request, and that thou mayest beware
By what is past, to thee I have revealed
What might have else to human race been hid;
The discord which befell, and war in heaven
Among the angelic powers, and the deep fall
Of those too high aspiring, who rebelled
With Satan, he who envies now thy state,
Who now is plotting how he may seduce
Thee also from obedience, that with him
Bereaved of happiness thou mayest partake
His punishment, eternal misery;
Which would be all his solace and revenge,
As a despite done against the most high,
Thee once to gain companion of his woe.
But listen not to his temptations, warn
Thy weaker; let it profit thee to have heard
By terrible example the reward
Of disobedience; firm they might have stood,
Yet fell; remember, and fear to transgress.'

BOOK VII

The Argument: Raphael at the request of Adam relates how and
wherefore this world was first created; that God, after the expel-
ling of Satan and his angels out of heaven, declared his pleasure to

create another world and other creatures to dwell therein; sends
his Son with glory and attendance of angels to perform the work of
creation in six days: the angels celebrate with hymns the performance thereof, and his reascension into heaven.

Descend from heaven Urania, by that name
If rightly thou art called, whose voice divine
Following, above the Olympian hill I soar,
Above the flight of Pegasean wing.
The meaning, not the name I call: for thou
Nor of the muses nine, nor on the top
Of old Olympus dwellest, but heavenly born,
Before the hills appeared, or fountain flowed,
Thou with eternal wisdom didst converse,
Wisdom thy sister, and with her didst play
In presence of the almighty father, pleased
With thy celestial song. Upled by thee
Into the heaven of heavens I have presumed,
An earthly guest, and drawn empyreal air,
Thy tempering; with like safety guided down
Return me to my native element:
Lest from this flying steed unreined, (as once
Bellerophon, though from a lower clime)
Dismounted, on the Aleian field I fall
Erroneous there to wander and forlorn.
Half yet remains unsung, but narrower bound
Within the visible diurnal sphere;
Standing on earth, not rapt above the pole,
More safe I sing with mortal voice, unchanged
To hoarse or mute, though fallen on evil days,
On evil days though fallen, and evil tongues;
In darkness, and with dangers compassed round,
And solitude; yet not alone, while thou
Visitest my slumbers nightly, or when morn
Purples the east: still govern thou my song,
Urania, and fit audience find, though few.

But drive far off the barbarous dissonance
Of Bacchus and his revelers, the race
Of that wild rout that tore the Thracian bard
In Rhodope, where woods and rocks had ears
To rapture, till the savage clamor drowned
Both harp and voice; nor could the muse defend
Her son. So fail not thou, who thee implores:
For thou art heavenly, she an empty dream.
    Say Goddess, what ensued when Raphael,
The affable archangel, had forewarned
Adam by dire example to beware
Apostasy, by what befell in heaven
To those apostates, lest the like befall
In Paradise to Adam or his race,
Charged not to touch the interdicted tree,
If they transgress, and slight that sole command,
So easily obeyed amid the choice
Of all tastes else to please their appetite,
Though wandering. He with his consorted Eve
The story heard attentive, and was filled
With admiration, and deep muse to hear
Of things so high and strange, things to their thought
So unimaginable as hate in heaven,
And war so near the peace of God in bliss
With such confusion: but the evil soon
Driven back redounded as a flood on those
From whom it sprung, impossible to mix
With blessedness. Whence Adam soon repealed
The doubts that in his heart arose: and now
Led on, yet sinless, with desire to know
What nearer might concern him, how this world
Of heaven and earth conspicuous first began,
When, and whereof created, for what cause,
What within Eden or without was done
Before his memory, as one whose drouth
Yet scarce allayed still eyes the current stream.

Whose liquid murmur heard new thirst excites,
Proceeded thus to ask his heavenly guest.
    'Great things, and full of wonder in our ears,
Far differing from this world, thou hast revealed
Divine interpreter, by favor sent
Down from the empyrean to forewarn
Us timely of what might else have been our loss,
Unknown, which human knowledge could not reach:
For which to the infinitely good we owe
Immortal thanks, and his admonishment
Receive with solemn purpose to observe
Immutably his sovereign will, the end
Of what we are. But since thou hast vouchsafed
Gently for our instruction to impart
Things above earthly thought, which yet concerned
Our knowing, as to highest wisdom seemed,
Deign to descend now lower, and relate
What may no less perhaps avail us known,
How first began this heaven which we behold
Distant so high, with moving fires adorned
Innumerable, and this which yields or fills
All space, the ambient air wide interfused
Embracing round this florid earth, what cause
Moved the creator in his holy rest
Through all eternity so late to build
In chaos, and the work begun, how soon
Absolved, if unforbid thou mayest unfold
What we, not to explore the secrets ask
Of his eternal empire, but the more
To magnify his works, the more we know.
And the great light of day yet wants to run
Much of his race though steep, suspense in heaven
Held by thy voice, thy potent voice he hears,
And longer will delay to hear thee tell
His generation, and the rising birth
Of nature from the unapparent deep:
Or if the star of evening and the moon

Haste to thy audience, night with her will bring
Silence, and sleep listening to thee will watch,
Or we can bid his absence, till thy song
End, and dismiss thee ere the morning shine.'
    Thus Adam his illustrious guest besought:
And thus the godlike angel answered mild.
    'This also thy request with caution asked
Obtain: though to recount almighty works
What words or tongue of seraph can suffice,
Or heart of man suffice to comprehend?
Yet what thou canst attain, which best may serve
To glorify the maker, and infer
Thee also happier, shall not be withheld
Thy hearing, such commission from above
I have received, to answer thy desire
Of knowledge within bounds; beyond abstain
To ask, nor let thine own inventions hope
Things not revealed, which the invisible king,
Only omniscient, hath suppressed in night,
To none communicable in earth or heaven:
Enough is left besides to search and know.
But knowledge is as food, and needs no less
Her temperance over appetite, to know
In measure what the mind may well contain,
Oppresses else with surfeit, and soon turns
Wisdom to folly, as nourishment to wind.
    'Know then, that after Lucifer from heaven
(So call him, brighter once amidst the host
Of angels, than that star the stars among)
Fell with his flaming legions through the deep
Into his place, and the great Son returned
Victorious with his saints, the omnipotent
Eternal father from his throne beheld
Their multitude, and to his Son thus spake.
    ' "At least our envious foe hath failed, who thought
All like himself rebellious, by whose aid
This inaccessible high strength, the seat

Of deity supreme, us dispossessed,
He trusted to have seized, and into fraud
Drew many, whom their place knows here no more;
Yet far the greater part have kept, I see,
Their station, heaven yet populous retains
Number sufficient to possess her realms
Though wide, and this high temple to frequent
With ministeries due and solemn rites:
But lest his heart exalt him in the harm
Already done, to have dispeopled heaven,
My damage fondly deemed, I can repair
That detriment, if such it be to lose
Self-lost, and in a moment will create
Another world, out of one man a race
Of men innumerable, there to dwell,
Not here, till by degrees of merit raised
They open to themselves at length the way
Up hither, under long obedience tried,
And earth be changed to heaven, and heaven to earth
One kingdom, joy and union without end.
Meanwhile inhabit lax, ye powers of heaven,
And thou my word, begotten Son, by thee
This I perform, speak thou, and be it done:
My overshadowing spirit and might with thee
I send along, ride forth, and bid the deep
Within appointed bounds be heaven and earth,
Boundless the deep, because I am who fill
Infinitude, nor vacuous the space.
Though I uncircumscribed myself retire,
And put not forth my goodness, which is free
To act or not, necessity and chance
Approach not me, and what I will is fate."
  'So spake the almighty, and to what he spake
His word, the filial Godhead, gave effect.
Immediate are the acts of God, more swift
Than time or motion, but to human ears
Cannot without process of speech be told,

So told as earthly notion can receive.
Great triumph and rejoicing was in heaven
When such was heard declared the almighty's will;
Glory they sung to the most high, good will
To future men, and in their dwellings peace:
Glory to him whose just avenging ire
Had driven out the ungodly from his sight
And the habitations of the just; to him
Glory and praise, whose wisdom had ordained
Good out of evil to create, instead
Of spirits malign a better race to bring
Into their vacant room, and thence diffuse
His good to worlds and ages infinite.
So sang the hierarchies: Meanwhile the Son
On his great expedition now appeared,
Girt with omnipotence, with radiance crowned
Of majesty divine, sapience and love
Immense, and all his father in him shone.
About his chariot numberless were poured
Cherub and seraph, potentates and thrones,
And virtues, winged spirits, and chariots winged,
From the armory of God, where stand of old
Myriads between two brazen mountains lodged
Against a solemn day, harnessed at hand,
Celestial equipage; and now came forth
Spontaneous, for within them spirit lived,
Attendant on their Lord: Heaven opened wide
Her ever during gates, harmonious sound
On golden hinges moving, to let forth
The king of glory in his powerful word
And spirit coming to create new worlds.
On heavenly ground they stood, and from the shore
They viewed the vast immeasurable abyss
Outrageous as a sea, dark, wasteful, wild,
Up from the bottom turned by furious winds
And surging waves, as mountains to assault
Heaven's height, and with the center mix the pole.

' "Silence, ye troubled waves, and thou deep, **peace**,"
Said then the omnific word, "your discord end:"
   'Nor stayed, but on the wings of cherubim
Uplifted, in paternal glory rode
Far into chaos, and the world unborn;
For chaos heard his voice: him all his train
Followed in bright procession to behold
Creation, and the wonders of his might.
Then stayed the fervid wheels, and in his hand
He took the golden compasses, prepared
In God's eternal store, to circumscribe
This universe, and all created things:
One foot he centered, and the other turned
Round through the vast profundity obscure,
And said, "thus far extend, thus far thy bounds,
This be thy just circumference, O world."
Thus God the heaven created, thus the earth,
Matter unformed and void: Darkness profound
Covered the abyss: but on the watery calm
His brooding wings the spirit of God outspread,
And vital virtue infused, and vital warmth
Throughout the fluid mass, but downward **purged**
The black tartareous cold infernal dregs
Adverse to life; then founded, then conglobed
Like things to like, the rest to several place
Disparted, and between spun out the air,
And earth self balanced on her center hung.
   ' "Let there be light," said God, and forthwith **light**
Ethereal, first of things, quintessence pure
Sprung from the deep, and from her native east
To journey through the airy gloom began,
Sphered in a radiant cloud, for yet the sun
Was not; she in a cloudy tabernacle
Sojourned the while. God saw the light was good;
And light from darkness by the hemisphere
Divided: light the day, and darkness night
He named. Thus was the first day even and morn:

Nor passed uncelebrated, nor unsung
By the celestial choirs, when orient light
Exhaling first from darkness they beheld:
Birthday of heaven and earth; with joy and shout
The hollow universal orb they filled,
And touched their golden harps, and hymning praised
God and his works, creator him they sung,
Both when first evening was, and when first morn.
  'Again, God said, "let there be firmament
Amid the waters, and let it divide
The waters from the waters:" and God made
The firmament, expanse of liquid, pure,
Transparent, elemental air, diffused
In circuit to the uttermost convex
Of this great round: partition firm and sure,
The waters underneath from those above
Dividing: for as earth, so he the world
Built on circumfluous waters calm, in wide
Crystalline ocean, and the loud misrule
Of chaos far removed, lest fierce extremes
Contiguous might distemper the whole frame:
And heaven he named the firmament: So even
And morning chorus sung the second day.
  'The earth was formed, but in the womb as yet
Of waters, embryon immature involved,
Appeared not: over all the face of earth
Main ocean flowed, not idle, but with warm
Prolific humor softening all her globe,
Fermented the great mother to conceive,
Satiate with genial moisture, when God said
"Be gathered now ye waters under heaven
Into one place, and let dry land appear."
Immediately the mountains huge appear
Emergent, and their broad bare backs upheave
Into the clouds, their tops ascend the sky:
So high as heaved the tumid hills, so low
Down sunk a hollow bottom broad and deep,

Capacious bed of waters: thither they
Hasted with glad precipitance, uprolled
As drops on dust conglobing from the dry;
Part rise in crystal wall, or ridge direct,
For haste; such flight the great command impressed
On the swift floods: as armies at the call
Of trumpet (for of armies thou hast heard)
Troop to their standard, so the watery throng,
Wave rolling after wave, where way they found.
If steep, with torrent rapture, if through plain,
Soft-ebbing; nor withstood them rock or hill,
But they, or underground, or circuit wide
With serpent error wandering, found their way,
And on the washy ooze deep channels wore;
Easy, ere God had bid the ground be dry,
All but within those banks, where rivers now
Stream, and perpetual draw their humid train.
The dry land, earth, and the great receptacle
Of congregated waters he called seas:
And saw that it was good, and said, "Let the earth
Put forth the verdant grass, herb yielding seed,
And fruit tree yielding fruit after her kind;
Whose seed is in herself upon the earth."
He scarce had said, when the bare earth, till then
Desert and bare, unsightly, unadorned,
Brought forth the tender grass, whose verdure clad
Her universal face with pleasant green,
Then herbs of every leaf, that sudden flowered
Opening their various colors, and made gay
Her bosom smelling sweet: and these scarce blown,
Forth flourished thick the clustering vine, forth crept
The smelling gourd, up stood the corny reed
Embattled in her field: and the humble shrub,
And bush with frizzled hair implicit: last
Rose as in dance the stately trees, and spread
Their branches hung with copious fruit; or gemmed
Their blossoms: with high woods the hills were crowned.

With tufts the valleys and each fountainside,
With borders long the rivers. That earth now
Seemed like to heaven, a seat where gods might dwell,
Or wander with delight, and love to haunt
Her sacred shades: though God had yet not rained
Upon the earth, and man to till the ground
None was, but from the earth a dewy mist
Went up and watered all the ground, and each
Plant of the field, which ere it was in the earth
God made, and every herb, before it grew
On the green stem; God saw that it was good:
So even and morn recorded the third day.
'Again the almighty spake: "Let there be lights
High in the expanse of heaven to divide
The day from night; and let them be for signs,
For seasons, and for days, and circling years,
And let them be for lights as I ordain
Their office in the firmament of heaven
To give light on the earth;" and it was so.
And God made two great lights, great for their use
To man, the greater to have rule by day,
The less by night altern: and made the stars,
And set them in the firmament of heaven
To illuminate the earth, and rule the day
In their vicissitude, and rule the night,
And light from darkness to divide. God saw,
Surveying his great work, that it was good:
For of celestial bodies first the sun
A mighty sphere he framed, unlightsome first,
Though of ethereal mold: then formed the moon
Globose, and every magnitude of stars,
And sowed with stars the heaven thick as a field:
Of light by far the greater part he took,
Transplanted from her cloudy shrine, and placed
In the sun's orb, made porous to receive
And drink the liquid light, firm to retain
Her gathered beams, great palace now of light.

Hither as to their fountain other stars
Repairing, in their golden urns draw light,
And hence the morning planet gilds her horns;
By tincture or reflection they augment
Their small peculiar, though from human sight
So far remote, with diminution seen.
First in his east the glorious lamp was seen,
Regent of day, and all the horizon round
Invested with bright rays, jocund to run
His longitude through heaven's high road: the gray
Dawn, and the Pleiades before him danced
Shedding sweet influence: less bright the moon,
But opposite in leveled west was set
His mirror with full face borrowing her light
From him, for other light she needed none
In that aspect, and still that distance keeps
Till night, then in the east her turn she shines,
Revolved on heaven's great axle, and her reign
With thousand lesser lights dividual holds,
With thousand thousand stars, that then appeared
Spangling the hemisphere: then first adorned
With her bright luminaries that set and rose,
Glad evening and glad morn crowned the fourth day.
   'And God said, "let the waters generate
Reptile with spawn abundant, living soul:
And let fowl fly above the earth, with wings
Displayed on the open firmament of heaven."
And God created the great whales, and each
Soul living, each that crept, which plenteously
The waters generated by their kinds,
And every bird of wing after his kind;
And saw that it was good, and blessed them, saying,
"Be fruitful, multiply, and in the seas
And lakes and running streams the waters fill;
And let the fowl be multiplied on the earth."
Forthwith the sounds and seas, each creek and bay
With fry innumerable swarm, and shoals

Of fish that with their fins and shining scales
Glide under the green wave, in sculls that oft
Bank the midsea: part single or with mate
Graze the seaweed their pasture, and through groves
Of coral stray, or sporting with quick glance
Show to the sun their waved coats dropped with gold,
Or in their pearly shells at ease, attend
Moist nutriment, or under rocks their food
In jointed armor watch: on smooth the seal,
And bended dolphins play: part huge of bulk
Wallowing unwieldly, enormous in their gait
Tempest the ocean: there leviathan
Hugest of living creatures, on the deep
Stretched like a promontory sleeps or swims,
And seems a moving land, and at his gills
Draws in, and at his trunk spouts out a sea.
Meanwhile the tepid caves, and fens and shores
Their brood as numerous hatch, from the egg that soon
Bursting with kindly rupture forth disclosed
Their callow young, but feathered soon and fledge
They summed their pens, and soaring the air sublime
With clang despised the ground, under a cloud
In prospect; there the eagle and the stork
On cliffs and cedar tops their aeries build:
Part loosely wing the region, part more wise
In common, ranged in figure wedge their way,
Intelligent of seasons, and set forth
Their airy caravan high over seas
Flying, and over lands with mutual wing
Easing their flight; so steers the prudent crane
Her annual voyage, borne on winds; the air
Floats, as they pass, fanned with unnumbered plumes:
From branch to branch the smaller birds with song
Solaced the woods, and spread their painted wings
Till even, nor then the solemn nightingale
Ceased warbling, but all night tuned her soft lays:
Others on silver lakes and rivers bathed

Their downy breast; the swan with arched neck
Between her white wings mantling proudly, rows
Her state with oary feet: yet oft they quit
The dank, and rising on stiff pennons, tower
The mid aerial sky: Others on ground
Walked firm; the crested cock whose clarion sounds
The silent hours, and the other whose gay train
Adorns him, colored with the florid hue
Of rainbows and starry eyes. The waters thus
With fish replenished, and the air with fowl,
Evening and morn solemnized the fifth day.
    The sixth, and of creation last arose
With evening harps and matin, when God said,
"Let the earth bring forth soul living in her kind,
Cattle and creeping things, and beast of the earth,
Each in their kind." The earth obeyed, and straight
Opening her fertile womb teemed at a birth
Innumerous living creatures, perfect forms,
Limbed and full-grown: out of the ground uprose
As from his lair the wild beast where he wons
In forest wild, in thicket, brake, or den;
Among the trees in pairs they rose, they walked:
The cattle in the fields and meadows green:
Those rare and solitary, these in flocks
Pasturing at once, and in broad herds upsprung.
The grassy clods now calved, now half appeared
The tawny lion, pawing to get free
His hinder parts, then springs as broke from bonds,
And rampant shakes his brinded mane; the ounce,
The libbard, and the tiger, as the mole
Rising, the crumbled earth above them threw
In hillocks; the swift stag from underground
Bore up his branching head: scarce from his mold
Behemoth biggest born of earth upheaved
His vastness: Fleeced the flocks and bleating rose,
As plants: ambiguous between sea and land
The river horse and scaly crocodile.

At once came forth whatever creeps the ground,
Insect or worm; those waved their limber fans
For wings, and smallest lineaments exact
In all the liveries decked of summer's pride
With spots of gold and purple, azure and green:
These as a line their long dimension drew,
Streaking the ground with sinuous trace; not all
Minims of nature; some of serpent kind
Wondrous in length and corpulence involved
Their snaky folds, and added wings. First crept
The parsimonious emmet, provident
Of future, in small room large heart enclosed,
Pattern of just equality perhaps
Hereafter, joined in her popular tribes
Of commonalty: swarming next appeared
The female bee that feeds her husband drone
Deliciously, and builds her waxen cells
With honey stored: the rest are numberless,
And thou their natures knowest, and gavest them names,
Needless to thee repeated; nor unknown
The serpent subtlest beast of all the field,
Of huge extent sometimes, with brazen eyes
And hairy mane terrific, though to thee
Not noxious, but obedient at thy call.
Now heaven in all her glory shone, and rolled
Her motions, as the great first mover's hand
First wheeled their course; earth in her rich attire
Consummate lovely smiled; air, water, earth,
By fowl, fish, beast, was flown, was swum, was walked
Frequent; and of the sixth day yet remained;
There wanted yet the master work, the end
Of all yet done; a creature who not prone
And brute as other creatures, but endued
With sanctity of reason, might erect
His stature, and upright with front serene
Govern the rest, self-knowing, and from thence
Magnanimous to correspond with heaven,

But grateful to acknowledge whence his good
Descends, thither with heart and voice and eyes
Directed in devotion, to adore
And worship God supreme, who made him chief
Of all his works: therefore the omnipotent
Eternal father (for where is not he
Present) thus to his Son audibly spake.
 ' "Let us make now man in our image, man
In our similitude, and let them rule
Over the fish and fowl of sea and air,
Beast of the field, and over all the earth,
And every creeping thing that creeps the ground."
This said, he formed thee, Adam, thee O man
Dust of the ground, and in thy nostrils breathed
The breath of life; in his own image he
Created thee, in the image of God
Express, and thou becamest a living soul.
Male he created thee, but thy consort
Female for race; then blessed mankind, and said,
"Be fruitful, multiply, and fill the earth,
Subdue it, and throughout dominion hold
Over fish of the sea, and fowl of the air,
And every living thing that moves on the earth."
Wherever thus created, for no place
Is yet distinct by name, thence, as thou knowest
He brought thee into this delicious grove,
This garden, planted with the trees of God,
Delectable both to behold and taste;
And freely all their pleasant fruit for food
Gave thee, all sorts are here that all the earth yields.
Variety without end; but of the tree
Which tasted works knowledge of good and evil,
Thou mayest not; in the day thou eatest, thou diest;
Death is the penalty imposed, beware,
And govern well thy appetite, lest sin
Surprise thee, and her black attendant death.
Here finished he, and all that he had made

Viewed, and behold all was entirely good;
So even and morn accomplished the sixth day:
Yet not till the creator from his work
Desisting, though unwearied, up returned
Up to the heaven of heavens his high abode,
Thence to behold this new created world
The addition of his empire, how it showed
In prospect from his throne, how good, how fair,
Answering his great idea. Up he rode
Followed with acclamation and the sound
Symphonious of ten thousand harps that tuned
Angelic harmonies: the earth, the air
Resounded, (thou rememberest, for thou heardst)
The heavens and all the constellations rung,
The planets in their stations listening stood,
While the bright pomp ascended jubilant.
"Open, ye everlasting gates," they sung,
"Open, ye heavens, your living doors; let in
The great creator from his work returned
Magnificent, his six days' work, a world;
Open, and henceforth oft; for God will deign
To visit oft the dwellings of just men
Delighted, and with frequent intercourse
Thither will send his winged messengers
On errands of supernal grace." So sung
The glorious train ascending: He through heaven,
That opened wide her blazing portals, led
To God's eternal house direct the way,
A broad and ample road, whose dust is gold
And pavement stars, as stars to thee appear,
Seen in the galaxy, that milky way
Which nightly as a circling zone thou seest
Powdered with stars. And now on earth the seventh
Evening arose in Eden, for the sun
Was set, and twilight from the east came on,
Forerunning night; when at the holy mount
Of heaven's high-seated top, the imperial throne

Of Godhead, fixed forever firm and sure,
The filial power arrived, and sat him down
With his great father, for he also went
Invisible, yet stayed (such privilege
Hath omnipresence) and the work ordained,
Author and end of all things, and from work
Now resting, blessed and hallowed the seventh day,
As resting on that day from all his work,
But not in silence holy kept; the harp
Had work and rested not, the solemn pipe,
And dulcimer, all organs of sweet stop,
All sounds on fret by string or golden wire
Tempered soft tunings, intermixed with voice
Choral or unison; of incense clouds
Fuming from golden censers hid the mount.
Creation and the six days' acts they sung,
"Great are thy works, Jehovah, infinite
Thy power; what thought can measure thee or tongue
Relate thee; greater now in thy return
Than from the giant angels; thee that day
Thy thunders magnified; but to create
Is greater than created to destroy.
Who can impair thee, mighty king, or bound
Thy empire? easily the proud attempt
Of spirits apostate and their counsels vain
Thou hast repelled, while impiously they thought
Thee to diminish, and from thee withdraw
The number of thy worshipers. Who seeks
To lessen thee, against his purpose serves
To manifest the more thy might: his evil
Thou usest, and from thence createst more good.
Witness this new-made world, another heaven
From heaven gate not far, founded in view
On the clear hyaline, the glassy sea;
Of amplitude almost immense, with stars
Numerous, and every star perhaps a world
Of destined habitation; but thou knowest

Their seasons: among these the seat of men,
Earth with her nether ocean circumfused,
Their pleasant dwelling place. Thrice happy men,
And sons of men, whom God hath thus advanced,
Created in his image, there to dwell
And worship him, and in reward to rule
Over his works, on earth, in sea, or air,
And multiply a race of worshipers
Holy and just: thrice happy if they know
Their happiness, and persevere upright."
   'So sung they, and the empyrean rung,
With hallelujahs: Thus was Sabbath kept.
And thy request think now fulfilled, that asked
How first this world and face of things began,
And what before thy memory was done
From the beginning, that posterity
Informed by thee, might know; if else thou seekest
Aught, not surpassing human measure, say.'

BOOK VIII

The Argument: Adam inquires concerning celestial motions, is
doubtfully answered, and exhorted to search rather things more
worthy of knowledge: Adam assents, and still desirous to detain
Raphael, relates to him what he remembered since his own creation,
his placing in Paradise, his talk with God concerning solitude and
fit society, his first meeting and nuptials with Eve, his discourse
with the angel thereupon; who after admonitions repeated departs.

   The angel ended, and in Adam's ear
So charming left his voice, that he a while
Thought him still speaking, still stood fixed to hear;
Then as new-waked thus gratefully replied.
   'What thanks sufficient, or what recompense

Equal have I to render thee, divine
Historian, who thus largely hast allayed
The thirst I had of knowledge, and vouchsafed
This friendly condescension to relate
Things else by me unsearchable, now heard
With wonder, but delight, and, as is due,
With glory attributed to the high
Creator; something yet of doubt remains,
Which only thy solution can resolve.
When I behold this goodly frame, this world
Of heaven and earth consisting, and compute,
Their magnitudes, this earth a spot, a grain,
An atom, with the firmament compared
And all her numbered stars, that seem to roll
Spaces incomprehensible (for such
Their distance argues and their swift return
Diurnal) merely to officiate light
Round this opacous earth, this punctual spot,
One day and night; in all their vast survey
Useless besides, reasoning I oft admire,
How nature wise and frugal could commit
Such disproportions, with superfluous hand
So many nobler bodies to create,
Greater so manifold to this one use,
For aught appears, and on their orbs impose
Such restless revolution day by day
Repeated, while the sedentary earth,
That better might with far less compass move,
Served by more noble than herself, attains
Her end without least motion, and receives,
As tribute such a sumless journey brought
Of incorporeal speed, her warmth and light;
Speed, to describe whose swiftness number fails.'
    So spake our sire, and by his countenance seemed
Entering on studious thoughts abstruse, which Eve
Perceiving where she sat retired in sight,
With lowliness majestic from her seat,

And grace that won who saw to wish her stay,
Rose, and went forth among her fruits and flowers,
To visit how they prospered, bud and bloom,
Her nursery; they at her coming sprung
And touched by her fair tendance gladlier grew.
Yet went she not, as not with such discourse
Delighted, or not capable her ear
Of what was high: such pleasure she reserved,
Adam relating, she sole auditress;
Her husband the relater she preferred
Before the angel, and of him to ask
Chose rather; he, she knew would intermix
Grateful digressions, and solve high dispute
With conjugal caresses, from his lip
Not words alone pleased her. O when meet now
Such pairs, in love and mutual honor joined?
With goddess-like demeanor forth she went;
Not unattended, for on her as queen
A pomp of winning graces waited still,
And from about her shot darts of desire
Into all eyes to wish her still in sight.
And Raphael now to Adam's doubt proposed
Benevolent and facile thus replied.

'To ask or search I blame thee not, for heaven
Is as the book of God before thee set,
Wherein to read his wondrous works, and learn
His seasons, hours, or days, or months, or years:
This to attain, whether heaven move or earth,
Imports not, if thou reckon right, the rest
From man or angel the great architect
Did wisely to conceal, and not divulge
His secrets to be scanned by them who ought
Rather admire; or if they list to try
Conjecture, he his fabric of the heavens
Hath left to their disputes, perhaps to move
His laughter at their quaint opinions wide
Hereafter, when they come to model heaven

And calculate the stars, how they will wield
The mighty frame, how build, unbuild, contrive
To save appearances, how gird the sphere
With centric and eccentric scribbled o'er,
Cycle and epicycle, orb in orb:
Already by thy reasoning this I guess,
Who art to lead thy offspring, and supposest
That bodies bright and greater should not serve
The less not bright, nor heaven such journeys run
Earth sitting still, when she alone receives
The benefit: consider first, that great
Or bright infers not excellence: the earth
Though, in comparison of heaven, so small,
Nor glistering, may of solid good contain
More plenty than the sun that barren shines,
Whose virtue on itself works no effect,
But in the fruitful earth; there first received
His beams, unactive else, their vigor find.
Yet not to earth are those bright luminaries
Officious, but to thee earth's habitant.
And for the heaven's wide circuit, let it speak
The maker's high magnificence, who built
So spacious, and his line stretched out so far;
That man may know he dwells not in his own;
An edifice too large for him to fill,
Lodged in a small partition, and the rest
Ordained for uses to his Lord best known.
The swiftness of those circles attribute,
Though numberless, to his omnipotence,
That to corporeal substances could add
Speed almost spiritual; me thou thinkest not slow,
Who since the morning hour set out from heaven
Where God resides, and ere midday arrived
In Eden, distance inexpressible
By numbers that have name. But this I urge,
Admitting motion in the heavens, to show
Invalid that which thee to doubt it moved;

Not that I so affirm, though so it seem
To thee who hast thy dwelling here on earth.
God to remove his ways from human sense,
Placed heaven from earth so far, that earthly sight,
If it presume, might err in things too high,
And no advantage gain. What if the sun
Be center to the world, and other stars
By his attractive virtue and their own
Incited, dance about him various rounds?
Their wandering course now high, now low, then hid,
Progressive, retrograde, or standing still,
In six thou seest, and what if seventh to these
The planet earth, so steadfast though she seem,
Insensibly three different motions move?
Which else to several spheres thou must ascribe,
Moved contrary with thwart obliquities,
Or save the sun his labor, and that swift
Nocturnal and diurnal rhomb supposed,
Invisible else above all stars, the wheel
Of day and night; which needs not thy belief,
If earth industrious of herself fetch day
Traveling east, and with her part averse
From the sun's beam meet night, her other part
Still luminous by his ray. What if that light
Sent from her through the wide transpicuous air,
To the terrestrial moon be as a star
Enlightening her by day, as she by night
This earth? reciprocal, if land be there,
Fields and inhabitants: Her spots thou seest
As clouds, and clouds may rain, and rain produce
Fruits in her softened soil, for some to eat
Allotted there; and other suns perhaps
With their attendant moons thou wilt descry
Communicating male and female light,
Which two great sexes animate the world,
Stored in each orb perhaps with some that live.
For such vast room in nature unpossessed

By living soul, desert and desolate,
Only to shine, yet scarce to contribute
Each orb a glimpse of light, conveyed so far
Down to this habitable, which returns
Light back to them, is obvious to dispute.
But whether thus these things, or whether not,
Whether the sun predominant in heaven
Rise on the earth, or earth rise on the sun,
He from the east his flaming road begin,
Or she from west her silent course advance
With inoffensive pace that spinning sleeps
On her soft axle, while she paces even,
And bears thee soft with the smooth air along,
Solicit not thy thoughts with matters hid,
Leave them to God above, him serve and fear;
Of other creatures, as him pleases best,
Wherever placed, let him dispose: joy thou
In what he gives to thee, this Paradise
And thy fair Eve; heaven is for thee too high
To know what passes there; be lowly wise:
Think only what concerns thee and thy being;
Dream not of other worlds, what creatures there
Live, in what state, condition or degree,
Contented that thus far hath been revealed
Not of earth only but of highest heaven.'
    To whom thus Adam cleared of doubt, replied.
'How fully hast thou satisfied me, pure
Intelligence of heaven, angel serene,
And freed from intricacies, taught to live,
The easiest way, nor with perplexing thoughts
To interrupt the sweet of life, from which
God hath bid dwell far off all anxious cares,
And not molest us, unless we ourselves
Seek them with wandering thoughts, and notions vain.
But apt the mind or fancy is to rove
Unchecked, and of her roving is no end;
Till warned, or by experience taught, she learn,

That not to know at large of things remote
From use, obscure and subtle, but to know
That which before us lies in daily life,
Is the prime wisdom, what is more, is fume,
Or emptiness, or fond impertinence,
And renders us in things that most concern
Unpracticed, unprepared, and still to seek.
Therefore from this high pitch let us descend
A lower flight, and speak of things at hand
Useful, whence hapiy mention may arise
Of something not unseasonable to ask
By sufferance, and thy wonted favor deigned.
Thee I have heard relating what was done
Ere my remembrance: now hear me relate
My story, which perhaps thou hast not heard;
And day is yet not spent; till then thou seest
How subtly to detain thee I devise,
Inviting thee to hear while I relate,
Fond, were it not in hope of thy reply:
For while I sit with thee, I seem in heaven,
And sweeter thy discourse is to my ear
Than fruits of palm-tree pleasantest to thirst
And hunger both, from labor, at the hour
Of sweet repast; they satiate, and soon fill,
Though pleasant, but thy words with grace divine
Imbued, bring to their sweetness no satiety.'
  To whom thus Raphael answered heavenly meek.
'Nor are thy lips ungraceful, sire of men,
Nor tongue ineloquent; for God on thee
Abundantly his gifts hath also poured
Inward and outward both, his image fair:
Speaking or mute all comeliness and grace
Attends thee, and each word, each motion forms.
Nor less think we in heaven of thee on earth
Than of our fellow servant, and inquire
Gladly into the ways of God with man:
For God we see hath honored thee, and set

On man his equal love: say therefore on;
For I that day was absent, as befell,
Bound on a voyage uncouth and obscure,
Far on excursion toward the gates of hell;
Squared in full legion (such command we had)
To see that none thence issued forth a spy,
Or enemy, while God was in his work,
Lest he incensed at such eruption bold,
Destruction with creation might have mixed.
Not that they durst without his leave attempt,
But us he sends upon his high behests
For state, as sovereign king, and to inure
Our prompt obedience. Fast we found, fast shut
The dismal gates, and barricadoed strong;
But long ere our approaching heard within
Noise, other than the sound of dance or song,
Torment, and loud lament, and furious rage.
Glad we returned up to the coasts of light
Ere Sabbath evening: so we had in charge.
But thy relation now; for I attend,
Pleased with thy words no less than thou with mine.
    So spake the godlike power, and thus our sire.
'For man to tell how human life began
Is hard; for who himself beginning knew?
Desire with thee still longer to converse
Induced me. As new waked from soundest sleep
Soft on the flowery herb I found me laid
In balmy sweat, which with his beams the sun
Soon dried, and on the reeking moisture fed.
Straight toward heaven my wondering eyes I turned,
And gazed a while the ample sky, till raised
By quick instinctive motion up I sprung,
As thitherward endeavoring, and upright
Stood on my feet; about me round I saw
Hill, dale, and shady woods, and sunny plains,
And liquid lapse of murmuring streams; by these,
Creatures that lived, and moved, and walked, or flew

Birds on the branches warbling; all things smiled,
With fragrance and with joy my heart o'erflowed.
Myself I then perused, and limb by limb
Surveyed, and sometimes went, and sometimes ran
With supple joints, as lively vigor led:
But who I was, or where, or from what cause,
Knew not; to speak I tried, and forthwith spake,
My tongue obeyed and readily could name
Whate'er I saw. "Thou sun," said I, "fair light,
And thou enlightened earth, so fresh and gay,
Ye hills and dales, ye rivers, woods, and plains,
And ye that live and move, fair creatures, tell,
Tell, if ye saw, how came I thus, how here?
Not of myself; by some great maker then,
In goodness and in power pre-eminent;
Tell me, how may I know him, how adore,
From whom I have that thus I move and live,
And feel that I am happier than I know."
While thus I called, and strayed I knew not whither,
From where I first drew air, and first beheld
This happy light, when answer none returned,
On a green shady bank profuse of flowers
Pensive I sat me down; there gentle sleep
First found me, and with soft oppression seized
My drowsed sense, untroubled, though I thought
I then was passing to my former state
Insensible, and forthwith to dissolve:
When suddenly stood at my head a dream,
Whose inward apparition gently moved
My fancy to believe I yet had being,
And lived: One came, methought, of shape divine,
And said, "thy mansion wants thee, Adam, rise,
First Man, of men innumerable ordained
First father, called by thee I come thy guide
To the garden of bliss, thy seat prepared."
So saying, by the hand he took me raised,
And over fields and waters, as in air

Smooth sliding without step, last led me up
A woody mountain; whose high top was plain,
A circuit wide, enclosed, with goodliest trees
Planted, with walks, and bowers, that what I saw
Of earth before scarce pleasant seemed. Each tree
Laden with fairest fruit that hung to the eye
Tempting, stirred in me sudden appetite
To pluck and eat; whereat I waked, and found
Before mine eyes all real, as the dream
Had lively shadowed: Here had new begun
My wandering, had not he who was my guide
Up hither, from among the trees appeared
Presence divine. Rejoicing, but with awe
In adoration at his feet I fell
Submiss: he reared me, and "Whom thou soughtest
Said mildly, "Author of all this thou seest
Above, or round about thee or beneath.
This Paradise I give thee, count it thine
To till and keep, and of the fruit to eat:
Of every tree that in the garden grows
Eat freely with glad heart; fear here no dearth:
But of the tree whose operation brings
Knowledge of good and ill, which I have set
The pledge of thy obedience and thy faith,
Amid the garden by the tree of life,
Remember what I warn thee, shun to taste,
And shun the bitter consequence: for know,
The day thou eatest thereof, my sole command
Transgressed, inevitably thou shalt die;
From that day mortal, and this happy state
Shalt lose, expelled from hence into a world
Of woe and sorrow." Sternly he pronounced
The rigid interdiction, which resounds
Yet dreadful in mine ear, though in my choice
Not to incur; but soon his clear aspect
Returned and gracious purpose thus renewed.
"Not only these fair bounds, but all the earth

To thee and to thy race I give; as lords
Possess it, and all things that therein live,
Or live in sea, or air, beast, fish, and fowl.
In sign whereof each bird and beast behold
After their kinds; I bring them to receive
From thee their names, and pay thee fealty
With low subjection; understand the same
Of fish within their watery residence,
Not hither summoned, since they cannot change
Their element to draw the thinner air."
As thus he spake, each bird and beast behold
Approaching two and two, these cowering low
With blandishment, each bird stooped on his wing.
I named them, as they passed, and understood
Their nature, with such knowledge God endued
My sudden apprehension: but in these
I found not what methought I wanted still;
And to the heavenly vision thus presumed.
    ' "O by what name, for thou above all these,
Above mankind, or aught than mankind higher,
Surpassest far my naming, how may I
Adore thee, author of this universe,
And all this good to man, for whose well being
So amply, and with hands so liberal
Thou hast provided all things: but with me
I see not who partakes. In solitude
What happiness, who can enjoy alone,
Or all enjoying, what contentment find?"
Thus I presumptuous; and the vision bright,
As with a smile more brightened, thus replied.
    ' "What callest thou solitude, is not the earth
With various living creatures, and the air
Replenished, and all these at thy command
To come and play before thee, knowest thou not
Their language and their ways, they also know,
And reason not contemptibly; with these
Find pastime, and bear rule; thy realm is large.'

So spake the universal lord, and seemed
So ordering. I with leave of speech implored,
And humble deprecation thus replied.
    ' "Let not my words offend thee, heavenly power,
My maker, be propitious while I speak.
Hast thou not made me here thy substitute,
And these inferior far beneath me set?
Among unequals what society
Can sort, what harmony or true delight?
Which must be mutual, in proportion due
Given and received; but in disparity
The one intense, the other still remiss
Cannot well suit with either, but soon prove
Tedious alike: Of fellowship I speak
Such as I seek, fit to participate
All rational delight, wherein the brute
Cannot be human consort; they rejoice
Each with their kind, lion with lioness;
So fitly them in pairs thou hast combined;
Much less can bird with beast, or fish with fowl
So well converse, nor with the ox the ape;
Worse then can man with beast, and least of all."
Whereto the almighty answered, not displeased.
"A nice and subtle happiness I see
Thou to thyself proposest, in the choice
Of thy associates, Adam, and wilt taste
No pleasure, though in pleasure, solitary.
What thinkest thou then of me, and this my state,
Seem I to thee sufficiently possessed
Of happiness, or not? who am alone
From all eternity, for none I know
Second to me or like, equal much less.
How have I then with whom to hold converse
Save with the creatures which I made, and those
To me inferior, infinite descents
Beneath what other creatures are to thee?"

'He ceased, I lowly answered. "To attain
The height and depth of thy eternal ways
All human thoughts come short, supreme of things;
Thou in thyself art perfect, and in thee
Is no deficience found; not so is man,
But in degree, the cause of his desire
By conversation with his like to help,
Or solace his defects. No need that thou
Shouldst propagate, already infinite;
And through all numbers absolute, though one;
But man by number is to manifest
His single imperfection, and beget
Like of his like, his image multiplied,
In unity defective, which requires
Collateral love, and dearest amity.
Thou in thy secrecy although alone,
Best with thyself accompanied, seekest not
Social communication, yet so pleased,
Canst raise thy creature to what height thou wilt
Of union or communion, deified;
I by conversing cannot these erect
From prone, nor in their ways complacence find."
Thus I emboldened spake, and freedom used
Permissive, and acceptance found, which gained
This answer from the gracious voice divine.
  ' "Thus far to try thee, Adam, I was pleased,
And find thee knowing not of beasts alone,
Which thou hast rightly named, but of thyself,
Expressing well the spirit within thee free,
My image, not imparted to the brute,
Whose fellowship therefore unmeet for thee
Good reason was thou freely shouldst dislike,
And be so minded still; I, ere thou spakest,
Knew it not good for man to be alone,
And no such company as then thou sawest
Intended thee, for trial only brought,
To see how thou couldst judge of fit and meet:

What next I bring shall please thee, be assured,
Thy likeness, thy fit help, thy other self,
Thy wish exactly to thy heart's desire."
    'He ended, or I heard no more, for now
My earthly by his heavenly overpowered,
Which it had long stood under, strained to the height
In that celestial colloquy sublime,
As with an object that excels the sense,
Dazzled and spent, sunk down, and sought repair
Of sleep, which instantly fell on me, called
By nature as in aid, and closed mine eyes.
Mine eyes he closed, but open left the cell
Of fancy my internal sight, by which
Abstracts as in a trance methought I saw,
Though sleeping, where I lay, and saw the shape
Still glorious before whom awake I stood;
Who stooping opened my left side, and took
From thence a rib, with cordial spirits warm;
And life blood streaming fresh; wide was the wound,
But suddenly with flesh filled up and healed:
The rib he formed and fashioned with his hands;
Under his forming hands a creature grew,
Manlike, but different sex, so lovely fair,
That what seemed fair in all the world, seemed now
Mean, or in her summed up, in her contained
And in her looks, which from that time infused
Sweetness into my heart, unfelt before,
And into all things from her air inspired
The spirit of love and amorous delight.
She disappeared, and left me dark, I waked
To find her, or forever to deplore
Her loss, and other pleasures all abjure:
When out of hope, behold her, not far off,
Such as I saw her in my dream, adorned
With what all earth or heaven could bestow
To make her amiable: On she came,
Led by her heavenly maker, though unseen,

And guided by his voice, nor uninformed
Of nuptial sanctity and marriage rites:
Grace was in all her steps, heaven in her eye,
In every gesture dignity and love.
I overjoyed could not forbear aloud.
   ' "This turn hath made amends; thou hast fulfilled
Thy words, creator bounteous and benign,
Giver of all things fair, but fairest this
Of all thy gifts, nor enviest. I now see
Bone of my bone, flesh of my flesh, myself
Before me; woman is her name, of man
Extracted; for this cause he shall forgo
Father and mother, and to his wife adhere;
And they shall be one flesh, one heart, one soul."
   'She heard me thus, and though divinely brought,
Yet innocence and virgin modesty,
Her virtue and the conscience of her worth,
That would be wooed, and not unsought be won,
Not obvious, not obtrusive, but retired,
The more desirable, or to say all,
Nature herself, though pure of sinful thought,
Wrought in her so, that seeing me, she turned;
I followed her, she what was honor knew,
And with obsequious majesty approved
My pleaded reason. To the nuptial bower
I led her blushing like the morn: all heaven,
And happy constellations on that hour
Shed their selectest influence; the earth
Gave sign of gratulation, and each hill;
Joyous the birds; fresh gales and gentle airs
Whispered it to the woods, and from their wings
Flung rose, flung odors from the spicy shrub,
Disporting, till the amorous bird of night
Sung spousal, and bid haste the evening star
On his hilltop to light the bridal lamp.
Thus have I told thee all my state, and brought
My story to the sum of earthly bliss

Which I enjoy, and must confess to find
In all things else delight indeed, but such
As used or not, works in the mind no change,
Nor vehement desire, these delicacies
I mean of taste, sight, smell, herbs, fruits, and **flowers,**
Walks, and the melody of birds; but here
Far otherwise, transported I behold,
Transported touch; here passion first I felt,
Commotion strange, in all enjoyments else
Superior and unmoved, here only weak
Against the charm of beauty's powerful glance.
Or nature failed in me, and left some part
Not proof enough such object to sustain,
Or from my side subducting, took perhaps
More than enough; at least on her bestowed
Too much of ornament, in outward show
Elaborate, of inward less exact.
For well I understand in the prime end
Of nature her the inferior, in the mind
And inward faculties, which most excel,
In outward also her resembling less
His image who made both, and less expressing
The character of that dominion given
O'er other creatures; yet when I approach
Her loveliness, so absolute she seems
And in herself complete, so well to know
Her own, that what she wills to do or say,
Seems wisest, virtuousest, discreetest, best;
All higher knowledge in her presence falls
Degraded, wisdom in discourse with her
Loses discountenanced, and like folly shows;
Authority and reason on her wait,
As one intended first, not after made
Occasionally; and to consummate all,
Greatness of mind and nobleness their seat
Build in her loveliest, and create an awe

About her, as a guard angelic placed.'
To whom the angel, with contracted brow.
   'Accuse not nature, she hath done her part;
Do thou but thine, and be not diffident
Of wisdom, she deserts thee not, if thou
Dismiss not her, when most thou needest her nigh,
By attributing overmuch to things
Less excellent, as thou thyself perceivest.
For what admirest thou, what transports thee so,
An outside? fair no doubt, and worthy well
Thy cherishing, thy honoring, and thy love,
Not thy subjection: weigh with her thyself;
Then value: Ofttimes nothing profits more
Than self esteem, grounded on just and right
Well managed; of that skill the more thou knowest,
The more she will acknowledge thee her head,
And to realities yield all her shows:
Made so adorn for thy delight the more,
So awful, that with honor thou mayest love
Thy mate, who sees when thou art seen least wise.
But if the sense of touch whereby mankind
Is propagated seem such dear delight
Beyond all other, think the same vouchsafed
To cattle and each beast; which would not be
To them made common and divulged, if aught
Therein enjoyed were worthy to subdue
The soul of man, or passion in him move.
What higher in her society thou findest
Attractive, human, rational, love still:
In loving thou dost well, in passion not,
Wherein true love consists not; love refines
The thoughts, and heart enlarges, hath his seat
In reason, and is judicious, is the scale
By which to heavenly love thou mayest ascend,
Not sunk in carnal pleasure, for which cause
Among the beasts no mate for thee was found.'

   To whom thus half abashed Adam replied.
'Neither her outside formed so fair, nor aught
In procreation common to all kinds
(Though higher of the genial bed by far,
And with mysterious reverence I deem)
So much delights me as those graceful acts,
Those thousand decencies that daily flow
From all her words and actions mixed with love
And sweet compliance, which declare unfeigned
Union of mind, or in us both one soul;
Harmony to behold in wedded pair
More grateful than harmonious sound to the ear.
Yet these subject not; I to thee disclose
What inward thence I feel, not therefore foiled,
Who meet with various objects, from the sense
Variously representing; yet still free
Approve the best, and follow what I approve.
To love thou blamest me not, for love thou sayest
Leads up to heaven, is both the way and guide;
Bear with me then, if lawful what I ask;
Love not the heavenly spirits, and how their love
Express they, by looks only, or do they mix
Irradiance, virtual or immediate touch?'
   To whom the angel with a smile that glowed
Celestial rosy red, love's proper hue,
Answered. 'Let it suffice thee that thou knowest
Us happy, and without love no happiness.
Whatever pure thou in the body enjoyest
(And pure thou wert created) we enjoy
In eminence, and obstacle find none
Of membrane, joint, or limb, exclusive bars:
Easier than air with air, if spirits embrace,
Total they mix, union of pure with pure
Desiring; nor restrained conveyance need
As flesh to mix with flesh, or soul with soul.
But I can now no more; the parting sun
Beyond the earth's green cape and verdant isles

Hesperean sets, my signal to depart.
Be strong, live happy, and love, but first of all
Him whom to love is to obey, and keep
His great command; take heed lest passion sway
Thy judgment to do aught, which else free will
Would not admit; thine and of all thy sons
The weal or woe in thee is placed; beware.
I in thy persevering shall rejoice,
And all the blest: stand fast; to stand or fall
Free in thine own arbitrament it lies.
Perfect within, no outward aid require;
And all temptation to transgress repel.'
    So saying, he arose; whom Adam thus
Followed with benediction. 'Since to part,
Go heavenly guest, ethereal messenger,
Sent from whose sovereign goodness I adore.
Gentle to me and affable hath been
Thy condescension, and shall be honored ever
With grateful memory: thou to mankind
Be good and friendly still, and oft return.'
    So parted they, the angel up to heaven
From the thick shade, and Adam to his bower.

BOOK IX

The Argument: Satan having compassed the earth, with medi-
ated guile returns as a mist by night into Paradise, enters into the
serpent sleeping. Adam and Eve in the morning go forth to their
labors, which Eve proposes to divide in several places, each labor-
ing apart: Adam consents not, alleging the danger, lest that enemy,
of whom they were forewarned, should attempt her found alone:
Eve loath to be thought not circumspect or firm enough, urges her
going apart, the rather desirous to make trial of her strength; Adam
at last yields: The serpent finds her alone; his subtle approach, first

gazing, then speaking, with much flattery extolling Eve above all
other creatures. Eve wondering to hear the serpent speak, asks how
he attained to human speech and such understanding not till now;
the serpent answers, that by tasting of a certain tree in the garden
he attained both to speech and reason, till then void of both: Eve
requires him to bring her to that tree, and finds it to be the tree of
knowledge forbidden: The serpent now grown bolder, with many
wiles and arguments induces her at length to eat; she pleased with
the taste deliberates a while whether to impart thereof to Adam or
not, at last brings him of the fruit, relates what persuaded her to
eat thereof: Adam at first amazed, but perceiving her lost, resolves
through vehemence of love to perish with her; and extenuating the
trespass, eats also of the fruit: The effects thereof in them both;
they seek to cover their nakedness; then fall to variance and accusa-
tion of one another.

No more of talk where God or angel guest
With man, as with his friend, familiar used
To sit indulgent, and with him partake
Rural repast, permitting him the while
Venial discourse unblamed: I now must change
Those notes to tragic; foul distrust, and breach
Disloyal on the part of man, revolt,
And disobedience: On the part of heaven
Now alienated, distance and distaste,
Anger and just rebuke, and judgment given,
That brought into this world a world of woe,
Sin and her shadow death, and misery
Death's harbinger: Sad task, yet argument
Not less but more heroic than the wrath
Of stern Achilles on his foe pursued
Thrice fugitive about Troy wall; or rage
Of Turnus for Lavinia disespoused,
Or Neptune's ire or Juno's, that so long
Perplexed the Greek and Cytherea's son:
If answerable style I can obtain
Of my celestial patroness, who deigns

Her nightly visitation unimplored,
And dictates to me slumbering, or inspires
Easy my unpremeditated verse:
Since first this subject for heroic song
Pleased me long choosing, and beginning late;
Not sedulous by nature to indite
Wars, hitherto the only argument
Heroic deemed, chief mastery to dissect
With long and tedious havoc fabled knights
In battles feigned; the better fortitude
Of patience and heroic martyrdom
Unsung; or to describe races and games,
Or tilting furniture, emblazoned shields,
Impreses quaint, caparisons and steeds;
Bases and tinsel trappings, gorgeous knights
At joust and tournament; then marshaled feast
Served up in hall with sewers, and seneshals;
The skill of artifice or office mean,
Not that which justly gives heroic name
To person or to poem. Me of these
Nor skilled nor studious, higher argument
Remains, sufficient of itself to raise
That name, unless an age too late, or cold
Climate, or years damp my intended wing
Depressed, and much they may, if all be mine,
Not hers who brings it nightly to my ear.
  The sun was sunk, and after him the star
Of Hesperus, whose office is to bring
Twilight upon the earth, short arbiter
Twixt day and night, and now from end to end
Night's hemisphere had veiled the horizon round:
When Satan who late fled before the threats
Of Gabriel out of Eden, now improved
In meditated fraud and malice, bent
On man's destruction, mauger what might hap
Of heavier on himself, fearless returned.
By night he fled, and at midnight returned

From compassing the earth, cautious of day,
Since Uriel regent of the sun descried
His entrance, and forewarned the cherubim
That kept their watch; thence full of anguish driven,
The space of seven continued nights he rode
With darkness, thrice the equinoctial line
He circled, four times crossed the car of night
From pole to pole, traversing each colure;
On the eighth returned, and on the coast averse
From entrance or cherubic watch, by stealth
Found unsuspected way. There was a place,
Now not, though sin, not time, first wrought the change,
Where Tigris at the foot of Paradise
Into a gulf shot under ground, till part
Rose up a fountain by the tree of life;
In with the river sunk, and with it rose
Satan involved in rising mist, then sought
Where to lie hid; sea he had searched and land
From Eden over Pontus, and the pool
Maeotis, up beyond the river Ob;
Downward as far antarctic; and in length
West from Orontes to the ocean barred
At Darien, thence to the land where flows
Ganges and Indus: thus the orb he roamed
With narrow search; and with inspection deep
Considered every creature, which of all
Most opportune might serve his wiles, and found
The serpent subtlest beast of all the field.
Him after long debate, irresolute
Of thoughts revolved, his final sentence chose
Fit vessel, fittest imp of fraud, in whom
To enter, and his dark suggestions hide
From sharpest sight: for in the wily snake,
Whatever sleights none would suspicious mark,
As from his wit and native subtlety
Proceeding, which in other beasts observed
Doubt might beget of diabolic power

Active within beyond the sense of brute.
Thus he resolved, but first from inward grief
His bursting passion into plaints thus poured:
　'O earth, how like to heaven, if not preferred
More justly, seat worthier of gods, as built
With second thoughts, reforming what was old!
For what god after better worse would build?
Terrestrial heaven, danced round by other heavens
That shine, yet bear their bright officious lamps,
Light above light, for thee alone, as seems,
In thee concentering all their precious beams
Of sacred influence: As God in heaven
Is center, yet extends to all, so thou
Centering receivest from all those orbs; in thee,
Not in themselves, all their known virtue appears
Productive in herb, plant, and nobler birth
Of creatures animate with gradual life
Of growth, sense, reason, all summed up in man.
With what delight could I have walked thee round,
If I could joy in aught, sweet interchange
Of hill and valley, rivers, woods and plains,
Now land, now sea, and shores with forest crowned,
Rocks, dens, and caves; but I in none of these
Find place or refuge; and the more I see
Pleasures about me, so much more I feel
Torment within me, as from the hateful siege
Of contraries; all good to me becomes
Bane, and in heaven much worse would be my state.
But neither here seek I, no nor in heaven
To dwell, unless by mastering heaven's supreme;
Nor hope to be myself less miserable
By what I seek, but others to make such
As I, though thereby worse to me redound:
For only in destroying I find ease
To my relentless thoughts; and him destroyed,
Or won to what may work his utter loss,
For whom all this was made, all this will soon

Follow, as to him linked in weal or woe,
In woe then; that destruction wide may range:
To me shall be the glory sole among
The infernal powers, in one day to have marred
What he almighty styled, six nights and days
Continued making, and who knows how long
Before had been contriving, though perhaps
Not longer than since I in one night freed
From servitude inglorious well-nigh half
The angelic name, and thinner left the throng
Of his adorers: he to be avenged,
And to repair his numbers thus impaired,
Whether such virtue spent of old now failed
More angels to create, if they at least
Are his created, or to spite us more,
Determined to advance into our room
A creature formed of earth, and him endow,
Exalted from so base original,
With heavenly spoils, our spoils; What he decreed
He effected; man he made, and for him built
Magnificent this world, and earth his seat,
Him Lord pronounced, and, O indignity!
Subjected to his service angel wings,
And flaming ministers to watch and tend
Their earthy charge: Of these the vigilance
I dread, and to elude, thus wrapped in mist
Of midnight vapor glide obscure, and pry
In every bush and brake, where hap may find
The serpent sleeping, in whose mazy folds
To hide me, and the dark intent I bring.
O foul descent! that I who erst contended
With gods to sit the highest, am now constrained
Into a beast, and mixed with bestial slime,
This essence to incarnate and imbrute,
That to the height of deity aspired;
But what will not ambition and revenge
Descend to? who aspires must down as low

As high he soared, obnoxious first or last
To basest things. Revenge, at first though sweet,
Bitter ere long back on itself recoils;
Let it; I reck not, so it light well aimed,
Since higher I fall short, on him who next
Provokes my envy, this new favorite
Of heaven, this man of clay, son of despite,
Whom us the more to spite his maker raised
From dust: spite then with spite is best repaid.'
   So saying, through each thicket dank or dry,
Like a black mist low creeping, he held on
His midnight search, where soonest he might find
The serpent: him fast sleeping soon he found
In labyrinth of many a round self rolled,
His head the midst, well stored with subtle wiles:
Not yet in horrid shade or dismal den,
Nor nocent yet, but on the grassy herb
Fearless unfeared he slept: in at his mouth
The devil entered, and his brutal sense,
In heart or head, possessing soon inspired
With act intelligential; but his sleep
Disturbed not, waiting close the approach of morn.
Now when as sacred light began to dawn
In Eden on the humid flowers, that breathed
Their morning incense, when all things that breathe,
From the earth's great altar send up silent praise
To the creator, and his nostrils fill
With grateful smell, forth came the human pair
And joined their vocal worship to the choir
Of creatures wanting voice, that done, partake
The season, prime for sweetest scents and airs:
Then commune how that day they best may ply
Their growing work: for much their work outgrew
The hands' dispatch of two gardening so wide.
And Eve first to her husband thus began.
   'Adam, well may we labor still to dress
This garden, still to tend plant, herb and flower,

Our pleasant task enjoined, but till more hands
Aid us, the work under our labor grows,
Luxurious by restraint; what we by day
Lop overgrown, or prune, or prop, or bind,
One night or two with wanton growth derides
'Tending to wild. Thou therefore now advise
Or hear what to my mind first thoughts present,
Let us divide our labors, thou where choice
Leads thee, or where most needs, whether to wind
The woodbine round this arbor, or direct
The clasping ivy where to climb, while I
In younder spring of roses intermixed
With myrtle, find what to redress till noon:
For while so near each other thus all day
Our task we choose, what wonder if so near
Looks intervene and smiles, or object now
Casual discourse draw on, which intermits
Our day's work brought to little, though begun
Early, and the hour of supper comes unearned.'
　　To whom mild answer Adam thus returned.
'Sole Eve, associate sole, to me beyond
Compare above all living creatures dear,
Well hast thou motioned, well thy thoughts employed
How we might best fulfill the work which here
God hath assigned us, nor of me shalt pass
Unpraised: for nothing lovelier can be found
In woman, than to study household good,
And good works in her husband to promote.
Yet not so strictly hath our Lord imposed
Labor, as to debar us when we need
Refreshment, whether food, or talk between,
Food of the mind, or this sweet intercourse
Of looks and smiles, for smiles from reason flow,
To brute denied, and are of love the food,
Love not the lowest end of human life.
For not to irksome toil, but to delight
He made us, and delight to reason joined.

These paths and bowers doubt not but our joint hands
Will keep from wilderness with ease, as wide
As we need walk, till younger hands erelong
Assist us: But if much converse perhaps
Thee satiate, to short absence I could yield.
For solitude sometimes is best society,
And short retirement urges sweet return.
But other doubt possesses me, lest harm
Befall thee severed from me; for thou knowest
What hath been warned us, what malicious foe
Envying our happiness, and of his own
Despairing, seeks to work us woe and shame
By sly assault; and somewhere nigh at hand
Watches, no doubt, with greedy hope to find
His wish and best advantage, us asunder,
Hopeless to circumvent us joined, where each
To other speedy aid might lend at need;
Whether his first design be to withdraw
Our fealty from God, or to disturb
Conjugal love, than which perhaps no bliss
Enjoyed by us excites his envy more;
Or this, or worse, leave not the faithful side
That gave thee being, still shades thee and protects.
The wife, where danger or dishonor lurks,
Safest and seemliest by her husband stays,
Who guards her, or with her the worst endures.'
    To whom the virgin majesty of Eve,
As one who loves, and some unkindness meets,
With sweet austere composure thus replied.
    'Offspring of heaven and earth, and all earth's lord,
That such an enemy we have, who seeks
Our ruin, both by thee informed I learn,
And from the parting angel overheard
As in a shady nook I stood behind,
Just then returned at shut of evening flowers.
But that thou shouldst my firmness therefore doubt
To God or thee, because we have a foe

May tempt it, I expected not to hear.
His violence thou fearest not, being such,
As we, not capable of death or pain,
Can either not receive, or can repel.
His fraud is then thy fear, which plain infers
Thy equal fear that my firm faith and love
Can by his fraud be shaken or seduced;
Thoughts, which how found they harbor in thy breast,
Adam, misthought of her to thee so dear?'
    To whom with healing words Adam replied.
'Daughter of God and man, immortal Eve,
For such thou art, from sin and blame entire:
Not diffident of thee do I dissuade
Thy absence from my sight, but to avoid
The attempt itself, intended by our foe.
For he who tempts, though in vain, at least asperses
The tempted with dishonor foul, supposed
Not incorruptible of faith, not proof
Against temptation: thou thyself with scorn
And anger wouldst resent the offered wrong,
Though ineffectual found: misdeem not then,
If such affront I labor to avert
From thee alone, which on us both at once
The enemy, though bold, will hardly dare,
Or daring, first on me the assault shall light.
Nor thou his malice and false guile contemn;
Subtle he needs must be, who could seduce
Angels, nor think superfluous others' aid.
I from the influence of thy looks receive
Access in every virtue, in thy sight
More wise, more watchful, stronger, if need were
Of outward strength; while shame, thou looking on,
Shame to be overcome or overreached
Would utmost vigor raise, and raised unite.
Why shouldst not thou like sense within thee feel
When I am present, and thy trial choose
With me, best witness of thy virtue tried.'

So spake domestic Adam in his care
And matrimonial love, but Eve, who thought
Less attributed to her faith sincere,
Thus her reply with accent sweet renewed.
    'If this be our condition, thus to dwell
In narrow circuit straitened by a foe,
Subtle or violent, we not endued
Single with like defense, wherever met,
How are we happy, still in fear of harm?
But harm precedes not sin: only our foe
Tempting affronts us with his foul esteem
Of our integrity: his foul esteem
Sticks no dishonor on our front, but turns
Foul on himself; then wherefore shunned or feared
By us? who rather double honor gain
From his surmise proved false, find peace within,
Favor from heaven, our witness from the event.
And what is faith, love, virtue unassayed
Alone, without exterior help sustained?
Let us not then suspect our happy state
Left so imperfect by the maker wise,
As not secure to single or combined.
Frail is our happiness, if this be so,
And Eden were no Eden thus exposed.'
    To whom thus Adam fervently replied.
'O woman, best are all things as the will
Of God ordained them, his creating hand
Nothing imperfect or deficient left
Of all that he created, much less man,
Or aught that might his happy state secure,
Secure from outward force; within himself
The danger lies, yet lies within his power:
Against his will he can receive no harm.
But God left free the will, for what obeys
Reason, is free, and reason he made right,
But bid her well beware, and still erect,
Lest by some fair appearing good surprised

She dictate false, and misinform the will
To do what God expressly hath forbid.
Not then mistrust, but tender love enjoins,
That I should mind thee oft, and mind thou me.
Firm we subsist, yet possible to swerve,
Since reason not impossibly may meet
Some specious object by the foe suborned,
And fall into deception unaware,
Not keeping strictest watch, as she was warned.
Seek not temptation then, which to avoid
Were better, and most likely if from me
Thou sever not: Trial will come unsought.
Wouldst thou approve thy constancy, approve
First thy obedience; the other who can know,
Not seeking thee attempted, who attest?
But if thou think, trial unsought may find
Us both securer than thus warned thou seemest,
Go; for thy stay, not free, absents thee more;
Go in thy native innocence, rely
On what thou hast of virtue, summon all,
For God towards thee hath done his part, do thine.
    So spake the patriarch of mankind, but Eve
Persisted, yet submiss, though last, replied.
    'With thy permission then, and thus forewarned
Chiefly by what thy own last reasoning words
Touched only, that our trial, when least sought,
May find us both perhaps far less prepared,
The willinger I go, nor much expect
A foe so proud will first the weaker seek;
So bent, the more shall shame him his repulse.'
Thus saying, from her husband's hand her hand
Soft she withdrew, and like a wood nymph light,
Oread or dryad, or of Delia's train,
Betook her to the groves, but Delia's self
In gait surpassed and goddess-like deport,
Though not as she with bow and quiver armed,
But with such gardening tools as art yet rude,

Guiltless of fire had formed, or angels brought
To Pales, or Pomona thus adorned,
Likeliest she seemed, Pomona when she fled
Vertumnus, or to Ceres in her prime,
Yet virgin of Proserpina from Jove.
Her long with ardent look his eye pursued
Delighted, but desiring more her stay.
Oft he to her his charge of quick return
Repeated, she to him as oft engaged
To be returned by noon amid the bower,
And all things in best order to invite
Noontide repast, or afternoon's repose.
O much deceived, much failing, hapless Eve,
Of thy presumed return! event perverse!
Thou never from that hour in Paradise
Foundest either sweet repast, or sound repose;
Such ambush hid among sweet flowers and shades
Waited with hellish rancor imminent
To intercept thy way, or send thee back
Despoiled of innocence, of faith, of bliss.
For now, and since first break of dawn the fiend,
Mere serpent in appearance, forth was come,
And on his quest, where likeliest he might find
The only two of mankind, but in them
The whole included race, his purposed prey.
In bower and field he sought, where any tuft
Of grove or garden plot more pleasant lay,
Their tendance or plantation for delight,
By fountain or by shady rivulet
He sought them both, but wished his hap might find
Eve separate, he wished, but not with hope
Of what so seldom chanced, when to his wish,
Beyond his hope, Eve separate he spies,
Veiled in a cloud of fragrance, where she stood,
Half spied, so thick the roses bushing round
About her glowed, oft stooping to support
Each flower of slender stalk, whose head though gay

Carnation, purple, azure, or specked with gold,
Hung drooping unsustained, them she upstays
Gently with myrtle band, mindless the while,
Herself, though fairest unsupported flower,
From her best prop so far, and storm so nigh.
Nearer he drew, and many a walk traversed
Of stateliest covert, cedar, pine, or palm,
Then voluble and bold, now hid, now seen
Among thick-woven arborets and flowers
Imbordered on each bank, the hand of Eve:
Spot more delicious than those gardens feigned
Or of revived Adonis, or renowned
Alcinous, host of old Laertes' son,
Or that, not mystic, where the sapient king
Held dalliance with his fair Egyptian spouse.
Much he the place admired, the person more.
As one who long in populous city pent,
Where houses thick and sewers annoy the air,
Forth issuing on a summer's morn to breathe
Among the pleasant villages and farms
Adjoined, from each thing met conceives delight,
The smell of grain, or tedded grass, or kine,
Or dairy, each rural sight, each rural sound;
If chance with nymphlike step fair virgin pass,
What pleasing seemed, for her now pleases more,
She most, and in her look sums all delight.
Such pleasure took the serpent to behold
This flowery plat, the sweet recess of Eve
Thus early, thus alone; her heavenly form
Angelic, but more soft, and feminine,
Her graceful innocence, her every air
Of gesture or least action overawed
His malice, and with rapine sweet bereaved
His fierceness of the fierce intent it brought:
That space the evil one abstracted stood
From his own evil, and for the time remained
Stupidly good, of enmity disarmed,

Of guile, of hate, of envy, of revenge;
But the hot hell that always in him burns,
Though in mid heaven, soon ended his delight,
And tortures him now more, the more he sees
Of pleasure not for him ordained: then soon
Fierce hate he recollects, and all his thoughts
Of mischief, gratulating, thus excites.
    'Thoughts, whither have ye led me, with what sweet
Compulsion thus transported to forget
What hither brought us, hate, not love, nor hope
Of Paradise for hell, hope here to taste
Of pleasure, but all pleasure to destroy,
Save what is in destroying, other joy
To me is lost. Then let me not let pass
Occasion which now smiles, behold alone
The woman, opportune to all attempts,
Her husband, for I view far round, not nigh,
Whose higher intellectual more I shun,
And strength, of courage haughty, and of limb
Heroic built, though of terrestrial mold,
Foe not informidable, exempt from wound,
I not; so much hath hell debased, and pain
Enfeebled me, to what I was in heaven.
She fair, divinely fair, fit love for gods,
Not terrible, though terror be in love
And beauty, not approached by stronger hate,
Hate stronger, under show of love well feigned,
The way which to her ruin now I tend.'
    So spake the enemy of mankind, enclosed
In serpent, inmate bad, and toward Eve
Addressed his way, not with indented wave,
Prone on the ground, as since, but on his rear,
Circular base of rising folds, that towered
Fold above fold a surging maze, his head
Crested aloft, and carbuncle his eyes;
With burnished neck of verdant gold, erect
Amidst his circling spires, that on the grass

Floated redundant: pleasing was his shape
And lovely, never since of serpent kind
Lovelier, not those that in Illyria changed
Hermione and Cadmus, or the god
In Epidaurus; nor to which transformed
Ammonian Jove, or Capitoline was seen,
He with Olympias, this with her who bore
Scipio the height of Rome. With tract oblique
At first, as one who sought access, but feared
To interrupt, sidelong he works his way.
As when a ship by skillful steersman wrought
Nigh river's mouth or foreland, where the wind
Veers oft, as oft so steers, and shifts her sail;
So varied he, and of his tortuous train
Curled many a wanton wreath in sight of Eve,
To lure her eye; she busied heard the sound
Of rustling leaves, but minded not, as used
To such disport before her through the field,
From every beast, more duteous at her call,
Than at Circean call the herd disguised.
He bolder now, uncalled before her stood;
But as in gaze admiring: Oft he bowed
His turret crest, and sleek enameled neck,
Fawning, and licked the ground whereon she trod.
His gentle dumb expression turned at length
The eye of Eve to mark his play; he glad
Of her attention gained, with serpent tongue
Organic, or impulse of vocal air,
His fraudulent temptation thus began.

   'Wonder not, sovereign mistress, if perhaps
Thou canst, who art sole wonder, much less arm
Thy looks, the heaven of mildness, with disdain,
Displeased that I approach thee thus, and gaze
Insatiate, I thus single, nor have feared
Thy awful brow, more awful thus retired.
Fairest resemblance of thy maker fair,
Thee all things living gaze on, all things thine

By gift, and thy celestial beauty adore
With ravishment beheld, there best beheld
Where universally admired: but here
In this enclosure wild, these beasts among,
Beholders rude, and shallow to discern
Half what in thee is fair, one man except,
Who sees thee? (and what is one?) who shouldst be seen
A goddess among gods, adored and served
By angels numberless, thy daily train.'
  So glozed the tempter, and his proem tuned;
Into the heart of Eve his words made way,
Though at the voice much marveling; at length
Not unamazed she thus in answer spake.
'What may this mean? Language of man pronounced
By tongue of brute, and human sense expressed?
The first at least of these I thought denied
To beasts, whom God on their creation-day
Created mute to all articulate sound;
The latter I demur, for in their looks
Much reason, and in their actions oft appears.
Thee, serpent, subtlest beast of all the field
I knew, but not with human voice endued;
Redouble then this miracle, and say,
How camest thou speakable of mute, and how
To me so friendly grown above the rest
Of brutal kind, that daily are in sight?
Say, for such wonder claims attention due.'
  To whom the guileful tempter thus replied.
'Empress of this fair world, resplendent Eve,
Easy to me it is to tell thee all
What thou commandest, and right thou shouldst be obeyed:
I was at first as other beasts that graze
The trodden herb, of abject thoughts and low,
As was my food, nor aught but food discerned
Or sex, and apprehended nothing high:
Till on a day roving the field, I chanced
A goodly tree far distant to behold

Laden with fruit of fairest colors mixed,
Ruddy and gold: I nearer drew to gaze;
When from the boughs a savory odor blown,
Grateful to appetite, more pleased my sense
Than smell of sweetest fennel or the teats
Of ewe or goat dropping with milk at even,
Unsucked of lamb or kid, that tend their play.
To satisfy the sharp desire I had
Of tasting those fair apples, I resolved
Not to defer; hunger and thirst at once,
Powerful persuaders, quickened at the scent
Of that alluring fruit, urged me so keen.
About the mossy trunk I wound me soon,
For high from ground the branches would require
Thy utmost reach or Adam's: round the tree
All other beasts that saw, with like desire
Longing and envying stood, but could not reach.
Amid the tree now got, where plenty hung
Tempting so nigh, to pluck and eat my fill
I spared not, for such pleasure till that hour
At feed or fountain never had I found.
Sated at length, erelong I might perceive
Strange alteration in me, to degree
Of reason in my inward powers, and speech
Wanted not long, though to this shape retained.
Thenceforth to speculations high or deep
I turned my thoughts, and with capacious mind
Considered all things visible in heaven,
Or earth, or middle, all things fair and good;
But all that fair and good in thy divine
Semblance, and in thy beauty's heavenly ray
United I beheld; no fair to thine
Equivalent or second, which compelled
Me thus, though importune perhaps, to come
And gaze, and worship thee of right declared
Sovereign of creatures, universal dame.'

So talked the spirited sly snake; and Eve
Yet more amazed unwary thus replied.
   'Serpent, thy overpraising leaves in doubt
The virtue of that fruit, in thee first proved:
But say, where grows the tree, from hence how far?
For many are the trees of God that grow
In Paradise, and various, yet unknown
To us, in such abundance lies our choice,
As leaves a greater store of fruit untouched,
Still hanging incorruptible, till men
Grow up to their provision, and more hands
Help to disburden nature of her bearth.'
   To whom the wily adder, blithe and glad.
'Empress, the way is ready, and not long,
Beyond a row of myrtles, on a flat,
Fast by a fountain, one small thicket past
Of blowing myrrh and balm; if thou accept
My conduct, I can bring thee thither soon.'
   'Lead then,' said Eve. He leading swiftly rolled
In tangles, and made intricate seem straight,
To mischief swift. Hope elevates, and joy
Brightens his crest, as when a wandering fire
Compact of unctuous vapor, which the night
Condenses, and the cold environs round,
Kindled through agitation to a flame,
Which oft, they say, some evil spirit attends,
Hovering and blazing with delusive light,
Misleads the amazed night-wanderer from his way
To bogs and mires, and oft through pond or pool,
There swallowed up and lost, from succor far.
So glistered the dire snake, and into fraud
Led Eve our credulous mother, to the tree
Of prohibition, root of all our woe;
Which when she saw, thus to her guide she spake.
   'Serpent, we might have spared our coming hither,
Fruitless to me, though fruit be here to excess,
The credit of whose virtue rest with thee.

Wondrous indeed, if cause of such effects.
But of this tree we may not taste nor touch ;
God so commanded, and left that command
Sole daughter of his voice; the rest, we live
Law to ourselves, our reason is our law.'
 To whom the tempter guilefully replied.
'Indeed? hath God then said that of the fruit
Of all these garden trees ye shall not eat,
Yet lords declared of all in earth or air?'
 To whom thus Eve yet sinless. 'Of the fruit
Of each tree in the garden we may eat,
But of the fruit of this fair tree amidst
The garden, God hath said, "Ye shall not eat
Thereof, nor shall ye touch it, lest ye die.' "
 She scarce had said, though brief, when now more bold
The tempter, but with show of zeal and love
To man, and indignation at his wrong,
New part puts on, and as to passion moved,
Fluctuates disturbed, yet comely, and in act
Raised, as of some great matter to begin.
As when of old some orator renowned
In Athens or free Rome, where eloquence
Flourished, since mute, to some great cause addressed,
Stood in himself collected, while each part,
Motion, each act won audience ere the tongue,
Sometimes in height began, as no delay
Of preface brooking through his zeal of right.
So standing, moving, or to height upgrown
The tempter all impassioned thus began.
 'O sacred, wise, and wisdom-giving plant,
Mother of science, now I feel thy power
Within me clear, not only to discern
Things in their causes, but to trace the ways
Of highest agents, deemed however wise.
Queen of this universe, do not believe
Those rigid threats of death; ye shall not die
How should ye? by the fruit? it gives you life

To knowledge: By the threatener, look on me,
Me who have touched and tasted, yet both live,
And life more perfect have attained than fate
Meant me, by venturing higher than my lot.
Shall that be shut to man, which to the beast
Is open? or will God incense his ire
For such a petty trespass, and not praise
Rather your dauntless virtue, whom the pain
Of death denounced, whatever thing death be,
Deterred not from achieving what might lead
To happier life, knowledge of good and evil;
Of good, how just? of evil, if what is evil
Be real, why not known, since easier shunned?
God therefore cannot hurt ye, and be just;
Not just, not God; not feared then, nor obeyed:
Your fear itself of death removes the fear.
Why then was this forbid? Why but to awe,
Why but to keep ye low and ignorant,
His worshipers; he knows that in the day
Ye eat thereof, your eyes that seem so clear,
Yet are but dim, shall perfectly be then
Opened and cleared, and ye shall be as gods,
Knowing both good and evil as they know.
That ye should be as gods, since I as man,
Internal man, is but proportion meet,
I of brute human, ye of human gods.
So ye shall die perhaps, by putting off
Human, to put on gods, death to be wished,
Though threatened, which no worse than this can bring.
And what are gods that man may not become
As they, participating godlike food?
The gods are first, and that advantage use
On our belief, that all from them proceeds;
I question it, for this fair earth I see,
Warmed by the sun, producing every kind,
Them nothing: If they all things, who encloses
Knowledge of good and evil in this tree.

That whoso eats thereof, forthwith attains
Wisdom without their leave? and wherein lies
The offense, that man should thus attain to know?
What can your knowledge hurt him, or this tree
Impart against his will if all be his?
Or is it envy, and can envy dwell
In heavenly breasts? these, these and many more
Causes import your need of this fair fruit.
Goddess humane, reach then, and freely taste.'
    He ended, and his words replete with guile
Into her heart too easy entrance won:
Fixed on the fruit she gazed, which to behold
Might tempt alone, and in her ears the sound
Yet rung of his persuasive words, impregned
With reason, to her seeming, and with truth;
Meanwhile the hour of noon drew on, and waked
An eager appetite, raised by the smell
So savory of that fruit, which with desire,
Inclinable now grown to touch or taste,
Solicited her longing eye; yet first
Pausing a while, thus to herself she mused.
    'Great are thy virtues, doubtless, best of fruits,
Though kept from man, and worthy to be admired,
Whose taste, too long forborne, at first assay
Gave elocution to the mute, and taught
The tongue not made for speech to speak thy praise:
Thy praise he also who forbids thy use,
Conceals not from us, naming thee the tree
Of knowledge, knowledge both of good and evil;
Forbids us then to taste, but his forbidding
Commends thee more, while it infers the good
By thee communicated, and our want:
For good unknown, sure is not had, or had
And yet unknown, is as not had at all.
In plain then, what forbids he but to know,
Forbids us good, forbids us to be wise?
Such prohibitions bind not. But if death

Bind us with after-bands, what profits then
Our inward freedom? In the day we eat
Of this fair fruit, our doom is, we shall die.
How dies the serpent? he hath eaten and lives,
And knows, and speaks, and reasons, and discerns,
Irrational till then. For us alone
Was death invented? or to us denied
This intellectual food, for beasts reserved?
For beasts it seems: yet that one beast which first
Hath tasted, envies not, but brings with joy
The good befallen him, author unsuspect,
Friendly to man, far from deceit or guile.
What fear I then, rather what know to fear
Under this ignorance of good and evil,
Of God or death, of law or penalty?
Here grows the cure of all, this fruit divine,
Fair to the eye, inviting to the taste,
Of virtue to make wise: what hinders then
To reach, and feed at once both body and mind?'

     So saying, her rash hand in evil hour
Forth reaching to the fruit, she plucked, she eat:
Earth felt the wound, and nature from her seat
Sighing through all her works gave signs of woe,
That all was lost. Back to the thicket slunk
The guilty serpent, and well might, for Eve
Intent now wholly on her taste, naught else
Regarded, such delight till then, as seemed,
In fruit she never tasted, whether true
Or fancied so, through expectation high
Of knowledge, nor was godhead from her thought.
Greedily she engorged without restraint,
And knew not eating death: Satiate at length,
And heightened as with wine, jocund and boon,
Thus to herself she pleasingly began.

     'O sovereign, virtuous, precious of all trees
In Paradise, of operation blessed
To sapience, hitherto obscured, infamed,

And thy fair fruit let hang, as to no end
Created; but henceforth my early care,
Not without song, each morning, and due praise
Shall tend thee, and the fertile burden ease
Of thy full branches offered free to all;
Till dieted by thee I grow mature
In knowledge, as the gods who all things know;
Though others envy what they cannot give;
For had the gift been theirs, it had not here
Thus grown. Experience, next to thee I owe,
Best guide; not following thee, I had remained
In ignorance, thou openest wisdom's way,
And givest access, though secret she retire.
And I perhaps am secret; heaven is high,
High and remote to see from thence distinct
Each thing on earth; and other care perhaps
May have diverted from continual watch
Our great forbidder, safe with all his spies
About him. But to Adam in what sort
Shall I appear? shall I to him make known
As yet my change, and give him to partake
Full happiness with me, or rather not,
But keep the odds of knowledge in my power
Without copartner? so to add what wants
In female sex, the more to draw his love,
And render me more equal, and perhaps,
A thing not undesirable, sometime
Superior: for inferior who is free?
This may be well: but what if God have seen,
And death ensue? then I shall be no more,
And Adam wedded to another Eve,
Shall live with her enjoying, I extinct;
A death to think. Confirmed then I resolve,
Adam shall share with me in bliss or woe:
So dear I love him, that with him all deaths
I could endure, without him live no life.'

So saying, from the tree her step she turned,
But first low reverence done, as to the power
That dwelt within, whose presence had infused
Into the plant sciential sap, derived
From nectar, drink of gods. Adam the while
Waiting desirous her return, had wove
Of choicest flowers a garland to adorn
Her tresses, and her rural labors crown
As reapers oft are wont their harvest queen.
Great joy he promised to his thoughts, and new
Solace in her return, so long delayed;
Yet oft his heart, divine of something ill,
Misgave him; he the faltering measure felt;
And forth to meet her went, the way she took
That morn when first they parted; by the tree
Of knowledge he must pass, there he her met,
Scarce from the tree returning; in her hand
A bough of fairest fruit that downy smiled,
New gathered, and ambrosial smell diffused.
To him she hasted, in her face excuse
Came prologue, and apology to prompt,
Which with bland words at will she thus addressed.

'Hast thou not wondered, Adam, at my stay?
Thee I have missed, and thought it long, deprived
Thy presence, agony of love till now
Not felt, nor shall be twice, for never more
Mean I to try, what rash untried I sought,
The pain of absence from thy sight. But strange
Hath been the cause, and wonderful to hear:
This tree is not as we are told, a tree
Of danger tasted, nor to evil unknown
Opening the way, but of divine effect
To open eyes, and make them gods who taste;
And hath been tasted such: the serpent wise,
Or not restrained as we, or not obeying,
Hath eaten of the fruit, and is become,
Not dead, as we are threatened, but thenceforth

Endued with human voice and human sense,
Reasoning to admiration, and with me
Persuasively hath so prevailed, that I
Have also tasted, and have also found
The effects to correspond, opener mine eyes,
Dim erst, dilated spirits, ampler heart,
And growing up to godhead; which for the
Chiefly I sought, without thee can despise.
For bliss, as thou hast part, to me is bliss,
Tedious, unshared with thee, and odious soon.
Thou therefore also taste, that equal lot
May join us, equal joy, as equal love;
Lest thou not tasting, different degree
Disjoin us, and I then too late renounce
Deity for thee, when fate will not permit.'

Thus Eve with countenance blithe her story told;
But in her cheek distemper flushing glowed.
On the other side, Adam, soon as he heard
The fatal trespass done by Eve, amazed,
Astonied stood and blank, while horror chill
Ran through his veins, and all his joints relaxed;
From his slack hand the garland wreathed for Eve
Down dropped, and all the faded roses shed:
Speechless he stood and pale, till thus at length
First to himself he inward silence broke.

'O fairest of creation, last and best
Of all God's works, creature in whom excelled
Whatever can to sight or thought be formed,
Holy, divine, good, amiable, or sweet!
How art thou lost, how on a sudden lost,
Defaced, deflowered, and now to death devote?
Rather how hast thou yielded to transgress
The strict forbiddance, how to violate
The sacred fruit forbidden! some cursed fraud
Of enemy hath beguiled thee, yet unknown,
And me with thee hath ruined, for with thee
Certain my resolution is to die;

How can I live without thee, how forgo
Thy sweet converse and love so dearly joined,
To live again in these wild woods forlorn?
Should God create another Eve, and I
Another rib afford, yet loss of thee
Would never from my heart; no no, I feel
The link of nature draw me: Flesh of flesh,
Bone of my bone thou art, and from thy state
Mine never shall be parted, bliss or woe.'
    So having said, as one from sad dismay
Recomforted, and after thoughts disturbed
Submitting to what seemed remediless,
Thus in calm mood his words to Eve he turned.
    'Bold deed thou hast presumed, adventurous Eve,
And peril great provoked, who thus hath dared
Had it been only coveting to eye
That sacred fruit, sacred to abstinence,
Much more to taste it under ban to touch.
But past who can recall, or done undo?
Not God omnipotent, nor fate, yet so
Perhaps thou shalt not die, perhaps the fact
Is not so heinous now, foretasted fruit,
Profaned first by the serpent, by him first
Made common and unhallowed ere our taste;
Nor yet on him found deadly, he yet lives,
Lives as thou saidst, and gains to live as man
Higher degree of life, inducement strong
To us, as likely tasting to attain
Proportional ascent, which cannot be
But to be gods, or angels demi-gods.
Nor can I think that God, creator wise,
Though threatening, will in earnest so destroy
Us his prime creatures, dignified so high,
Set over all his works, which in our fall,
For us created, needs with us must fail,
Dependent made; so God shall uncreate,
Be frustrate, do, undo, and labour lose,

Not well conceived of God, who though his power
Creation could repeat, yet would be loath
Us to abolish, lest the adversary
Triumph and say; "Fickle their state whom God
Most favors, who can please him long? Me first
He ruined, now mankind; whom will he next?"
Matter of scorn, not to be given the foe.
However I with thee have fixed my lot,
Certain to undergo like doom, if death
Consort with thee, death is to me as life;
So forcible within my heart I feel
The bond of nature draw me to my own,
My own in thee, for what thou art is mine;
Our state cannot be severed, we are one,
One flesh; to lose thee were to lose myself.'

  So Adam, and thus Eve to him replied.
'O glorious trial of exceeding love,
Illustrious evidence, example high!
Engaging me to emulate, but short
Of thy perfection, how shall I attain,
Adam, from whose dear side I boast me sprung,
And gladly of our union hear thee speak,
One heart, one soul in both; whereof good proof
This day affords, declaring thee resolved,
Rather than death or aught than death more dread
Shall separate us, linked in love so dear,
To undergo with me one guilt, one crime,
If any be, of tasting this fair fruit,
Whose virtue, for of good still good proceeds,
Direct, or by occasion hath presented
This happy trial of thy love, which else
So eminently never had been known.
Were it I thought death menaced would ensue
This my attempt, I would sustain alone
The worst, and not persuade thee, rather die
Deserted, than oblige thee with a fact
Pernicious to thy peace, chiefly assured

Remarkably so late of thy so true,
So faithful love unequaled; but I feel
Far otherwise the event, not death, but life
Augmented, opened eyes, new hopes, new joys,
Taste so divine, that what of sweet before
Hath touched my sense, flat seems to this, and harsh.
On my experience, Adam, freely taste,
And fear of death deliver to the winds.'

So saying, she embraced him, and for joy
Tenderly wept, much won that he his love
Had so ennobled, as of choice to incur
Divine displeasure for her sake, or death.
In recompense (for such compliance bad
Such recompense best merits) from the bough
She gave him of that fair enticing fruit
With liberal hand: he scrupled not to eat
Against his better knowledge, not deceived,
But fondly overcome with female charm.
Earth trembled from her entrails, as again
In pangs, and nature gave a second groan,
Sky loured and muttering thunder, some sad drops
Wept at completing of the mortal sin
Original; while Adam took no thought,
Eating his fill, nor Eve to iterate
Her former trespass feared, the more to soothe
Him with her loved society, that now
As with new wine intoxicated both
They swim in mirth, and fancy that they feel
Divinity within them breeding wings
Wherewith to scorn the earth: but that false fruit
Far other operation first displayed,
Carnal desire inflaming, he on Eve
Began to cast lascivious eyes, she him
As wantonly repaid; in lust they burn:
Till Adam thus 'gan Eve to dalliance move.

'Eve, now I see thou art exact of taste,
And elegant, of sapience no small part,

Since to each meaning savor we apply,
And palate call judicious; I the praise
Yield thee, so well this day thou hast purveyed.
Much pleasure we have lost, while we abstained
From this delightful fruit, nor known till now
True relish, tasting; if such pleasure be
In things to us forbidden, it might be wished,
For this one tree had been forbidden ten.
But come, so well refreshed, now let us play,
As meet is, after such delicious fare;
For never did thy beauty since the day
I saw thee first and wedded thee, adorned
With all perfections, so inflame my sense
With ardor to enjoy thee, fairer now
Than ever, bounty of this virtuous tree.'
    So said he, and forbore not glance or toy
Of amorous intent, well understood
Of Eve, whose eye darted contagious fire.
Her hand he seized, and to a shady bank.
Thick overhead with verdant roof embowered
He led her nothing loath; flowers were the couch,
Pansies, and violets, and asphodel,
And hyacinth, earth's freshest softest lap.
There they their fill of love and love's disport
Took largely, of their mutual guilt the seal,
The solace of their sin, till dewy sleep
Oppressed them, wearied with their amorous play.
Soon as the force of that fallacious fruit,
That with exhilarating vapor bland
About their spirits had played, and inmost powers
Made err, was now exhaled, and grosser sleep
Bred of unkindly fumes, with conscious dreams
Encumbered, now had left them, up they rose
As from unrest, and each the other viewing,
Soon found their eyes how opened, and their minds
How darkened; innocence, that as a veil
Had shadowed them from knowing ill, was gone.

Just confidence, and native righteousness,
And honor from about them, naked left
To guilty shame he covered, but his robe
Uncovered more. So rose the Danite strong
Herculean Samson from the harlot-lap
Of Philistean Dalilah, and waked
Shorn of his strength, they destitute and bare
Of all their virtue: silent, and in face
Confounded long they sat, as stricken mute,
Till Adam, though not less than Eve abashed,
At length gave utterance to these words constrained.

'O Eve, in evil hour thou didst give ear
To that false worm, of whomsoever taught
To counterfeit man's voice, true in our fall,
False in our promised rising; since our eyes
Opened we find indeed, and find we know
Both good and evil, good lost, and evil got,
Bad fruit of knowledge, if this be to know,
Which leaves us naked thus, of honor void,
Of innocence, of faith, of purity,
Our wonted ornaments now soiled and stained,
And in our faces evident the signs
Of foul concupiscence; whence evil store;
Even shame, the last of evils; of the first
Be sure then. How shall I behold the face
Henceforth of God or angel, erst with joy
And rapture so oft beheld? those heavenly shapes
Will dazzle now this earthly, with their blaze
Insufferably bright. O might I here
In solitude live savage, in some glade
Obscured, where highest woods impenetrable
To star or sunlight, spread their umbrage broad,
And brown as evening: Cover me ye pines,
Ye cedars, with innumerable boughs
Hide me, where I may never see them more.
But let us now, as in bad plight, devise
What best may for the present serve to hide

The parts of each from other, that seem most
To shame obnoxious, and unseemliest seen,
Some tree whose broad smooth leaves together sewed,
And girded on our loins, may cover round
Those middle parts, that this new comer, shame,
There sit not, and reproach us as unclean.'
    So counseled he, and both together went
Into the thickest wood, there soon they chose
The fig tree, not that kind for fruit renowned,
But such as at this day to Indians known
In Malabar or Decan spreads her arms
Branching so broad and long, that in the ground
The bended twigs take root, and daughters grow
About the mother tree, a pillared shade
High overarched, and echoing walks between;
There oft the Indian herdsman shunning heat
Shelters in cool, and tends his pasturing herds
At loopholes cut through thickest shade: Those leaves
They gathered, broad as Amazonian targe,
And with what skill they had, together sewed,
To gird their waist, vain covering if to hide
Their guilt and dreaded shame; O how unlike
To that first naked glory. Such of late
Columbus found the American so girt
With feathered cincture, naked else and wild
Among the trees on isles and woody shores.
Thus fenced, and as they thought, their shame in part
Covered, but not at rest or ease of mind,
They sat them down to weep, nor only tears
Rained at their eyes, but high winds worse within
Began to rise, high passions, anger, hate,
Mistrust, suspicion, discord, and shook sore
Their inward state of mind, calm region once
And full of peace, now tossed and turbulent:
For understanding ruled not, and the will
Heard not her lore, both in subjection now
To sensual appetite, who from beneath

Usurping over sovereign reason claimed
Superior sway: from thus distempered breast,
Adam, estranged in look and altered style,
Speech intermitted thus to Eve renewed.

    'Would thou hadst harkened to my words, and stayed
With me, as I besought thee, when that strange
Desire of wandering this unhappy morn,
I know not whence possessed thee; we had then
Remained still happy, not as now, despoiled
Of all our good, shamed, naked, miserable.
Let none henceforth seek needless cause to approve
The faith they owe; when earnestly they seek
Such proof, conclude, they then begin to fail.'

    To whom soon moved with touch of blame thus Eve.
'What words have passed thy lips, Adam severe,
Imputest thou that to my default, or will
Of wandering, as thou callest it, which who knows
But might as ill have happened thou being by,
Or to thyself perhaps: hadst thou been there,
Or here the attempt, thou couldst not have discerned
Fraud in the serpent, speaking as he spake;
No ground of enmity between us known,
Why he should mean me ill, or seek to harm.
Was I to have never parted from thy side?
As good have grown there still a lifeless rib.
Being as I am, why didst not thou the head
Command me absolutely not to go,
Going into such danger as thou saidst?
Too facile then thou didst not much gainsay,
Nay didst permit, approve, and fair dismiss
Hadst thou been firm and fixed in thy dissent,
Neither had I transgressed, nor thou with me.'

    To whom then first incensed Adam replied.
'Is this the love, is this the recompense
Of mine to thee, ingrateful Eve, expressed
Immutable when thou wert lost, not I,
Who might have lived and joyed immortal bliss,

Yet willingly chose rather death with thee;
And am I now upbraided, as the cause
Of thy transgressing? not enough severe,
It seems, in thy restraint: what could I more?
I warned thee, I admonished thee, foretold
The danger, and the lurking enemy
That lay in wait; beyond this had been force,
And force upon free will hath here no place.
But confidence then bore thee on, secure
Either to meet no danger, or to find
Matter of glorious trial; and perhaps
I also erred in overmuch admiring
What seemed in thee so perfect, that I thought
No evil durst attempt thee, but I rue
That error now, which is become my crime,
And thou the accuser. Thus it shall befall
Him who to worth in women overtrusting
Lets her will rule; restraint she will not brook,
And left to herself, if evil thence ensue,
She first his weak indulgence will accuse.'

    Thus they in mutual accusation spent
The fruitless hours, but neither self-condemning,
And of their vain contest appeared no end.

BOOK X

The Argument: Man's transgression known, the guardian angels
forsake Paradise, and return up to heaven to approve their vigilance,
and are approved, God declaring that the entrance of Satan could
not be by them prevented. He sends his Son to judge the trans-
gressors, who descends and gives sentence accordingly; then in pity
clothes them both, and reascends. Sin and death sitting till then at
the gates of hell, by wondrous sympathy feeling the success of Satan
in this new world, and the sin by man there committed, resolve to

sit no longer confined in hell, but to follow Satan their sire up to the
place of man: To make the way easier from hell to this world to
and fro, they pave a broad highway or bridge over chaos, according
to the track that Satan first made; then preparing for earth, they
meet him proud of his success returning to hell; their mutual
gratulation. Satan arrives at Pandemonium, in full of assembly re-
lates with boasting his success against man; instead of applause is
entertained with a general hiss by all his audience, transformed with
himself also suddenly into serpents, according to his doom given in
Paradise; then deluded with a show of the forbidden tree springing
up before them, they greedily reaching to take of the fruit, chew
dust and bitter ashes. The proceedings of sin and death; God fore-
tells the final victory of his Son over them, and the renewing of all
things; but for the present commands his angels to make several
alterations in the heavens and elements. Adam more and more per-
ceiving his fallen condition heavily bewails, rejects the condolement
of Eve; she persists and at length appeases him: then to evade the
curse likely to fall on their offspring, proposes to Adam violent ways,
which he approves not, but conceiving better hope, puts her in
mind of the late promise made them, that her seed should be re-
venged on the serpent, and exhorts her with him to seek peace of the
offended deity, by repentance and supplication.

> Meanwhile the heinous and despiteful act
> Of Satan done in Paradise, and how
> He in the serpent, had perverted Eve,
> Her husband she, to taste the fatal fruit,
> Was known in heaven; for what can scape the eye
> Of God all-seeing, or deceive his heart
> Omniscient, who in all things wise and just,
> Hindered not Satan to attempt the mind
> Of man, with strength entire, and free will armed,
> Complete to have discovered and repulsed
> Whatever wiles of foe or seeming friend.
> For still they knew, and ought to have still remembered
> The high injunction not to taste that fruit,
> Whoever tempted; which they not obeying,

Incurred, what could they less, the penalty,
And manifold in sin, deserved to fall.
Up into heaven from Paradise in haste
The angelic guards ascended, mute and sad
For man, for of his state by this they knew,
Much wondering how the subtle fiend had stolen
Entrance unseen. Soon as the unwelcome news
From earth arrived at heaven gate, displeased
All were who heard, dim sadness did not spare
That time celestial visages, yet mixed
With pity, violated not their bliss.
About the new-arrived, in multitudes
The ethereal people ran, to hear and know
How all befell: they towards the throne supreme
Accountable made haste to make appear
With righteous plea, their utmost vigilance,
And easily approved; when the most high
Eternal father from his secret cloud,
Amidst in thunder uttered thus his voice.

   'Assembled angels, and ye powers returned
From unsuccessful charge, be not dismayed,
Nor troubled at these tidings from the earth,
Which your sincerest care could not prevent,
Foretold so lately what would come to pass,
When first this tempter crossed the gulf from hell.
I told ye then he should prevail and speed
On his bad errand, man should be seduced
And flattered out of all, believing lies
Against his maker; no decree of mine
Concurring to necessitate his fall,
Or touch with lightest moment of impulse
His free will, to her own inclining left
In even scale. But fallen he is, and now
What rests but that the mortal sentence pass
On his transgression, death denounced that day,
Which ne presumes already vain and void,
Because not yet inflicted, as he feared.

By some immediate stroke; but soon shall find
Forbearance no acquittance ere day end.
Justice shall not return as bounty scorned.
But whom send I to judge them? whom but thee
Vicegerent Son, to thee I have transferred
All judgment whether in heaven, or earth, or hell.
Easy it may be seen that I intend
Mercy colleague with justice, sending thee
Man's friend, his mediator, his designed
Both ransom and redeemer voluntary,
And destined man himself to judge man fallen.'
 So spake the father, and, unfolding bright
Toward the right hand his glory, on the Son
Blazed forth unclouded deity; he full
Resplendent all his father manifest
Expressed, and thus divinely answered mild.
 'Father eternal, thine is to decree,
Mine both in heaven and earth to do thy will
Supreme, that thou in me thy son beloved
Mayest ever rest well pleased. I go to judge
On earth these thy transgressors, but thou knowest,
Whoever judged, the worst on me must light,
When time shall be, for so I undertook
Before thee; and not repenting, this obtain
Of right, that I may mitigate their doom
On me derived, yet I shall temper so
Justice with mercy, as may illustrate most
Them fully satisfied, and thee appease.
Attendance none shall need, nor train, where none
Are to behold the judgment, but the judged,
Those two; the third best absent is condemned,
Convict by flight, and rebel to all law
Conviction to the serpent none belongs.'
 Thus saying, from his radiant seat he rose
Of high collateral glory: him thrones and powers,
Princedoms, and dominations ministrant
Accompanied to heaven gate, from whence

Eden and all the coast in prospect lay.
Down he descended straight; the speed of gods
Time counts not, though with swiftest minutes winged
Now was the sun in western cadence low
From noon, and gentle airs due at their hour
To fan the earth now waked, and usher in
The evening cool when he from wrath more cool
Came the mild judge and intercessor both
To sentence man: the voice of God they heard
Now walking in the garden, by soft winds
Brought to their ears, while day declined, they heard,
And from his presence hid themselves among
The thickest trees, both man and wife, till God
Approaching, thus to Adam called aloud.

'Where art thou Adam, wont with joy to meet
My coming seen far off? I miss thee here,
Not pleased, thus entertained with solitude,
Where obvious duty erewhile appeared unsought:
Or come I less conspicuous, or what change
Absents thee, or what chance detains? Come forth.'
He came, and with him Eve, more loath, though first
To offend, discountenanced both, and discomposed;
Love was not in their looks, either to God
Or to each other, but apparent guilt,
And shame, and perturbation, and despair,
Anger, and obstinacy, and hate, and guile.
Whence Adam, faltering long, thus answered brief.

'I heard thee in the garden, and of thy voice
Afraid, being naked, hid myself.' To whom
The gracious judge without revile replied.

'My voice thou oft hast heard, and hast not feared,
But still rejoiced, how is it now become
So dreadful to thee? that thou art naked, who
Hath told thee? hast thou eaten of the tree
Whereof I gave thee charge thou shouldst not eat?'

To whom thus Adam sore beset replied.
'O heaven! in evil strait this day I stand

Before my judge, either to undergo
Myself the total crime, or to accuse
My other self, the partner of my life;
Whose failing, while her faith to me remains,
I should conceal, and not expose to blame
By my complaint; but strict necessity
Subdues me, and calamitous constraint,
Lest on my head both sin and punishment,
However insupportable, be all
Devolved; though should I hold my peace, yet thou
Wouldst easily detect what I conceal.
This woman whom thou madest to be my help,
And gavest me as thy perfect gift, so good,
So fit, so acceptable, so divine,
That from her hand I could suspect no ill,
And what she did, whatever in itself,
Her doing seemed to justify the deed;
She gave me of the tree, and I did eat.'
  To whom the sovereign presence thus replied.
'Was she thy God, that her thou didst obey
Before his voice, or was she made thy guide,
Superior, or but equal, that to her
Thou didst resign thy manhood, and the place
Wherein God set thee above her made of thee,
And for thee, whose perfection far excelled
Hers in all real dignity: Adorned
She was indeed, and lovely to attract
Thy love, not thy subjection, and her gifts
Were such as under government well seemed,
Unseemly to bear rule, which was thy part
And person, hadst thou known thyself aright.'
  So having said, he thus to Eve in few:
'Say Woman, what is this which thou hast done?'
  To whom sad Eve with shame nigh overwhelmed
Confessing soon, yet not before her judge
Bold or loquacious, thus abashed replied.
  'The serpent me beguiled and I did eat.'

Which when the Lord God heard, without delay
To judgment he proceeded on the accused
Serpent though brute, unable to transfer
The guilt on him who made him instrument
Of mischief, and polluted from the end
Of his creation; justly then accursed,
As vitiated in nature: more to know
Concerned not man (since he no further knew)
Nor altered his offense; yet God at last
To Satan first in sin his doom applied,
Though in mysterious terms, judged as then best:
And on the serpent thus his curse let fall

'Because thou hast done this, thou art accursed
Above all cattle, each beast of the field;
Upon thy belly groveling thou shalt go,
And dust shalt eat all the days of thy life.
Between thee and the woman I will put
Enmity, and between thine and her seed;
Her seed shall bruise thy head, thou bruise his heel.'

So spake this oracle, then verified
When Jesus son of Mary second Eve,
Saw Satan fall like lightning down from heaven,
Prince of the air; then rising from his grave
Spoiled principalities and powers, triumphed
In open show, and with ascension bright
Captivity led captive through the air,
The realm itself of Satan long usurped,
Whom he shall tread at last under our feet;
Even he who now foretold his fatal bruise,
And to the woman thus his sentence turned.

'Thy sorrow I will greatly multiply
By thy conception; children thou shalt bring
In sorrow forth, and to thy husband's will
Thine shall submit, he over thee shall rule.'

On Adam last thus judgment he pronounced.
'Because thou hast hearkened to the voice of thy wife,
And eaten of the tree concerning which

'I charged thee, saying: Thou shalt not eat thereof.
Cursed is the ground for thy sake, thou in sorrow
Shalt eat thereof all the days of thy life;
Thorns also and thistles it shall bring thee forth
Unbid, and thou shalt eat the herb of the field,
In the sweat of thy face thou shalt eat bread,
Till thou return unto the ground, for thou
Out of the ground wast taken, know thy birth,
For dust thou art, and shalt to dust return.'
　　So judged he man, both judge and saviour sent,
And the instant stroke of death denounced that day
Removed far off; then pitying how they stood
Before him naked to the air, that now
Must suffer change, disdained not to begin
Thenceforth the form of servant to assume,
As when he washed his servants' feet, so now
As father of his family he clad
Their nakedness with skins of beasts, or slain,
Or as the snake with youthful coat repaid;
And thought not much to clothe his enemies:
Nor he their outward only with the skins
Of beasts, but inward nakedness, much more
Opprobrious, with his robe of righteousness,
Arraying covered from his father's sight.
To him with swift ascent he up returned,
Into his blissful bosom reassumed
In glory as of old, to him appeased
All, though all-knowing, what had passed with man
Recounted, mixing intercession sweet.
Meanwhile ere thus was sinned and judged on earth,
Within the gates of hell sat sin and death,
In counterview within the gates, that now
Stood open wide, belching outrageous flame
Far into chaos, since the fiend passed through,
Sin opening, who thus now to death began.
　　'O son, why sit we here each other viewing
Idly, while Satan our great author thrives

In other worlds, and happier seat provides
For us his offspring dear? It cannot be
But that success attends him; if mishap,
Ere this he had returned, with fury driven
By his avengers, since no place like this
Can fit his punishment, or their revenge.
Methinks I feel new strength within me rise,
Wings growing, and dominion given me large
Beyond this deep; whatever draws me on,
Or sympathy, or some connatural force
Powerful at greatest distance to unite
With secret amity things of like kind
By secretest conveyance. Thou my shade
Inseparable must with me along:
For death from sin no power can separate.
But lest the difficulty of passing back
Stay his return perhaps over this gulf
Impassable, impervious, let us try
Adventurous work, yet to thy power and mine
Not unagreeable, to found a path
Over this main from hell to that new world
Where Satan now prevails, a monument
Of merit high to all the infernal host,
Easing their passage hence, for intercourse,
Of transmigration, as their lot shall lead.
Nor can I miss the way, so strongly drawn
By this new felt attraction and instinct.'
    Whom thus the meager shadow answered soon.
'Go whither fate and inclination strong
Leads thee, I shall not lag behind, nor err
The way, thou leading, such a scent I draw
Of carnage, prey innumerable, and taste
The savor of death from all things there that live:
Nor shall I to the work thou enterprisest
Be wanting, but afford thee equal aid,'
    So saying, with delight he snuffed the smell
Of mortal change on earth. As when a flock

Of ravenous fowl, though many a league remote,
Against the day of battle, to a field,
Where armies lie encamped, come flying, lured
With scent of living carcasses designed
For death, the following day, in bloody fight.
So scented the grim feature, and upturned
His nostril wide into the murky air,
Sagacious of his quarry from so far.
Then both from out hell gates into the waste
Wide anarchy of chaos damp and dark
Flew diverse, and with power (their power was great)
Hovering upon the waters; what they met
Solid or slimy, as in raging sea
Tossed up and down, together crowded drove
From each side shoaling towards the mouth of hell.
As when two polar winds blowing adverse
Upon the Cronian sea, together drive
Mountains of ice, that stop the imagined way
Beyond Petsora eastward, to the rich
Cathaian coast. The aggregated soil
Death with his mace petrific, cold and dry,
As with a trident smote, and fixed as firm
As Delos floating once; the rest his look
Bound with Gorgonian rigor not to move,
And with asphaltic slime; broad as the gate,
Deep to the roots of hell the gathered beach
They fastened, and the mole immense wrought on
Over the foaming deep high arched, a bridge
Of length prodigious joining to the wall
Immovable of this now fenceless world
Forfeit to death; from hence a passage broad,
Smooth, easy, inoffensive down to hell.
So, if great things to small may be compared,
Xerxes, the liberty of Greece to yoke,
From Susa his Memnonian palace high
Came to the sea, and over Hellespont
Bridging his way, Europe with Asia joined,

And scourged with many a stroke the indignant waves.
Now had they brought the work by wondrous art
Pontifical, a ridge of pendent rock
Over the vexed abyss, following the track
Of Satan, to the selfsame place where he
First lighted from his wing, and landed safe
From out of chaos to the outside bare
Of this round world: with pins of adamant
And chains they made all fast, too fast they made
And durable; and now in little space
The confines met of empyrean heaven
And of this world, and on the left hand hell
With long reach interposed; three several ways
In sight, to each of these three places led.
And now their way to earth they had descried,
To Paradise first tending, when behold
Satan in likeness of an angel bright
Betwixt the Centaur and the Scorpion steering
His zenith, while the sun in Aries rose:
Disguised he came, but those his children dear
Their parent soon discerned, though in disguise.
He after Eve seduced, unminded slunk
Into the wood fast by, and changing shape
To observe the sequel, saw his guileful act
By Eve, though all unwitting, seconded
Upon her husband, saw their shame that sought
Vain covertures; but when he saw descend
The Son of God to judge them terrified
He fled, not hoping to escape, but shun
The present, fearing guilty what his wrath
Might suddenly inflict; that past, returned
By night, and listening where the hapless pair
Sat in their sad discourse, and various plaint,
Thence gathered his own doom, which understood
Not instant, but of future time. With joy
And tidings fraught, to hell he now returned,
And at the brink of chaos, near the foot

Of this new wondrous pontifice, unhoped
Met who to meet him came, his offspring dear.
Great joy was at their meeting, and at sight
Of that stupendous bridge his joy increased.
Long he admiring stood, till sin, his fair
Enchanting daughter, thus the silence broke.
    'O parent, these are thy magnific deeds,
Thy trophies, which thou viewest as not thine own,
Thou art their author and prime architect:
For I no sooner in my heart divined,
My heart, which by a secret harmony
Still moves with thine, joined in connection sweet,
That thou on earth hadst prospered, which thy looks
Now also evidence, but straight I felt
Though distant from thee worlds between, yet felt
That I must after thee with this thy son;
Such fatal consequence unites us three:
Hell could no longer hold us in her bounds,
Nor this unvoyageable gulf obscure
Detain from following thy illustrious track.
Thou hast achieved our liberty, confined
Within hell gates till now, thou us empowered
To fortify thus far, and overlay
With this portentous bridge the dark abyss.
Thine now is all this world, thy virtue hath won
What thy hands builded not, thy wisdom gained
With odds what war hath lost, and fully avenged
Our foil in heaven; here thou shalt monarch reign,
There didst not; there let him still victor sway,
As battle hath adjudged, from this new world
Retiring, by his own doom alienated,
And henceforth monarchy with thee divide
Of all things parted by the empyreal bounds,
His quadrature, from thy orbicular world,
Or try thee now more dangerous to his throne.'
    Whom thus the prince of darkness answered glad
'Fair daughter, and thou son and grandchild both,

High proof ye now have given to be the race
Of Satan (for I glory in the name,
Antagonist of heaven's almighty king)
Amply have merited of me, of all
The infernal empire, that so near heaven's door
Triumphal with triumphal act have met,
Mine with this glorious work, and made one realm
Hell and this world, one realm, one continent
Of easy thoroughfare. Therefore while I
Descend through darkness, on your road with ease
To my associate powers, them to acquaint
With these successes, and with them rejoice,
You two this way, among these numerous orbs
All yours, right down to Paradise descend;
There dwell and reign in bliss, thence on the earth
Dominion exercise and in the air,
Chiefly on man, sole lord of all declared,
Him first make sure your thrall, and lastly kill.
My substitutes I send ye, and create
Plenipotent on earth, of matchless might
Issuing from me: on your joint vigor now
My hold of this new kingdom all depends,
Through sin to death exposed by my exploit.
If your joint power prevails, the affairs of hell
No detriment need fear, go and be strong.'
    So saying he dismissed them, they with speed
Their course through thickest constellations held
Spreading their bane; the blasted stars looked wan,
And planets, planet-struck, real eclipse
Then suffered. The other way Satan went down
The causey to hell-gate; on either side
Disparted chaos over built exclaimed,
And with rebounding surge the bars assailed,
That scorned his indignation: through the gate,
Wide open and unguarded, Satan passed,
And all about found desolate; for those
Appointed to sit there, had left their charge,

Flown to the upper world; the rest were all
Far to the inland retired, about the walls
Of Pandemonium, city and proud seat
Of Lucifer, so by allusion called,
Of that bright star to Satan paragoned.
There kept their watch the legions, while the grand
In council sat, solicitous what chance
Might intercept their emperor sent, so he
Departing gave command, and they observed.
As when the Tartar from his Russian foe
By Astracan over the snowy plains
Retires, or Bactrian Sophi from the horns
Of Turkish crescent, leaves all waste beyond
The realm of Aladule, in his retreat
To Tauris or Casbeen. So these the late
Heaven-banished host, left desert utmost hell
Many a dark league, reduced in careful watch
Round their metropolis, and now expecting
Each hour their great adventurer from the search
Of foreign worlds: he through the midst unmarked,
In show plebeian angel militant
Of lowest order, passed; and from the door
Of that Plutonian hall, invisible
Ascended his high throne, which under state
Of richest texture spread, at the upper end
Was placed in regal luster. Down a while
He sat, and round about him saw unseen:
At last as from a cloud his fulgent head
And shape star bright appeared, or brighter, clad
With what permissive glory since his fall
Was left him, or false glitter: All amazed
At that so sudden blaze the Stygian throng
Bent their aspect, and whom they wished beheld,
Their mighty chief returned: loud was the acclaim:
Forth rushed in haste the great consulting peers,
Raised from their dark divan, and with like joy

Congratulant approached him, who with hand
Silence, and with these words attention won.
    'Thrones, dominations, princedoms, virtues, powers,
For in possession such, not only of right,
I call ye and declare ye now, returned
Successful beyond hope, to lead ye forth
Triumphant out of this infernal pit
Abominable, accursed, the house of woe,
And dungeon of our tyrant: Now possess,
As lords, a spacious world, to our native heaven
Little inferior, by my adventure hard
With peril great achieved. Long were to tell
What I have done, what suffered, with what pain
Voyaged the unreal, vast, unbounded deep
Of horrible confusion, over which
By sin and death a broad way now is paved
To expedite your glorious march; but I
Toiled out my uncouth passage, forced to ride
The untractable abyss, plunged in the womb
Of unoriginal night and chaos wild,
That jealous of their secrets fiercely opposed
My journey strange, with clamorous uproar
Protesting fate supreme; thence how I found
The new created world, which fame in heaven
Long had foretold, a fabric wonderful
Of absolute perfection, therein man
Placed in a paradise, by our exile
Made happy: Him by fraud I have seduced
From his creator, and the more to increase
Your wonder, with an apple; he thereat
Offended, worth your laughter, hath given up
Both his beloved man and all his world,
To sin and death a prey, and so to us,
Without our hazard, labor, or alarm,
To range in, and to dwell, and over man
To rule, as over all he should have ruled.
True is, me also he hath judged, or rather

Me not, but the brute serpent in whose shape
Man I deceived: that which to me belongs,
Is enmity, which he will put between
Me and mankind; I am to bruise his heel;
His seed, when is not set, shall bruise my head:
A world who would not purchase with a bruise,
Or much more grievous pain? Ye have the account
Of my performance: What remains, ye gods,
But up and enter now into full bliss.'
    So having said, a while he stood, expecting
Their universal shout and high applause
To fill his ear, when contrary he hears
On all sides, from innumerable tongues
A dismal universal hiss, the sound
Of public scorn; he wondered, but not long
Had leisure, wondering at himself now more;
His visage drawn he felt to sharp and spare,
His arms clung to his ribs, his legs entwining
Each other, till supplanted down he fell
A monstrous serpent on his belly prone,
Reluctant, but in vain, a greater power
Now ruled him, punished in the shape he sinned,
According to his doom: he would have spoke,
But hiss for hiss returned with forked tongue
To forked tongue, for now were all transformed
Alike, to serpents all as accessories
To his bold riot: dreadful was the din
Of hissing through the hall, thick swarming now
With complicated monsters head and tail,
Scorpion and asp, and Amphisbaena dire,
Cerastes horned, Hydrus, and Ellops drear,
And Dipsas (not so thick swarmed once the soil
Bedropped with blood of Gorgon, or the isle
Ophiusa) but still greatest he the midst,
Now dragon grown, larger than whom the sun
Engendered in the Pythian vale on slime,
Huge Python, and his power no less he seemed

Above the rest still to retain; they all
Him followed issuing forth to the open field,
Where all yet left of that revolted rout
Heaven-fallen, in station stood or just array,
Sublime with expectation when to see
In triumph issuing forth their glorious chief;
They saw, but other sight instead, a crowd
Of ugly serpents; horror on them fell,
And horrid sympathy; for what they saw,
They felt themselves now changing; down their arms,
Down fell both spear and shield, down they as fast,
And the dire hiss renewed, and the dire form
Catched by contagion, like in punishment,
As in their crime. Thus was the applause they meant,
Turned to exploding hiss, triumph to shame
Cast on themselves from their own mouths. There stood
A grove hard by, sprung up with this their change,
His will who reigns above, to aggravate
Their penance, laden with fair fruit, like that
Which grew in Paradise, the bait of Eve
Used by the tempter: on that prospect strange
Their earnest eyes they fixed, imagining
For one forbidden tree a multitude
Now risen, to work them further woe or shame;
Yet parched with scalding thirst and hunger fierce,
Though to delude them sent, could not abstain,
But on they rolled in heaps, and up the trees
Climbing, sat thicker than the snaky locks
That curled Megaera: greedily they plucked
The fruitage fair to sight, like that which grew
Near that bituminous lake where Sodom flamed;
This more delusive, not the touch, but taste
Deceived; they fondly thinking to allay
Their appetite with gust, instead of fruit
Chewed bitter ashes, which the offended taste
With spattering noise rejected: oft they assayed,
Hunger and thirst constraining, drugged as oft,

With hatefulest disrelish writhed their jaws
With soot and cinders filled; so oft they fell
Into the same illusion, not as man
Whom they triumphed once lapsed. Thus were they plagued
And worn with famine, long and ceaseless hiss,
Till their lost shape, permitted, they resumed,
Yearly enjoined, some say, to undergo
This annual humbling certain numbered days,
To dash their pride, and joy for man seduced.
However some tradition they dispersed
Among the heathen of their purchase got,
And fabled how the serpent, whom they called
Ophion with Eurynome, the wide-
Encroaching Eve perhaps, had first the rule
Of high Olympus, thence by Saturn driven
And Ops, ere yet Dictaean Jove was born.
Meanwhile in Paradise the hellish pair
Too soon arrived, sin there in power before,
Once actual, now in body, and to dwell
Habitual habitant; behind her death
Close following pace for pace, not mounted yet
On his pale horse: to whom sin thus began.
    'Second of Satan sprung, all conquering death,
What thinkest thou of our empire now, though earned
With travail difficult, not better far
Than still at hell's dark threshold to have sat watch,
Unnamed, undreaded, and thyself half starved?'
    Whom thus the sin-born monster answered soon.
'To me, who with eternal famine pine,
Alike is hell, or Paradise, or heaven,
There best, where most with ravin I may meet;
Which here, though plenteous, all too little seems
To stuff this maw, this vast unhide-bound corpse.'
    To whom the incestuous mother thus replied.
'Thou therefore on these herbs, and fruits, and flowers
Feed first, on each beast next, and fish, and fowl,
No homely morsels, and whatever thing

The scythe of time mows down, devour unspared,
Till I in man residing through the race,
His thoughts, his looks, words, actions all infect,
And season him thy last and sweetest prey.'

   This said, they both betook them several ways,
Both to destroy, or unimmortal make
All kinds, and for destruction to mature
Sooner or later; which the almighty seeing,
From his transcendent seat the saints among,
To those bright orders uttered thus his voice.

   'See with what heat these dogs of hell advance
To waste and havoc yonder world, which I
So far and good created, and had still
Kept in that state, had not the folly of man
Let in these wasteful furies, who impute
Folly to me, so doth the prince of hell
And his adherents, that with so much ease
I suffer them to enter and possess
A place so heavenly, and conniving seem
To gratify my scornful enemies,
That laugh, as if transported with some fit
Of passion, I to them had quitted all,
At random yielded up to their misrule;
And know not that I called and drew them thither
My hell-hounds, to lick up the draff and filth
Which man's polluting sin with taint hath shed
On what was pure, till crammed and gorged, nigh burst
With sucked and glutted offal, at one sling
Of thy victorious arm, well-pleasing Son,
Both sin, and death, and yawning grave at last
Through chaos hurled, obstruct the mouth of hell
Forever, and seal up his ravenous jaws.
Then heaven and earth renewed shall be made pure
To sanctity that shall receive no stain:
Till then the curse pronounced on both precedes.'

   He ended, and the heavenly audience loud
Sung hallelujah, as the sound of seas,

Through multitude that sung: 'Just are thy ways,
Righteous are thy decrees on all thy works;
Who can extenuate thee? Next, to the Son,
Destined restorer of mankind, by whom
New heaven and earth shall to the ages rise,
Or down from heaven descend.' Such was their song,
While the creator calling forth by name
His mighty angels gave them several charge,
As sorted best with present things. The sun
Had first his precept so to move, so shine,
As might affect the earth with cold and heat
Scarce tolerable, and from the north to call
Decrepit winter, from the south to bring
Solstitial summer's heat. To the blanc moon
Her office they prescribed, to the other five
Their planetary motions and aspects,
In sextile, square, and trine, and opposite,
Of noxious efficacy, and when to join
In synod unbenign, and taught the fixed
Their influence malignant when to shower,
Which of them rising with the sun, or falling,
Should prove tempestuous: To the winds they set
Their corners, when with bluster to confound
Sea, air, and shore, the thunder when to roll
With terror through the dark aerial hall.
Some say he bid his angels turn askance
The poles of earth twice ten degrees and more
From the sun's axle; they with labor pushed
Oblique the centric globe: Some say the sun
Was bid turn reins from the equinoctial road
Like distant breadth to Taurus with the seven
Atlantic sisters, and the Spartan twins
Up to the tropic Crab; then down amain
By Leo and the Virgin and the Scales,
As deep as Capricorn, to bring in change
Of seasons to each clime; else had the spring
Perpetual smiled on earth with vernant flowers,

Equal in days and nights, except to those
Beyond the polar circles; to them day
Had unbenighted shone, while the low sun
To recompense his distance, in their sight
Had rounded still the horizon, and not known
Or east or west, which had forbid the snow
From cold Estotiland, and south as far
Beneath Magellan. At that tasted fruit
The sun, as from Thyestean banquet, turned
His course intended; else how had the world
Inhabited, though sinless, more than now,
Avoided pinching cold and scorching heat?
These changes in the heavens, though slow, produced
Like change on sea and land, sideral blast,
Vapor, and mist, and exhalation hot,
Corrupt and pestilent: Now from the north
Of Norumbega, and the Samoed shore
Bursting their brazen dungeon, armed with ice
And snow and hail and stormy gust and flaw,
Boreas and Caecias and Argestes loud
And Thrascias rend the woods and seas upturn;
With adverse blasts upturns them from the south
Notus and Afer black with thunderous clouds
From Sierra Leone; thwart of these as fierce
Forth rush the Levant and the Ponent winds
Eurus and Zephyr with their lateral noise,
Sirocco, and Libecchio. Thus began
Outrage from lifeless things; but discord first
Daughter of sin, among the irrational,
Death introduced through fierce antipathy:
Beast now with beast gan war, and fowl with fowl,
And fish with fish; to graze the herb all leaving,
Devoured each other; nor stood much in awe
Of man, but fled him, or with countenance grim
Glared on him passing: these were from without
The growing miseries, which Adam saw
Already in part, though hid in gloomiest shade,

To sorrow abandoned, but worse felt within,
And in a troubled sea of passion tossed,
Thus to disburden sought with sad complaint.

   'O miserable of happy! is this the end
Of this new glorious world, and me so late
The glory of that glory, who now become
Accursed of blessed, hide me from the face
Of God, whom to behold was then my height
Of happiness: yet well, if here would end
The misery, I deserved it, and would bear
My own deservings; but this will not serve;
All that I eat or drink, or shall beget,
Is propagated curse. O voice once heard
Delightfully, "Increase and multiply,"
Now death to hear! for what can I increase
Or multiply, but curses on my head?
Who of all ages to succeed, but feeling
The evil on him brought by me, will curse
My head, "Ill fare our ancestor impure,
For this we may thank Adam;" but his thanks
Shall be the execration; so besides
Mine own that bide upon me, all from me
Shall with a fierce reflux on me redound,
On me as on their natural center light
Heavy, though in their place. O fleeting joys
Of Paradise, dear bought with lasting woes!
Did I request thee, maker, from my clay
To mold me man, did I solicit thee
From darkness to promote me, or here place
In this delicious garden? as my will
Concurred not to my being, it were but right
And equal to reduce me to my dust,
Desirous to resign, and render back
All I received, unable to perform
Thy terms too hard, by which I was to hold
The good I sought not. To the loss of that,
Sufficient penalty, why hast thou added

The sense of endless woes? inexplicable
Thy justice seems; yet to say truth, too late,
I thus contest; then should have been refused
Those terms whatever, when they were proposed:
Thou didst accept them; wilt thou enjoy the good,
Then cavil the conditions? and though God
Made thee without thy leave, what if thy son
Prove disobedient, and reproved, retort,
"Wherefore didst thou beget me? I sought it not"
Wouldst thou admit for his contempt of thee
That proud excuse? yet him not thy election,
But natural necessity begot.
God made thee of choice his own, and of his own
To serve him, thy reward was of his grace,
Thy punishment then justly is at his will.
Be it so, for I submit, his doom is fair,
That dust I am, and shall to dust return:
O welcome hour whenever! why delays
His hand to execute what his decree
Fixed on this day? why do I overlive,
Why am I mocked with death, and lengthened out
To deathless pain? how gladly would I meet
Mortality my sentence, and be earth
Insensible, how glad would lay me down
As in my mother's lap? there I should rest
And sleep secure; his dreadful voice no more
Would thunder in my ears, no fear of worse
To me and to my offspring would torment me
With cruel expectation. Yet one doubt
Pursues me still, lest all I cannot die,
Lest that pure breath of life, the spirit of man
Which God inspired, cannot together perish
With this corporeal clod; then in the grave,
Or in some other dismal place who knows
But I shall die a living death? O thought
Horrid, if true! yet why? it was but breath
Of life that sinned; what dies but what had life

And sin? the body properly hath neither.
All of me then shall die: let this appease
The doubt, since human reach no further knows.
For though the Lord of all be infinite,
Is his wrath also? be it, man is not so,
But mortal doomed. How can he exercise
Wrath without end on man whom death must end?
Can he make deathless death? that were to make
Strange contradiction, which to God himself
Impossible is held, as argument
Of weakness, not of power. Will he, draw out,
For anger's sake, finite to infinite
In punished man, to satisfy his rigor
Satisfied never; that were to extend
His sentence beyond dust and nature's law,
By which all causes else according still
To the reception of their matter act,
Not to the extent of their own sphere. But say
That death be not one stroke, as I supposed,
Bereaving sense, but endless misery
From this day onward, which I feel begun
Both in me, and without me, and so last
To perpetuity; aye me, that fear
Comes thundering back with dreadful revolution
On my defenseless head; both death and I
Am found eternal, and incorporate both,
Nor I on my part single, in me all
Posterity stands cursed: Fair patrimony
That I must leave ye, sons; O were I able
To waste it all myself, and leave ye none!
So disinherited how would ye bless
Me now your curse! Ah, why should all mankind
For one man's fault thus guiltless be condemned,
If guiltless? But from me what can proceed,
But all corrupt, both mind and will depraved,
Not to do only, but to will the same
With me? how can they then acquitted stand

In sight of God? Him after all disputes
Forced I absolve: all my evasions vain,
And reasonings, though through mazes, lead me still
But to my own conviction: first and last
On me, me only, as the source and spring
Of all corruption, all the blame lights due;
So might the wrath. Fond wish! couldst thou suppor'
That burden heavier than the earth to bear
Than all the world much heavier, though divided
With that bad woman? Thus what thou desirest
And what thou fearest, alike destroys all hope
Of refuge, and concludes thee miserable
Beyond all past example and future,
To Satan only like both crime and doom.
O conscience, into what abyss of fears
And horrors hast thou driven me; out of which
I find no way, from deep to deeper plunged!'
    Thus Adam to himself lamented loud
Through the still night, not now, as ere man fell,
Wholesome and cool, and mild, but with black air
Accompanied, with damps and dreadful gloom,
Which to his evil conscience represented
All things with double terror: On the ground
Outstretched he lay, on the cold ground, and oft
Cursed his creation, death as oft accused
Of tardy execution, since-denounced
The day of his offense. 'Why comes not death,'
Said he, 'with one thrice acceptable stroke
To end me? Shall truth fail to keep her word,
Justice divine not hasten to be just?
But death comes not at all, justice divine
Mends not her slowest pace for prayers or cries.
O woods, O fountains, hillocks, dales and bowers,
With other echo late I taught your shades
To answer, and resound far other song.'
Whom thus afflicted when sad Eve beheld,
Desolate where she sat, approaching nigh,

Soft words to his fierce passion she assayed:
But her with stern regard he thus repelled.

'Out of my sight, thou serpent, that name best
Befits thee with him leagued, thyself as false
And hateful; nothing wants, but that thy shape,
Like his, and color serpentine may show
Thy inward fraud, to warn all creatures from thee
Henceforth; lest that too heavenly form, pretended
To hellish falsehood, snare them. But for thee
I had persisted happy, had not thy pride
And wandering vanity, when least was safe,
Rejected my forewarning, and disdained
Not to be trusted, longing to be seen
Though by the devil himself, him overweening
To overreach, but with the serpent meeting
Fooled and beguiled, by him thou, I by thee,
To trust thee from my side, imagined wise,
Constant, mature, proof against all assaults,
And understood not all was but a show
Rather than solid virtue, all but a rib
Crooked by nature, bent, as now appears,
More to the part sinister from me drawn,
Well if thrown out, as supernumerary
To my just number found. O why did God,
Creator wise, that peopled highest heaven
With spirits masculine, create at last
This novelty on earth, this fair defect
Of nature, and not fill the world at once
With men as angels without feminine,
Or find some other way to generate
Mankind? this mischief had not then befallen,
And more that shall befall, innumerable
Disturbances on earth through female snares,
And strait conjunction with this sex: for either
He never shall find out fit mate, but such
As some misfortune brings him, or mistake,
Or whom he wishes most shall seldom gain

Through her perverseness, but shall see her gained
By a far worse, or if she love, withheld
By parents, or his happiest choice too late
Shall meet, already linked and wedlock-bound
To a fell adversary, his hate or shame:
Which infinite calamity shall cause
To human life, and household peace confound.'

He added not, and from her turned, but Eve
Not so repulsed, with tears that ceased not flowing,
And tresses all disordered, at his feet
Fell humble, and embracing them, besought
His peace, and thus proceeded in her plaint.

'Forsake me not thus, Adam, witness heaven
What love sincere, and reverence in my heart
I bear thee, and unweeting have offended,
Unhappily deceived; thy suppliant
I beg, and clasp thy knees; bereave me not,
Whereon I live, thy gentle looks, thy aid,
Thy counsel in this uttermost distress,
My only strength and stay: forlorn of thee,
Whither shall I betake me, where subsist?
While yet we live, scarce one short hour perhaps,
Between us two let there be peace, both joining,
As joined in injuries, one enmity
Against a foe by doom express assigned us,
That cruel serpent: On me exercise not
Thy hatred for this misery befallen,
On me already lost, me than thyself
More miserable; both have sinned, but thou
Against God only, I against God and thee,
And to the place of judgment will return,
There with my cries importune heaven, that all
The sentence from thy head removed may light
On me, sole cause to thee of all this woe,
Me me only just object of his ire.'

She ended weeping, and her lowly plight,
Immovable till peace obtained from fault

Acknowledged and deplored, in Adam wrought
Commiseration; soon his heart relented
Towards her, his life so late and sole delight,
Now at his feet submissive in distress,
Creature so fair his reconcilement seeking,
His counsel whom she had displeased, his aid;
As one disarmed, his anger all he lost,
And thus with peaceful words upraised her soon.
   'Unwary, and too desirous, as before,
So now of what thou knowest not, who desirest
The punishment all on thyself; alas,
Bear thine own first, ill able to sustain
His full wrath whose thou feelest as yet least part,
And my displeasure bearest so ill. If prayers
Could alter high decrees, I to that place
Would speed before thee, and be louder heard,
That on my head all might be visited,
Thy frailty and infirmer sex forgiven,
To me committed and by me exposed.
But rise, let us no more contend, nor blame
Each other, blamed enough elsewhere, but strive
In offices of love, how we may lighten
Each other's burden in our share of woe;
Since this day's death denounced, if aught I see,
Will prove no sudden, but a slow-paced evil,
A long day's dying to augment our pain,
And to our seed (O hapless seed!) derived.'
   To whom thus Eve, recovering heart, replied.
'Adam, by sad experiment I know
How little weight my words with thee can find,
Found so erroneous, thence by just event
Found so unfortunate; nevertheless,
Restored by thee, vile as I am, to place
Of new acceptance, hopeful to regain
Thy love, the sole contentment of my heart
Living or dying, from thee I will not hide
What thoughts in my unquiet breast are risen,

Tending to some relief of our extremes,
Or end, though sharp and sad, yet tolerable,
As in our evils, and of easier choice.
If care of our descent perplex us most,
Which must be born to certain woe, devoured
By death at last, and miserable it is
To be to others cause of misery,
Our own begotten, and of our loins to bring
Into this cursed world a woeful race,
That after wretched life must be at last
Food for so foul a monster, in thy power
It lies, yet ere conception to prevent
The race unblest, to being yet unbegot.
Childless thou art, childless remain:
So death shall be deceived his glut, and with us two
Be forced to satisfy his ravenous maw.
But if thou judge it hard and difficult,
Conversing, looking, loving, to abstain
From love's due rites, nuptial embraces sweet,
And with desire to languish without hope,
Before the present object languishing
With like desire, which would be misery
And torment less than none of what we dread,
Then both ourselves and seed at once to free
From what we fear for both, let us make short,
Let us seek death, or he not found, supply
With our own hands his office on ourselves;
Why stand we longer shivering under fears,
That show no end but death, and have the power,
Of many ways to die the shortest choosing,
Destruction with destruction to destroy.'

   She ended here, or vehement despair
Broke off the rest; so much of death her thoughts
Had entertained, as dyed her cheeks with pale.
But Adam with such counsel nothing swayed,
To better hopes his more attentive mind
Laboring had raised, and thus to Eve replied.

'Eve, thy contempt of life and pleasure seems
To argue in thee something more sublime
And excellent than what thy mind contemns;
But self-destruction therefore sought, refutes
That excellence thought in thee, and implies,
Not thy contempt, but anguish and regret
For loss of life and pleasure overloved.
Or if thou covet death, as utmost end
Of misery, so thinking to evade
The penalty pronounced, doubt not but God
Hath wiselier armed his vengeful ire than so
To be forestalled; much more I fear lest death
So snatched will not exempt us from the pain
We are by doom to pay; rather such acts
Of contumacy will provoke the highest
To make death in us live: Then let us seek
Some safer resolution, which methinks
I have in view, calling to mind with heed
Part of our sentence, that thy seed shall bruise
The serpent's head; piteous amends, unless
Be meant, whom I conjecture, our grand foe
Satan, who in the serpent hath contrived
Against us this deceit: to crush his head
Would be revenge indeed; which will be lost
By death brought on ourselves, or childless days
Resolved, as thou proposest; so our foe
Shall scape his punishment ordained, and we
Instead shall double ours upon our heads.
No more be mentioned then of violence
Against ourselves, and willful barrenness,
That cuts us off from hope, and savors only
Rancor and pride, impatience and despite,
Reluctance against God and his just yoke
Laid on our necks. Remember with what mild
And gracious temper he both heard and judged
Without wrath or reviling; we expected
Immediate dissolution, which we thought

Was meant by death that day, when lo, to thee
Pains only in child-bearing were foretold,
And bringing forth, soon recompensed with joy,
Fruit of thy womb: On me the curse aslope
Glanced on the ground, with labor I must earn
My bread; what harm? Idleness had been worse;
My labor will sustain me; and lest cold
Or heat should injure us, his timely care
Hath unbesought provided, and his hands
Clothed us unworthy, pitying while he judged;
How much more, if we pray him, will his ear
Be open, and his heart to pity incline,
And teach us further by what means to shun
The inclement seasons, rain, ice, hail and snow,
Which now the sky with various face begins
To show us in this mountain, while the winds
Blow moist and keen, shattering the graceful locks
Of these fair spreading trees; which bids us seek
Some better shroud, some better warmth to cherish
Our limbs benumbed, ere this diurnal star
Leave cold the night, how we his gathered beams
Reflected, may with matter sere foment,
Or by collision of two bodies grind
The air attrite to fire, as late the clouds
Justling or pushed with winds rude in their shock
Tine the slant lightning, whose thwart flame driven down
Kindles the gummy bark of fir or pine,
And sends a comfortable heat from far,
Which might supply the sun: such fire to use,
And what may else be remedy or cure
To evils which our own misdeeds have wrought,
He will instruct us praying, and of grace
Beseeching him, so as we need not fear
To pass commodiously this life, sustained
By him with many comforts, till we end
In dust, our final rest and native home.
What better can we do, than to the place

Repairing where he judged us, prostrate fall
Before him reverent, and there confess
Humbly our faults, and pardon beg, with tears
Watering the ground, and with our sighs the air
Frequenting, sent from hearts contrite, in sign
Of sorrow unfeigned, and humiliation meek.
Undoubtedly he will relent and turn
From his displeasure; in whose look serene,
When angry most he seemed and most severe,
What else but favor, grace, and mercy shone?'
    So spake our father penitent, nor Eve
Felt less remorse: they forthwith to the place
Repairing where he judged them prostrate fell
Before him reverent, and both confessed
Humbly their faults, and pardon begged, with tears
Watering the ground, and with their sighs the air
Frequenting, sent from hearts contrite, in sign
Of sorrow unfeigned, and humiliation meek.

BOOK XI

The Argument: The Son of God presents to his father the prayers
of our first parents now repenting, and intercedes for them: God
accepts them, but declares that they must no longer abide in Para-
dise; sends Michael with a band of cherubim to dispossess them;
but first to reveal to Adam future things: Michael's coming down.
Adam shows to Eve certain ominous signs; he discerns Michael's
approach, goes out to meet him: the angel denounces their de-
parture. Eve's lamentation. Adam pleads, but submits: The angel
leads him up to a high hill, sets before him in vision what shall
happen till the flood.

    Thus they in lowliest plight repentant stood
Praying, for from the mercy-seat above
Prevenient grace descending had removed
The stony from their hearts, and made new flesh

Regenerate grow instead, that sighs now breathed
Unutterable, which the spirit of prayer
Inspired, and winged for heaven with speedier flight
Than loudest oratory: yet their port
Not of mean suitors, nor important less
Seemed their petition, than when the ancient pair
In fables old, less ancient yet than these,
Deucalion and chaste Pyrrha to restore
The race of mankind drowned, before the shrine
Of Themis stood devout. To heaven their prayers
Flew up, nor missed the way, by envious winds
Blown vagabond or frustrate: in they passed
Dimensionless through heavenly doors; then clad
With incense, where the golden altar fumed,
By their great intercessor, came in sight
Before the father's throne: Them the glad Son
Presenting, thus to intercede began.

'See father, what first fruits on earth are sprung
From thy implanted grace in man, these sighs
And prayers, which in this golden censer, mixed
With incense, I thy priest before thee bring,
Fruits of more pleasing savor from thy seed
Sown with contrition in his heart, than those
Which his own hand manuring all the trees
Of Paradise could have produced, ere fallen
From innocence. Now therefore bend thine ear
To supplication, hear his sighs though mute;
Unskillful with what words to pray, let me
Interpret for him, me his advocate
And propitiation, all his works on me
Good or not good ingraft, my merit those
Shall perfect, and for these my death shall pay.
Accept me, and in me from these receive
The smell of peace toward mankind, let him live
Before thee reconciled, at least his days
Numbered, though sad, till death, his doom (which I

To mitigate thus plead, not to reverse)
To better life shall yield him, where with me
All my redeemed may dwell in joy and bliss,
Made one with me as I with thee am one.'
    To whom the father, without cloud, serene.
'All thy request for man, accepted Son,
Obtain, all thy request was my decree:
But longer in that Paradise to dwell,
The law I gave to nature him forbids:
Those pure immortal elements that know
No gross, no unharmonious mixture foul,
Eject him tainted now, and purge him off
As a distemper, gross to air as gross,
And mortal food, as may dispose him best
For dissolution wrought by sin, that first
Distempered all things, and of incorrupt
Corrupted. I at first with two fair gifts
Created him endowed, with happiness
And immortality: that fondly lost,
This other served but to eternize woe;
Till I provided death; so death becomes
His final remedy, and after life
Tried in sharp tribulation, and refined
By faith and faithful works, to second life,
Waked in the renovation of the just,
Resigns him up with heaven and earth renewed.
But let us call to synod all the blest
Through heaven's wide bounds; from them I will not hide.
My judgments, how with mankind I proceed,
As how with peccant angels late they saw;
And in their state, though firm, stood more confirmed.'
    He ended, and the Son gave signal high
To the bright minister that watched, he blew
His trumpet, heard in Oreb since perhaps
When God descended, and perhaps once more
To sound at general doom. The angelic blast

Filled all the regions: from their blissful bowers
Of amaranthine shade, fountain or spring,
By the waters of life, where'er they sat
In fellowships of joy: the sons of light
Hasted, resorting to the summons high,
And took their seats; till from his throne supreme
The almighty thus pronounced his sovereign will.
  'O sons, like one of us man is become
To know both good and evil, since his taste
Of that defended fruit; but let him boast
His knowledge of good lost, and evil got,
Happier, had it sufficed him to have known
Good by itself, and evil not at all.
He sorrows now, repents, and prays contrite,
My motions in him, longer than they move,
His heart I know, how variable and vain
Self-left. Lest therefore his now bolder hand
Reach also of the tree of life, and eat,
And live forever, dream at least to live
Forever, to remove him I decree,
And send him from the garden forth to till
The ground whence he was taken, fitter soil.
  'Michael, this my behest have thou in charge,
Take to thee from among the cherubim
Thy choice of flaming warriors, lest the fiend
Or in behalf of man, or to invade
Vacant possession some new trouble raise:
Haste thee, and from the Paradise of God
Without remorse drive out the sinful pair,
From hallowed ground the unholy, and denounce
To them and to their progeny from thence
Perpetual banishment. Yet lest they faint
At the sad sentence rigorously urged,
For I behold them softened and with tears
Bewailing their excess, all terror hide.
If patiently thy bidding they obey,
Dismiss them not disconsolate; reveal

To Adam what shall come in future days,
As I shall thee enlighten, intermix
My covenant in the woman's seed renewed;
So send them forth, though sorrowing, yet in peace:
And on the east side of the garden place,
Where entrance up from Eden easiest climbs,
Cherubic watch, and of a sword the flame
Wide waving, all approach far off to fright,
And guard all passage to the tree of life:
Lest Paradise a receptacle prove
To spirits foul, and all my trees their prey,
With whose stolen fruit man once more to delude.'
　　He ceased; and the archangelic power prepared
For swift descent, with him the cohort bright
Of watchful cherubim; four faces each
Had, like a double Janus, all their shape
Spangled with eyes more numerous than those
Of Argus, and more wakeful than to drowse,
Charmed with Arcadian pipe, the pastoral reed
Of Hermes, or his opiate rod. Meanwhile
To resalute the world with sacred light
Leucothea waked, and with fresh dews embalmed
The earth, when Adam and first matron Eve
Had ended now their orisons, and found
Strength added from above, new hope to spring
Out of despair, joy, but with fear yet linked;
Which thus to Eve his welcome words renewed.
　　'Eve, easily may faith admit, that all
The good which we enjoy, from heaven descends;
But that from us aught should ascend to heaven
So prevalent as to concern the mind
Of God high-blest, or to incline his will,
Hard to belief may seem; yet this will prayer,
Or one short sigh of human breath, upborne
Even to the seat of God. For since I sought
By prayer the offended deity to appease,
Kneeled and before him humbled all my heart,

Methought I saw him placable and mild,
Bending his ear; persuasion in me grew
That I was heard with favor; peace returned
Home to my breast, and to my memory
His promise, that thy seed shall bruise our foe;
Which then not minded in dismay, yet now
Assures me that the bitterness of death
Is past, and we shall live. Whence hail to thee,
Eve rightly called, mother of all mankind,
Mother of all things living, since by thee
Man is to live, and all things live for man.'

    To whom thus Eve with sad demeanor meek.
'Ill worthy I such title should belong
To me transgressor, who for thee ordained
A help, became thy snare; to me reproach
Rather belongs, distrust and all dispraise:
But infinite in pardon was my judge,
That I who first brought death on all, am graced
The source of life; next favorable thou,
Who highly thus to entitle me vouchsafest,
Far other name deserving. But the field
To labor calls us now with sweat imposed,
Though after sleepless night; for see the morn,
All unconcerned with our unrest, begins
Her rosy progress smiling; let us forth,
I never from thy side henceforth to stray,
Where'er our day's work lies, though now enjoined
Laborious, till day droop; while here we dwell,
What can be toilsome in these pleasant walks?
Here let us live, though in fallen state, content.'

    So spake, so wished much-humbled Eve, but fate
Subscribed not; nature first gave signs, impressed
On bird, beast, air, air suddenly eclipsed
After short blush of morn; nigh in her sight
The bird of Jove, stooped from his airy tour,
Two birds of gayest plume before him drove:
Down from a hill the beast that reigns in woods

First hunter then, pursued a gentle brace,
Goodliest of all the forest, hart and hind;
Direct to the eastern gate was bent their flight.
Adam observed, and with his eye the chase
Pursuing, not unmoved to Eve thus spake.

'O Eve, some further change awaits us nigh,
Which heaven by these mute signs in nature shows
Forerunners of his purpose, or to warn
Us haply too secure of our discharge
From penalty, because from death released
Some days; how long, and what till then our life,
Who knows, or more than this, that we are dust,
And thither must return and be no more.
Why else this double object in our sight
Of flight pursued in the air and o'er the ground
One way the selfsame hour? why in the east
Darkness ere day's mid-course, and morning light
More orient in yon western cloud that draws
O'er the blue firmament a radiant white,
And slow descends, with something heavenly fraught

He erred not, for by this the heavenly bands
Down from a sky of jasper lighted now
In Paradise, and on a hill made halt,
A glorious apparition, had not doubt
And carnal fear that day dimmed Adam's eye.
Not that more glorious, when the angels met
Jacob in Mahanaim, where he saw
The field pavilioned with his guardians bright;
Nor that which on the flaming mount appeared
In Dothan, covered with a camp of fire,
Against the Syrian king, who to surprise
One man, assassin-like had levied war,
War unproclaimed. The princely hierarch
In their bright stand, there left his powers to seize
Possession of the garden; he alone,
To find where Adam sheltered, took his way,

Not unperceived of Adam, who to Eve,
While the great visitant approached, thus spake.
   'Eve, now expect great tidings, which perhaps
Of us will soon determine, or impose
New laws to be observed; for I descry
From yonder blazing cloud that veils the hill
One of the heavenly host, and by his gait
None of the meanest, some great potentate
Or of the thrones above, such majesty
Invests him coming; yet not terrible,
That I should fear, nor sociably mild,
As Raphael, that I should much confide,
But solemn and sublime, whom not to offend,
With reverence I must meet, and thou retire.'
He ended; and the archangel soon drew nigh,
Not in his shape celestial, but as man
Clad to meet man; over his lucid arms
A military vest of purple flowed
Livelier than Meliboean, or the grain
Of Sarra, worn by kings and heroes old
In time of truce; Iris had dipped the woof;
His starry helm unbuckled showed him prime
In manhood where youth ended; by his side
As in a glistening zodiac hung the sword,
Satan's dire dread, and in his hand the spear.
Adam bowed low, he kingly from his state
Inclined not, but his coming thus declared.
   'Adam, heaven's high behest no preface needs:
Sufficient that thy prayers are heard, and death,
Then due by sentence when thou didst transgress,
Defeated of his seizure many days
Given thee of grace, wherein thou mayest repent,
And one bad act with many deeds well done
Mayest cover: well may then thy Lord appeased
Redeem thee quite from death's rapacious claim;
But longer in this Paradise to dwell
Permits not; to remove thee I am come,

And send thee from the garden forth to till
The ground whence thou wast taken, fitter soil.'
    He added not, for Adam at the news
Heart-struck with chilling grip of sorrow stood,
That all his senses bound; Eve, who unseen
Yet all had heard, with audible lament
Discovered soon the place of her retire.
    'O unexpected stroke, worse than of death!
Must I thus leave thee Paradise? thus leave
Thee native soil, these happy walks and shades,
Fit haunt of gods? where I had hope to spend,
Quiet though sad, the respite of that day
That must be mortal to us both. O flowers,
That never will in other climate grow,
My early visitation, and my last
At even, which I bred up with tender hand
From the first opening bud, and gave ye names,
Who now shall rear ye to the sun, or rank
Your tribes, and water from the ambrosial fount?
Thee lastly nuptial bower, by me adorned
With what to sight or smell was sweet; from thee
How shall I part, and whither wander down
Into a lower world, to this obscure
And wild, how shall we breathe in other air
Less pure, accustomed to immortal fruits?'
    Whom thus the angel interrupted mild.
'Lament not Eve, but patiently resign
What justly thou hast lost; nor set thy heart,
Thus overfond, on that which is not thine;
Thy going is not lonely, with thee goes
Thy husband, him to follow thou art bound;
Where he abides, think there thy native soil.'
    Adam by this from the cold sudden damp
Recovering, and his scattered spirits returned,
To Michael thus his humble words addressed.
    'Celestial, whether among the thrones, or named
Of them the highest, for such of shape may seem

Prince above princes, gently hast thou told
Thy message, which might else in telling wound,
And in performing end us; what besides
Of sorrow and dejection and despair
Our frailty can sustain, thy tidings bring,
Departure from this happy place, our sweet
Recess, and only consolation left
Familiar to our eyes, all places else
Inhospitable appear and desolate,
Nor knowing us nor known: and if by prayer
Incessant I could hope to change the will
Of him who all things can, I would not cease
To weary him with my assiduous cries:
But prayer against his absolute decree
No more avails than breath against the wind,
Blown stifling back on him that breathes it forth:
Therefore to his great bidding I submit.
This most afflicts me, that departing hence,
As from his face I shall be hid, deprived
His blessed countenance; here I could frequent,
With worship, place by place where he vouchsafed
Presence divine, and to my sons relate;
"On this mount he appeared, under this tree
Stood visible, among these pines his voice
I heard, here with him at this fountain talked:"
So many grateful altars I would rear
Of grassy turf, and pile up every stone
Of luster from the brook, in memory,
Or monument to ages, and thereon
Offer sweet smelling gums and fruits and flowers:
In yonder nether world where shall I seek
His bright appearances, or footstep trace?
For though I fled him angry, yet recalled
To life prolonged and promised race, I now
Gladly behold though but his utmost skirts
Of glory, and far off his steps adore.'

To whom thus Michael with regard benign.
'Adam, thou knowest heaven his, and all the earth.
Not this rock only; his omnipresence fills
Land, sea, and air, and every kind that lives,
Fomented by his virtual power and warmed:
All the earth he gave thee to possess and rule,
No despicable gift; surmise not then
His presence to these narrow bounds confined
Of Paradise or Eden: this had been
Perhaps thy capital seat, from whence had spread
All generations, and had hither come
From all the ends of the earth, to celebrate
And reverence thee their great progenitor.
But this pre-eminence thou hast lost, brought down
To dwell on even ground now with thy sons:
Yet doubt not but in valley and in plain
God is as here, and will be found alike
Present, and of his presence many a sign
Still following thee, still compassing thee round
With goodness and paternal love, his face
Express, and of his steps the track divine.
Which that thou mayest believe, and be confirmed
Ere thou from hence depart, know I am sent
To show thee what shall come in future days
To thee and to thy offspring; good with bad
Expect to hear, supernal grace contending
With sinfulness of men; thereby to learn
True patience, and to temper joy with fear
And pious sorrow, equally inured
By moderation either state to bear,
Prosperous or adverse: so shalt thou lead
Safest thy life, and best prepared endure
Thy mortal passage when it comes. Ascend
This hill; let Eve (for I have drenched her eyes)
Here sleep below while thou to foresight wakest,
As once thou sleptst, while she to life was formed.'
    To whom thus Adam gratefully replied.

'Ascend, I follow thee, safe guide, the path
Thou leadest me, and to the hand of heaven submit,
However chastening, to the evil turn
My obvious breast, arming to overcome
By suffering, and earn rest from labor won,
If so I may attain.' So both ascend
In the visions of God: It was a hill
Of Paradise the highest, from whose top
The hemisphere of earth in clearest ken
Stretched out to the amplest reach of prospect lay.
Not higher that hill nor wider looking round,
Whereon for different cause the tempter set
Our second Adam in the wilderness,
To show him all earth's kingdoms and their glory.
His eye might there command wherever stood
City of old or modern fame, the seat
Of mightiest empire, from the destined walls
Of Cambalu, seat of Cathaian khan
And Samarkand by Oxus, Temir's throne,
To Paquin of Sinaean kings, and thence
To Agra and Lahor of great Mogul
Down to the golden Chersonese, or where
The Persian in Ecbatan sat, or since
In Hispahan, or where the Russian ksar
In Moscow, or the sultan in Bizance,
Turkestan-born; nor could his eye not ken
The empire of Negus to his utmost port
Ercoco and the less maritime kings
Mombasa, and Quiloa, and Melind,
And Sofala thought Ophir, to the realm
Of Congo, and Angola farthest south;
Or thence from Niger flood to Atlas mount
The kingdoms of Almansor, Fez and Sus,
Morocco and Algiers, and Tremisen;
On Europe thence, and where Rome was to sway
The world: in spirits perhaps he also saw
Rich Mexico the seat of Montezume,

And Cusco in Peru, the richer seat
Of Atabalipa, and yet unspoiled
Guiana, whose great city Geryon's sons
Call El Dorado: but to nobler sights
Michael from Adam's eyes the film removed
Which that false fruit that promised clearer sight
Had bred; then purged with euphrasy and rue
The visual nerve, for he had much to see;
And from the well of life three drops instilled.
So deep the power of these ingredients pierced,
Even to the inmost seat of mental sight,
That Adam now enforced to close his eyes,
Sunk down and all his spirits became entranced:
But him the gentle angel by the hand
Soon raised, and his attention thus recalled.
   'Adam, now ope thine eyes, and first behold
The effects which thy original crime hath wrought
In some to spring from thee, who never touched
The excepted tree, nor with the snake conspired,
Nor sinned thy sin, yet from that sin derive
Corruption to bring forth more violent deeds.'
   His eyes he opened, and beheld a field,
Part arable and tilth, whereon were sheaves
New reaped, the other part sheep-walks and folds;
In the midst an altar as the landmark stood
Rustic, of grassy sward; thither anon
A sweaty reaper from his tillage brought
First-fruits, the green ear, and the yellow sheaf,
Unculled, as came to hand; a shepherd next
More meek came with the firstlings of his flock
Choicest and best; then sacrificing, laid
The inwards and their fat, with incense strewed,
On the cleft wood, and all due rites performed.
His offering soon propitious fire from heaven
Consumed with nimble glance, and grateful steam;
The other's not, for his was not sincere;
Whereat he inly raged, and as they talked,

Smote him into the midriff with a stone
That beat out life; he fell, and deadly pale
Groaned out his soul with gushing blood effused.
Much at that sight was Adam in his heart
Dismayed, and thus in haste to the angel cried.

'O Teacher, some great mischief hath befallen
To that meek man, who well had sacrificed;
Is piety thus and pure devotion paid?'

To whom Michael thus, he also moved, replied.
'These two are brethren, Adam, and to come
Out of thy loins; the unjust the just hath slain,
For envy that his brother's offering found
From heaven acceptance; but the bloody fact
Will be avenged, and the other's faith approved
Lose no reward, though here thou see him die,
Rolling in dust and gore.' To which our sire.

'Alas, both for the deed and for the cause!
But have I now seen death? Is this the way
I must return to native dust? O sight
Of terror, foul and ugly to behold,
Horrid to think, how horrible to feel!'

To whom thus Michael. 'Death thou hast seen
In his first shape on man; but many shapes
Of death, and many are the ways that lead
To his grim cave, all dismal; yet to sense
More terrible at the entrance than within.
Some, as thou sawest, by violent stroke shall die,
By fire, flood, famine, by intemperance more
In meats and drinks, which on the earth shall bring
Diseases dire, of which a monstrous crew
Before thee shall appear; that thou mayest know
What misery the inabstinence of Eve
Shall bring on men.' Immediately a place
Before his eyes appeared, sad, noisome, dark,
A lazar-house it seemed, wherein were laid
Numbers of all diseased, all maladies
Of ghastly spasm. or racking torture, qualms

Of heart-sick agony, all feverous kinds,
Convulsions, epilepsies, fierce catarrhs,
Intestine stone and ulcer, colic pangs,
Demoniac phrenzy, moping melancholy
And moon-struck madness, pining atrophy,
Marasmus, and wide-wasting pestilence,
Dropsies, and asthmas, and joint-racking rheums.
Dire was the tossing, deep the groans, despair
Tended the sick busiest from couch to couch;
And over them triumphant death his dart
Shook, but delayed to strike, though oft invoked
With vows, as their chief good, and final hope.
Sight so deform what heart of rock could long
Dry-eyed behold? Adam could not, but wept,
Though not of woman born; compassion quelled
His best of man, and gave him up to tears
A space, till firmer thoughts restrained excess,
And scarce recovering words his plaint renewed.

'O miserable mankind, to what fall
Degraded, to what wretched state reserved!
Better end here unborn. Why is life given
To be thus wrested from us? rather why
Obtruded on us thus? who if we knew
What we receive, would either not accept
Life offered, or soon beg to lay it down,
Glad to be so dismissed in peace. Can thus
The image of God in man created once
So goodly and erect, though faulty since,
To such unsightly sufferings be debased
Under inhuman pains? Why should not man,
Retaining still divine similitude
In part, from such deformities be free,
And for his maker's image sake exempt?'

'Their maker's image,' answered Michael, 'then
Forsook them, when themselves they vilified
To serve ungoverned appetite, and took
His image whom they served, a brutish vice,

Inductive mainly to the sin of Eve.
Therefore so abject is their punishment,
Disfiguring not God's likeness, but their own,
Or if his likeness, by themselves defaced
While they pervert pure nature's healthful rules
To loathsome sickness, worthily, since they
God's image did not reverence in themselves.'

'I yield it just,' said Adam, 'and submit.
But is there yet no other way, besides
These painful passages, how we may come
To death, and mix with our connatural dust?'

'There is,' said Michael, 'if thou well observe
The rule of not too much, by temperance taught
In what thou eatest and drinkest, seeking from thence
Due nourishment, not gluttonous delight,
Till many years over thy head return:
So mayest thou live, till like ripe fruit thou drop
Into thy mother's lap, or be with ease
Gathered, not harshly plucked, for death mature:
This is old age; but then thou must outlive
Thy youth, thy strength, thy beauty, which will change
To withered weak and gray; thy senses then
Obtuse, all taste of pleasure must forgo,
To what thou hast, and for the air of youth
Hopeful and cheerful, in thy blood will reign
A melancholy damp of cold and dry
To weigh thy spirits down, and last consume
The balm of life.' To whom our ancestor.

'Henceforth I fly not death, nor would prolong
Life much, bent rather how I may be quit
Fairest and easiest of this cumbrous charge,
Which I must keep till my appointed day
Of rendering up, and patiently attend
My dissolution.' Michael replied,

'Nor love thy life, nor hate; but what thou livest
Live well, how long or short permit to heaven:
And now prepare thee for another sight.'

He looked and saw a spacious plain, whereon
Were tents of various hue; by some were herds
Of cattle grazing: others, whence the sound
Of instruments that made melodious chime
Was heard, of harp and organ; and who moved
Their stops and chords was seen: his volant touch
Instinct through all proportions low and high
Fled and pursued transverse the resonant fugue.
In other part stood one who at the forge
Laboring, two massy clods of iron and brass
Had melted (whether found where casual fire
Had wasted woods on mountain or in vale,
Down to the veins of earth, thence gliding hot
To some cave's mouth, or whether washed by stream
From underground) the liquid ore he drained
Into fit molds prepared; from which he formed
First his own tools; then, what might else be wrought
Fusile or graven in metal. After these,
But on the hither side a different sort
From the high neighboring hills, which was their seat,
Down to the plain descended: by their guise
Just men they seemed, and all their study bent
To worship God aright, and know his works
Not hid, nor those things last which might preserve
Freedom and peace to men: they on the plain
Long had not walked, when from the tents behold
A bevy of fair women, richly gay
In gems and wanton dress; to the harp they sung
Soft amorous ditties, and in dance came on:
The men though grave, eyed them, and let their eyes
Rove without rein, till in the amorous net
Fast caught, they liked, and each his liking chose;
And now of love they treat till the evening star
Love's harbinger appeared; then all in heat
They light the nuptial torch, and bid invoke
Hymen, then first to marriage rites invoked;
With feast and music all the tents resound.

Such happy interview and fair event
Of love and youth not lost, songs, garlands, flowers,
And charming symphonies attached the heart
Of Adam, soon inclined to admit delight,
The bent of nature; which he thus expressed.

'True opener of mine eyes, prime angel blest,
Much better seems this vision, and more hope
Of peaceful days portends, than those two past;
Those were of hate and death, or pain much worse,
Here nature seems fulfilled in all her ends.'

To whom thus Michael. 'Judge not what is best
By pleasure, though to nature seeming meet,
Created, as thou art, to nobler end
Holy and pure, conformity divine.
Those tents thou sawest so pleasant, were the tents
Of wickedness, wherein shall dwell his race
Who slew his brother; studious they appear
Of arts that polish life, inventors rare,
Unmindful of their maker, though his spirit
Taught them, but they his gifts acknowledged none.
Yet they a beauteous offspring shall beget;
For that fair female troop thou sawest, that seemed
Of goddesses, so blithe, so smooth, so gay,
Yet empty of all good wherein consists
Woman's domestic honor and chief praise;
Bred only and completely to the taste
Of lustful appetence, to sing, to dance,
To dress, and troll the tongue, and roll the eye.
To these that sober race of men, whose lives
Religious titled them the sons of God,
Shall yield up all their virtue, all their fame
Ignobly, to the trains and to the smiles
Of these fair atheists, and now swim in joy,
(Erelong to swim at large) and laugh; for which
The world erelong a world of tears must weep.'

To whom thus Adam of short joy bereft.
'O pity and shame, that they who to live well

Entered so fair, should turn aside to tread
Paths indirect, or in the midway faint!
But still I see the tenor of man's woe
Holds on the same, from woman to begin.'
     'From man's effeminate slackness it begins,'
Said the angel, 'who should better hold his place
By wisdom, and superior gifts received.
But now prepare thee for another scene.'
     He looked and saw wide territory spread
Before him, towns, and rural works between,
Cities of men with lofty gates and towers,
Concourse in arms, fierce faces threatening war,
Giants of mighty bone, and bold emprise;
Part wield their arms, part curb the foaming steed,
Single or in array of battle ranged
Both horse and foot, nor idly mustering stood;
One way a band select from forage drives
A herd of beeves, fair oxen and fair kine
From a fat meadow ground; or fleecy flock,
Ewes and their bleating lambs over the plain,
Their booty; scarce with life the shepherds fly,
But call in aid, which makes a bloody fray;
With cruel tournament the squadrons join;
Where cattle pastured late, now scattered lies
With carcasses and arms the ensanguined field
Deserted: Others to a city strong
Lay siege, encamped; by battery, scale, and mine,
Assaulting; others from the wall defend
With dart and javelin, stones and sulphurous fire;
On each hand slaughter and gigantic deeds.
In other part the sceptered heralds call
To council in the city gates: anon
Gray-headed men and grave, with warriors mixed,
Assemble, and harangues are heard, but soon
In factious opposition, till at last
Of middle age one rising, eminent
In wise deport, spake much of right and wrong,

Of justice, of religion, truth and peace,
And judgment from above: him old and young
Exploded and had seized with violent hands,
Had not a cloud descending snatched him thence
Unseen amid the throng: so violence
Proceeded, and oppression, and sword-law
Through all the plain, and refuge none was found.
Adam was all in tears, and to his guide
Lamenting turned full sad; 'O what are these,
Death's ministers, not men, who thus deal death
Inhumanly to men, and multiply
Ten thousandfold the sin of him who slew
His brother; for of whom such massacre
Make they but of their brethren, men of men?
But who was that just man, whom had not heaven
Rescued, had in his righteousness been lost?'
     To whom thus Michael. 'These are the product
Of those ill-mated marriages thou sawest:
Where good with bad were matched, who of themselves
Abhor to join; and by imprudence mixed,
Produce prodigious births of body or mind.
Such were these giants, men of high renown;
For in those days might only shall be admired,
And valor and heroic virtue called;
To overcome in battle, and subdue
Nations, and bring home spoils with infinite
Manslaughter, shall be held the highest pitch
Of human glory, and for glory done
Of triumph, to be styled great conquerors,
Patrons of mankind, gods, and sons of gods,
Destroyers rightlier called and plagues of men.
Thus fame shall be achieved, renown on earth,
And what most merits fame in silence hid.
But he the seventh from thee, whom thou beheldest
The only righteous in a world perverse,
And therefore hated, therefore so beset
With foes for daring single to be just,

And utter odious truth, that God would come
To judge them with his saints: Him the most high
Rapt in a balmy cloud with winged steeds
Did, as thou sawest, receive, to walk with God
High in salvation and the climes of bliss,
Exempt from death; to show thee what reward
Awaits the good, the rest what punishment?
Which now direct thine eyes and soon behold.'
    He looked, and saw the face of things quite changed,
The brazen throat of war had ceased to roar,
All now was turned to jollity and game,
To luxury and riot, feast and dance,
Marrying or prostituting, as befell,
Rape or adultery, where passing fair
Allured them; thence from cups to civil broils.
At length a reverend sire among them came,
And of their doings great dislike declared,
And testified against their ways; he oft
Frequented their assemblies, whereso met,
Triumphs or festivals, and to them preached
Conversion and repentance, as to souls
In prison under judgments imminent:
But all in vain: which when he saw, he ceased
Contending, and removed his tents far off;
Then from the mountain hewing timber tall,
Began to build a vessel of huge bulk,
Measured by cubit, length, and breadth, and height,
Smeared round with pitch, and in the side a door
Contrived, and of provisions laid in large
For man and beast: when lo a wonder strange!
Of every beast, and bird, and insect small
Came sevens, and pairs, and entered in, as taught
Their order: last the sire, and his three sons
With their four wives; and God made fast the door.
Meanwhile the south wind rose, and with black wings
Wide hovering, all the clouds together drove
From under heaven; the hills to their supply

, and exhalation dusk and moist,
up amain; and now the thickened sky
a dark ceiling stood; down rushed tne rain
Impetuous, and continued till the earth
No more was seen; the floating vessel swum
Uplifted; and secure with beaked prow.
Rode tilting o'er the waves, all dwellings else
Flood overwhelmed, and them with all their pomp
Deep under water rolled; sea covered sea,
Sea without shore; and in their palaces
Where luxury late reigned, sea-monsters whelped
Ano stabled; of mankind, so numerous late,
All left, in one small bottom swum embarked.
How didst thou grieve then, Adam, to behold
The end of all thy offspring, end so sad,
Depopulation; thee another flood,
Of tears and sorrow a flood thee also drowned,
And sunk thee as thy sons; till gently reared
By the angel, on thy feet thou stoodest at last,
Though comfortless, as when a father mourns
His children, all in view destroyed at once;
And scarce to the angel utteredst thus thy plaint.

'O visions ill foreseen! better had I
Lived ignorant of future, so had borne
My part of evil only, each day's lot
Enough to bear; those now, that were dispensed
The burden of many ages, on me light
At once, by my foreknowledge gaining birth
Abortive, to torment me ere their being,
With thought that they must be. Let no man seek
Henceforth to be foretold what shall befall
Him or his children, evil he may be sure,
Which neither his foreknowing can prevent,
And he the future evil shall no less
In apprehension than in substance feel
Grievous to bear: but that care now is past,
Man is not whom to warn; those few escaped

Famine and anguish will at last consume
Wandering that watery desert: I had hope
When violence was ceased, and war on earth,
All would have then gone well, peace would have crowned
With length of happy days the race of man;
But I was far deceived; for now I see
Peace to corrupt no less than war to waste.
How comes it thus? unfold, celestial guide,
And whether here the race of man will end.'
To whom thus Michael. 'Those whom last thou sawest
In triumph and luxurious wealth, are they
First seen in acts of prowess eminent
And great exploits, but of true virtue void;
Who having spilt much blood, and done much waste
Subduing nations, and achieved thereby
Fame in the world, high titles, and rich prey,
Shall change their course to pleasure, ease, and sloth,
Surfeit, and lust, till wantonness and pride
Raise out of friendship hostile deeds in peace.
The conquered also, and enslaved by war
Shall with their freedom lost all virtue lose
And fear of God, from whom their piety feigned
In sharp contest of battle found no aid
Against invaders; therefore cooled in zeal
Thenceforth shall practice how to live secure,
Worldly or dissolute, on what their lords
Shall leave them to enjoy; for the earth shall bear
More than enough, that temperance may be tried:
So all shall turn degenerate, all depraved,
Justice and temperance, truth and faith forgot;
One man except, the only son of light
In a dark age, against example good,
Against allurement, custom, and a world
Offended; fearless of reproach and scorn,
Or violence, he of their wicked ways
Shall them admonish, and before them set
The paths of righteousness, how much more safe,

And full of peace, denouncing wrath to come
On their impenitence; and shall return
Of them derided, but of God observed
The one just man alive; by his command
Shall build a wondrous ark, as thou beheldest,
To save himself and household from amidst
A world devote to universal wrack.
No sooner he with them of man and beast
Select for life shall in the ark be lodged,
And sheltered round, but all the cataracts
Of heaven set open on the earth shall pour
Rain day and night, all fountains of the deep
Broke up, shall heave the ocean to usurp
Beyond all bounds, till inundation rise
Above the highest hills: then shall this mount
Of Paradise by might of waves be moved
Out of his place, pushed by the horned flood,
With all his verdure spoiled, and trees adrift
Down the great river to the opening gulf,
And there take root an island salt and bare,
The haunt of seals and orcs, and sea-mews' clang.
To teach thee that God attributes to place
No sanctity, if none be thither brought
By men who there frequent, or therein dwell.
And now what further shall ensue, behold.'
    He looked, and saw the ark hull on the flood,
Which now abated, for the clouds were fled,
Driven by a keen north-wind, that blowing dry
Wrinkled the face of deluge, as decayed;
And the clear sun on his wide watery glass
Gazed hot, and of the fresh wave largely drew,
As after thirst, which made their flowing shrink
From standing lake to tripping ebb, that stole
With soft foot towards the deep, who now had stopped
His sluices, as the heaven his windows shut.
The ark no more now floats, but seems on ground
Fast on the top of some high mountain fixed.

And now the tops of hills as rocks appear;
With clamor thence the rapid currents drive
Towards the retreating sea their furious tide.
Forthwith from out the ark a raven flies,
And after him, the surer messenger,
A dove sent forth once and again to spy
Green tree or ground whereon his foot may light;
The second time returning, in his bill
An olive leaf he brings, pacific sign:
Anon dry ground appears, and from his ark
The ancient sire descends with all his train;
Then with uplifted hands, and eyes devout,
Grateful to heaven, over his head beholds
A dewy cloud, and in the cloud a bow
Conspicuous with three listed colors gay,
Betokening peace from God, and covenant anew.
Whereat the heart of Adam erst so sad
Greatly rejoiced, and thus his joy broke forth.

  'O thou who future things canst represent
As present, heavenly instructor, I revive
At this last sight, assured that man shall live
With all the creatures, and their seed preserve.
Far less I now lament for one whole world
Of wicked sons destroyed, than I rejoice
For one man found so perfect and so just,
That God vouchsafes to raise another world
From him, and all his anger to forget.
But say, what mean those colored streaks in heaven,
Distended as the brow of God appeased,
Or serve they as a flowery verge to bind
The fluid skirts of that same watery cloud,
Lest it again dissolve and shower the earth?'

  To whom the archangel. 'Dextrously thou aimest;
So willingly doth God remit his ire,
Though late repenting him of man depraved,
Grieved at his heart, when looking down he saw

The whole earth filled with violence, and all flesh
Corrupting each their way; yet those removed.
Such grace shall one just man find in his sight,
That he relents, not to blot out mankind,
And makes a covenant never to destroy
The earth again by flood, nor let the sea
Surpass his bounds, nor rain to drown the world
With man therein or beast; but when he brings
Over the earth a cloud, will therein set
His triple-colored bow, whereon to look
And call to mind his covenant: Day and night,
Seed time and harvest, heat and hoary frost
Shall hold their course, till fire purge all things new,
Both heaven and earth, wherein the just shall dwell.'

BOOK XII

The Argument: The angel Michael continues from the flood to re-
late what shall succeed; then, in the mention of Abraham, comes
by degrees to explain, who that seed of the woman shall be, which
was promised Adam and Eve in the fall; his incarnation, death,
resurrection, and ascension; the state of the Church till his second
coming. Adam greatly satisfied and recomforted by these relations
and promises descends the hill with Michael; wakens Eve, who
all this while had slept, but with gentle dreams composed to quiet-
ness of mind and submission. Michael in either hand leads them out
of Paradise, the fiery sword waving behind them, and the cherubim
taking their stations to guard the place.

As one who in his journey baits at noon,
Though bent on speed, so here the archangel paused
Betwixt the world destroyed and world restored.
If Adam aught perhaps might interpose;
Then with transition sweet new speech resumes.

'Thus thou hast seen one world begin and end;
And man as from a second stock proceed.
Much thou hast yet to see, but I perceive
Thy mortal sight to fail; objects divine
Must needs impair and weary human sense:
Henceforth what is to come I will relate,
Thou therefore give due audience, and attend.
This second source of men, while yet but few;
And while the dread of judgment past remains
Fresh in their minds, fearing the deity,
With some regard to what is just and right
Shall lead their lives, and multiply apace,
Laboring the soil, and reaping plenteous crop,
Corn, wine and oil; and from the herd or flock,
Oft sacrificing bullock, lamb, or kid,
With large wine-offerings poured, and sacred feast,
Shall spend their days in joy unblamed, and dwell
Long time in peace by families and tribes
Under paternal rule; till one shall rise
Of proud ambitious heart, who not content
With fair equality, fraternal state,
Will arrogate dominion undeserved
Over his brethren, and quite dispossess
Concord and law of nature from the earth,
Hunting (and men not beasts shall be his game)
With war and hostile snare such as refuse
Subjection to his empire tyrannous:
A mighty hunter thence he shall be styled
Before the Lord, as in despite of heaven,
Or from heaven claiming second sovereignty;
And from rebellion shall derive his name,
Though of rebellion others he accuse.
He with a crew, whom like ambition joins
With him or under him to tyrannize,
Marching from Eden towards the west, shall find
The plain, wherein a black bituminous gurge
Boils out from under ground, the mouth of hell;

Of brick, and of that stuff they cast to build
A city and tower, whose top may reach to heaven,
And get themselves a name, lest far dispersed
In foreign lands their memory be lost
Regardless whether good or evil fame.
But God who oft descends to visit men
Unseen, and through their habitations walks
To mark their doings, them beholding soon,
Comes down to see their city, ere the tower
Obstruct heaven towers, and in derision sets
Upon their tongues a various spirit to rase
Quite out their native language, and instead
To sow a jangling noise of words unknown:
Forthwith a hideous gabble rises loud
Among the builders; each to other calls
Not understood, till hoarse, and all in rage,
As mocked they storm; great laughter was in heaven
And looking down, to see the hubbub strange
And hear the din; thus was the building left
Ridiculous, and the work confusion named.'
  Whereto thus Adam fatherly displeased.
'O execrable son so to aspire
Above his brethren, to himself assuming
Authority usurped, from God not given:
He gave us only over beast, fish, fowl
Dominion absolute; that right we hold
By his donation; but man over men
He made not lord; such title to himself
Reserving, human left from human free.
But this usurper his encroachment proud
Stays not on man; to God his tower intends
Siege and defiance: Wretched man! what food
Will he convey up thither to sustain
Himself and his rash army, where thin air
Above the clouds will pine his entrails gross,
And famish him of breath, if not of bread?'

To whom thus Michael. 'Justly thou abhorrest
That son, who on the quiet state of men
Such trouble brought, affecting to subdue
Rational liberty; yet know withal,
Since thy original lapse, true liberty
Is lost, which always with right reason dwells
Twinned, and from her hath no dividual being:
Reason in man obscured, or not obeyed,
Immediately inordinate desires
And upstart passions catch the government
From reason, and to servitude reduce
Man till then free. Therefore since he permits
Within himself unworthy powers to reign
Over free reason, God in judgment just
Subjects him from without to violent lords;
Who oft as undeservedly enthrall
His outward freedom: Tyranny must be,
Though to the tyrant thereby no excuse.
Yet sometimes nations will decline so low
From virtue, which is reason, that no wrong,
But justice, and some fatal curse annexed
Deprives them of their outward liberty,
Their inward lost: Witness the irreverent son
Of him who built the ark, who for the shame
Done to his father, heard this heavy curse,
"Servant of servants," on his vicious race.
Thus will this latter, as the former world,
Still tend from bad to worse, till God at last
Wearied with their iniquities, withdraw
His presence from among them, and avert
His holy eyes; resolving from thenceforth
To leave them to their own polluted ways;
And one peculiar nation to select
From all the rest, of whom to be invoked,
A nation from one faithful man to spring:
Him on this side Euphrates yet residing,
Bred up in idol worship; O that men

(Canst thou believe?) should be so stupid grown,
While yet the patriarch lived, who scaped the flood,
As to forsake the living God, and fall
To worship their own work in wood and stone
For gods! yet him God the most high vouchsafes
To call by vision from his father's house,
His kindred and false gods, into a land
Which he will show him, and from him will raise
A mighty nation, and upon him shower
His benediction so, that in his seed
All nations shall be blest; he straight obeys,
Not knowing to what land, yet firm believes:
I see him, but thou canst not, with what faith
He leaves his gods, his friends, and native soil
Ur of Chaldaea, passing now the ford
To Haran, after him a cumbrous train
Of herds and flocks, and numerous servitude;
Not wandering poor, but trusting all his wealth
With God, who called him, in a land unknown.
Canaan he now attains, I see his tents
Pitched about Sechem, and the neighboring plain
Of Moreh; there by promise he receives
Gift to his progeny of all that land;
From Hamath northward to the desert south
(Things by their names I call, though yet unnamed)
From Hermon east to the great western sea,
Mount Hermon, yonder sea, each place behold
In prospect, as I point them; on the shore
Mount Carmel; here the double-founted stream
Jordan, true limit eastward; but his sons
Shall dwell to Senir, that long ridge of hills.
This ponder, that all nations of the earth
Shall in his seed be blessed; by that seed
Is meant thy great deliverer, who shall bruise
The serpent's head; whereof to thee anon
Plainlier shall be revealed. This patriarch blest,
Whom faithful Abraham due time shall call,

A son, and of his son a grandchild leaves,
Like him in faith, in wisdom, and renown;
The grandchild with twelve sons increased, departs
From Canaan, to a land hereafter called
Egypt, divided by the river Nile;
See where it flows, disgorging at seven mouths
Into the sea: to sojourn in that land
He comes invited by a younger son
In time of dearth, a son whose worthy deeds
Raise him to be the second in that realm
Of Pharaoh: there he dies, and leaves his race
Growing into a nation, and now grown
Suspected to a sequent king, who seeks
To stop their overgrowth, as inmate guests
Too numerous; whence of guests he make them slaves
Inhospitably, and kills their infant males:
Till by two brethren (those two brethren call
Moses and Aaron) sent from God to claim
His people from enthrallment, they return
With glory and spoil back to their promised land.
But first the lawless tyrant, who denies
To know their God, or message to regard,
Must be compelled by signs and judgments dire;
To blood unshed the rivers must be turned,
Frogs, lice and flies must all his palace fill
With loathed intrusion, and fill all the land;
His cattle must of rot and murrain die,
Botches and blains must all his flesh emboss,
And all his people; thunder mixed with hail,
Hail mixed with fire must rend the Egyptian sky
And wheel on the earth, devouring where it rolls;
What it devours not, herb, or fruit, or grain,
A darksome cloud of locusts swarming down
Must eat, and on the ground leave nothing green:
Darkness must overshadow all his bounds,
Palpable darkness, and blot out three days;
Last with one midnight stroke all the first-born

Of Egypt must lie dead. Thus with ten wounds
The river-dragon tamed at length submits
To let his sojourners depart, and oft
Humbles his stubborn heart, but still as ice
More hardened after thaw, till in his rage
Pursuing whom he late dismissed, the sea
Swallows him with his host, but them lets pass
As on dry land between two crystal walls,
Awed by the rod of Moses so to stand
Divided, till his rescued gain their shore:
Such wondrous power God to his saint will lend,
Though present in his angel, who shall go
Before them in a cloud, and pillar of fire,
By day a cloud, by night a pillar of fire,
To guide them in their journey, and remove
Behind them, while the obdurate king pursues:
All night he will pursue, but his approach
Darkness defends between till morning watch;
Then through the fiery pillar and the cloud
God looking forth will trouble all his host
And craze their chariot-wheels: when by command
Moses once more his potent rod extends
Over the sea; the sea his rod obeys;
On their embattled ranks the waves return,
And overwhelm their war: the race elect
Safe towards Canaan from the shore advance
Through the wild desert, not the readiest way,
Lest entering on the Canaanite alarmed
War terrify them inexpert, and fear
Return them back to Egypt, choosing rather
Inglorious life with servitude; for life
To noble and ignoble is more sweet
Untrained in arms, where rashness leads not on.
This also shall they gain by their delay
In the wide wilderness, there they shall found
Their government, and their great senate choose
Through the twelve tribes, to rule by laws ordained:

God from the Mount of Sinai, whose gray top
Shall tremble, he descending, will himself
In thunder lightning and loud trumpet's sound
Ordain them laws; part such as appertain
To civil justice, part religious rites
Of sacrifice, informing them, by types
And shadows, of that destined seed to bruise
The serpent, by what means he shall achieve
Mankind's deliverance. But the voice of God
To mortal ear is dreadful; they beseech
That Moses might report to them his will,
And terror cease; he grants what they besought
Instructed that to God is no access
Without mediator, whose high office now
Moses in figure bears, to introduce
One greater, of whose day he shall foretell,
And all the prophets in their age the times
Of great Messiah shall sing. Thus laws and rites
Established, such delight hath God in men
Obedient to his will, that he vouchsafes
Among them to set up his tabernacle,
The holy one with mortal men to dwell:
By his prescript a sanctuary is framed
Of cedar, overlaid with gold, therein
An ark, and in the ark his testimony,
The records of his covenant, over these
A mercy-seat of gold between the wings
Of two bright cherubim, before him burn
Seven lamps as in a zodiac representing
The heavenly fires; over the tent a cloud
Shall rest by day, a fiery gleam by night,
Save when they journey, and at length they come,
Conducted by his angel to the land
Promised to Abraham and his seed: the rest
Were long to tell, how many battles fought,
How many kings destroyed, and kingdoms won,
Or how the sun shall in mid heaven stand still

A day entire, and night's due course adjourn,
Man's voice commanding, "Sun in Gibeon stand,
And thou moon in the vale of Aialon,
Till Israel overcome;" so call the third
From Abraham, son of Isaac, and from him
His whole descent, who thus shall Canaan win."
　　Here Adam interposed. 'O sent from heaven,
Enlightener of my darkness, gracious things
Thou hast revealed, those chiefly which concern
Just Abraham and his seed: now first I find
Mine eyes' true opening, and my heart much eased,
Erewhile perplexed with thoughts what would become
Of me and all mankind; but now I see
His day, in whom all nations shall be blest
Favor unmerited by me, who sought
Forbidden knowledge by forbidden means.
This yet I apprehend not, why to those
Among whom God will deign to dwell on earth
So many and so various laws are given;
So many laws argue so many sins
Among them; how can God with such reside?'
　　To whom thus Michael. 'Doubt not but that sin
Will reign among them, as of thee begot;
And therefore was law given them to evince
Their natural pravity, by stirring up
Sin against law to fight; that when they see
Law can discover sin, but not remove,
Save by those shadowy expiations weak,
The blood of bulls and goats, they may conclude
Some blood more precious must be paid for man,
Just for unjust, that in such righteousness
To them by faith imputed, they may find
Justification towards God, and peace
Of conscience, which the law by ceremonies
Cannot appease, nor man the moral part
Perform, and not performing cannot live.
So law appears imperfect, and but given

With purpose to resign them in full time
Up to a better covenant, disciplined
From shadowy types to truth, from flesh to spirit,
From imposition of strict laws, to free
Acceptance of large grace, from servile fear
To filial, works of law to works of faith.
And therefore shall not Moses, though of God
Highly beloved, being but the minister
Of law, his people into Canaan lead;
But Joshua whom the Gentiles Jesus call,
His name and office bearing, who shall quell
The adversary serpent, and bring back
Through the world's wilderness long wandered man
Safe to eternal Paradise of rest.
Meanwhile they in their earthly Canaan placed
Long time shall dwell and prosper, but when sins
National interrupt their public peace,
Provoking God to raise them enemies:
From whom as oft he saves them penitent
By judges first, then under kings; of whom
The second, both for piety renowned
And puissant deeds, a promise shall receive
Irrevocable, that his regal throne
Forever shall endure; the like shall sing
All prophecy, that of the royal stock
Of David (so I name this king) shall rise
A son, the woman's seed to thee foretold,
Foretold to Abraham, as in whom shall trust
All nations, and to kings foretold, of kings
The last, for of his reign shall be no end.
But first a long succession must ensue,
And his next son for wealth and wisdom famed,
The clouded ark of God till then in tents
Wandering, shall in a glorious temple enshrine.
Such follow him, as shall be registered
Part good, part bad, of bad the longer scroll,
Whose foul idolatries, and other faults

Heaped to the popular sum, will so incense
God, as to leave them, and expose their land,
Their city, his temple, and his holy ark
With all his sacred things, a scorn and prey
To that proud city, whose high walls thou sawest
Left in confusion, Babylon thence called.
There in captivity he lets them dwell
The space of seventy years, then brings them back,
Remembering mercy, and his covenant sworn
To David, stablished as the days of heaven.
Returned from Babylon by leave of kings
Their lords, whom God disposed, the house of God
They first re-edify, and for a while
In mean estate live moderate, till grown
In wealth and multitude, factious they grow;
But first among the priests dissension springs,
Men who attend the altar, and should most
Endeavor peace: their strife pollution brings
Upon the temple itself: at last they seize
The scepter, and regard not David's sons,
Then lose it to a stranger, that the true
Anointed king Messiah might be born
Barred of his right; yet at his birth a star
Unseen before in heaven proclaims him come,
And guides the eastern sages, who inquire
His place, to offer incense, myrrh, and gold;
His place of birth a solemn angel tells
To simple shepherds, keeping watch by night;
They gladly thither haste, and by a choir
Of squadroned angels hear his carol sung.
A virgin is his mother, but his sire
The power of the most high; he shall ascend
The throne hereditary, and bound his reign
With earth's wide bounds, his glory with the heavens.ᶜ

He ceased, discerning Adam with such joy
Surcharged, as had like grief been dewed in tears,
Without the vent of words, which these he breathed.

'O prophet of glad tidings, finisher
Of utmost hope! now clear I understand
What oft my steadiest thoughts have searched in vain,
Why our great expectation should be called
The seed of woman: Virgin mother, hail,
High in the love of heaven, yet from my loins
Thou shalt proceed, and from thy womb the Son
Of God most high; so God with man unites.
Needs must the serpent now his capital bruise
Expect with mortal pain: say where and when
Their fight, what stroke shall bruise the victor's heel.'
     To whom thus Michael. 'Dream not of their fight,
As of a duel, or the local wounds
Of head or heel: not therefore joins the Son
Manhood to godhead, with more strength to foil
Thy enemy; nor so is overcome
Satan, whose fall from heaven, a deadlier bruise,
Disabled not to give thee thy death's wound:
Which he, who comes thy Saviour, shall recure,
Not by destroying Satan, but his works
In thee and in thy seed: nor can this be,
But by fulfilling that which thou didst want,
Obedience to the law of God, imposed
On penalty of death, and suffering death,
The penalty to thy transgression due,
And due to theirs which out of thine will grow:
So only can high justice rest appaid.
The law of God exact he shall fulfill
Both by obedience and by love, though love
Alone fulfill the law; thy punishment
He shall endure by coming in the flesh
To a reproachful life and cursed death,
Proclaiming life to all who shall believe
In his redemption, and that his obedience
Imputed becomes theirs by faith, his merits
To save them, not their own, though legal works.
For this he shall live hated, be blasphemed,

Seized on by force, judged, and to death condemned
A shameful and accursed, nailed to the cross
By his own nation, slain for bringing life;
But to the cross he nails thy enemies,
The law that is against thee, and the sins
Of all mankind, with him there crucified,
Never to hurt them more who rightly trust
In this his satisfaction; so he dies,
But soon revives, death over him no power
Shall long usurp; ere the third dawning light
Return, the stars of morn shall see him rise
Out of his grave, fresh as the dawning light,
Thy ransom paid, which man from death redeems,
His death for man, as many as offered life
Neglect not, and the benefit embrace
By faith not void of works: this godlike act
Annuls thy doom, the death thou shouldst have died,
In sin forever lost from life; this act
Shall bruise the head of Satan, crush his strength
Defeating sin and death, his two main arms,
And fix far deeper in his head their stings
Than temporal death shall bruise the victor's heel,
Or theirs whom he redeems, a death like sleep,
A gentle wafting to immortal life.
Nor after resurrection shall he stay
Longer on earth than certain times to appear
To his disciples, men who in his life
Still followed him; to them shall leave in charge
To teach all nations what of him they learned
And his salvation, them who shall believe
Baptizing in the profluent stream, the sign
Of washing them from guilt of sin to life
Pure, and in mind prepared, if so befall,
For death, like that which the Redeemer died.
All nations they shall teach; for from that day
Not only to the sons of Abraham's loins
Salvation shall be preached, but to the sons

Of Abraham's faith wherever through the world;
So in his seed all nations shall be blest.
Then to the heaven of heavens he shall ascend
With victory, triumphing through the air
Over his foes and thine; there shall surprise
The serpent, prince of air, and drag in chains
Through all his realm, and there confounded leave;
Then enter into glory, and resume
His seat at God's right hand, exalted high
Above all names in heaven; and thence shall come,
When this world's dissolution shall be ripe,
With glory and power to judge both quick and dead,
To judge the unfaithful dead, but to reward
His faithful, and receive them into bliss,
Whether in heaven or earth, for then the earth
Shall be all Paradise, far happier place
Than this of Eden, and far happier days.'

　　So spake the archangel Michael, then paused,
As at the world's great period; and our sire
Replete with joy and wonder thus replied.
　　'O goodness infinite, goodness immense!
That all this good of evil shall produce,
And evil turn to good; more wonderful
Than that which by creation first brought forth
Light out of darkness! full of doubt I stand,
Whether I should repent me now of sin
By me done and occasioned, or rejoice
Much more, that much more good thereof shall spring,
To God more glory, more good will to men
From God, and over wrath grace shall abound.
But say, if our deliverer up to heaven
Must reascend, what will betide the few
His faithful, left among the unfaithful herd,
The enemies of truth; who then shall guide
His people, who defend? will they not deal
Worse with his followers than with him they dealt?'

'Be sure they will,' said the angel; 'but from heaven
He to his own a comforter will send,
The promise of the father, who shall dwell
His spirit within them, and the law of faith
Working through love, upon their hearts shall write,
To guide them in all truth, and also arm
With spiritual armor, able to resist
Satan's assaults, and quench his fiery darts,
What man can do against them, not afraid,
Though to the death, against such cruelties
With inward consolations recompensed,
And oft supported so as shall amaze
Their proudest persecutors: for the spirit
Poured first on his apostles, whom he sends
To evangelize the nations, then on all
Baptized, shall them with wondrous gifts endue
To speak all tongues, and do all miracles,
As did their Lord before them. Thus they win
Great numbers of each nation to receive
With joy the tidings brought from heaven: at length
Their ministry performed, and race well run,
Their doctrine and their story written left,
They die; but in their room, as they forewarn,
Wolves shall succeed for teachers, grievous wolves,
Who all the sacred mysteries of heaven
To their own vile advantages shall turn
Of lucre and ambition, and the truth
With superstitions and traditions taint,
Left only in those written records pure,
Though not but by the spirit understood.
Then shall they seek to avail themselves of names,
Places and titles, and with these to join
Secular power, though feigning still to act
By spiritual, to themselves appropriating
The spirit of God, promised alike and given
To all believers; and from that pretense,
Spiritual laws by carnal power shall force

On every conscience; laws which none shall find
Left them enrolled, or what the spirit within
Shall on the heart engrave. What will they then
But force the spirit of grace itself, and bind
His consort liberty; what, but unbuild
His living temples, built by faith to stand,
Their own faith not another's: for on earth
Who against faith and conscience can be heard
Infallible? yet many will presume:
Whence heavy persecution shall arise
On all who in the worship persevere
Of spirit and truth; the rest, far greater part,
Will deem in outward rites and specious forms
Religion satisfied; truth shall retire
Bestuck with slanderous darts, and works of faith
Rarely be found: so shall the world go on,
To good malignant, to bad men benign,
Under her own weight groaning till the day
Appear of respiration to the just,
And vengeance to the wicked, at return
Of him so lately promised to thy aid
The woman's seed, obscurely then foretold,
Now amplier known thy Saviour and thy Lord,
Last in the clouds from heaven to be revealed
In glory of the father, to dissolve
Satan with his perverted world, then raise
From the conflagrant mass, purged and refined,
New heavens, new earth, ages of endless date
Founded in righteousness and peace and love
To bring forth fruits, joy and eternal bliss.'
    He ended; and thus Adam last replied.
'How soon hath thy prediction, seer blest,
Measured this transient world, the race of time,
Till time stand fixed: beyond is all abyss,
Eternity, whose end no eye can reach.
Greatly instructed I shall hence depart,
Greatly in peace of thought, and have my fill

Of knowledge, what this vessel can contain;
Beyond which was my folly to aspire.
Henceforth I learn, that to obey is best,
And love with fear the only God, to walk
As in his presence, ever to observe
His providence, and on him sole depend,
Merciful over all his works, with good
Still overcoming evil, and by small
Accomplishing great things, by things deemed weak
Subverting worldly strong, and worldly wise
By simply meek; that suffering for truth's sake
Is fortitude to highest victory,
And to the faithful death the gate of life;
Taught this by his example whom I now
Acknowledge my redeemer ever blest.'
    To whom thus also the angel last replied:
'This having learned, thou hast attained the sum
Of wisdom; hope no higher, though all the stars
Thou knewest by name, and all the ethereal powers,
All secrets of the deep, all nature's works,
Or works of God in heaven, air, earth, or sea,
And all the riches of this world enjoyedst,
And all the rule, one empire; only add
Deeds to thy knowledge answerable, add faith,
Add virtue, patience, temperance, add love,
By name to come called charity, the soul
Of all the rest: then wilt thou not be loth
To leave this Paradise, but shalt possess
A paradise within thee, happier far.
Let us descend now therefore from this top
Of speculation; for the hour precise
Exacts our parting hence; and see the guards,
By me encamped on yonder hill, expect
Their motion, at whose front a flaming sword,
In signal of remove, waves fiercely round;
We may no longer stay: go, waken Eve;
Her also I with gentle dreams have calmed

Portending good, and all her spirits composed
To meek submission: thou at season fit
Let her with thee partake what thou hast heard,
Chiefly what may concern her faith to know,
The great deliverance by her seed to come
(For by the woman's seed) on all mankind.
That ye may live, which will be many days,
Both in one faith unanimous though sad,
With cause for evils past, yet much more cheered
With meditation on the happy end.'

    He ended, and they both descend the hill;
Descended, Adam to the bower where Eve
Lay sleeping ran before, but found her waked;
And thus with words not sad she him received.

    'Whence thou returnest, and whither wentest, I know;
For God is also in sleep, and dreams advise,
Which he hath sent propitious, some great good
Presaging, since with sorrow and heart's distress
Wearied I fell asleep: but now lead on;
In me is no delay; with thee to go,
Is to stay here; without thee here to stay,
Is to go hence unwilling; thou to me
Art all things under heaven, all places thou,
Who for my willful crime art banished hence.
This further consolation yet secure
I carry hence; though all by me is lost,
Such favor I unworthy am vouchsafed,
By me the promised seed shall all restore.'

    So spake our mother Eve, and Adam heard
Well pleased, but answered not; for now too nigh
The archangel stood, and from the other hill
To their fixed station, all in bright array
The cherubim descended; on the ground
Gliding meteorous, as evening mist
Risen from a river o'er the marish glides,
And gathers ground fast at the laborer's heel
Homeward returning. High in front advanced,

The brandished sword of God before them blazed
Fierce as a comet; which with torrid heat,
And vapor as the Libyan air adust,
Began to parch that temperate clime; whereat
In either hand the hastening angel caught
Our lingering parents, and to the eastern gate
Led them direct, and down the cliff as fast
To the subjected plain; then disappeared.
They looking back, all the eastern side beheld
Of Paradise, so late their happy seat,
Waved over by that flaming brand, the gate
With dreadful faces thronged and fiery arms:
Some natural tears they dropped, but wiped them soon;
The world was all before them, where to choose
Their place of rest, and providence their guide:
They hand in hand with wandering steps and slow,
Through Eden took their solitary way.